A NOVEL OF REVOLUTION

FACTION 9

HE'S WATCHING YOU

BUT NOW
SOMEONE'S
WATCHING HIM!

JAMES FIRELOCKE

ISBN Paperback: 978-0-9995682-9-3
ISBN eBook: 978-0-9995682-8-6

Printed in the United States of America

Cover art by Steve Thomas.
Cover and interior design by Ghislain Viau.

I believe it, because it is impossible…it is true,
because it is absurd.
—Tertullian

The death of democracy is the birth of revolution.
Hatred of greed is the salvation of love.
—21st Century Revolutionary Slogan

I am now quite certain that the crimes of this guilty land
can never be purged away but with blood.
—Abolitionist John Brown, minutes before his execution

CONTENTS

Phase Three: Psycho Pietá

Meet the Federal Security Agency

The Northeast Field Office of the Federal Security Agency in lower Manhattan is a ten-story structure that resembles an old warehouse.

But this appearance is a deception.

The building's walls are fifteen feet thick and made of ferro-concrete quadruple-reinforced with titanium bars. Its frame consists of a densely interlocking network of ultrastrong, flexible supersteel, while its windows are transparent shields of a foot-thick, virtually indestructible polymer. The top ten floors are entirely uninhabited; only the seventeen subfloors contain workspaces. The whole formidable monolith is designed to withstand a direct hit from a fifty-megaton nuclear warhead. Even if all of Manhattan were reduced to radioactive rubble, the bureaucrats of the Federal Security Agency's Northeast Field Office would be able to continue their work protecting America.

One of the workers in the Security Agency building, Jack Tone, had his office on subfloor -16. Jack, badge number 2076, was a GS-13

1

Security Officer whose job was to manipulate a battery of databases, culling information on citizens, legal residents, and non-citizens, and writing assessments on them. He was thirty years old, romantically unattached, and without any close family ties. He had been at the Security Agency for five years and was considered an outstanding worker by his supervisors. Every year since the start of his employment, he had achieved an employment rating of "Surpassing Excellent." He performed his work dutifully and scrupulously and, unlike some other Security Officers, he never caused his supervisors unnecessary trouble.

There was only one problem with Jack.

He was slowly losing his mind.

Jack was somewhat introverted, though not entirely antisocial. He had previously worked as an editor at a small company that published New Age books, but this company had been taken over by a corporate publisher and then phased out of existence. Suddenly jobless, Jack had searched online every day for a new position, but the nation's plunging literacy rates, along with the absorption of once-independent publishing houses into global media conglomerates, made it a bleak market for unemployed editors.

On the recommendation of one of his deceased parents' old colleagues, Jack applied for a Security Officer position that had appeared in a public job announcement. He had been hired after an accelerated fifteen-month background check.

He lived in a small apartment near Van Vorst Park in Jersey City, and took the ferry across the Hudson every day to Manhattan. He caught the northbound 2 line and entered the SA building from Oversight Street.

Like all Security Agency employees, Jack carried five pieces of personal identification with him at all times: his badge, his credential, his electromagnetic ID card, his retina, and his DNA. After passing through the front doors of the SA building, he took the employee's path through Biometrics Screening. Helmeted, unsmiling guards in the black-and-gold uniforms of the Security Agency Police watched him, while Identity Officers in Plexiglas consoles confirmed his identity. He showed his badge, flashed his credential, inserted his EMID into a slot, then stared into a retinal scanner. Only if one of these resulted in a Negative would he be required to provide a DNA sample for instant analysis. This rarely happened, and when it did, it was usually due to electrical storms.

Having been cleared through Biometrics Screening, Jack took the elevator down to floor -16 and entered his office. Though he was several hundred feet below the surface of the Earth, his wall had a virtual window showing pink sand, a green ocean, and swaying palm trees. Reproductions of the Constitution and the Declaration of Independence were on his wall. On his desk was a bobblehead doll of Andrew Carnegie that he had won during an office raffle—the highlight of a rather drab holiday party during which division director Sonny Vargas Schicklegruber had unsmilingly handed everyone a candy cane.

One gray January morning of the unexpectedly cold Alternative Year 2041, Jack went through this routine as he had every other day of his federal career, with the exception that on this particular day, he had a premonition that something was very, *very* wrong, that something terrible was about to happen—a feeling that fate had finally directed its eyes upon him and was now about to unleash a program of mind-boggling craziness that it had kept in reserve for most of Jack's thirty years of existence.

Phase One

The Demon in the Whirlwind

CHAPTER ONE

Hell on Earth

On that day, Jack's premonitions of doom were aggravated by the jitteriness of the Security Officer in the room next door who was pacing back and forth. Stanley Spork had been with the Security Agency for ten years and, to Jack's mind, was showing troubling signs of burnout. Jack tried not to think about it and to concentrate instead on his own work, but Stanley frequently bustled into his office uninvited.

As he did just now.

"Have you met that new officer?" Stanley asked, looking around furtively.

"You mean Jill Jones? Yes."

"I think she's a ghoster."

"Stan, you think everybody's a ghoster," said Jack.

"This one for sure."

"You can't have all ghosters in one office. If we're all spying on each other, then none of us can spy on the public. It makes no sense."

"I quite understand that, sir," said Stanley testily. Like government employees from the time of the Ming Empire, Stan had a weird tendency to shift to formal locution when defensive.

"So what are you worried about?" asked Jack. "We know there are ghosters in the office. I could be a ghoster. You could be a ghoster. There's nothing we can do about it. Let's just get back to work and not worry about these things."

Jack stared at his monitor and pretended to be reading the latest convoluted and incomprehensible Policy Clarification.

"They say that as many as 10 percent of the employees of a federal office may consist of ghosters," continued Stan. "Yet I've never heard of an opening for one in this office. You have to be selected, they say. I've never been approached about being a ghoster. Have you ever been approached?"

"No."

"But of course neither of us could say if we had been approached, could we?"

"We could not."

"So the information exchanged in this conversation is essentially useless," concluded Stan.

"It probably is, Stan. But I have some work to do."

Stan did not take the hint. He stood hovering in Jack's doorway. "They have certain tells, though, that give them away," he said, half to himself. "Friendly, outgoing types. That's why I don't think you're a ghoster, Tone. Because you're as non-outgoing as they get."

"I know. But I have ten assessments to finish, Stan. And three were returned by supervisors for revisions, so I have to work on them as well."

Stan frowned. "Good day, sir," he said brusquely. To Jack's great relief, he finally returned to his own office.

But now Jack was starting to feel even more gloomy and paranoid than when he first came in to work. All this talk of ghosters rattled him. "Ghoster" was the colloquial term for Security Officers whose job was to spy on their fellow Security Officers. Technically they were referred to as Office Safety Officers, or OSOs. Though they were scattered among the various divisions of the Security Agency, they had their own division and answered to their own mysterious hierarchy of supervisors.

You weren't supposed to talk about ghosters. You certainly weren't supposed to use the word, which was considered impolitic or even offensive, like using a racial slur. During the ten months Jack had spent at Security Officer Basic Training, he and his fellow students had been told several times that OSOs were there for the benefit of the employees, not to spy on them. Examples were given of how, through their diligence, OSOs had intervened to save Security Officers from potentially career-destroying vices such as alcoholism, drug use, prostitution, and gambling.

By sheer force of will, Jack directed his mind away from the subject of ghosters, including the alleged new ghoster, Jill Jones—a twenty-something with a fresh-faced, bubbly personality. He had to finish his checks and write his assessments. This required conducting searches in several databases: the Crime, Aggression, and Insanity Resource for Biometrics Only (CAIRBO), a law-enforcement database; the Curriculum Regulation and University Metric (CRUM), which was used to track the activities of college students; the Social Contact Register for Undesirables (SCRU), a clearinghouse database for social media usage by right-wing groups; the Radical Entity

Directory (RED), which did the same for left-wing organizations; the Financial Underworld and Corporation Jeopardizing Operations Book (always referred to as FJOB), a list of militants and activists hostile to corporate power; the Antisocial and Nonconformist Educator List (ANEL), which was self-explanatory; the Objectionable, Nonproductive, and Antisocial Artists Numeration (ONAAN); the Interagency Database on Fundamentalists, Atheists, and Other Social Deviants (IADOFAOSD); the Acquired Sickness, Epidemic, and Cancer Researchers Undocumentation Directory (ASECRUD), which monitored rogue scientists whose activities threatened the profits and sustainability of the pharmaceutical conglomerates; and finally the most important database of all: the Personal Identification System Information Bank (PISIBANK). This was the most protected and sensitive of all government databases, because it contained uncensored and detailed personal and financial information on everyone in the country, without exception, including all politicians.

The PISIBANK would have been the gold standard of government databases, had it been publicly known. As it stood, it was the most carefully guarded of all the Security Agency's databases. Security Officers were strictly forbidden by secret internal policy memos (which had the force of law) from speaking about it outside the SA building. In fact, they were even forbidden from *thinking* about the PISIBANK, and each Security Officer received special DuplexThink™ psych training to accomplish this.

Every morning, Jack checked his Register of Suspects (ROS). First he ran them through CAIRBO, printing out the results and making five copies, initialed in red, green, black, purple, and blue ink, respectively. Three of these copies were filed with his supervisor with an Introduction to Suspects (ITS) memo. One was placed in the

DDS (the Document Destruction Slot). The fifth was fed mechanically into the CRUM database, which processed the information and cross-checked it on both SCRU and RED. Jack then wrote a brief Basic Detection and Security Memo that incorporated all relevant findings up until this point. He made a date-stamped copy for his supervisor to sign. When this was done, he manually produced a punch-card transliteration that was processed through FJOB. Any hits or non-hits were automatically fed into ANEL, and then uploaded into ONAAN. A magnetic-strip data card was generated through a 3-D printer, which Jack had to take by hand down to Operations Oversight Section (OOS) for confirmation. Once the chip had been validated, it was scanned through IADOFAOSD using the office Cryptometric Regulation and Processing Unit (CRAPU). The ASECRUD run-through completed the process, at which point the Assessment, now fully coded onto the chip key, had to be conveyed by hand to the PISIBANK within ten minutes, or the whole process had to be repeated, which required Review and Authorization from Headquarters in Washington, DC.

Because of this time constraint, Security Officers were continually dashing down the long hallway to the station where the PISIBANK installation was located. The hallway that led to the PISIBANK was winding and about fifty yards long—meaning that there were often collisions as Security Officers tried to get their chip keys down in time. Occasionally a Security Officer would hit a wall and fall down, in which case other Security Officers, glancing down and determining that their fallen comrade was not in danger, would rush by them, or leap over them, so they could get to the PISIBANK promptly. There were rarely fights or physical altercations between Security Officers, as it was assumed that some of them were ghosters...and you didn't want to punch a ghoster—a sure way of being declared a Suppressive Employee if there ever was one.

Once he reached the PISIBANK, Jack would insert his chip key into a slot and wait impatiently while the large, blinking, mainframe tower generated the assessment, which was generally about fifteen pages long and had to be manually copyedited before final submission to a supervisor.

Jack went through this entire process ten times a day.

On that particular day in February, he left the office feeling frazzled, unsteady—like he was losing his mind. He decided to stop off at Egan's Bar for a drink.

He wasn't paying much attention as he crossed Oversight Street, and when he looked up, he saw a large KrunchyKake delivery truck bearing down on him. He heard the screech of the truck's brakes and the screams of other pedestrians. The blazing white headlights filled up his whole field of vision.

Jack Tone saw the face of death.

CHAPTER TWO

Death Comes for the Bureaucrat

Jack's whole life rushed before his eyes like a river of driver ants—
and what a purposeless, pathetic life it appeared to him now,
observed from this precarious vantage point between here and the
hereafter, with black-robed Charon taking him by the arm and whispering into his ear, its breath as dry as the plague winds of Babylon.
At that instant Jack realized that his life as a security bureaucrat was
meaningless, and that his office was a kind of supernatural Auschwitz
to which he transported his soul and spirit every single day to be
gassed—a Groundhog Day of existential horror that cycled over and
over again. A Samsara wheel from which he could not break free.
Interminable cruelty—self-inflicted!

Suddenly death, in the chariot of the KrunchyKake delivery
truck, took on a friendly face. Death's whisper became a song of
seduction against which Jack could not prevail.

And then he was hit—not by the delivery truck, but by a good Samaritan who, standing in the middle of the street and facing him, had seen the tragedy that was about to occur. With incredible speed, this man dashed forward and bodily knocked Jack out of the path of the truck, just as it screeched to a stop. Stunned, Jack lay sprawled on the ground. Just before the stranger had tackled him, Charon had assumed the form of the PISIBANK computer, its jaws open in frustrated rage. It evaporated like a dream phantom, and its shriek became the buzz of alarmed pedestrians.

"My dear fellow, you must watch where you are going!" said the man, who now helped Jack to his feet.

Jack stood there, still shocked and very shaky. The man steadied him with a strong grip on his arm. He was very tall—a few inches taller than Jack, who was about five eleven—with broad shoulders, black hair, and handsome angular features. He appeared to be of East Asian ancestry. His eyes were dark and authoritative in a steady, unflinching sort of way, like those of a mounted general on the front lines, calmly ignoring the whistle of the enemy's shells, or a fleet commander issuing orders as cannonballs crashed into the masts. He wore a neat suit and an overcoat with a flat-brimmed hat.

"Are you okay, my friend?" he asked, his grip still firm on Jack's arm.

Jack muttered something.

"I think you need to sit down," suggested the stranger. "*That* was a close one! You were almost smashed into atoms. You came pretty close to transitioning into the other world."

Jack nodded numbly.

"I think you require a restorative," said the man. "Do you drink?"

"Sometimes," mumbled Jack.

Jack followed the stranger across the street to Egan's Bar. At a side table, the man ordered two Scotches—one for himself and one for Jack.

Jack gulped his down. His wits were beginning to return to him. He looked up at the man across the table. "I was almost killed…I owe you my life," he said.

"Nonsense," said the man, waving his hand nonchalantly. "You would have done the same for me."

"No, but really, I would have been *killed*."

"We live and die a thousand times every day," said the man philosophically, while adjusting his tie. "It's not *death* we should fear, but what happens *after* death."

Jack was still a little woozy. "What's your name?" he asked.

The man ordered another round of Scotches. "You can call me…" He paused. "Andronicus."

"*Andronicus?*"

He handed Jack a card, which said:

PETER ANDRONICUS

CERTIFIED PUBLIC ACCOUNTANT

15 CALLOWHILL STREET

PHILADELPHIA, PENNA

Jack noticed the Victorian script, the archaic abbreviation of "Pennsylvania." To the right of the script was a wispy drawing of a dapper fellow in a colonial tricorne hat and waistcoat, giving a victorious thumbs-up as if to reassure potential customers that he had the moxie to get their taxes done. To the left was the Liberty Bell with an exaggerated crack.

"I'm in the city for business," said Andronicus. "Leaving on the 9:57 Northeast Flyer from Penn Station."

Jack took the card and nodded. "I'm Jack Tone."

"So what do you do, Jack?"

"I work for U.S. Customs. I'm an inspector." Even now, in his rattled mental state, he automatically gave his cover position.

"We both have very exciting jobs, then. You are a customs inspector and I am an accountant. But we earn a living, right?" Andronicus smiled with his dark eyes and lifted his glass of Scotch.

"Yes, we do," Jack replied.

"And life is the most important thing, isn't it?"

"It is."

"To life," said Andronicus, clinking his glass on Jack's.

They drank.

"Tell me something, Jack. I'm thinking of taking a trip to Korea to visit my father's family. Strange to say, I haven't been out of the U.S. since I was a teenager. While there, I'll undoubtedly be plied with gifts. Do I have to pay a duty on gifts when I return?"

Again speaking automatically, Jack said, "Well, you will at least have to *declare* them—*and* any purchases you bring back—on the CBP declaration form 2729B1. For anything you have bought, you should have a proof of purchase or receipt. As for the gifts, the customs inspector will determine fair market value."

"Hmmm," said Andronicus, looking reflectively at the ice in his glass. He seemed suddenly uninterested in the answer to his own inquiry. "Well, I've got to get going, my friend. You *are* all right now, aren't you? You're looking much better already. Good luck to you."

Andronicus stood up, and so did Jack. They shook hands, and Andronicus left the bar quickly.

Through the dirty window, Jack watched his tall figure as it vanished into the crowd.

As part of his Security Officer job, Jack was occasionally called upon to interview criminal detainees. From this, he had learned a thing or two about credibility. This fellow Andronicus had definite elements of the Philadelphia accent in his speech. But as for his profession, Jack strongly suspected he was absolutely lying.

F9

Under normal circumstances, Jack would have reported the incident to his supervisor. In fact, it might well have been recorded by security cameras outside the SA Building. However, for the time being he chose to say nothing. This "Andronicus" fellow had saved his life after all, and once the SA had designated you an Active Subject in its data-processing machines, you were under their Eye for good. In the worst-case scenario, SA processing could have a terrible effect on your ability to find a job—or to keep a job if you had one. Your credit rating plummeted. Forget about loans to buy a house or start a business. And if you were self-employed, your business would dry up.

Not all Active Subjects suffered these dire consequences, only those perceived to be the most dangerous. But Jack didn't know anything at all about Andronicus, and he was reluctant to do anything that might jeopardize the man who had just saved his life from a rampaging KrunchyKake delivery truck.

F9

Two weeks passed rather quickly. Jack put the whole incident out of his mind, burying himself in his job. Having been saved from the jaws of death gave to him a new energy—a new optimism, even. For as oppressive as his job was, it was better than the abyss of nonexistence. He now chastised himself for his past dissatisfaction, and resolved to be an even better federal employee—more conscientious, more diligent, more selfless in his time and energy.

And then, one evening while he was standing in Penn Station, he heard someone call his name.

"Jack! Jack Tone! How *are* you?"

Andronicus came up and shook his hand vigorously.

"Peter...nice to see you..."

"Call me Andronicus; everybody does. 'Peter' is essentially a throwaway name. Listen, Jack, it's great we stumbled across each other like this. You see, I've got another customs-related question. There's a little bar over here—a dingy old place, but private. If you don't mind...my inquiry is a little, shall we say, *sensitive*..."

Andronicus suddenly paused, still looking at Jack. Two blue-uniformed National Police officers were passing, lightly swinging their neural truncheons. It was unusual to see only two NPs on a patrol, but then Jack noticed a man following behind them wearing drab business attire and opaque, perfectly round spectacles. He briefly glanced at Jack. A drone the size of a ping-pong ball circled the man's head like a satellite.

Jack realized that this third man was probably an agent of the Mind Police, as they were colloquially called. Technically, they were the Committee of Commercial Security. They had begun as the private consumer-surveillance arm of the Chamber of Commerce, and had evolved into Wall Street's most secretive intelligence gathering organization, an American Gestapo dedicated to rooting out ConsumerCrime among the citizenry. The Security Agency had little to do with them, other than trying to hack their databases for information, which was easily enough done, as the Lords of the Chamber of Commerce were very easily paid off.

In any case, concluded Jack, some low-level citizen was probably about to be arrested for Product Slander.

"Sure," he said to Andronicus, as soon as the three men had passed. "I'd be happy to answer your question."

"Capital fellow!" replied Andronicus cheerfully.

Jack hoped the question wouldn't be too complicated. As part of his official cover, he had been instructed in the basic laws and regulations governing customs. But he was by no means an expert.

Jack followed Andronicus towards The Cock and Bull bar, which stood between a gun shop called Hang 'Em High and an unnamed store displaying refurbished pharmatainment equipment. They went all the way to the back of The Cock and Bull, where they sat down at a small table against the wall.

With his dark eyes, Andronicus looked at Jack searchingly. He cleared his voice and spoke softly, virtually in a whisper. "Do you mind if we put our phones in this special lead-lined case?" he asked, taking a small box out of his suitcase and placing it on the table.

Jack stared, surprised. "Why?"

Andronicus winked and nodded towards the little box. Jack stared. Andronicus nodded again.

"There's nothing to worry about," said Jack. "My phone is off. I pay the monthly Off Tax just so it doesn't continually bug me with advertisements. Anything we discuss is confidential."

Andronicus took a Cock and Bull paper napkin, clicked his pen, and drew a dialogue bubble next to the rooster's beak. Inside the bubble, he wrote: *Nothing Is Ever Off, Jack.*

The brashly grinning rooster seemed to be looking directly at Jack as it perched on the horn of the fat, slumbering bull. The effect was weird.

"Trust the rooster, Jack," said Andronicus softly.

Keeping his eyes on Andronicus, Jack slowly took his communicator out of his pocket and placed it in the box. It lay there like a playing card made of very thin black plastic. Andronicus did the same with his own phone, which turned out to be the pen he had just written with.

"What's your question?" asked Jack warily.

Andronicus smiled smugly and sat back, reaching into his overcoat and removing a pack of cigarettes. "Do you mind if I smoke?"

Jack shrugged. "I don't. The bar owner might, though."

Andronicus drew out a cigarette and then said, "Oh, I forgot, I don't smoke." He threw the cigarette on the floor, crushed the packet in one hand, and dropped it on the table. "In fact, I've *never* smoked in my life. Strange, isn't it, Jack. *I've never smoked.* I find the whole idea of smoking repulsive. And yet here I am with a cigarette pack in my pocket. So maybe I *do* smoke. Maybe my memories have been altered, and so this thing, this cigarette pack, now seems like an alien object when in fact it is a close friend."

Jack looked at him evenly. "What's your point?"

"My point is that sometimes people plant things on us that we don't want. Things, or memories. I seem to recall, Jack, that you wanted to be an archeologist when you were young."

"How the *hell* would you know that?"

"And here you are, a customs inspector. In your youth, you dreamed of digging through the ruins of ancient civilizations, but now you dig through people's luggage."

Jack's unease was quickly escalating. This conversation was not going quite the way he had anticipated. "Listen, Andronicus, you may have saved my life, but that doesn't give you the right to intrude in it. Have you been researching my background?"

"My friend, my friend...*no*," said Andronicus soothingly. "I didn't have to research your background. Look at the world we live in. Information flows here, flows there. It flows up and down, it turns around. Webs. Internets. The Deep Net. Metanets. Clouds drifting along. Candy Castles in the sky. We see *everything* from a variety of political, social, biological, economic, and spiritual perspectives now, and in the end, so far as I can recollect, we don't really *know* much of anything, do we?"

Jack blinked again, and tried to keep calm, though he appeared to be facing a madman.

"There is an active World Mind," continued Andronicus, "and anyone can tap into it to find what they want. Curious about the man whose life I had saved from the Darkness of Existential Extinction, I did a little poking here and there. I found a very pleasant photo of a younger and somewhat awkward-looking Jack Tone. A yearbook photo from St. Peter's Prep in Jersey City. It said, 'Jack Tone wants to be an archeologist.' That's all it said. You were not really active in any clubs, other than the Archeology Club, which you founded and of which you, apparently, were the one and only member."

"I don't know if you are prepping me for a threat, or a bribe, or what. But this conversation is over and I must go." Jack made to stand up.

Andronicus sat back, smiled, and then assumed a square-shouldered, officious posture. He made his voice theatrically deep: "I'm Security Officer Jack." He saluted.

Jack narrowed his eyes. "What did you just say?"

Andronicus raised his eyebrows innocently. "What—did I say something to distress you, Security Officer Jack?"

"You didn't get *that* information from my *high school yearbook.*"

"No. But I *did* get it from the World Mind. Any and all information about any and all people is either available on the World Mind or can be deduced from the information that is there, with 99.9 percent accuracy. *Our people* have become experts at navigating the informational labyrinth, Jack. You spy on us, we spy on you."

"Who the hell are you?" replied Jack, his voice rising. "And what do you mean by '*our people*'?"

"You have your people, we have ours. Your people are the servitors of the Corporate-Government alliance, the federal stooges of the Wall Street Werewolves, the Corporationist Creeps, and the Banker Gangsters—the Greedheads. We represent the people of Earth, the citizens of the Human Nation. Decide which side you are on, Security Officer Jack Tone, General Schedule 13. But choose carefully. In the end, you are nothing to them. No degrading vice, no filthy passion, no heartless cruelty, no bigoted impulse, no exploitive program, no godless blasphemy, no agonizing disease is off-limits to the American Corporate Capitalist. The bull-worshipping pigs will take any of these things, or all of them, and attempt to turn a Profit. When you cease to be profitable, you too will be discarded. It's the American Way, and it has been so since America was founded on the rape of indigenous people and slaves. America must be re-founded anew, this time on the pure ideals of liberty and life."

Jack nodded. Now he understood. Andronicus was an Undesirable. And Jack had fallen for a trap—a very dangerous trap. "Good day, sir."

Jack stood up and made to leave the table, but Andronicus jumped up and blocked him. "Ask yourself one question before you go. Are you *happy* in your work? If so—if you are a happy man, a happy employee, and a happy citizen—don't call the number stored on this disposable cell phone. I repeat, do not call this number." Andronicus held out the phone.

Jack took the phone and dropped it on the table. "Who are you to presume anything about my professional happiness?"

Andronicus held his arms out wide. "I am no one to presume anything. But something tells me that going into an office every day to run endless illogical security checks, to file reams of paper and write yards of memos, to race like a rat with other Security Officers to the PISIBANK computer—all this is starting to erode your sanity. Am I wrong, Jack?"

"How do you know about PISIBANK?"

"Is PISIBANK driving you crazy, Jack? What if I were to tell you that PISIBANK is not just a database, but also an artificial intelligence? Would you believe me?"

"*How do you know about PISIBANK?!*"

"Let's just say that one of your ghosters *isn't* a ghoster. Let's conjecture that they work for us."

"You keep saying 'we,' 'us.' Who is this 'we'? Who are you working for?"

"I'm going out on a limb here, Jack—because I suspect that you, in your heart of hearts, are with us. That you will join us and win your freedom. We are not a terrorist group. We condemn *all* violence." Andronicus held up a finger. Behind him, Jack could see the happy hour patrons at the bar and tables, drinking and chattering away the day's concerns, gazing half-insensate at 3-D telescreens. But he couldn't hear any noise, only Andronicus's voice. It was as if the interior of the bar was simply a scene whose purpose was to frame Andronicus.

"We possess no weapons other than Truth," Andronicus continued gravely. "We are a political action organization, dedicated to the peaceful and legitimate overthrow of the Corporationist state. There is nothing illegal about us at all. But there is no place for us in America's stagnant political system. So we are obliged to operate in the shadows. We call ourselves The Friendly Neighborhood Political Discussion Group."

Jack's mind started racing. He knew all of the allegedly nonviolent dissident political groups—those that were not terroristic and not affiliated with any of the banned "Non-Patriotic" parties. But he had never heard of "The Friendly Neighborhood Political Discussion Group," had never encountered it in any database, had never seen mention of it in any generated report. Either this group was very new or it didn't really exist.

"What do you want from me, Andronicus?"

"I just want you to come to a meeting, that's all. It's perfectly legal. You actually have a constitutional right to go to political meetings and discuss things, even if most citizens nowadays refrain from exercising this right because of fear of retaliation from the Corporatocracy. Call the number on that phone, and you will hear the time, place, and date of the meeting. I strongly encourage you to attend, Jack. After all, if the Great Spirit is active in the world, then surely he made me his instrument in saving you, and he did so for a reason. I hardly think he spared you from death because he wanted you to continue to mentally disintegrate in the Security Agency. You have nothing to lose but the chains that are dragging you into the abyss of slavery and insanity."

Andronicus took his own phone out of the box and walked away. Jack waited a few moments and then picked up his phone. He hesitated a split second before bending down and snatching Andronicus's disposable phone from the table, slipping it furtively into his coat pocket.

F9

The next evening, while returning by the ferry to his apartment in Jersey City, Jack dialed the number on the disposable phone. He heard Andronicus's recorded voice:

"Jack, if you've called this number, that means you are seriously interested in attending our meeting. I am honored. This Saturday, take the two p.m. Amtrak Great North Unlimited from Penn Station to 30th Street Station in Philadelphia. When you arrive at 30th Street, ascend to the main level of the station. You will see a statue of an angel holding a fallen soldier. Exit the station on that side. Take care crossing the street, and proceed until you come to a bridge spanning the Schuylkill River. Cross that bridge on the left side. Continue along JFK Boulevard until you come to the corner of the large Masonic temple, across from City Hall. Wait there, and a courier will meet you. And Jack, please take care. I don't want to alarm you, but I think you may be in great danger. If you see any tall, gaunt-looking characters in dark federal suits with broad-brimmed fedoras, do not in any way let on that you have noticed them." There was a pause, but by this time Jack had concluded that Andronicus was a dangerous nutjob. First thing in the morning, he would report this whole episode to a supervisor.

Andronicus spoke again: "And Jack, I have information about the circumstances of your parents' deaths."

Jack was not expecting this. He winced, as if the phone had delivered him a physical shock.

"Godspeed, Jack. Oh, one more thing: as you have probably anticipated, this disposable phone will now self-neutralize."

"*Jesus Christ*," cried Jack, as the phone suddenly grew hot and began to vibrate. He looked around wildly. The ferry was still approaching the Paulus Hook Terminal, so he dropped the phone into the river.

He thought he saw the sleek form of a bull shark just beneath the surface, but he couldn't be sure.

🕈9

On Friday, Jack boarded the train to Philadelphia, a city he had not visited in a long time. He didn't particularly like Philadelphia—he thought the inhabitants were not very friendly, and were even a little hostile to outsiders. Certainly this was true at their sports venues, where they had a tendency to behave like rampaging barbarians or xenophobic tribesmen. But he was determined to resolve this situation, and he wasn't going to turn back now. At 30th Street Station, he walked towards the somewhat ghoulish statue of the angel cradling the dead soldier, exited as instructed, and crossed the bridge over the river. A cold wind was blowing, and the sky above the city was pewter gray. There were no other pedestrians on the bridge, and, as far as he could tell, he was not being followed—certainly not by any gaunt figures in suits and fedoras. Jack continued for several blocks along JFK Boulevard, passing a park on his left, and finally reached the corner of a castlelike structure across the street from what he assumed was City Hall.

He stood there for ten minutes in the chill wind, looking around him, scanning every person who walked by: students and commuters mostly, all of them walking at a fast clip. Two steely-eyed National Police patrollers with neuron guns slung over their shoulders briefly glanced at him as they passed, both wearing uniforms with the NP's distinctive black, white, and blue American Flag patch. Other than this, no one provoked Jack's suspicion. Finally someone tugged on his sleeve. Startled, he turned and found himself facing a scruffy-looking and possibly homeless person in a green Eagles ski cap. His face was deeply lined, his eyes a pale green.

"Yes?" inquired Jack.

"Follow, stranger."

Even in those two words, Jack detected a sharp Philadelphia twang. He trailed after the man along the narrow, unfamiliar streets, until they came to a modest-looking café called the Trappist Tavern. The man turned around and made a quick jerking motion with his thumb. "Go in there, stranger, all the way to the back, and knock on the door with the 'PRIVATE' sign." As he spoke, the man was not looking directly at Jack, but rather over his shoulder and down the street they had just come. "Hurry, stranger. Hurry."

And then the man was off, turning the corner, his rags fluttering in the cold wind.

Jack entered the tavern. A dark passage led to a door—like a speakeasy entrance with a large, grilled peephole. Jack's guide knocked, and the peephole slid open from the inside.

"Who is it?" came a voice from inside.

"It's the plumber," said the guide. "I've come to fix the sink."

The man behind the door opened it to admit them. Immediately beyond was a small interior with a bar and an enclosed area near a bay window where Philadelphians were hunched over beers, conversing sullenly with each other. The place was packed with surly men and women of all ages; all drank dark, strong Belgian ales, their eyes shifting from side to side as they spoke, as if they were all anticipating some invader to burst in at any moment.

For a creepy instant their conversation ceased and they all looked up at him.

Jack thought he should leave, but just as quickly they all looked away, resuming their conversations over their beers and their pots of steamed mussels.

Although he was in the heart of the City of Brotherly Love, all he could feel was paranoia.

He went down a passage, passing a few more tables, trying to press his way politely through the crowd without provoking any unnecessary hostility, until he came to a back room, where even more customers sat in tight groups sipping from large, tulip-shaped glasses of Belgian ale. There was another small bar in the back room; the bartender did not look at him as he knocked on the door with the "Private" sign.

Jack heard the sound of a heavy deadbolt sliding. The door swung open, and Andronicus pulled him inside. "Welcome, friend, welcome!"

Andronicus took his coat and ushered him to a seat. "Friends," said Andronicus, "this is Jack, who is considering joining the Friendly Neighborhood Political Discussion Group. He came all the way from Jersey City. Let's give him a warm hello."

There were several other men and women in the group, who now eyed Jack suspiciously, as if he were some kind of hostile intruder. Andronicus did not introduce them, and they did not introduce themselves. Feeling very uncomfortable, Jack took a chair, and Andronicus handed him a large glass of Chimay.

"Friend Emily owns this restaurant," explained Andronicus, gesturing to a green-haired, violet-eyed, brown-complexioned young woman in riding boots sitting directly across from Jack, who decided her hair and eye color were probably the result of one of those gene-mods that were popular among twenty-somethings. "Emily generously lets us use this room for our meetings. Now, then…where were we?"

The several members of the group were sitting in an irregular circle around a small table, on which were bottles of ale, a bottle of carbonated spring water, a bowl of pretzels, a can of nuts, and a basket of potato chips. No one said anything, but he could feel them appraising him in silence. He was acutely conscious of his outsider status.

"I believe we were talking about *Mission:Impossible* films," said a broad-shouldered, dark-haired man with a Slavic accent. "And cultural memes thereof."

"Ah, yes, Friend Taras," nodded Andronicus. "So we were…so we were…and you were observing…?"

"Only that," replied Taras, raising his eyes musingly, "it demonstrates great capacity of American people for uncritical absorption of cultural ludicrousness that this…this dramatic device, if I will call it that, in which main private agent of movie so effectively disguises face with rubber mask, which in reality would convince no one and simply make him look like monster. Only my point." Taras shrugged.

"I agree," said Emily Bombsinger emphatically, flashing a strange look at Jack. "At key intervals in the story, the bad guy comes in, and then sort of peels off his rubber mask, and, surprise: it turns out to be the Impossible Mission Force agent. I always thought it would be interesting if after that, he peeled off his face again, and it was back to the bad guy. Maybe it's been done."

"I would take it one step further," said a bald man in a clerical collar, as he generously filled up his glass with more Chimay.

"Please elaborate, Friend Doublecross," said Andronicus.

Jack kept his hands locked on his lap. *Who the hell were these freaks?*

The priest took a long swig of his Belgian ale. "Well, what I mean is that the Bad Guy would first take off his rubber face, revealing himself to be the Impossible Mission Force agent. Then he would take off his face again, as Emily indicated, revealing himself to be the Bad Guy again. But what if he were to keep doing this? What would the reaction of the audience be?"

"I have observed human beings enough over the years to answer that," said another woman. She had black hair and wore a high-collared, form-fitting coat with silver buttons. She had a sharp jaw, high cheekbones, and a prominent nose. Something about her immediately struck Jack as predatory, and competing elements of his primal male brainstem seemed conflicted about whether or not she was attractive.

"Friend Polyvox, please share your thoughts," said Andronicus.

"First the people in the audience would laugh, of course. But if the face-stripping continued, they would become confused, and then angry. The accepted action movie paradigm would have been violated. Some would shout their objections directly at the screen; others would walk out of the theater. Predictable human behaviors."

"Friend Polyvox has a good point," nodded Andronicus.

"Especially if the face-stripping were to continue indefinitely," said a burly man with a black, grey-speckled beard. This guy reminded Jack of the twentieth-century TV mountain man Grizzly Adams, whose ancient reruns he had watched with his father. The mountain man tugged thoughtfully at his beard. "If he were to keep taking off rubber faces—Bad Guy, Agent, Bad Guy, Agent, Bad Guy, Agent, Bad Guy, Agent—until this big mound of discarded rubber masks started rising from the floor."

"Precisely," said Emily Bombsinger. "And that's where you have to introduce the change. So suddenly the mask is torn off, and it's not the Bad Guy or the Secret Agent. This time it's Gandhi."

"And then crowd is like, *What effing is going on?*" observed Taras.

An elderly, professorial man in a tweed vest lifted his hand from his brass duck head cane and flourished it languidly. "And then, beneath Gandhi, there is Jesus, called the Christ."

"And then Joseph Stalin."

"And beneath Stalin, Adolf Hitler."

"And then Mao."

"Donald Duck comes next."

"Then Scrooge McDuck, that corporationist pig."

"And then George Washington."

"Thomas Jefferson would be under there as well."

"And then the final revelation," said Grizzly Adams. "The last mask is torn off, revealing the visage of Satan, who then turns to face the audience, breaking the fourth wall, and intoning: '*Beneath me—is you.*'"

Everyone except Jack broke into loud peals of laughter. The laughter ceased as soon as it had begun, and all the members of the Friendly Neighborhood Political Discussion Group fixed their eyes on Jack with pure Philadelphia xenophobia.

"Well," said Andronicus, standing and clapping his hands once. "We didn't get to talk about Marx as much tonight as I had hoped, but maybe next time. Good night, everyone. Be safe."

The various members of the discussion group finished off their glasses, put on their coats, and said good night to each other, leaving Jack bewildered and alone in the back room with Andronicus.

"Well, my friend," said Andronicus with an urbane smile, "what do you think of our cozy little coffee klatch?"

"Is this some kind of joke?" sputtered Jack angrily. "You brought me all the way down here to talk about…about *Scrooge McDuck?* What's going on here?"

Quietly, Andronicus opened up a lead-lined box on the table. He placed his phone inside of it. Impatiently, Jack did the same.

Andronicus closed the box. "That was a decoy conversation. You are an officer with the U.S. Security Agency. Every single phone call you have is monitored, and every conversation anywhere near your cell phone is recorded as well."

"My phone was off. And it's not my work phone."

"As you know, neither fact makes any difference."

"Whatever. And just who was that gang of eccentrics?"

"Possibly fellow travelers, possibly actors hired by me. Possibly both. Philadelphia hasn't yet been completely sanitized by Corporate Power, as has Manhattan—that wealthy, shiny, sterile playground for the Moneyed Classes. There are many misfits around here who, in one way or another, believe in The Cause. But the Enemy advances inexorably, I'm afraid."

"I assume we may speak freely now, here in your den of revolution. Tell me once and for all what it is you want."

"First, and just so I am on the level with you, I must make it abundantly clear that there is a dangerous game afoot in our country today—a very perilous game. And I will simply not be able to reveal every detail of what we know, or suspect, at once. I will reveal things to you as they are needed."

"Why?" asked Jack.

"Because what is happening in America today is so insane, so mind-boggling, that the full truth, or what we suspect to be the full truth, will simply be shut out of your brain by your reasoning faculties. If I told you right now, you would leave this place laughing contemptuously and never come back. Therefore the particulars must be revealed to you gradually, Jack, in the same way that a mountain climber must acclimate slowly to changing conditions during his ascent. The mind, like the body, must encounter new worlds slowly."

Jack scrutinized Andronicus, as if seeing him for the first time. Previously Jack had judged him to be about forty, but now he thought he might be younger, possibly closer to thirty. It was really impossible to say. His black hair was short but thick and hung in locks over a clear forehead. His expression revealed absolutely nothing.

"And what *can* you reveal to me?" asked Jack. "I insist on knowing more. I won't cooperate with you otherwise. Tell me what you know about my parents' deaths. You have an obligation to tell me, and I have a right to know."

Andronicus shook his head equably and gave a gentle shrug. "I can't give you the particulars. I will *not* give them to you, for your own sake. All I can say is that some years ago, something was discovered—something that had been intentionally hidden from the common people, but that might now be revealed. The discovery was astounding, in the same way a scientific or archeological discovery is astounding, with the potential to remake the world. However, it was buried, and the discoverers destroyed. Imagine if a new planet were discovered, but the governments of the world, operating under the directives of the Oligarchs and Money Elites, kept it secret. Imagine if a cure for cancer were finally achieved, but the Elites quashed it."

"An old conspiracy theory, never established by facts."

Andronicus ignored this and continued: "You know, of course, about the Terracotta Army in China, which was discovered in the late twentieth century."

Jack was taken aback. Was the man mad? "What does *that* have to do with anything?"

"Legions of life-size warriors, marching before the tomb of the ancient emperor Qin Shi. They had been buried in an underground necropolis for over two thousand years: spearmen, archers, officers, generals, horses, chariots—a whole army! But they had been forgotten. They are now admired by hundreds of thousands of visitors a year, but suppose the governments of the world had reburied the secret, worried that such a glorious glimpse into another reality might inspire people to rise up against the cabals of evil—greedy, bloodthirsty, and completely unscrupulous rulers that will stop at nothing to maintain their domination. It is the objective of the Global Elites to force most of humanity into a state of utter serfdom and enslavement. And you, Jack Tone, must help us identify the ringleader."

Jack took this in. He waited a moment, then said, "All that sounds a little far-fetched."

"Does it, Jack? You work for the government, but do you trust your government?"

Jack shrugged. "Yes."

"But it doesn't trust you, does it? Trust must go both ways, otherwise it's false. If your government trusts you, then why do they scan you like cyborgs every time you enter your office?"

"Because I might not be me, I could be an infiltrator."

"But once you are in the office, they know who you are. And yet they continuously monitor you through the ghosters."

"How do you know about all that, anyway?"

"As I believe I indicated to you before, we have an agent, Jack. One of your ghosters works for us."

"Who?"

Andronicus smiled. "We have established that your government doesn't trust you. It doesn't trust you as an employee, and it certainly doesn't trust you as a citizen. In fact, you are a citizen in name only. A democratic government, by definition, should be of the people, by the people, and for the people. Ours is no longer any of these. Ours is a government of the rich and powerful, by the rich and powerful, and for the rich and powerful. You are not a citizen—you are a serf in the corporate state."

"I would contest that."

"Do so, but the fact remains money is the expression of freedom in our country today. Each resident has as many rights and freedoms as his or her money can buy. Even with your GS-13 salary, you can't buy much, can you, Jack?"

"I buy what I need."

"Every serf is given what he or she needs in order to exist and produce profit for the overlords. Even our elected officials aren't free anymore. Take the Senate. Do you know what the Money Elites call senators?"

"No." Jack yawned and placed his hand over his mouth. Somewhere outside the room, he could hear a woman singing.

"They call them 'servitors.' It's true...I'm not making this up. In exclusive clubs across the land, on landed estates, in mansions and yachts, U.S. senators are contemptuously referred to as servitors by the Money Elites. The relationship between the Money Elites to U.S. senators is that of lords to vassals. Every senator—that is, every servitor—must pay obeisance to a member of the Money Elite, to his or her overlord. This is because the three most important components of the U.S. Government—the White House, the Congress, and the Federal Courts—answer to the U.S. Chamber of Commerce. The Chamber of Commerce, in turn, answers to a secret organization called the North American Capital Committee. Also known as the Billionaires' Guild."

Jack sighed. "I believe you are a fantasist, Andronicus. But you're an entertaining one! And to whom does this North American Billionaires' Guild answer? The Pope?"

Andronicus chuckled. "The Pope is an outlier. The North American Billionaires' Guild is one of the twelve such Guilds that operate in the world, each governing its own Pharmatainment Zone with supreme authority: North America, South America, Russia, Sino-Japan, Oceania, Indo-Pakistan, Greater Arabia, Greater Africa, Europe, and the Lunar Company. Note that a particular billionaires' guild may have authority over countries that are hostile to each other politically, as in Indo-Pakistan and Sino-Japan. You can trust that the leaders of each Guild are above such rivalries, and are united like siblings in the Pursuit of Profit."

"I wonder why I have never heard of this ridiculous global guild system. Maybe because I don't read comic books anymore, or troll the Metanets for screwball ideas."

"As I said, it's secret."

"Oh, come on, Andronicus. Such a thing could never be kept secret. And besides, what's to keep these various Guilds and 'Pharmatainment Zones' from betraying each other and blowing the whole global conspiracy?"

A broad smile spread across Andronicus's face. "Now, my friend, you are beginning to think like a political discussion group member!

You are correct that, in due time, the various Guilds and Pharma-tainment Zones would go to war, because they are creations of the corporationists, and the nature of corporationist culture is competition and extermination. The most savage wolf is a corporationist pig, though I must apologize for denigrating wolves and pigs in my mixed metaphor. But the fact is that something prevents the various wolf packs from turning on each other. Only something very powerful and influential could do this. What do you think it is?"

"The Trilateral Commission?"

"Not exactly."

"The Loyal Order of the Moose?"

"Negative."

"Good, because I just filled out my application. The Elders of Zion?"

Andronicus gave a somber chuckle. "On the contrary, in certain of the Control Zones, the Enemy highly values the Jews as a default scapegoat during periods of social or economic unrest. That's why every Dictator-Plutocrat keeps a copy of that old anti-Semitic Tsarist fiction in his back pocket. Guess again."

"Doctor Moriarty? Ming the Merciless? Xenu? How the hell should I know?"

"None of the above, I'm afraid. It's The World Committee of Financial Security."

"That was going to be my next guess. They meet in the Hague, right?"

"We don't know where they meet. I doubt they gather together in one place very often. They are a kind of supreme politburo of the most powerful corporate heads. These people—whoever they are, and however many they are, neither of which we know—rule the world."

"One world-government," nodded Jack, his voice edged with sarcasm. "I should have seen this coming. It's all falling into place now."

"We still have many world governments, but we have *one-world rule*."

"When did all this happen? When did these structures of power come into being without anyone even noticing? It's really quite remarkable."

"It began with the Blue War, and continued through the White War and the Red War. It was all part of a long-term Corporationist scheme."

Now Jack was truly flabbergasted. He stepped back from Andronicus. "The Wars were planned by corporations?" he blurted, practically laughing in Andronicus's face. "The wars that pitched the *whole world* into chaos, famine, mass death? The wars that almost precipitated climate catastrophe and the near extinction of humanity—all the fault of *corporations…?*" Jack's voice trailed off. He was old enough to remember the tail end of the Red War, the political and economic upheaval that attended it, the popular panic, the execrable cowardice of Congress and the thunderous silence from the White House, the protests and riots, the mass hysteria that humanity was on the brink of nuclear Armageddon, the equally intense mass euphoria when the world's largest corporations came together and, through force bordering on violence, compelled the corrupt politicians of the world to broker peace. He remembered it as a child, and he had studied it in high school and college. He had seen countless dramas dedicated to The Salvation, as it was called. What Andronicus was alleging was both unjust and treasonous!

"Global corporations *saved* the world from political paralysis, Andronicus. Everyone knows that. And here you are saying that the

Wars were *intentional.* I've got no more to discuss with you. Give me my phone and show me out of this place now. I demand it."

"Of course the wars were intentional," Andronicus fired back. "Crawl out of your cocoon, Jack Tone. The Wars were planned from soup to nuts to achieve exactly what they did: one, *profit;* two, *reduction in the Earth's population;* three, *abolishment of the old political orders and the establishment of one-world corporationist rule.* That's why in political discussion circles, we call them the Wars of the Great Betrayal. Humanity was betrayed—by a brood of the most venal, parasitical, money-crazed Wall Street and international greedheads ever to claw their way hissing and jerking out of a jackal's bloody womb."

"You really *are* insane!" replied Jack, stepping even farther back from Andronicus, until he was almost against the wall. "You actually believe all of this demented nonsense? How are you privileged to know this information, anyway?"

"I was in the Red War...as second lieutenant just out of the academy. I was on the staff of a prominent general, and had access to critical information. Near the conclusion of the war, that general was assassinated, and several of us in the officer corps began to piece things together and realize what was going on. Of course, by that time it was too late. These wheels had been turning since before we were born, Jack."

"I don't believe you, not for a minute. Both my parents served during the Wars. They never said anything about this at all, and they were liberals, very progressive. They would have spoken out if they had known of such betrayal."

"Liberals, progressives," Andronicus sneered. "Absolutely meaningless terms. As meaningless as the Nobel Peace Prize. What did your parents do during the Wars, anyway?"

"They were civilian geologists in the Army Corps of Engineers," said Jack, insulted. He was proud of the fact, and still treasured their commendations.

"That was a rhetorical question. You don't think I know who your parents were? We did our homework on you, Jack." Andronicus paused, as if waiting for Jack's response, but Jack did not oblige him. He continued, "Well, the general I worked under met regularly with the U.S. National Security Council. I knew things your parents never even dreamed of…at first." Andronicus made an expression of regret. "But now that you mention it, I must now broach this most painful subject—that of your parents."

Jack said nothing.

"They died…" began Andronicus solemnly.

"They died in an accident when I was eighteen. So what of it? What does that have to do with anything?"

"Your mother and father were murdered—murdered by the State. They were the discoverers of the Dangerous Secret I mentioned earlier."

"Oh my God… It's time for me to go." Jack struggled for words, and then said, "My parents were working for the U.S. Geologic Survey when they died. What the hell kind of dangerous secret could they have discovered? A new fault line in the North American Plate?"

Andronicus placed a hand on Jack's arm. "Seventeen years ago they discovered what we call 'The Plot' and courageously sought to do something about it. As a result, they and several of their closest associates were taken out."

Jack laughed mirthlessly and shook his head. "No, my parents were killed in a car accident."

"The accident was contrived." Andronicus placed a fat file on the table. "This report was completed by two of our most trusted analysts, who assiduously and tirelessly deduced the truth from the World Mind. It was reviewed by Number One."

"Number One?"

"You might call him our leader."

"Okay, now I've heard everything."

"All of the peaceful, non-terrorist, politically dissident organizations on the East Coast—or most of them—regardless of their political philosophies, acknowledge the status of Number One as a wise and authoritative personage. He or she—Number One's identity is concealed from us—is a mathematician and master logician. When there are disputes between the factions, Number One is the final arbiter. Number One personally reviewed this report. You should read it, but before you do, I will summarize what it says."

"Don't bother. I'm not in the mood for any more of your fiction."

Andronicus again ignored him. "Your father and mother, both in the Federal Senior Executive Service, were killed because of what they knew. Your old company, where you worked as an editor, did not go out of business because of financial misadventure, but was killed off intentionally, compelling you to seek the only other employment you thought would be gainful—federal employment, following in the steps of your parents. You were hired by the government because they wanted to keep an eye on you, as the son of two eliminated troublemakers. As it turned out, you were a dutiful and scrupulous employee. You now have the highest performance rating, and access to the PISIBANK database. They see you as a success. They see you as someone transformed. It is important for them to continue to believe both these things, for what they have done to you—destroying your family and winning your total loyalty—is what they wish to do to all of humanity. They wish to separate us from all bonds but those of the Corporate State. They wish to destroy love. So far, this pride, this conceit, has prevented them from suspecting that you are in any way wavering in your loyalty to the Corporate State."

"Total nonsense," blurted Jack. In truth, he wasn't sure what to think.

Andronicus held up a finger. "Let me continue. The very fact that your behavior pattern has recently been characterized by anomalies means that you will be discovered quite shortly, and you will be eliminated. Therefore, you must do something very dangerous to save your country and to save yourself. You must generate a complete assessment on Senator Lance Boyler of Pennsylvania—one of the most venal and corrupt human beings ever to be born of woman. He is a Servitor's Servitor, a slavish vassal of an as-of-yet unidentified Corporate Overlord. Faction Nine believes, and Number One concurs, that Boyler's corporate overlord is the mastermind behind the Plot. We must learn who that corporate overlord is. You, with your access to PISIBANK, can provide information that will reveal this person's true identity."

"Faction Nine?" asked Jack.

"Excuse me?"

"You said 'Faction Nine.' What's that?"

"Oh, that's just shorthand for The Friendly Neighborhood Political Discussion Group." Andronicus waved a dismissive hand. "If you don't mind, let's get back to the question of PISIBANK access."

Jack looked at Andronicus searchingly.

"Is something the matter?" asked Andronicus.

"You don't seem delirious," said Jack, "even though you sound it."

"Read the report yourself," replied Andronicus, holding out an old-fashioned paper file bound with plastic fasteners.

Jack took it, flipping through it cursorily, stopping when he came to a section of photographs, which he dared not look at—images of two wrapped bodies, presumably burned beyond recognition. He had a sick feeling that Andronicus was not lying to him.

"Can you do a security rundown on Lance Boyler?" asked Andronicus.

"I don't think you have any comprehension of what a tortuous labyrinth the security bureaucracy is. It is intentionally that way, so that anyone navigating its booby-trapped tunnels without authorization will ultimately come to a grisly end. This is the whole purpose of bureaucracy: Control through Chaos. What you are requesting is impossible, Andronicus."

"Perhaps, but it is our only hope. The Plot nears maturity. Something terrible is about to happen."

"Why can't your infiltrator, your spy in my office, do this work for you?"

"Because that person, as a ghoster, has no real access to PISI-BANK or any of the security databases. They only have access to their own databases—databases on you and your fellow Security Officers. Our operative does have one additional power, though...."

Andronicus paused; his eyes became icy. He crossed his arms over his chest, and his voice lost its timber of reasonable appeal. It was suddenly hard—ruthlessly hard. "Our operative has the means to designate you, Jack Tone, a Suppressive Employee of the Federal Government. I can only conjecture that once this designation is finalized, there will follow interrogation, incarceration, and other unpleasant things."

Jack was no longer angry, or amused. He felt cold. He felt dead already.

"Tell me this," he said to Andronicus. "Who was driving the KrunchyKake delivery truck that almost 'hit' me?"

Andronicus looked thoughtfully at Jack. "You think that was a setup? You're too suspicious, Jack. Follow my instructions carefully, and everything will be okay. You will survive, and then we will bring you fully into the democratic underground, where the tentacles of the Corporatocracy will never find you. Do you accept the mission?"

Jack swallowed hard. "No! I don't accept the mission. I don't even know what you're talking about—all this is too crazy. I don't even know who you are, Andronicus."

The chill evaporated from Andronicus's eyes. He was again the genial friend, the guiding older brother, the concerned persuader. "My friend, you are very tired. Sleep on the matter, and we can continue the discussion in the morning."

Andronicus showed Jack to a small room on the fourth floor, with a single window that looked out onto a narrow alleyway. There was a bed, a nightstand, and a bathroom with a sink whose outdated fixtures looked like relics from the turn of the century. When the door closed behind Andronicus, Jack was glad to be alone again. Though he had been defiant, even rude, to Andronicus, his mind was in turmoil, and he regarded the bound paper report in his hands with a mixture of curiosity and dread.

¶9

Andronicus returned to the meeting room, where he poured himself a Scotch and dropped into one of the chairs. The door opened, and the tall, dark-haired woman with the high-collared coat came in. She sat down in the chair across from Andronicus, but said nothing. Andronicus did not immediately raise his eyes to connect with hers. Instead, he kept looking at the far wall, as if he were contemplating something of critical importance, some matter of which she might or might not be aware. However, he was perfectly sensible to the fact that she was there, that she had just come in and seated herself across from him.

Karin Polyvox had first come to the discussion group about a year ago, with a letter of recommendation from Number One. She had requested a "transfer" from the Anarchist Faction Six, after having had some kind of disagreement with its brilliant but erratic leader Bluebeard. Number One had provided few explanatory details, but had asked Andronicus to take her in. Number One had no real authority in such matters, but he or she was so esteemed among most of the factions that any such letter would have been treated more or less like a direct order. Andronicus complied.

Polyvox had proven to be a very efficient and capable field operative, sometimes going away for weeks at a time, but always coming back with extremely valuable information. Her ability in this regard was a bit uncanny. But to Andronicus, she was as cold and unemotional as a vampire. His cunning for getting into people's heads had failed with her, and she was as much a mystery to him now as the day she had walked through the door of the Trappist Tavern. He knew only that she was Canadian, that she had been raised in some quasi-religious community of political radicals with its own bizarre origin myth, and that she had spent a lot of time overseas.

It was that origin myth that he at once believed and disbelieved.

She refused to carry any kind of weapon other than a telescoping battle staff that could deliver both lethal and non-lethal shocks. She always wore the same long coat with the high collar, and black boots. At first he'd quietly resented her presence, but Max Blackshield,

Faction Nine's director of intelligence, regarded her highly, and she remained. Andronicus suspected that she and Blackshield had worked together before, but he never inquired more deeply. Over time Polyvox had revealed some things about herself to Andronicus, things that would have shed light on her peculiar demeanor and frame of mind—had he believed them. Yet the order she belonged to was apparently very rich, and provided Faction Nine with essential financial and technological support. Because of this, Number One's recommendation, and Blackshield's approval, Andronicus did not probe too deeply into her origins. But he never relinquished his suspicions.

Finally, he looked up and nodded at her. "Good evening, my friend."

"Have you turned him yet?" she asked bluntly, looking at him with eyes of frosty gunmetal gray.

"I'm working on it. A drink?"

She shook her head.

"Doctor Krypton's psych-report gave us the heads-up," he continued. "Tone is the kind of introvert who on the surface seems a pushover, but who at his core is much harder to crack. A small percentage of federal employees fall into this category."

"The stubborn ox posing as a milquetoast," she said. "As opposed to the standard milquetoast."

"Exactly. It's a defense mechanism. Confronted with an absurd order by a bureaucratic superior, you obsequiously consent, and then you find a way around it. But I assume you were listening to our conversation, anyway."

She nodded. "We need him to do one thing, and one thing only, Andronicus. If we can get him to do that, success will be ours."

"Are you implying he's expendable?"

"He is a tool of the Enemy, is he not?" replied Polyvox.

"Well..." Andronicus finished off his Scotch and shrugged noncommittally. "The whole world is a tool of the Enemy."

"You showed him the report on his parents' death," she said.

"Of course."

"He will read it tonight, or at least leaf through it. He will think about it. I suspect this will push him over the edge of his indecision and into our hands. He strikes me as depressive. This will work to our advantage."

"What do you mean by 'depressive'?"

"Krypton is clear on this. Tone is in a state of existential crisis. Though highly intelligent, his sanity is eroding and he's beginning to wonder whether existence is in fact worth all the trouble. I think you understand what I'm getting at, Andronicus. We have a certain window of opportunity here, after which Tone will no longer be of any use to us because dead men make lousy informants."

"I feel a bit sorry for him," said Andronicus, staring dismally into his empty glass. Outside, in the main bar of the Trappist Tavern, they could hear the murmur of the patrons.

"If I'm not mistaken," she said flatly, "pity is what occasioned your downfall in your previous life. Please don't let your objectivity be subverted by emotionality, my friend. As a human being, Tone of course has inherent value, but for us he must be a means to an end, so that we can preserve the lives of many millions more. I think it is one of your own who said it is proper that one should die for the good of the many."

Polyvox stood up from her chair, reached into her pocket, removed black gloves and a watch cap, and pulled them on. "It's cold out there. It's bleak. But at the same time, there's something beautiful about this cold. I think I'll take a walk. Want to come with me?"

Andronicus weighed the invitation. The Northern Hemisphere was currently in the Diablo III Weather Cycle, where scorching hot summers quickly gave way to bitterly cold winters punctuated by violent snowstorms. So far they had been spared any major blizzards, but meteorologists were predicting a real monster before the spring equinox, one that might even compromise the massive levees that flanked the coastal cities.

"I'll pass," he said. "Rather, I thought we might share a drink outside at the bar. Emily is singing tonight. 'Classics from the Great American Songbook.'"

"It's late. I'm tired. I'm going back to my apartment. Where are you sleeping tonight?"

"I'll stay in one of the rooms here."

"You should come back with me. I have many rooms, as you know, and they are very quiet."

"I want to be here when Tone gets up, to continue our conversation."

"Of course." Polyvox walked over to where Andronicus was sitting. "Would you like some free advice? Give Tone some food in the morning. Your kind always gets more pliable with a good meal in the stomach. An egg sandwich, perhaps. Krypton's report indicated that he likes egg sandwiches. But no bacon or sausage. Krypton also determined that he is pre-vegetarian, with an emerging revulsion for animal flesh."

"A strange man, that Tone."

"Krypton's report also indicates that he underwent therapy in the wake of his parents' murder."

"I've read the report, Polyvox. Apparently, however, not as closely as you have."

She placed a hand on his shoulder and squeezed it tightly, which was the extent of her displayed of camaraderie. "Good luck going in for the kill, Andronicus. We are at that critical juncture where small actions are crucial, and this time *everything* will depend upon what you say to him tomorrow."

Andronicus took a deep breath. He stood up and walked with her through the main bar of the Trappist Tavern. Green-haired Emily Bombsinger was behind the bar, chatting with a drunk customer while Petriv sat nearby, his burly Ukrainian hands shoved in his pockets. Emily smiled at them as they passed. They went through the exit door, down a little hallway, and out onto the street. It was bitterly cold, and snowflakes swirled down from the buildings above. They stood for a few moments on the street, next to each other, saying nothing. Only a few autocabs passed, and there were no pedestrians. Philadelphia, unlike its more flamboyant eastern cousins, actually enjoyed going to sleep at night, although it didn't necessarily wake up the better for it in the morning.

Polyvox turned to him. "I'll consult with you in the morning about the matter of Jack Tone. Good luck. And remember, Andronicus: *La seule chose immuable sur la nature humaine est son caractère changeant. Ce qui refuse de changer, doit mourir.*"

"The only thing unchangeable about human nature is its change-ability—what doesn't change, must die. Who said that, Voltaire?"

"No, me. *Long* before Voltaire."

Andronicus stood there watching as Polyvox walked down the street and turned the corner. Sometimes he worried about her frame of mind, but he never worried about more mundane things, like the possibility that she might be—as they said in this town—"jumped."

Any pathetic criminal fool unfortunate enough to assault Polyvox might very quickly find himself in the Other World.

Andronicus went back into the Trappist Tavern. He sat at the bar next to Taras Petriv. "My usual," he said to Bombsinger.

Bombsinger scrutinized Andronicus for a moment and then slid him a glass of seltzer with lemon in it.

He pushed it back. "That's not what I ordered."

"Good friend," said Petriv, "Emily and I are in agreements—that woman makes you drink too much."

"Bear in mind, *that woman* has performed invaluable services for The Cause," replied Andronicus, taking Petriv's vodka bottle and pouring a pony shot into his seltzer. "*That woman* was recommended to our faction by Number One."

Emily Bombsinger leaned forward, her genetically engineered green hair rather unkempt from a day of tending her bar. "Just the same," she said with a humorless smile, "we don't like her." She exchanged a meaningful glance with Petriv.

"I know, I know," said Andronicus sympathetically. "But try to remember, comrades, that Polyvox is our sister in The Cause, that life is very, very short, and that the enemy of our Enemy is our friend. We can't afford to let petty personality frictions undermine group integrity."

"Oh, I just remembered, your sister came in today, Andronicus," said Emily quickly.

"What?"

"She said you had not visited your mother in several weeks."

"Indeed, I haven't," growled Andronicus. "Why can't that busy-body understand I'm trying to save the world?"

Emily raised both of her hands in a defensive gesture. "I'm just relaying the message. She wanted to know if you will be attending the Strawbridge's Hunt."

"No, I most certainly will not be attending the *Strawbridge's Hunt*! My mother knows The Cause takes up all of my time, and that I can't waste a single precious second getting on a horse and chasing after a mechanical fox in some antiquated, bourgeois, Anglo-Saxon ritual. If my sister returns, kindly convey that message to her, Emily." He scrunched his brow, then added, "And tell her to stay away from this tavern. It's not safe."

"And what of Jack Tone?" asked Taras Petriv softly.

"Tomorrow he either walks out of here committed to work for us"—Andronicus downed his vodka seltzer in one gulp—"or he doesn't walk out of here at all."

He stood up from the bar and went straight to his room, where he fell into bed and immediately into a turbulent sleep.

CHAPTER THREE

The Conspirators

Jack spent the night in the small apartment above the Trappist Tavern. He tried to peruse the report that Andronicus had given him, but was unable to bring himself to study the photographs of the rusted hulk of his parents' car, or to read the clinical but grotesque descriptions of their deaths. He put the report aside, perversely hoping that it was all just a cruel ploy to coerce him.

The room was small with a narrow bed and an old night table with a single lamp on it. Though he was exhausted, he did not sleep well. Were it not for all these insinuations about his parents' murder, Jack would have fled in the darkness and reported this oddball collection of dissidents to his supervisors at the Security Agency.

But something held him back.

His parents' deaths had been a terrible shock to him at the time, and he had never really recovered from the tragic incident, the hole in his life that had been gouged by that seemingly random event. In retrospect, that period of mourning had been marked by irregularities—a lack of details about the manner in which his parents had perished, the evasiveness of the police, the hurried way in which his parents' old friends had advised him to move on, to continue with his life. About the accident itself there had been many unanswered questions, though in his grief he had not dwelled on them. The car crash had taken place in a part of central Pennsylvania that his parents had never been to before, and they had not even mentioned to him that they were travelling there. And in the months before the accident, both his mother and father had seemed preoccupied with something. He had often heard hushed conversations, and then when they noticed him, abruptly acting as if everything was all right. More than once, strangers had visited their house, retreating with his parents into their office for long talks.

Suppose what Andronicus was saying was right?

Suppose their deaths had not been an accident, but had involved state-sponsored foul play?

Could he actually be an employee of the very government that had murdered them?

And if so, could he really betray his own Agency? A few generations ago, a presidential candidate—Jack couldn't recall the name—had asserted that "corporations were people," and thereby helped sink his own candidacy among an electorate that still despised corporate power. Corporations and government agencies might not be people, but they were *composed of* people. He thought of Spork, Jill Jones, Modell (his supervisor), even the SA guards with their shiny helmets—they were his co-workers, people with photographs of their family members on their desks, people who picked up their kids from school. Each one was a little cog in the vast state security bureaucracy, but each was a *person*.

Could he betray them? His colleagues and coworkers?

In the morning, Andronicus came by with an egg sandwich and a cup of coffee. Jack, who had been sitting on the edge of his bed, stood up, but Andronicus gestured for him to sit down. "You've had a trying few days, Jack. Eat, and restore your strength."

Jack munched on the egg sandwich and sipped the coffee. Andronicus, still standing, watched him for a few moments with intense, penetrating eyes. At length Andronicus asked, "Are you with us?"

"I need more time to think, Andronicus."

"There is no time."

Jack snapped, "What you are asking me to do is unthinkable—to pilfer sensitive information from the Federal Government, information pertaining to a well-known and powerful senator! I'm sworn to defend my government, my country. You want me to become a traitor. You want me to betray my country and the people I work with—I won't do it."

"I'm asking you to act out of love for your country, Jack—out of love for democracy. This is the opposite of treason."

"That's good, because I won't betray my country. I would die first. I am an American, and nothing can make me betray her."

"You speak as if this is what I want. Betrayal. Treason." Andronicus looked scornful. "Perhaps, Jack Tone, you should know that this is *my* country as much as it is yours. It is my mother's ancestral country and my father's adopted one. Both were fervent patriots. I find treason, the betrayal of one's homeland, as repulsive as you do. Benedict Arnold was no hero in my book, even though he felt compelled to act as he did by men who had betrayed *him*."

Jack finished the egg sandwich and gulped down the rest of the coffee. He stood up, glancing out of the room's single window. Below was a cobblestone alley, still deep in shadow. Above, the morning sun was beginning to creep down a wall of sooty red brick. How old was that wall? he wondered. A hundred, two hundred, three hundred years? He imagined the workers of a long-dead generation carefully placing their plumb lines, meticulously laying each brick. Immigrant men with calloused hands, families to support, and all the private aspirations that every human heart traps like a locked box. What would these men think of the alien America of today, the America where the box of the human heart was no longer locked, where greedy eyes stared into it, and grasping hands reached in—all with the blessing of the State? Maybe Andronicus was right after all. Maybe we had forgotten what we had lost. Then Jack saw a figure pass in the alley. It paused; it looked briefly up at the window. Jack realized, in the end, he could trust no one.

"I think you misunderstand me, Andronicus. I wish to go. I'm not saying yes or no to your offer. I need more time to think. I'll get back to you."

"Before you go, let me make one observation, Jack. I know who you are. You are a good man, a man of integrity. You're not some young, sniveling, disaffected jackass of a punk who has been brainwashed by demonically possessed online terrorists into killing innocent people. All we're asking is that you help us in restoring our country's sacred freedoms, to help us save our fellow American citizens from the combined forces of decomposing government and tyrannical commercialism that have slowly insinuated themselves, like poison gas, into the hearts of once-free men and women, inducing societal paralysis, provoking a culture of fear that is now blatantly evident everywhere. What can be the harm in this, and in avenging your parents' cruel murder? That alone should be reason enough for you. It's a question of honor. Your honor as a son, and your honor as a citizen."

"Honor? What do you think I do as a Security Officer, Andronicus? I work tirelessly to destroy fear, to root out the Enemy so that people can live in peace."

"No, Jack," said Andronicus grimly. "You work for the Enemy. You work to promote fear. As a wise man once said, fear is the enemy. The modern Corporationist State employs fear to keep its citizens in a condition of endless subservience: fear of outsiders, fear of each other, fear of God, fear of death, fear of sadness, fear of loneliness, fear of disease. For each of these fears it offers a convenient antidote, but at a price. A new drug, a new movie, a new TV series, a new Pharmatainment Module, a new virtual reality game, a new form of pornography, a new religion, a new obsession, a new manner of death. The American Corporationist State is the master manipulator of fear, and you are one of its drones."

Jack stared straight ahead, avoiding Andronicus's eyes.

"Your great-great-grandfather was in the war, wasn't he?" asked Andronicus.

Jack frowned; this man had a disconcerting habit of hopping from one subject to another. "Which war?"

"The Big One—the major war of the last century."

"He was. But what are you getting at *now*?"

"I mean nothing at all. My mother's great-grandfather was an officer in that war, a West Point graduate. He survived its horrors. A world away, my father's grandfather conspired against the Japanese occupiers. He was captured, tortured, but he too survived. If I'm not mistaken, your great-great-grandfather did not survive. He died at Normandy."

"How do you know that? You apparently invade the sanctity of other people's private lives as nonchalantly as the government."

"America is no longer the country that your grandfather's grandfather died for on blood-soaked Omaha Beach, Jack," said Andronicus forcefully. "Your great-great-grandfather sacrificed his life for something. He died, but not in vain, cut in half at age thirty by some sociopathic, Pervitin-crazed Nazi soldier's bone-saw MG42 machine gun. Lying on a cold foreign beach, his guts spilling out of him."

Jack grimaced—Andronicus's imagery repulsed him. "Do you have to be so graphic?"

"I know war, Jack. Oh yes, I know what happens in war." There was an unexpected passion in Andronicus's voice now. He came closer, leaning down slightly to address Jack. "Your great-great-grandfather might have died in agony, but at least he died for something. He didn't die to make people rich. He didn't die satisfying the Hollywood war fantasies of a rich brat president and his cabal of devious advisors. America may not have been a perfect country then, but at least it was striving to improve itself, to make itself a place where every man and woman was a citizen with rights. America has long since gone the other way. It has become a land where most people are serfs in a neo-manorial system, where every person's essential worth is calculated by how much gold they can pump up into the corrupted gizzards of Wall Street bloodsuckers, for whom even an infinite amount of wealth is never enough. In helping us, Jack, you would no more be a traitor than the Founders were traitors. In 1770, a British colonial officer named Washington was still toasting to the health of his sovereign King George. A few short years later he was ordering his soldiers to fire upon soldiers of that same monarch. Was he a traitor?"

"I don't need a grade school history lesson from you."

"Here's something more recent: your parents didn't die right away in that wreck. They burned to death—agonizingly, screaming. And no doubt thinking of you, their beloved only son. You have a chance to bring those perpetrators to justice, Jack. Have you no interest in that?" Andronicus paused, and when he next spoke, there was an uncharacteristic acid in his tone. "Maybe you have no honor after all."

Jack closed his eyes and kneaded his fingers into his brow. He felt Andronicus's hand on his shoulder. "My friend, it gives me no pleasure to speak of these painful things, to provoke these sad memories within you. Tell me your answer now, and let's be done with this conversation once and for all."

"You'll just kill me if I say no."

"Incorrect. You will return to your government sinecure, your decent benefits, your final retirement, and your inevitable death at the local euthanasia center—a more painless end than your parents suffered, I suppose. *We*, on the other hand, will disappear, and you will never hear from us again. We will be more invisible to you than the ghosters who haunt you at your job. We are masters at hiding in plain sight. In the end, we will die, too. Perhaps not painlessly, but certainly not like obedient serfs put down by their masters."

Jack thought of his parents in that car, of the flames consuming them until they were ashes and bone. He thought of the evil American agents who had consigned them to those flames. He did not know if he trusted Andronicus or not. But he trusted his own passions, his desire to see justice brought upon the heads of those who had incinerated his parents. He did not know what form that justice would take, and he was not by nature a violent man. But in the gloom and misery of that moment, he made a fateful decision.

"Tell me what you want me to do," he said resignedly.

"Every detail has been planned out," said Andronicus brightly. "Listen, my friend, and I shall explain."

F9

"The operation has to be completed by Monday night," said Andronicus. "You'll return to New York tonight. On Monday morning, you'll go to work as normal. You'll perform the security rundown for Lance Boyler, but of course you won't take the printed report generated by PISIBANK to a supervisor for review. Instead, you'll put the report into your briefcase and take it with you when you leave work at your normal departure hour. Don't leave before that. Do not deviate from any element of your typical routine on that day. Nothing you do must provoke suspicion."

"I don't carry a briefcase. I wear a backpack. And there is a possibility I might be called over for secondary exit inspection before leaving the SA Field Office building. If they find the report in my backpack, it's over."

"How often have you been routed through secondary exit inspection before?"

"Never. But it is a possibility. In any case, every employee is scanned on the way out. We're not supposed to be taking any documents home. I have never done so, and the scanner memory banks will be aware of this, because normally I just keep my lunch and a plastic water bottle in my backpack. If the scanners suddenly detect a wad of papers, that might set off a red flag and I could be called over for secondary exit inspection. The most dangerous part of this operation will be getting the report out of the SA building. The security rundown is nothing compared to that."

Andronicus considered this for a moment, scratching his chin and peering at the floor. "Okay, this is what we'll do. We'll postpone the operation for two days. I'll give you a couple of copies of *Model Railroader* magazine to carry in your backpack, along with your foodstuffs, on Monday and Tuesday. See if you are called over. If not, on Wednesday, you do the rundown. Leave the *Model Railroader* magazines in your desk and replace them with the unedited assessment. Do you understand?"

"Yes."

"Once you are on Oversight Street, walk down a half block to the intersection with Sarick Street. Stand there. A nondescript blue car driven by a gray-haired woman of handsome appearance will pull up to you with the back window down. Throw your backpack into the backseat. The car will move on."

"And what about me?"

"A large black SUV will come up to you a few minutes later, driven by one of the people you met last night: the tall woman in the high-collared coat. Her operating name is Karin Polyvox. Get in the car with Polyvox, and she'll escort you to safety. Oh, by the way, how was that egg sandwich?"

"It was fine."

There he went again, changing the subject on a dime. "Good. Those were Amish organic eggs from the Reading Terminal Market. They were not produced by Big Agra."

"Fascinating, but let's stick to the subject at hand. So my safety will be in the hands of this Polyvox. She struck me as a little odd. A strange look. Is there anything you're not telling me about her?"

"You have nothing to worry about on her account. She is a member of a very ancient order of contemplative revolutionaries. Everything is going to work out perfectly fine. I have no apprehensions, and neither should you."

"An ancient, revolutionary order of contemplative revolutionaries?"

Andronicus lifted his hands. "Humans have been scheming to overthrow their governments for thousands of years, Jack. Is it really so surprising?"

F9

On Monday was Jack's first dry run, whose purpose was to verify the government was not already on to him. He would perform it exactly as instructed by Andronicus. He went to work that day, kept a low profile, and completed all of his security checks in an efficient and timely manner. Evening came. He took the elevator up to the lobby. As he was preparing to leave the SA building, the Sergeant of the Guard waved him over.

Jack went cold. This had never happened before. During all his years of employment at the Security Agency, he had *never* been called over for secondary exit inspection.

The Sergeant of the Guard was towering and bull-faced, his helmet low over his eyebrows. The Security Agency Police wore black uniforms with gold trim. The American Flag patch on their uniform shoulder had a black field, gold stars, and alternating black and gold stripes. This distinguished them from other organizations, such as the feared Warforce branch of the FBI, whose uniforms were black and red and whose American Flag had alternating red, white, and black stripes, or the National Police, whose uniform and American Flag were black, white, and blue.

"Good evening, sir," said the sergeant. He stepped forward, the heels of his polished jackboots cracking precisely against the marble floor. "Do you mind if we take a look in your backpack?"

"No, not at all."

Jack tried not to swallow, not to manifest any of the tiny facial gestures that were now being scanned by invisible computers and human analysts of the SA Protective Services. He unzipped his backpack, and the Sergeant of the Guard removed his lunch bag, his water bottle, and the two copies of *Model Railroader*. He flipped through the magazines, and then quickly returned everything to Jack.

"Thank you, sir, you may continue."

Jack nodded, walked out into the icy winter night, and immediately stopped off at Ryan's for a calming beer.

On Tuesday night, it happened all over again. The Sergeant of the Guard summoned him over as he was about to exit. The sergeant removed the contents of Jack's backpack and flipped through the two magazines.

"Model railroad aficionado, eh?" observed the sergeant.

"I am." Jack swallowed, in spite of himself. It was as if he didn't have control of his throat muscles. He himself had been trained to identify compulsive gulping as a possible indicator of a deceiver. "It's a soothing hobby," he added awkwardly.

The Sergeant of the Guard said nothing and replaced the magazines. He handed Jack his backpack. "Good night, sir."

"Good night."

"What scale do you prefer?" the sergeant asked suddenly.

Jack was caught off guard by the question. "Scale?" he blurted.

"Modeling scale."

He cleared his throat, his mind racing. "I prefer HO scale. But my apartment is small, so I primarily work with N."

"Have a good night, sir," said the sergeant. "Take care outside, there's a nasty bite to the wind this evening."

Jack returned to his apartment in Jersey City and sat there in the semi-darkness, a single halogen lamp burning behind a shabby lampshade. Across the room, gazing at him like some bug-eyed, tentacled hydra that had attached itself to his telescreen, was an inert JollyJoy™ Pharmatainment unit that he had not used in years. The endless security dramas, porn documentaries, megapreachers, and skeptic comics not only bored him, but they also struck him as thoroughly idiotic. He had even cancelled his Pharmatainment subscription, which meant he had to pay a monthly cancellation fee, but it was worth it just to know that he wouldn't waste hours every evening hunched over in a headset, losing himself in some semi-real world of sickly, lurid color and abrasive sound. For a while after the cancellation, he had started to read again, but even this had stopped. Now he just tended to sit in the darkness, drowsy with post-bureaucratic brain fatigue, fighting sleep until it was time to get up, wash his face, brush his teeth, and go to bed.

Jack listened. He thought he heard someone walking down the hallway outside, opening a door. His neighbors kept to themselves, and he barely recognized their faces, let alone knew their names. On the coffee table in front of him was a slightly faded photograph of himself and his parents: his father dark complexioned, tall and strong, with a wide cheerful smile; his mother pretty, with sandy hair and pale blue eyes, her face wind-burned. They were standing on a rocky shore somewhere, but Jack couldn't remember where since he was only about four in the photo. His hair was lighter, and he was smiling too, or laughing. He had discovered the picture after his parents had died in the accident. It was one of the few things that the transportation investigators had not taken.

In the years immediately after their deaths, Jack had sometimes silently conversed with his parents in the photo, asking them questions, bouncing ideas off of their static images. At first it gave him a strange kind of comfort, but after a while it had become no more meaningful than a security drama or an infomercial. He was projecting too much of what he thought they would say to him, had they still been alive, and this was being dishonest, disrespectful of their memory. He didn't think about his parents too much anymore, and when he did, he tried to remember his father's strong arms lifting him up to pluck a toy down from a shelf, or his mother holding him close, carrying him down the street to the park, where he remembered throwing crumbs to the ducks.

Now Jack's mind was slowly drawn back to the present moment, to the task he had taken on. He wondered why he had been stopped *twice* for secondary exit inspection. The first time he could understand—the guards had noticed the magazines. But why the second time? The second search might simply have been random—but probably not. Jack concluded that the expression recognition technology had noted some anomaly. At that moment, he caught himself grinding his jaws—something he did when he was very tense or nervous. The sensors had probably picked up the clenching of his jaw muscles and indicated a very low-level non-sensitive concern to the guards, who had then performed a perfunctory bag search. Yes, that had to be it.

Tomorrow was Wednesday. Would the Security Agency Police look in his backpack a third time? Andronicus had warned him not to go ahead if he were subjected to two consecutive exit searches. But the suspense and stress of this whole operation were starting to corrode his sanity. He had to bring it to some kind of completion. Tomorrow was the day. He resolved to go ahead with the plan, and if he were caught and declared a Suppressive Federal Employee, then, well, maybe he could claim these radicals of The Friendly Neighborhood Political Discussion Group were threatening to kill him or something. It would be a pathetic excuse, and it would demonstrate his inferior employment caliber. But he no longer cared. It was time to rush forward, to make a mad dash for freedom at his own personal Checkpoint Charlie, to leap over the barbed wire, dodge the machine gun spray, and win his freedom. Or at least to strike a blow for freedom—a symbolic blow—even if he personally lost.

He had come to that critical point to which all citizens of a degraded political system ultimately come, even if they never admit it to themselves. In this, Andronicus was correct, however crazy he might be in other respects.

Jack had nothing to lose but his chains.

F9

Wednesday, February 15, of the year 2041, dawned cold and clear over the Newark–New York designated census area. And yet never had Jack Tone awakened with such a feeling of dread in the pit of his stomach.

On the ferry ride across the Hudson that morning, the water was black and cold, and Jack imagined the bull sharks churning menacingly beneath the hull. The massive levee pumps seemed louder than ever as they worked continuously to keep the city from being submerged. His sense of foreboding only increased as the subway rattled around him—a segmented, impersonal serpent writhing its way along endless troglodytic tunnels. When he ascended to the surface and saw the SA Northeast Field Office, it had a grim aspect to it, as if every false window was peering at him calculatedly, striving to read his thoughts. It was the visage of a devil with a hundred eyes—each one blind, each one penetrating with its gaze deep into the recesses of his soul.

He entered. The guards stood watching icily. He flashed his badge, displayed his credential, swiped his ID, and presented his retina.

Cleared for admission, he took the elevator down to floor -16.

The elevator music that day consisted of Johnny Kenwood saxophone solos. As the elevator descended into the deepest levels of the SA building, Jack stood next to other silent employees, all of them wearing their IDs on lanyards around their necks, all of them staring straight ahead, like seagulls on the beach.

One by one they exited, until Jack was alone on the elevator, accompanied only by the undulating pop melodies of Johnny Kenwood's saxophone. Jack, a passionate saxophonist himself, tried not to wince at Kenwood's insipid noodlings.

The elevator rang at floor -16, and Jack stepped off, entering his place of work within the security bureaucracy: the ultra-secret Directorate of Privacy Protection. He followed the hallway to his office. Stanley Spork was at his desk, staring pensively at his monitor. The new officer, Jill Jones, gave Jack a sprightly "hello."

He sat at his desk. He was surprised to notice that his hands were sweating as he logged into his terminal. He had to get the security rundown on Lance Boyler done quickly. There must be no delays. The first thing to be done was a manual name and date-of-birth search on the General Register of Suspects, which theoretically included all U.S. citizens and permanent residents.

A message bar flashed across his monitor:

YOUR TERMINAL PASSWORD HAS EXPIRED.

PLEASE REQUEST RESET.

Jack cursed under his breath. He headed down to the office of one of the supervisors, Pannwitz.

"Good morning, Jack."

"Good morning, sir. I need a terminal password reset."

Pannwitz removed a Form G-169a from his desk, checked the appropriate boxes, and gave it to Jack to sign. Pannwitz signed it himself and date-stamped it. "Take this over to Raeder in IT Security. Once he has authorized it, make two copies. One for HQ and one to be fed into your Document Destruction Slot."

Jack took the Form G-169a. "Thanks."

Raeder was sitting at his desk stirring cream into his coffee. He looked up as Jack entered holding the Form G-169a. "I need a password reset," said Jack.

Raeder took the form and glanced at it. "This isn't notarized."

"Excuse me?"

"This form has to be notarized by the Hand Scan people first. Normally you have to schedule that four days in advance."

"Okay, but I just found out this morning that my terminal password had expired."

"You must have ignored the notices."

"Listen, Raeder, I really need this to be done today. I have a backlog of assessments to complete this week. It's urgent."

"Looks like somebody is in danger of losing his Surpassing Excellent performance rating," sighed Raeder, adjusting the round steel-rimmed glasses on his nose as he continued to stare at his own monitor. "What shall we do…what shall we do…" Raeder's fingers jabbed rapidly onto his keyboard. "There, I've sent a message to Greim at Hand Scanning, floor -14. Take the form up to him, then bring it back to me once it has been notarized."

Jack took the elevator to -14 and found Greim in his cubicle. "I need a Hand Scan and notarization for this Form G-169a."

"You have to schedule an appointment four days in advance," said Greim.

"I know, sorry about that. Raeder said to come to you. I need the Hand Scan notarization now."

Greim frowned and checked his e-mails. "Looks like Raeder sent an Expedited Scan request for you. But he didn't attach a G-244 Expedited Hand Scan Request Form. I'm e-mailing him now. Go back to Raeder and get the G-244, sign it, and return it to me."

Greim took a sip of coffee and a bite out of his egg sandwich.

Jack returned to floor -15 and went into Raeder's office. Raeder wasn't looking at him, but he held out the G-244 Expedited Hand Scan Request Form. Jack took it, signed it, and brought it back to Greim on floor -14.

"We can now expedite the Hand Scan," Greim said, taking the G-244 from Jack. "However, new regulations from the Department of Hygiene require that you apply sanitizer to your hands before the scan."

"Fine. Give me some sanitizer. I have to get this done."

"I only have Type III Sanitizer. New regulations require that all employees being Hand Scanned use Type IV Sanitizer."

"Where do I get that?"

"You have to go up to Commissary on floor -9."

"Why can't I just use Type III?"

"Sorry, Tone. Those are the regs. I don't write them, and I can't change them. Ask for Mannstein in the Commissary. Tell him I sent you. He'll give you a bottle of Type IV, then you can come right back here and I'll get you scanned pronto."

Jack went up to floor -9 and tracked down Mannstein behind the counter at the Commissary. "I need a bottle of Type IV hand sanitizer…it's urgent."

Mannstein was unmoved. "And I need an S-4578 requisition form signed by your supervisor." Mannstein handed him the blank form.

Tone returned to Pannwitz, who signed and date-stamped the S-4578. He took the form back up to -9, where Mannstein signed it, date-stamped it, and made three copies, one of which he fed into his Document Destruction Slot. He handed another copy to Jack. "Keep this for your personal file."

Mannstein disappeared behind some shelves and returned a few moments later with a purple squirt bottle of Type IV Hygienic Lotion. Jack took the lotion down to Greim in Hand Scanning. Greim watched attentively as Jack smeared it all over his hands. It had a strong, unnatural raspberry aroma. Greim instructed Jack to place both hands on the glass scanner surface. There was a flash of light, and the G-169a emerged from a slot with two tiny handprints in a box on the lower right.

"Can I see your ID?" said Greim. "For the notarization."

Jack showed Greim his badge and credential. Greim looked from the photo on the credential up to Jack. "The person in the picture looks thinner than you," said Greim. "I can't be certain of your identity."

"Come on, Greim, it's me, Jack Tone. This is my credential. You know who I am."

"I really should send you up to ID Verification to get a Credential Verification Certificate," said Greim.

"It's me, dammit. Jack Tone. This is the badge and credential I used to get into the building this morning. Please just go ahead with the notarization."

"I'm afraid I can't do that, Tone. I'll need that Credential Verification Certificate after all."

Jack leaned across Greim's desk. "This morning I received a Security Assessment order marked 'Highest Urgency.' I have to complete the assessment by close of business."

"That's your concern. Mine is the safety of America."

"If I don't complete the assessment by COB, then I'll have to complete a Tardiness Explanation Report. I don't want to have to say that Biometrics Specialist Greim contributed to the delay by insisting, against all reason, that I obtain a Credential Verification Certificate. But be assured I will include that detail prominently in my Tardiness Explanation Report."

"Are you threatening me by form? If so, I am within my rights to complete an SA-1492 Form Abuse Form."

"Interpret it as you will."

Greim selected a stamp from a revolving rack, notarized the G-169a, and then shoved the document back to Jack. "Good day."

Jack took the hand-scanned and notarized G-169a down to Raeder in IT Security. Raeder removed a magnifying glass from his drawer and studied the two little handprints on the form. "Initial here, to verify that these are your handprints."

Jack quickly scribbled his initials. Raeder nodded, and made two copies of the G-169a, feeding one into his Document Destruction Slot, and scanning the other to HQ.

"Give it about an hour. The password reset ribbon will prompt you to reset the password. You can't use any of the previous fifty passwords you've used this year."

"Thanks," said Jack.

An hour later Jack was able to log in to his computer. It was almost ten o'clock. He had spent two hours resetting his password.

F9

A strange calm and concentration of purpose came over Jack as he typed the name and DOB of Lance Boyler into the Register of Suspects. He knew at this point there was no going back, for this was a completely unauthorized search. Not only did he risk being declared a Suppressive Employee, but unauthorized searches were themselves punishable by dishonorable separation from the agency, loss of all benefits, a hefty fine, and imprisonment in the supermax prison at Florence, Arizona.

ROS generated an Identity String for Boyler, which Jack then ran through CAIRBO. He initialed the five copies in red, green, black, purple, and blue ink. Now came the tricky part. He had to file three of these with a supervisor, accompanied by an Introduction to Suspects memo. Normally the supervisors were so frazzled and busy that they just signed off, as hundreds of ITS memos came across their desks each day.

Instead of going back to Supervisor Pannwitz, Jack went to Guderian. She was on the phone having an animated conversation. Guderian glanced over the memo and signed off. Jack, his heart pounding, returned to his office and fed all of the copies except one into his Document Destruction Slot. The fifth he entered manually into the CRUM database. The information on Boyler was processed and cross-checked on SCRU and RED.

Jack sat at his desk, nervously drumming his fingers until the SCRU and RED results were burped out. He dashed out a Brief of Detection and Security Memo and date-stamped a copy for Guderian to sign. This time Guderian was off the phone.

"Look, I'm pretty busy right now," she said to Jack. "Can you have Modell sign that?"

"Sure," said Jack.

He took the Brief of Detection and Security Memo down to Modell, who was adjusting a framed print depicting Lee's surrender at Appomattox Court House on his wall. Modell took the memo from Jack and looked over it. He picked up his pen, and then paused, squinting at the document before him with technocratic intensity.

Modell was a relatively new supervisor, just a few years older than Jack himself—perhaps only thirty-five. He had graduated from one of the most prestigious law schools in the United States and was already vying to become Subdirector of Privacy Protection. To the Security Officers below him, Modell attempted affability, and usually bungled it, but in a way that made the officers pity more than despise him. To management officials above, he was as deferential as a virgin pledge trying to ingratiate his way into the inner fraternity of the alpha males.

To Jack, the most obnoxious thing about Modell was his inept attempts not to come off as obnoxious.

But he was a supervisor. And in the Federal Government, a supervisor had *power*. Perhaps a mere morsel of power, like a tiny nugget in the pocket of a grizzled, arthritic prospector. But gold was gold, and power was power, and you jealously guarded whatever miniscule bit that fate had bestowed upon you.

Modell was taking a very long time reading the memo. "Lance Boyler... *Senator* Lance Boyler?" He looked questioningly at Jack.

Jack shrugged and tried to sound slightly bored. "It came in this morning with an 'urgent' tag."

Jack kept his hands behind his back, rubbing them convulsively, while Modell pursed his lips and studied the memo. "I don't know, Tone…I almost think this should have a Supplementary VIP Vetting Memo from HQ. Don't you?"

"I don't think that's necessary, sir…"

"But this guy is a U.S. *Senator*. When's the last time we did a rundown on a senator?"

Modell took out the 78 Code of Federal Regulations and flipped through it. He read out loud:

Section 5, Subsection I, Clause (g), Subclause (34), Item (HH), Subitem (dd): In all cases where a Security Assessment is requested for a Person of Prominence (POP), a Very Important Person (VIP), and a Person of Outstanding and Overwhelming Fame (POOF), the Security Officer may, at his or her discretion, write a supplementary VIP Vetting Memo to be sent to HQ with the Brief of Detection and Security Memo. This is not obligatory, and in each instance concerning a POP, a VIP, and a POOF, a prudential and discretionary judgment should be made by the Security Officer in consultation with the Supervisory Security Officer.

Modell frowned. "That doesn't tell us much, does it? But certainly Lance Boyler would qualify as a POP or a VIP, though possibly not a POOF. No, I think we should write up the VIP Memo and submit it to HQ in DC, ASAP."

Jack tried not to display his anxiety, digging his fingernails into the palms of his hands. Why the hell had he even come to Modell? He should have known better. Modell was obsessive about the regulations. He practically had them all memorized.

"With respect, sir, I don't think Boyler can be considered a POP any more than he can be considered a POOF. A VIP, sure, but that's just one of the three categories. And if you look at the wording, it says a POP, a VIP, *and* a POOF, not a POP, a VIP, *or* a POOF. Boyler would be excluded from this classification simply on account of not being a POOF."

"I disagree, Tone. We're obliged in circumstances like this to follow the Plain English Protocols issued by HQ. The Plain English meaning of this regulation is that being a POP, a VIP, *or* a POOF is sufficient for the classification to be valid. But I agree that there is some ambiguity in the way the regulation is written. I'm going to ask you to complete an AS-1066 Plain English Clarification Request and submit that to HQ. As soon as the PECR results come back, we can proceed. Make three copies and feed one into your Document Destruction Slot."

"Sir, it could take several days for a response. As I said, this was tagged as 'urgent.'"

"May I remind you that we're public servants, Tone? Nothing is so urgent that the regulations can simply be disregarded."

Someone cleared his voice loudly behind them. Modell stood up and saluted crisply. Jack turned and saw Schicklegruber, the Director. How long had he been standing there?

"Sorry to interrupt this water-cooler chat," said Schicklegruber gruffly, "but I have to speak to you about your Assessment Numbers, Modell. They're low again for the second month in a row. Forget about that VIP memo. Sign off on the goddamn BDSM and let's keep the balls rolling."

"But sir—"

"You heard what I said. Sign off, and then report to my office immediately."

Modell reluctantly wrote his signature at the bottom of the BDSM and handed it to Jack, who, nodding with submissive gratitude at the Director, fled back into his office.

His brow was drenched with sweat. By sheer chance he had been saved from the maw of almost certain disaster. He quickly produced a punch-card transliteration of the report and processed it through FJOB, ANEL, and ONAAN. Jack took the magnetic strip from the 3-D printer, and then hurried down to Operations Oversight Section for confirmation. Badolio validated the chip immediately, and Jack brought it back to be scanned through IADOFAOSD at the CRAPU station. After the ASECRUD run-through, he took the fully coded Assessment key down to PISIBANK.

Five other Security Officers were ahead of him, like impatient customers lined up at an ATM machine. Stanley Spork seemed to be having some trouble at PISIBANK. He was frowning and shaking his head.

"Come on, Spork," said Derzhinksy, "you're holding up the line. The clock is ticking. We've all got time-sensitive assessments to run. If you haven't gotten your ducks lined up, go back to your office and realign them."

Tone did not particularly like Derzhinksy. He had a reputation for being abrasive and sneaky. But right now he was speaking for all of the other Security Officers in the Directorate of Privacy Protection who were waiting in line to use PISIBANK. None of them could afford to let the ten-minute window expire on their coded keys. They all had too many cases to do.

Spork threw up his hands in frustration, cursed, and stormed away. The line moved quickly after that. One by one the Security Officers inserted their coded chip keys and generated their un-copyedited reports.

The report on Lance Boyler was fifty pages—far longer than a typical assessment, but that was to be expected for a politician of his high status.

Jack took the sheaf of papers and returned to his office, looking neither to the right nor the left. He closed his office door, sat down at his desk, and took deep, long breaths.

For ten minutes his hands shook uncontrollably.

But he wasn't out of the forest yet.

9

He resisted the impulse to leave work early, to claim he was sick. That would set off red flags for sure, and he had already strewn a trail of potential red flags in his bureaucratic wake. It was only a matter of time before behavior algorithms or the ghosters took note of his extraordinarily unusual patterns today. In the Federal Government, you were always being watched.

As usual Jack ate his lunch at his desk, but he did not register the taste of the sandwich he had prepared. He sipped compulsively from his water bottle and tried not to look at the clock. Even now, in his office, he was in danger of being observed by the ghosters.

He did seven more assessments, and every second of every minute of the remainder of his workday, he feared that Security Agency Police would rush into his office and arrest him. The hours dragged on—a torture in itself. Did OSO already know of his malfeasance? Were they waiting until he tried to leave to nab him? Or would they arrest him on the street?

The uncertainty was unbearable, crushing…

Finally it was ten minutes until his scheduled departure time. Jack, feeling as if he had been hit with a severe bout of the flu, turned off his office light with a quaking hand. Removing the copies of *Model Railroader* from his backpack, he quickly replaced them with the thick PISIBANK report on Lance Boyler. He zipped up his backpack, put on his coat, and slung the backpack over his shoulder.

Jill Jones had already left, but Stan Spork was still in his office.

"Good night, Stan," he said as he passed.

He did not hear Stan reply, which troubled him. Could Stan be a ghoster? Did Stan know exactly what was going on?

Jack took the elevator up to the lobby of the Field Office. As he approached the exit station, his legs seemed resistant. Every nerve and muscle in his body was rebelling against his brain, trying to compel him to turn around, to go back to his office, to somehow undo everything he had done today.

For what he had done had made him a criminal.

An Enemy of the State.

He saw the guards in their black-and-gold uniforms. He saw the Sergeant of the Guard standing beside the X-ray machine and the metal detector. Jack joined a group of exiting employees, hoping to escape with the herd.

"One moment, sir!" said the Sergeant of the Guard.

Jack turned his head in horror. The Sergeant was gesturing for him to come over.

"Good evening, Sergeant," said Jack, his throat dry as sandpaper.

The Sergeant was holding a copy of *Railroad Model Craftsman*. "You mentioned you have a small apartment. There's an interesting article in this issue about efficient N-Gauge track layout in small spaces."

"Thanks, Sergeant, thanks very much. Good night to you."

Jack hurried out of the field office building, his knees wobbly. He walked down to the intersection of Sarick and Oversight. A pale blue car pulled up, the back window down. The gray-haired woman behind the wheel did not look at him. Jack tossed his backpack through the window, and the car gently rolled away. He waited for the black SUV.

And waited.

It did not come. He glanced around in disbelief. Every time a vehicle that even remotely resembled a black SUV came into sight, he stared at it intently.

After a half hour, he came to the blood-chilling realization that he had been taken for a fool.

The Friendly Neighborhood Political Discussion Group—Faction Nine, that was—had used him and betrayed him, leaving him to the wolves.

CHAPTER FOUR

Betrayed

Jack was now a hunted beast—he had no choice but to flee. The security bureaucracy, inefficient as it was, never slept. The wheels of its brain turned slowly, and often erratically, but their rotations were constant, and when some pebble of suspicion fell into their works, the whole thing shuddered violently and alarms went off. It was only a matter of time—perhaps hours—until the dull but unblinking eyes of the bureaucracy would turn their gaze on Jack's malfeasance, at which point the whole apparatus would open wide its mouth and unleash a swarm of agents and investigators to track him down.

And the most terrifying of these hunters were the so-called external ghosters—the mysterious agents whose exclusive task was to apprehend renegade federal employees and return them for secret interrogation and punishment. For them, the Constitution meant nothing and civil rights were nonexistent. Clandestine, independent judicial panels appointed by the most powerful moneyed interests in the United States provided legal justification for all their actions; and secret prisons, run at great profit by the Federal-Oligarchic establishment, were authorized to detain suspects indefinitely in their Inquisition-style dungeons.

Jack resisted the impulse to run. He walked briskly down the sidewalk until he came to the subway. He went down the steps and stood impatiently on the platform, his hands shoved deep into his pockets.

He heard the *clip-clop* of jackboots and, out of the corner of his eyes, saw the crowd part instinctively for two patrolling National Police officers armed with sidearms and neural batons. Jack glanced at them and then looked quickly away.

A mistake! National Police officers were trained to react like guard dogs to the merest hint of suspicious behavior.

Suddenly both officers were standing next to him in their heavy winter uniforms—so close that Jack could see the woven synthetic fabric of their black, white, and blue American Flag patches.

"Your Identity Documents, sir," said one of them.

Jack struggled to remain calm, to suppress the urge to bolt back up the stairs and onto the street. These cops were asking for *Identity Documents*, nothing more, he told himself. No need to panic. It was probably just a random Racial Registry Check, which were common on the subway. Race was assigned at birth—a legal process initiated several generations ago when Congress, in a failed attempt to maintain a majority European demographic, officially began to designate as "white" some U.S. citizens of mixed or non-European ancestry. The registry was, of course, controversial, and was ultimately taken over by marketing corporations. For average citizens to change their assignments involved a long and tedious process with high fees. So people unsatisfied with their racial assignments often carried false documents. A portion of the hefty fines for Race Registry Violations went to the National Police.

Jack's official racial identity, based vaguely on his family history, was Teutonic-Celtic-Congolese. Dear God, he hoped that was all these officers were interested in. Could his crime have been discovered already? Could an APB have been sent out?

"Is something the matter, Officers?" Jack asked, swallowing, trying to look slightly bored.

"Your Identity Documents," the officer repeated, this time more firmly.

Jack removed his SA badge and credential and handed it over. The officer's otherwise stolid face twitched very slightly in surprise. He removed a pen scanner from his pocket and ran it over the credential, then handed it back. "Thank you, sir," said the NP officer. He and his partner lifted their neural batons to their caps in a quick salute. "And God Bless America."

"God Bless America to you," replied Jack. "And thank you for your diligent service."

Just as the NP officers walked away, the train rolled up to the platform. Feeling lightheaded, Jack stepped on. He took the train to the ferry station and boarded the next ferry to Paulus Hook in Jersey City. By now it was dark, but there was a full moon, and as he stood on the ferry and gazed bleakly into the frigid, choppy Hudson, he could see the bull sharks turning over, flashing their terrible serrated jaws in the moonlight.

Jack gripped the railing of the ferry as he looked down, the bitter winter wind stinging his skin. Suddenly he saw a churning commotion, a turmoil of dorsal fins, white eyes, thrashing tails, and triangular teeth. Most likely a seal had been hit, and the bull sharks had moved in, ripping chunks of flesh from the miserable doomed creature, until the moonlit swells were dark from the profusion of blood. Tearing his eyes away from the sickening scene, he looked up and saw the glittering towers of Wall Street—the empyreal castles of the Aristocracy of America.

He retreated into the ferry and sat, compulsively rubbing his hands. In fact, the National Police were the least of his worries. He tried to identify ghosters in the crowd of commuters, but of course he knew they would conceal themselves as civilians. The ghosters might be young or old, women or men; some might possibly appear to be teenagers. They could be watching him even now.

A mad thought occurred to him: jump into the river and attempt to swim ashore. Of course, he would perish in seconds, overcome by the cold or chewed to death by the ravenous bull sharks. But maybe that was a better fate than falling into the hands of the dreaded secret federal agents of the U.S. Government, for whom mercy was weakness, and justice an absurd joke—a phony idea to be proclaimed like the pulpit preachments of a secretly degenerate and hypocritical clergyman.

He disembarked at the Paulus Hook ferry station and headed for his apartment near Van Vorst Park. He had formulated a plan: he would pack only what he needed, including his passport, and take the train to Canada. Once there, he would figure out what to do next.

On the way to his apartment building he heard footsteps behind him. Turning around, he thought he saw a shadowy figure slink out of view. He kept watching for a minute, but saw nothing more. He had to get a grip on himself. If he reacted like a paranoiac to every sound or shadow, he would go completely insane—and then he would start making mistakes.

He proceeded on to his apartment building, forcing himself not to hurry. Once inside, he did not take off his coat or hat, but pulled out an old suitcase and threw a change of clothes into it. His possessions were few, and his room sparse. He packed a few books, the only photo he had of his parents, some bottles of water. He deliberated on whether to take his saxophone. He had played since high school, and it was one of his few sources of pure, aesthetic happiness. But it was also large and bulky, and he feared that it might unnecessarily set off metal detectors at the border. It was a risk he could not take.

With deep and painful reluctance, he set it lovingly on his bed.

To soothe his nerves, he drank a beer from his refrigerator.

He had grown up in Jersey City and was now about to leave it for good, but before he left, he had to make one last stop. It was irrational, he knew, but he had to go there.

The cemetery.

F9

In the moonlight, Holy Name Cemetery was a place of shadows and gloom, where stone saints and angels stood silent watch over the sleeping dead. His parents' headstone was a modest one, with the Archangel Michael looking down at the plot, armed with a spear, his eyes heavy-lidded, his face sorrowful. Jack had personally chosen this stone, a traumatic responsibility for an eighteen-year-old. The shadow of the angel fell across him as he muttered a prayer, though in his heart he felt nothing—no supernatural presence, no guiding hand of destiny or purpose. Here in this place, all he felt was the emptiness of death, the oppressive tombs of expired lives and extinct dreams.

The cold wind shook the bare branches of a tree. It made a forlorn whistling sound as it whipped around the broken angel wings and sharp finials of the gothic monuments. Jack felt the presence of death, the final inward suck of air before a body became a corpse. Despondency and weariness overcame him; he resigned himself to his fate. He considered abandoning the whole thing, going into work in the morning and confessing his crime to his superiors. He felt ashamed of what he had done. He would go to Guderian—the least fanatical of the supervisors. He would offer to cooperate in the investigation of Andronicus and his minions. He would betray Faction Nine, just as they had betrayed him.

And then he heard a whispered word: "Jack."

Startled, Jack turned. Fifty feet away, standing by a crooked tombstone, was a tall, gaunt figure in a broad-brimmed fedora and a dark suit. He could barely make out the face of this person, though it seemed unnaturally white. Jack's blood ran cold.

"Jack," came the voice again—a weird whispering hiss. Jack shook his head and blinked. Now the figure was gone.

He turned to leave the cemetery, but as he headed for the gate he saw the figure again, standing there.

It approached him with unnatural speed, as if it were floating over the ground. Crying out, Jack swung his suitcase. It connected, making a weird dry crunching sound. The figure said nothing, but crumpled into a heap of black shadows.

Jack ran for the cemetery gate and the sidewalk. Looking behind him, he saw the black heap where he had left it. Suddenly it rose up again, like a collapsed scarecrow suddenly drawn up to its full height by invisible strings, its unnaturally long arms outstretched, its fingers wriggling slowly, like a sea urchin's spines.

What the hell, thought Jack.

It rushed at him as if it were being whipped forward in a strong wind. Jack ran, dropped his suitcase, and stumbled. Turning to look up, he saw his pursuer fully for the first time: a cadaverous white face, bloodshot yellow eyes, arms stretched out, and fingers splayed like a bogeyman's claws. He could not believe what he was seeing—it made no sense.

What was this thing? Its ghoulishly humanoid aspect certainly didn't fit his conception of an external ghoster, who more often looked like the neighborhood grocer or even the kid on the powered skateboard. But he didn't know what the hell else to call it.

Whatever it was, it was about to pounce when Jack saw a bright gleam of metal. It struck the ghoster full on in the face. The ghoster emitted a shrieking sound and retreated back into the cemetery, where, as Jack watched, it vanished into the shadows of the tombs.

Above him stood the woman from the Trappist Tavern, the one whom Andronicus had identified as Karin Polyvox. She wore her long black coat and was carrying a gleaming tactical baton, which she quickly collapsed and concealed. She reached down to take his hand.

"Hurry, Jack Tone," she said, helping him to his feet. "That was just a scout. It has already signaled others, and soon they will swarm, like hornets alerted by pheromone discharges." She reached into his pocket and took his cell phone, dropping it on the ground and crushing it with the heel of her boot.

What she had just said was almost as insane as the creature itself, but he had no time for questions. Jack grabbed his suitcase and followed Polyvox to an SUV. He threw his suitcase on the backseat and got in on the passenger side.

Polyvox backed up down the street, spun around, and tore away from the cemetery.

"Where were you before?" he asked. "I waited for you in the city."

"Traffic accident. You should have waited longer. Revolutionaries must be patient, Tone. We are not terrorists, savage and impatient. We wait and watch."

"I thought you had abandoned me."

She glanced at him, her eyes bright and steely.

"Faction Nine never abandons its own."

F9

Jack said nothing for a while, as she drove slowly down one street and then another. "Where are we going?" he finally asked, stealing a look at her, noticing in particular a distinctively strong profile.

"Where did you intend to go?"

"I was going to take the train to Montreal, and then Quebec City."

"Then they will have anticipated that, I'm afraid."

"Are you saying the Federal Government can read minds? We may have other powers, but I can assure you we can't do that."

"Not yet, but they're working on it. The Government, in league with Big Pharma and social-media corporations, is working on the problem of mind-reading and control and hopes to have a profitable solution within a decade. But as for now, they can read your mind in the same way Orwell's Thought Police could: by using supercomputers to make highly accurate statistical inferences about your future behavior. They already know everything there is to know about you. Why did you choose Quebec City, anyway?"

"I went to a shrine there with my parents when I was a boy."

"Very well, it can be assumed that they know that. But what did you intend to do once you got there, seeing as how you can't even speak French?"

"I can speak French…my mother was born in Quebec."

"Another reason for them to follow you there. You might as well have left a sign on your office door saying you were heading to Quebec. Would you have attempted to contact your Canadian relatives?"

"I don't have any relatives that I know of. My mother's closest family members are all dead. I've never met my cousins."

"This was a dangerously half-baked plan of yours, Tone. The good thing is, *we* know that *they* know where you intended to flee. We have to make sure they think you are going there."

"And where will we go, back to Philadelphia?"

"Absolutely not. Andronicus has forbidden it. At the moment, you are like a radioactive lightbulb—visible from all points, hidden from none. No, we will gradually make our way to Quebec and hide for a while in plain sight."

"What? Why Quebec? You just said they would know I'm going there."

"You will not travel as Jack Tone. You will travel under a revolutionary alias. Do you have any suggestions?"

"What kind of suggestions?"

"Suggestions for a *nom de guerre*. You can choose an historic revolutionary if you want to."

He paused to think first. "How about Roger Casement?"

"Well, he was executed, for one thing, which is not very propitious. In fact, a name has already been chosen for you. Thomas Darwin Payne. That's your pseudonym."

"I thought you were going to let me choose the name. I'm a bit confused."

"You're a government employee, so that's not surprising."

"We're not all confused," said Jack defensively. "Clearly the feds chasing me know what they're doing."

"This is what will happen. I will set things up to confirm that you are going to Quebec. We will wait two weeks, and then you will travel as this man." She reached into her coat and handed Jack a false passport with his picture, though he was bearded with long hair. The name of the passport holder was Thomas Darwin Payne.

"A beard, long hair—but it still looks like me," said Jack. "What good will this do? Canadian biometric detectors are as good as ours. Once they scan this photo, they will know immediately that it's me. Trust me, I'm a Security Officer. This plan of yours is full of holes."

"You underestimate us, Tone. First, the photo is overlaid on a subsurface image. When the scanners read the image, they will register this hidden secondary image, that of the bearded Thomas Darwin Payne—a fictional U.S. citizen whose appearance, strikingly similar to your own, has been implanted by one of our Canadian operatives in the Joint American-Canadian Collaborative Antirevolutionary Security System. This will bring up a set of fictional biographical details about Thomas Darwin Payne, a geophysicist."

"Fine, but what happens when Canadian border officials actually see me? I can tell you that they've already been alerted by the U.S. authorities. Even as we speak, they're looking over electronic wanted posters with my picture. They're not going to fall for the beard-and-long-hair trick. The wanted posters will include this permutation of my appearance, along with a bald Jack Tone, a Jack Tone with glasses, a Jack Tone with sunglasses, a Jack Tone with his hair dyed, a Jack Tone with a different skin complexion, and a Jack Tone with slightly puffed-out cheeks and bad teeth."

"Certainly they'll anticipate all of that. But contemporary human nature is sufficiently deformed, Thomas, that when their computers tell them that you are not in fact Jack Tone, the border officials will let you pass through the checkpoint. Human intellection has long since decayed to the point where people now trust their machines far more than each other—more than their own instincts, more than themselves. It's the beginning of the Singularity."

"If you say so." Jack sounded gloomy. He didn't really understand what she was talking about. There was something not quite right about this Polyvox—an oddness analogous to a movie where the speech of an actor is not completely in sync with the movement of their lips. He tried to relax. The Faction Nine people claimed to have thought this whole thing out carefully. But still he was nervous. He imagined the U.S.-Canadian border checkpoint bristling with armed guards and crawling with security officials. It seemed inconceivable that he could just slip across, despite their reassurances.

F9

Polyvox drove the car into an underground garage, and from there they took the elevator to an apartment on the fifteenth floor. There were two bedrooms, a bathroom, and one window, whose blinds were drawn. On the wall was a picture of a lighthouse battered by waves.

"We made it," she sighed, securing the door behind her. She led him down a short hallway to the living room of the apartment. "Would you care for a drink?" She gestured to a dry bar.

"No."

"Very well. I might have one myself. Finding you was a bit nerve-wracking." She poured herself a glass of blue liqueur and tossed it back. "This bottle is mine, by the way, for when I visit. It's very strong and might make you sick, so don't try it. And that bedroom is mine. You must never go in there."

Tone looked carefully at this odd person who had rescued him from the sinister attacker in the cemetery. Jack was not quite six feet tall; she was several inches taller. Her hair was dark, her eyes nickel gray. She wore a long black coat with gold buttons and a hood at the back. On her feet were black boots. She had a quick, lithe manner of moving. He could detect no element of friendliness or warmth in her, but at the same time she did not strike him as callous or cruel.

"Where are we?" he asked.

"I can only tell you that we're somewhere in the area of Newark," said Polyvox. She shrugged. "Sorry. They say hell is a place much like it."

"It's gotten much better over the years," said Jack defensively. His father's family was from Newark. "Gentrification and all that."

"Quite. In any case, this safe house was specifically chosen because of its obscurity. There are reading materials for you, and a 3-D telescreen. There is enough food in the refrigerator for two weeks, but don't be too gluttonous. I'll check in on you every couple of days. Don't open the door for anyone, ever. Don't go out into the hallway. Don't open the blinds or look out the window. Random informers are always on the prowl, as you know. External ghosters and so forth."

Jack didn't like the sound of all this. He didn't like being cooped up, and he especially didn't like her mention of ghosters. "I wanted to ask you about that. In my office, ghosters are people who pose as Security Officers, but who are actually tasked with spying on their fellow employees. But that…that *thing* that came after me in the cemetery, what was that?"

"Just an *external* ghoster," replied Polyvox, looking away evasively.

"No, it wasn't. External ghosters are spies trained to keep watch over government employees outside of the workplace. An external ghoster looks like the pizza delivery girl, not a ghoul in a suit. That thing we encountered definitely didn't look completely human."

"It was a man, Thomas Payne. That's all."

"Please don't call me Thomas Payne. Call me Jack Tone."

"Jack, it was a *man*."

"It was not a man! And if you are not forthright with me about the nature of these things, how can I be prepared for them?"

"Very well." Polyvox put her glass down on the dry bar. "Andronicus has authorized me to explain the situation, if you insisted, which he suspected you would. The creature that came after you in the cemetery *was* human—at one time. We don't know much about them other than the fact that they appear to be the monstrous product of some secret Defense Department experiment headed by the notorious biochemist Doctor Ignatz Gottlieb Farben. One theory is that the first generation were terrorists detained by the U.S. Government who were then subjected to a radical form of experimentation designed to turn them into peaceful and complacent world citizens. Things went horribly awry, and the result was a batch of violent, howling maniacs. The remedy involved the implantation of a synthetic organ, derived through genetic alteration of a pig's pituitary gland, which generates a continuous small supply of methamphetamine. In any event, the new beings proved to be very ruthless, obedient, and efficient slave warriors, like Hitler's Pervitin-drugged soldiers during the Blitzkrieg. This is our main theory, at any rate."

"And what are the alternative theories?"

"There are none. We call them 'Plutocroids,' perhaps a neologism coined by Number One, who might have made it up—or who might have learned the name from his own private sources."

"And these spooks are just running around our cities, towns, playgrounds, and cemeteries?"

"Hardly. They are almost always dispatched at night. They are very adept at keeping to the shadows. If compelled to be in public, they will wear their hats low and their collars up, but will move quickly to conceal themselves—down an alley, in a Dumpster, even under water. They have been known to cling like bats to rafters for hours at a time, until the coast is clear for them to slip away."

Jack shuddered. "So is this the dark secret, the terrible conspiracy, uncovered by my parents? These Plutocroids?"

Polyvox looked at him with her hard gray eyes. She smiled slightly. "Hardly. What they discovered is far, far more bizarre, dangerous, and mind-boggling."

"Can you tell me what it is?"

"Alas, that information can only be given out on a need-to-know basis, Security Officer Tone. And for you, that is not currently authorized." She handed him a plastic button on a lanyard. "Wear this around your neck at all times, even in the shower. Press it immediately if you suspect the approach of Plutocroids or any other enemy agents. Now I have to go scatter some red herrings."

Polyvox walked swiftly down the hallway to the door and exited the apartment. Jack heard the door lock behind her.

CHAPTER FIVE

The Flight

Polyvox emerged from Van Vorst Park and entered Jack's apartment building. His door was unlocked, and she easily gained access to his apartment, giving it a quick survey. Not surprisingly, the Plutocroids had already been there. The room had been torn apart and was a complete mess. Even the mattress had been ripped open and gutted. They had picked the place clean of every scrap of information that might lead them to Tone.

In the middle of the floor was a saxophone, but it had been vindictively stomped on and smashed. Polyvox nodded. She knew why.

She picked up the flattened saxophone. Then she carefully laid a receipt for a train ticket to Quebec City on the night table. She placed a glass on it so it wouldn't blow onto the floor. Leaving the door partly open, she left. At some point, the Plutocroids would return, and see the door was ajar. They would notice the receipt on the nightstand and immediately conclude that renegade Security Officer Tone was trying to deceive them, to make them think he was going to Quebec, which of course he was not.

Except, of course, he really was.

She slipped quietly out of the apartment building, moving like a shadow herself, and concealed herself in the park across the street. Pulling up her hood, she watched patiently in the cold. She did not doze, and never took her eyes off the entrance to the building which until now Tone had called home. Sometime after midnight, three weirdly slender, slightly elongated figures in black hats crept along the sidewalk and entered the apartment building. A few minutes later, they silently rushed out.

F9

For the first three days, Jack remained alone in his safe house. He paced, he tried to watch television, he tried to read. He dozed at odd hours. He let his beard start to grow out, and he avoided the ever-escalating temptation to peer through the blinds or to go into Polyvox's room. Every noise, every sound in the hallway, every blast of winter wind against the window made him start.

On the fourth day, he heard the sound of the locks clicking in the door. Polyvox came in and quickly closed the door behind her. He could smell the cold winter air on her coat. Jack was sitting on the couch, looking scruffy and disheveled. In front of him was a bottle of beer and the last of his hard pretzels on a plate.

"Excellent," she said, nodding approvingly as she looked at him. "Neat bureaucrat Jack has been replaced by slovenly rebel Jack. This will do nicely. A casual acquaintance would not recognize you on the street."

"I wish to speak to Andronicus," said Jack, who had been brooding about his situation.

"Why?"

"I want to know exactly what's going to happen to me."

"You have to disappear first, from the radar of the government. Then you will see Andronicus."

She unbuttoned her coat and threw it over the back of an armchair. Jack studied her peculiar attire underneath.

Polyvox was wearing a chest protector that resembled a traditional black vest or waistcoat, with a silver watch on a fob, as well as breeches made of a very sheer, silklike material. Her boots had knee cops and were tied with strings at the back. Her bare arms were marked with several logic-symbol tattoos in various colors, including vividly illuminated runes. Strapped to her thigh was some kind of silver baton with engraved markings in it. She seemed even taller with her coat off than with it on, with solid shoulders, long athletic legs, and smoothly defined musculature.

"This is the field habit of my order," she said, as if perceiving that he found her attire strange. "We are trained from childhood to be immune to extremes of temperature, as well as extremes of pleasure and pain. This is one of the benefits of transcendental exercise—the concentration of the will to the objective of detachment and perfection."

Jack nodded uncomfortably and tried to concentrate on the blank television screen. Polyvox sat down in a chair and crossed her legs.

"It's important that we respect each other, Jack, since we'll be in each other's company for some time now."

"Of course. I wasn't aware that I was being disrespectful."

"I perceived that—just perhaps—you were being disrespectful with your eyes."

"I assure you I wasn't being disrespectful with my eyes or any other part of my body, including my brain." He nervously crossed his own legs and kept his eyes on the television.

Suddenly Polyvox placed a crushed saxophone on the coffee table in front of him. He looked down on it in horror and sadness.

"Is this yours?" she asked.

He nodded.

"The Plutocroids hate these things. At least the Type II, III, and IV Plutocroids. I'm not sure about the Type Is, but probably so."

"They hate saxophones? Why?"

Polyvox shrugged. "The sound has a peculiar effect on them. It drives them mad with anguish. Some say it is just an auditory-neurological effect. Others say that the plaintive harmonies of the instrument evoke deeply embedded remembrances of their lost humanity. Either way, the Defense Department has been utterly unable to counter the effect. They say music soothes the savage beast. In this case, a certain type of music disables them. It's too bad you left it in your apartment. Why did you?"

Jack shook his head. "I didn't want to, I just thought it would encumber me—it might set off alarms."

"I will talk to Andronicus about getting you another saxophone, as a proper defense against Plutocroids."

"A defense?"

"A sidearm of song, in case you are attacked."

"Surely you don't expect me to just stop in my tracks and belt out a tune if those *monsters* are coming after me? I would prefer to run like hell."

"Few humans can outrun a Plutocroid. Not only must you belt out a saxophone tune, but you must do so from the heart, with feeling. Blowing random notes is useless—that will just anger them more. The best kind of music appears to be jazzy improvisation. Classical improvisation works as well. After that, set pieces can be effective. As a last resort you can play pop standards along the lines of Johnny Kenwood."

"I've never played Johnny Kenwood in my life."

"If your life depends upon it, you will."

"This is all so insane. Music is about peace, not war."

"Music, my friend, is about *everything*."

Jack looked glumly down on his squashed saxophone.

"I would like to leave for Quebec tomorrow," said Polyvox.

"Why? Didn't you say they are expecting me to go there?"

"They were, but that has changed. They now think you want them to think you are heading there, if you follow."

"Not really."

"Plus, I don't want to miss the Winter Carnival in Quebec City."

"Is that really essential to establishing the Dictatorship of the Proletariat?"

"No, but while the festivities are taking place, I must attend a secret conference with the members of my order. We'll leave tomorrow morning on the Iceliner Limited from New York to Quebec City. We will be traveling as Thomas and Mary Payne, independent geophysicists on our way to a research station in Nunavut Territory. We'll stay in Quebec for a week, and then travel by train to our next destination. You'll be happy to know that our sources tell us that the government believes you've fled to Europe, possibly with the intention of seeking asylum in Russia."

Jack let this information sink in for a minute. "Suppose someone asks us a question about geophysics?"

"No one is going to ask us any questions about geophysics, Jack. I chose that field precisely because it is so obscure to the average layperson. Besides, I have studied up on the subject and can easily bluff my way through any situation that might arise. And your parents were geologists, so you probably know more than you think."

Jack sighed. "I wish I were as confident as you sound."

F9

The Iceliner Limited left Penn Station, slowly slithering along its ancient tunnel, then breaking to the surface as it crawled past New York and headed north. Jack and Polyvox sat next to each other in a train cabin near the back of the car. Jack sat by the window, staring out at the passing landscape—first the brick, steel, and stone of the city, then its leafy suburbs, then the snow-covered hills of upstate New York and Vermont. Polyvox did not seem interested in anything outside of the train, but instead read a magazine.

Jack was too nervous to read. He felt disoriented without his phone. He alternated between looking out the window and anxiously watching the faces of people passing the cabin door, or scrutinizing those who entered and sat across from them in the opposite seats. Luckily, none of them attempted to make conversation, although a few of the male passengers studied Polyvox with what he perceived to be lecherous curiosity.

The train stopped at Brattleboro, Vermont. Jack turned to Polyvox and said, "What *is* that you're reading? It looks like cuneiform."

"I'm a member of the Neo-Sumerian Revival League. There are about a thousand of us worldwide, and we publish *The New Sumerian* four times a year."

He was about to respond, when an elderly couple entered the cabin and sat down across from them.

They nodded in greeting, and Jack immediately suspected they were chatterers. He looked out the window and tried to avoid making eye contact. The train lurched into motion again, and soon exited the station. They continued heading north, towards the Vermont-Quebec border...and the dreaded border check station.

Jack looked fixedly out the window. Polyvox was absorbed in her magazine. Out of the corner of his eye, he could sense the new couple looking at them, eager to initiate a conversation. He must not, under any circumstance, make eye contact.

Suddenly, the man sneezed. Jack made the fatal mistake of glancing over and muttering "*Gesundheit.*"

"It's a bit frosty up here," said the man cheerfully, speaking with a Southern accent. "Isn't it?" He rubbed his hands in imitation of a person fending off the cold. "Brrrrrrrrr!"

"We're from Birmingham, Alabama," added the woman. "Where are you folks from?"

Jack waited for Polyvox to answer, but she did not. She merely peered, smiling, over the top of *The New Sumerian*. Finally she answered, "We're from New Hope, Pennsylvania."

"Oh, New Hope!" cried the woman in delight. "I have a cousin who lives there. It's a very pretty little town. Whereabouts in New Hope do you live?"

"Right on the canal," said Polyvox.

"I'm Lafayette Calhoun," said the man, "and this is my wife Beatrice."

"Mary and Thomas Payne," said Polyvox, lowering her magazine. They shook hands.

Beatrice adjusted her purse on her lap. "Lafayette just retired and we're both heading up to Montreal. We've never been there. It's quite nice, they say. We especially wanted to see it in winter. I know that sounds strange, but I suppose Lafayette and I have always been just a couple of queer ducks."

Beatrice and Lafayette chuckled together, and held hands. They chuckled again.

Jack watched them morosely.

"Oh, Montreal is a lovely city," said Polyvox. "I strongly recommend the *Musée des Beaux Arts*."

Why is she engaging them in conversation? Jack wondered.

He forced himself to smile.

"And what do you do for a living, Thomas?" asked Lafayette.

"My wife and I are geophysicists, heading to a research station in Nunavut."

Lafayette and Beatrice looked at each other with wide-eyed surprise. Lafayette clapped his hands together. "Geophysicists? Well, how about that! I was just saying to Beatrice the other day how I wished I knew a geophysicist. I have so many questions to ask."

Jack watched the man stolidly.

"Lafayette always wanted to be a geophysicist," explained Beatrice, patting her husband's hand. "In the end, he wound up working in sales for Little Suzie Snack Foods."

"My specialty was the Cosmic Brownie," said Lafayette, chuckling self-deprecatingly. "But I was always passionate about my hobby, geophysics. This idea of tectonic plate movement always intrigued me. I never quite understood exactly how the continents move like they do. It frankly has always struck me as absurd that entire continents could shift from their original positions. Can you explain that, Thomas?"

Lafayette was looking directly at Jack through his round-rimmed glasses, his eyes watery but curious.

Jack cleared his throat. "Yes, of course. It's quite a complicated process. In fact, that's my wife's specialty. I deal more with…igneous rocks, and that sort of thing. You know, volcanic activity and so forth." Jack turned to Polyvox. "Mary?"

Polyvox smiled equably, but Jack thought he noticed an element of annoyance in her expression. "And what is it, sir, that you would like to know?"

"Oh, how the continents move. I could never quite get my head around that. How does something so vast and huge as a continent actually *move*? It would seem that, if the Good Lord created the Earth a certain way, then such titanic movements would be precluded, possibly even a violation of His Divine Plan."

"Well, to put it rather simply," Polyvox explained, "the top layer of the Earth's crust, called the lithosphere, is harder and cooler than the asthenosphere below it, which manifests more fluidlike properties. The lithosphere sort of rests or floats on the asthenosphere, so to speak. But the lithosphere has two parts: the continents and the ocean floors. The continents are mostly granite, while the seafloors are made of denser, heavier basalt. So the continents are lighter and float higher, while the heavier seafloors are lower. As the continents move over the asthenosphere, the basalt ocean floors are forced under them, or subducted. That means the seafloors kind of grind beneath the granite edges of the continents. In this way, over the course of hundreds of millions of years, the continents move and shift, and sometimes collide."

"Fascinating," said Lafayette without much enthusiasm. "Quite fascinating." He pursed his lips and looked away.

Beatrice smiled, but there was coolness in her demeanor, and Jack suddenly perceived that this apparently harmless couple might actually be a pair of external ghosters—the more human kind, that was, not the mutant Plutocroid hunters. Both of them now fell silent. After a while, Beatrice dozed, while Lafayette took out a battered paperback of *Gone with the Wind*. They no longer seemed interested in conversation with Jack and Polyvox.

Polyvox returned to her Sumerian magazine, but Jack shifted uneasily in his seat, considering their predicament, trying to make an objective determination. He was now convinced that these two were ghosters, and that it was only a matter of time before other agents closed in for the arrest. After a few moments he said, "My dear, let's go up to the observation car."

"Whatever for?" replied Polyvox.

"I'd like to stretch my legs." He tried to communicate the urgency of his request through the intensity of his stare.

Polyvox put down her magazine, and together they went to the observation car, where they sat down and ordered tea.

"That was quite a performance—you know your geophysics all right," said Jack. "But you know what I'm thinking."

Polyvox raised her eyebrows in a question.

"That couple down there—very friendly, then suddenly very aloof."

"The thought did cross my mind. But I think there is another explanation. They're creationists, and they were not pleased when

I mentioned that tectonic movements take place over the course of hundreds of millions of years. This conflicts with their biblical understanding that the Earth was created by an omnipotent god in six days."

Jack shook his head. "I think we're dealing with more than a couple of creationists."

"It could be, but I doubt it."

"I want to get off the train at the next station."

"Keep calm, Jack. Honestly, how could someone as jumpy as you have worked as a Security Officer?"

"I was an analyst. I was never assigned to the field as an agent. The most I did was go to prisons and detention centers to conduct interviews."

"The prison-industrial complex," said Polyvox grimly.

Jack saw something. He lowered his voice: "Don't look now, but the Calhouns have just arrived in the observation car."

"Then we can perform a test," said Polyvox. "Let's hold hands and kiss each other. If they are creationists, then they will be put off or embarrassed by this open display of romantic affection. They may not even return to our cabin, feeling uncomfortable about being around us. But if they're agents, they will find a seat to the side and unobtrusively wait for us to finish."

Jack had no time to object—Polyvox leaned across the table, pressing her lips to his, and sucker-punching him with a fiery, passionate, deeply penetrating kiss that caused strange electrical currents to surge up and down his body, rendering him almost blind and helpless to react. When she broke the kiss and pulled back from him, he had no idea how much time had passed, but he sensed it had been several minutes.

His head still spinning, Jack looked across the aisle. Lafayette and Beatrice Calhoun were sitting patiently at their table, sipping tea, pretending not to notice.

"Oh, hello, friends," said Beatrice, suddenly turning away from the window. "We didn't even see you there."

They stood up together. Their coats were buttoned, and they had their luggage with them. "We've decided to get off at the next stop to visit an old colleague of Lafayette's, but before we go, we wanted to give this to you."

Lafayette reached into his breast pocket. Jack noticed that Polyvox had quietly slipped her hand under her own coat—poised to draw her baton? But Lafayette only removed a small paper pamphlet and handed it to Jack. It was a fundamentalist comic strip warning against the error of evolution. It had vivid sketches of pitchfork-wielding devils cackling gleefully as they tossed scientists holding *The Origin of Species* into the fires of hell.

"God bless you, friends," said Beatrice, as she and her husband walked away. "We hope you find the way."

After they were gone, Polyvox laughed.

Jack was angry, but tried not to look at Polyvox. Her kiss had been cold, alien, and passionate, and he now felt himself shaking, as if he had consumed too much caffeine and red wine at the same time. "So you think it's funny?" he blurted at her. His thoughts were confused. "I'm a devout lapsed Catholic and those damned fundamentalist fanatics gave me a good scare. Not only that, but I thought for sure they were ghosters."

Polyvox stopped laughing, but her mirth still showed in her gunmetal gray eyes. "They weren't so bad—besides, I'd take a fundamentalist fanatic over a Wall Street werewolf any day." She looked at him steadily. "A biblical literalist at least believes in something higher than himself, but a hedge fund manager is the closest a human being can come to being the Devil incarnate."

"So you believe in the Devil."

"I believe in devils."

"How about God?"

"My god is a god who throws a grappling hook on the high and mighty and brings them crashing down. A god who avenges the suffering of the downtrodden and the innocent, who pours out his wrath upon the greedy oppressor; a god who rebuilds humanity with bricks baked in the furnace of justice. But I've yet to find that god among most of the human beings I've met."

"Yes, yes, whatever," muttered Jack. "God, I just want to get off this train."

F9

The train finally arrived at St. Albans, Vermont—the border crossing point. Jack and Polyvox were again alone in their cabin. "We're almost there," said Polyvox. "Once we're in Canada, we can lie low for a few weeks. I myself am looking forward to sleeping in a nice comfortable bed."

A voice came over the train's intercom: "Good afternoon, passengers. This is your engineer speaking. We apologize for the inconvenience, but officials of the U.S. Government will now be boarding the train to review the documents of everyone continuing on to Canada. This is merely a security precaution and there is no need to be alarmed. Thanks for your cooperation, and God bless America."

"We have to get off now, Polyvox. We can make a run for it."

"Take it easy, Jack. We've got everything covered. The passports are foolproof."

But he could sense her tension. "I'll be right back," she said, getting out of her seat and leaving the cabin. She returned a few minutes later and announced, "Border Patrol and Security Agency officials have boarded."

"My own agency…this is it, this is the end."

"They're going down the trains, car by car, cabin by cabin, checking passports and doing instant retinal and hand scans. But don't worry, I have a kit."

"A kit?"

"An identity kit, provided by Max Blackshield, Andronicus's spymaster. Maybe you remember him from the Trappist Tavern. A thin, quiet man with dark hair and an olive complexion." She took out a small plastic case and a bottle of hand sanitizer from her coat. "Squirt this on your hands and let them dry. Quickly—the federal agents are just a few cabins away."

While Jack briskly rubbed the sanitizer on his hands and waved them dry, she opened the disposable contact lens case. "I assume you can apply contact lenses."

"No, I've never used contact lenses. How are contact lenses going to be of any use for a retinal scan?"

"These contact lenses are coded with a false retinal image that will be picked up by the scanner. For goodness' sake, Jack, stop asking questions and put in the contact lenses."

They could hear gruff voices in the hallway and knuckles rapping against the cabin doors.

"How do you put in a contact lens?"

"You remove it like this, then hold it on the tip of your finger concave side up. Then you sort of brace open your upper and lower eyelid—then apply. *Voila!*" Polyvox had taken one of the disposable lenses, popped it into her own eye, and then popped it out. "It's so easy…it's child's play."

This was not the best metaphor for Jack, as it reminded him of a creepy old horror movie about a demonic doll that hacked people's faces. He tried not to blink as he pushed a fresh contact lens against one eye, and then the other. It felt unnatural, like he had sand stuck in both eyes. Polyvox pushed his head back, forcing open his eyes and squirting eye drops into them.

"It stings!" cried Jack, covering both eyes with his hands.

"Jack, give me your hands," she said, pulling them away from his face. "I have to spray them with the false handprint primer."

But it was too late. They heard footsteps outside, a knock on the cabin door. Polyvox quickly concealed the kit in her coat and removed a flask of whisky, splashing it on Jack's neck and chest. He had no idea what she was doing, wondering if she had gone mad, but he had no time to say anything. There was another harsh knock on the cabin door. Without waiting for a reply, the people outside slid the door open. A man in a gray suit entered, followed by two uniformed Border Patrol agents.

"Your passports please," said the man in the gray suit, holding out a badge with a credential from the U.S. Security Agency. Through his bleary, bloodshot eyes, Jack immediately realized that he was a Field Officer, though one he did not know personally.

"Here you are, Officer," said Polyvox, handing him both of their passports. "Is there some trouble?"

"Nothing to worry about..."—the SA officer looked at her passport—"...Ms. Payne. Just a routine random check." He looked at Jack's fake passport, then up at Jack, then down at the passport again, then back to Jack.

His eyes narrowed.

"I apologize," said Polyvox. "We've been drinking a bit. My husband can't hold his liquor."

She laughed lightly, but the SA officer looked grim. "Mr. Thomas Darwin Payne?"

"Yes, that's me."

"Would you mind standing up please, sir?"

Now the two burly Border Patrol officers entered the cabin and positioned themselves with their arms crossed. Another SA officer—a woman in a dark blue suit—appeared at the door.

"What's the purpose of your travel, Mr. Payne?" asked the male SA officer, handing the passport to the officer who was standing in the door. She inserted it into a passport reader.

"We're heading up to a geology research station in Nunavut." Jack rubbed his eyes, which burned. "But we're stopping off at Quebec City first, for the Winter Carnival."

"Where were you born, Mr. Payne?" asked the woman.

"Eugene, Oregon."

"Where did you go to school?"

"Undergraduate or graduate?"

"Undergraduate."

"The University of Oregon."

She looked at her colleague and nodded.

"Would you mind stepping out into the hallway, Mr. Payne?" asked the male SA officer.

Sensing clouds of doom gathering over him, Jack followed him into the hallway.

The female officer said, "Mr. Payne, I'm just going to do a quick retinal scan. Would you mind opening your right eye very wide?"

"You're going to shine that thing into my eye?"

"It will just take a second."

"Is there any chance of being blinded? Is that a laser?"

"I assure you, there is zero chance of blinding. Please keep your right eye wide open."

Jack opened his eye and she flashed her penlight-sized scanner into it.

"Would you mind placing your right hand on this screen?" asked the male SA officer.

"What is that?"

"Just a simple hand scanner."

Now Polyvox stood up. "You should know that my husband has a dermatological lotion on his hand. Unfortunately, we both picked up scabies a few days ago in a motel. I kept telling Thomas not to scratch his groin, but he did, and now they're in his hands, too."

The male SA officer backed up slightly and frowned almost imperceptibly. "Scabies?"

"You know, the contagious skin infection caused by infestation of the *Sarcoptes scabiei* mite. Normally the little critters confine themselves to your armpits and groin, but unfortunately they spread to Thomas's hands. He scratches his groin when he gets nervous. I don't think he's infectious now, because he's been using the lotion—when he remembers. But he does have that greasy insecticide on his hands at the moment, to help prevent crusting."

One of the Border Patrol agents stumbled against the seat as he instinctively backed up.

"Well, everything checks out anyway," said the male SA officer. "That should be it for now. Thanks for your cooperation." He handed the passports to Polyvox.

The four federals quickly retreated from the cabin and moved on. Jack dropped into his seat.

"Keep those in your eyes," whispered Polyvox. "They might come back."

Jack waited another half hour, until the train lurched forward, to take the contact lenses out. Within two hours they had arrived at Central Station in Montreal, where they were immediately escorted to Secondary Inspection and Biometrics Screening. Jack felt only dread as he and Polyvox sat down across from the Canadian Border Services officer and again presented their documents.

"What is your purpose in coming to Canada—business or plea-sure?" asked the officer. Jack swallowed hard as she ran their passports through what he knew was the Joint American-Canadian Collabora-tive Antirevolutionary Security System biometrics reader.

Polyvox reached over and squeezed Jack's hand. "Thomas and I have wanted to experience the Winter Carnival for a long time now. It's the fulfillment of a dream." She kissed him on the cheek with uncharacteristic warmth.

"Yes," said Jack, his face reddening.

"*Bienvenue au Canada!*" said the guard, handing their passports back to them.

They rented a car and Polyvox drove the rest of the way to Quebec City and their hotel, which was on a narrow cobblestone street in the Old Town, overlooked by the towers of the elegant Hotel Frontenac.

They had reached the end of their journey.

For now.

CHAPTER SIX

Living on the Lam

Their room was in the back, on the third floor, with two windows that looked out onto a stone-walled garden where a Venus fountain was now half-buried under a deep layer of snow. Polyvox had chosen this room, where she had stayed before, because prying eyes on the street level could not peer in. But in fact, she was no longer really too worried about that.

"We've made it," she sighed. "Safe and sound."

"How can you be sure?"

"No one followed us on the highway to Quebec. And once we returned the car to the rental place, no one followed us as we walked here through the crowds of revelers. The hounds have certainly lost the scent and will be looking for you on other continents."

"How long must we stay here?"

"A couple of weeks. To let things cool off even more, out of prudence. Also, I have to meet with my sisters in the Order."

Jack surveyed the room. He had been hoping for something more spacious and modern. "There's only one bed."

Polyvox gave a dry laugh. "It's big enough for both of us, and as the mission consumes all of my physical and spiritual energy, I won't be interrupting your sleep with any unwanted mating overtures."

"I wasn't worrying about mating overtures," said Jack, who was uncomfortable precisely because he had been worrying about them. "All the same, maybe we can request a room with two beds. I prefer privacy."

"I did make such a request, and they said they had none. Agents across the world are looking for you, Jack. You are in a hideaway, while the wolves are prowling elsewhere. After some time, they will stop looking for you with such intensity. They will move on to other more immediate threats. Now that you are in this hideaway, you must blend in. Do not walk too quickly or present any outward signs of nervousness or suspicion. Avoid all confrontations, and if you are accosted by drunkards, celebratory overenthusiasts, or young bucks jealously guarding their females, suppress your masculine instincts—frankly, you don't seem afflicted by excessive testosterone production—and back down politely. There is an art to living on the lam, and you must learn it. But the art requires self-deprecation. I don't think *you* should have trouble with that."

"Are *you* living on the lam, Polyvox?"

"Pardon me?"

"Surely 'Polyvox' is not your real name, any more than 'Andronicus' is *his* name."

Polyvox smiled. "The revolutionary's life is lived beyond the boundaries of the political order. Now, we had a long trip on that stinking train. I'm going to bathe for an hour, unless you want to use the bathroom first. Then we can go out to eat and drink, and pretend we are normal again—docile, obedient citizens of the world, enjoying our simple pleasures when we can grab them."

Polyvox unbuttoned her coat and threw it on the bed. While Jack tried not to watch, she took off her protective vest, her watch and fob, her boots and her baton, and her sheer black breeches. Her clothing she dumped unceremoniously in the corner, but her tactical baton she laid carefully on the table. She proceeded, naked, to the bathroom.

When he heard the water running in the bath, Jack sat down. He was exhausted but wired. He folded his hands on his lap and closed his eyes. He dozed, and dreamed of a gaunt, pallid-faced figure in a black suit creeping up the stairway to their room, its long spindly hand closing around the knob and pushing the door open.

Startled, Jack opened his eyes. There was no Plutocroid: their room was empty and quiet. He heard Polyvox splashing softly in the tub and saw light fanning out from under the bathroom door. It was dark outside, but through the window he could faintly hear sounds of merriment, as festive crowds roamed the streets, defying the cruel winter with torches, songs, and cheers.

Gleaming in the lamplight, the tactical baton lay on the table. He picked it up to examine it. It was not quite as long as a nightstick, and was more slender. Engraved into its silver surface were unfamiliar runic markings—some blocklike, others a flowing cursive. He slapped it in his open palm. It was weighty—it could render a good headache, to be sure, or maim an assailant. He shuddered. He did not particularly like weapons. He had been cursorily trained in their use, though as a desk officer he did not "carry" and had never had any occasion to make practical use of his training, which had been fine with him. But of all the simple armaments he had been trained to use, the tactical baton, which could be employed effectively in nonlethal counterattack, struck him as the most practical.

Whatever that meant.

He slapped it in his palm again.

Suddenly it expanded into a ten-foot pole-arm, similar to a *guandao* or a glaive, with a blade at one end and a hard glowing blue orb at the other—the whole thing vibrating with currents of energy. Startled, Jack flung the weapon away from him. He winced as it rang loudly on the floor and rolled against the wall. Casting a panicked glance at the bathroom door, he jumped out of his seat and grabbed the shiny metal shaft—shaking it, squeezing it, throttling it, trying desperately to get it to contract back to its original size.

What the hell did she have this thing for? And where was such a weapon manufactured to begin with?

Gripping it with both hands, he twisted it and felt a click. Finally, it contracted. He placed it back on the table and dropped into the seat just as Polyvox emerged from the bathroom, wrapped in a towel.

She paused, her eyes settling on the tactical baton. "Please don't touch my things."

"What do you mean?"

"That's a very dangerous instrument. It takes novices many, many years to even begin to perfect its use."

"I'm sorry. I thought it was a flashlight or something."

A tense silence fell between them.

"Listen, Polyvox," he said uneasily, "you can go out to get something to eat. I'm tired. I just want to sleep."

"Very well. Do you want me to bring something back for you?"

"No…well, just a bottle of water and a light snack if you can find something. Some cookies if they have them. Like those Dad's oatmeal cookies we saw in the Montreal train station. If you can't find anything don't worry."

"Very well." Polyvox dressed and left the room, taking her tactical baton with her.

F9

Jack was so tired he immediately fell into a deep sleep, this time untroubled by nightmares of Plutocroids. When he woke up, Polyvox was lying naked next to him, uncovered by the sheets, which in his sleep he had wrapped exclusively around himself. Another man might not have objected to finding himself in this situation—waking up alongside a six-foot-four, Amazonlike warrior woman. But Jack was not like other men. He had been married once, deeply in love the whole time, but things had not ended well. Now he had a kind of paranoia about women, a permanently unsettled feeling about their motives and methods of operation. He fully recognized that this was his own fault, not that of women in general, and unlike most men with such struggles, he felt no resentment towards them, only detachment.

Or so he told himself. In fact, sometimes he felt the opposite.

Polyvox was lying on her back, straight as an arrow, her hands locked over her stomach. Suddenly her steely gray eyes popped open. "Ah, morning," she sighed.

She threw her long legs over the edge of the bed and sprang to her feet. Pulling on her boots, she patted her stomach. "I'm pretty hungry. And you?"

"Yes," he replied, crawling out of bed and rubbing his new growth of beard uneasily. There was a bottle of water on his nightstand, along with a packet of Dad's oatmeal cookies. He reached for the bottle, opened it, and drank. "Has Andronicus contacted you, Polyvox?"

"We don't have phones, so how could he contact us? The plan is for us to remain out of communication for several weeks."

"But how do we know what he wants us to do?"

"He wants us to make decisions on our own. Andronicus is not our dictator. He is a true democrat, with a lowercase 'd.'"

They dressed, put on their coats, and went down to the hotel's tiny dining room, where they had strong coffee and maple-syrup-drenched crepes. Though it was only nine o'clock, on the street they could see Winter Festival revelers staggering along in a state of apparent intoxication.

"Maybe it wasn't a good idea to hide out in this city, at this particular time," said Jack, looking dubiously out the window.

"On the contrary, this is the *best* sort of place to hide. It's much easier for spies, agents, and government trackers to conceal themselves among drab crowds of commuters than among those engaged in riot and revel. Not to mention, the North American motherhouse of my order is located in the vicinity of this city, and I must pay them a visit."

"What kind of order do you belong to, anyway?" asked Jack. "Is it religious?"

Polyvox shrugged. "Well, that all depends on how you define religion."

"Do you have rituals dedicated to the service or placation of divine beings?"

"Even if we did have such rituals—and I'm not saying we do or do not—that's not really what you're asking, is it? What you want to know is the history and philosophy of my order, which is secret and cannot be divulged. Let's just say, we value justice and compassion, and we hate cruelty and injustice with equal passion."

"So if you tell me about the true nature of your compassionate order, you'll have to kill me. I understand."

"You have your secrets, I have mine, and Andronicus has his—just as everyone else in the world does. We respect each other by honoring these secrets and not inquiring too much about them."

They finished their breakfast and went out onto the street. A light snow was falling and the sky was gray. Following the crowd, they came to a park full of ice castles and glittering carvings. The people suddenly cried out together in joy, pointing to the Hotel Frontenac. Perched on one of its lofty towers was a great winged bird—a Phoenix of ice with scintillating silver plumage. It stretched its wings and glided down towards a Snow Village with an Ice Castle at its center. The people followed the wondrous bird with their eyes, transfixed by its splendor and beauty.

As it passed overhead, stirring up a strong breeze, it dropped a blizzard of tiny crystals. Some fell in the snow; others were caught by onlookers. They were translucent liquor candies. Polyvox popped one in her mouth and handed another to Jack. Warily, he bit down. The crystal cracked and the sweet liquor flowed over his tongue and down his throat. Instantly, his dour mood was buoyed and he grinned foolishly.

The Queen of Winter, in flowing silver robes, a snowflake diadem on her brow, dismounted from the back of the Ice Phoenix and addressed the crowd in French.

"Welcome, friends! We call upon the gods of ice and the gods of snow to bless us with their manifold graces, to purify our hearts with the Sacred Frost of the new year, and to build for us during these festival days a palace of Joy and Companionship in the heart of Winter."

"Look out!" cried Polyvox, yanking Jack out of the way.

A parade was approaching, led by a squad of fire-breathing snowmen. They spun in circles as they waddled forward, shooting jets of colored fire from their mouths. Behind them came several huge animatronic polar bears, with howdahs on their backs filled with fantastic and grotesque creatures that showered the mob with maple cookies.

Jack and Polyvox wandered the streets of the Snow Village. There were taverns carved of ice, and channels along which flowed various flavored vodkas and traditional liquors. Merchants sold piping-hot food and souvenirs; bartenders filled ice goblets with dark, rich ales. Snow maidens and snow lads ladled out molten maple syrup onto big cups of fresh snow, creating maple taffy. Marionettes frolicked and engaged in mock battles for cheering children. Dancers and street performers seemed to be leaping in every direction, so that Jack frequently found himself flailing his arms, believing he was about to be pounced upon. At the edge of the Snow Village was a huge basin of water: an artificial lake. Polyvox insisted that they board one of the Ice Swans that was conveying people across the basin to the other side.

By now Jack was starting to feel the effects of the liquors, *bières*, vodkas, whiskies, maple cookies, maple taffies, and crepes—of which he had, perhaps injudiciously, oversampled. The Ice Swan rocked with a queasy, sickening motion as it plied across the choppy waters, piloted by two snowmen. For Jack, the journey evoked the frigid Hudson and his old morning commute—which now seemed an experience of another age, a time in which he was still a drone of society, and not a confused and disoriented revolutionary.

"Are you okay, Jack?" asked Polyvox. "You're sort of weaving in your seat."

"Yes, I am fine, but no more alcohol…"

"Of course, of course. We'll get something to eat—soon."

The Ice Swan reached the other side of the basin, where Jack stumbled as he disembarked. Snow maidens in white bikinis and boots of fake fur steadied him and helped him across the gangplank. A two-seater Ice Flume was waiting. Polyvox pulled Jack in beside her. The flume took off, cranking and rattling as it carried them up a steep incline, from which they could see the whole vast and colorful spectacle of the Winter Festival below. There was the Hotel Frontenac, now draped in streamers. There were the upper and lower sections of the Old City, festooned with sparkling lights. Every street and alley teemed with people; fireworks exploded; the Ice Phoenix circled overhead, casting a gigantic shadow. The great St. Lawrence River flowed wide and majestic towards the North Atlantic, its surface covered by drifting chunks of ice. By now the gray clouds had parted and the bright winter sun streamed down, illuminating everything with a lovely cold fire.

The Ice Flume teetered at its apex. Without warning, Polyvox pulled Jack close and whispered in his ear.

"Here we are at the top of the world—no cell phones, no way of connecting with anything or anyone, completely off the radar of the government or any other controlling powers. No one knows who we are, or where we are. This is true freedom—the freedom of obscurity!"

The Ice Phoenix, the flowing colored vodkas and whiskies, the dancers and puppets and animatronic polar bears, the liquor candies dropping from the sky, the fire, frost, and phantasms of the Winter Festival—Jack's head was spinning from it all, and all he could reply was, "Whatever you say, Ms. Polyvox."

The flume went crashing down, splashing them with a wave of frigid water. They stepped out of the flume. Polyvox took off her coat and began shaking the water off of it, while Jack spun around dizzily and tumbled into a snow bank.

Jack did not quite remember how he got back to the hotel. He vaguely recalled Polyvox pulling him by the wrist through the surging mobs, the thronged streets, thrusting off boozy lechers with powerful swipes of her free arm. Then he was in bed, on his stomach, overcome by a profound and dreamless slumber.

Polyvox watched him for some time. His breathing became deep and steady. Satisfied that he was out for the night, she withdrew a timepiece from her cloak and glanced at it. She needed to hurry, or she would be late. She left the hotel and vanished down a narrow, forgotten alleyway.

CHAPTER SEVEN

The State of the Apes

Opening a grate at the end of the alley, Polyvox descended a long, long flight of stone steps until she came to a brick-lined tunnel. An old sign screwed into the wall said, in French and English:

CAUTION!
ABANDONED SEWERS
WALLS MAY COLLAPSE
DO NOT ENTER
DANGER OF DEATH!

She followed it for at least a mile as it wormed its way deeper into the earth, branching to the right and the left. Finally she reached a rocky dead end. She tapped a touch-code on the rock, which slid away, revealing a heavy door reinforced with bands of metal. She placed her palm against a shiny plate on the door. It opened, but she left it ajar after passing through. She now paused to listen at the entrance of a labyrinth. She made her way through the labyrinth, whose bewildering complex of tunnels she knew by heart, until she came to an underground chamber.

The chamber was illuminated by large blue orbs on stone mounts. Directly in front of Polyvox, on a high chair, sat the Superior of the North American Motherhouse of the Order of Cosmic Justice. She had a solemn face and silver hair. Like Polyvox, she wore a hooded, high-collared cloak, knee-high boots, and black formfitting breeches. A sash over her chest was covered in luminous hieroglyphs.

On the wall behind her was a disk that resembled both a sunburst and an immensely complicated clock. It featured a sparkling galactic multitude of dials, gears, coils, wheels, rods, pallets, hooks, pawls, levers, springs, studs, pinions, rods, bobs, and other intricately configured moving parts.

To the right and the left of the Superior sat other figures, similar in appearance to Polyvox, all of them garbed in cloaks and formfitting black garments. They were both male and female—tall, athletic, nubile, human yet somehow not human, like the titans that strode the Earth in the time before time. They ranged in age from teenagers to adults. Their appearance was at once savage and civilized, exotic and puritanical.

Everyone, including the Superior, stood up when Polyvox entered. One of the younger sisters came up to Polyvox and offered her a goblet full of wine. She took it, drank it all down, and handed back the empty cup.

"Greetings, Polyvox," said the Superior, who stood over seven feet tall. "We have been waiting eagerly for some news from you. Please give us an account of your work among the Human Apes."

"The Human Apes are still divided against themselves, my lady, as always. Divisions are growing, unrest is increasing. Perhaps revolution

is brewing. Various factions vie with one another for advantage. There
are the Money Elites, the Governments, the Political Dissidents, the
Terrorists, the Religious Fanatics, the Social Deconstructionists, the
Gender Revolutionaries, the Ecophiles, the Scientists, the Mutants,
and the Restive Masses."

"And what of the Human Ape Nations themselves? Can you
report on them?"

"I will do so now."

🜚

Report of Sister Polyvox
To the Revolutionary Order of Cosmic Justice
On the State of the Apes
January, Alternative Human Year 2041
10,925,677 PCE (Post-Cataclysm, Estimated)

Polyvox closed her eyes and gathered her thoughts, for she had
quite a few decades of Ape History to cover—almost a century.
Presently, she began to speak.

"The Continental Empire of the Warlike Apes to our south
continues its reverse evolution into a nation of Plutocratic Slaver
Apes, even as it grows more paranoid about its loss of greatness
following the failed wars initiated generations ago by their former
incompetent leader, the Idiot Ape of Texas, and the subsequent
horrendous misrule of the Tower Ape, also called the Orangutan.
Its citizens are now little better than serfs, which is the intention of
the elites who control the country. In addition, the Warlike Apes
are challenged both militarily and economically by the dramatic
rise of the Red Apes of the East, who still revere their founder, the
Serene and Crazy Ape, and who have assembled a vast war machine

on land and sea. Many of their leaders, in fact, work for the Red Apes of the East."

Polyvox paused to clear her throat and gauge the effects of her words upon her listeners. They looked back at her stoically, but she could detect their deep disquiet.

"To the west of the Red Apes are the Apes of the Double Eagle, whose land was once ruled, as we recall, by the tyrannical and bloodthirsty Ape of Steel. There are countless other nations of Apes, such as the Apes of the Three Crosses, whose empire is now extinct. The powerful Economic Union of Apes continues to wield some global influence, but these Apes have a low birthrate and they are spiritually depleted. At the heart of this Economic Union are the Teutonic Apes, who were briefly ruled, as we know, by the Ape of the Twisted Cross—a slobbering, gesticulating mad-ape who believed in the patently absurd idea that some Apes were innately superior to others, and who embarked on a program of extermination which we at that time were powerless to stop."

From the gathered sisters and brothers there now came a strange sound, gray and forlorn—something between grumbling and mirthless laughter. Polyvox politely waited for this to pass, and then continued.

"Further south, the Levantine Apes are in upheaval and spilling out of their borders in mass migrations, while the corrupt leaders of the Great Southern Apes and the Postcolonial Apes continue to torment their subjects. The island-dwelling Ingenious Apes, who in many ways are most like us in temperament, are experiencing population decline and becoming economically enervated. The subcontinental Caste Apes are intelligent and thoughtful, but their huge population is riven by sectarian, ethnic, gender-based, and political divisions. The Oceanic Apes observe the world around them guardedly, fearful of the coming cataclysm."

"Cataclysm?" asked the Superior.

Despite her own inherent modesty, Polyvox realized that she was enjoying being the center of attention, even in her capacity as Bringer of Bad News. She stroked her chin, musing thoughtfully for a minute. And then she said:

"Here is the real danger, brothers and sisters. The Human Apes continue to evolve. Increasingly one encounters individuals who have been genetically modified, along with rapidly emerging Artificial Ape Intelligence. We cannot rule out the emergence of a race of cybernetic Super Apes. This, my sisters and brothers, is the current state of the Apes."

"Welcome to the monkey house," observed the Superior, shaking her head ruefully. "It is difficult to believe that these savage brutes are the descendants of the docile simians who once gathered fruit peacefully outside the walls of our former cities."

"Indeed, my lady. And to this day, most of the Apes despise and mistrust each other with a passion that is difficult for us to comprehend. All across the globe, it is Ape versus Ape, constantly. But this is the intention of the ruling Plutocrat Apes, who hold all the power."

"And how does this ongoing situation influence our dilemma, Sister Polyvox?"

"There is so much unrest in the world, so much inequality, that more and more Ape factions are breaking onto the scene, creating a welter of ideologies, some of which have more merit than others. Since I last reported to you some time ago, I have forged bonds with one dissident faction in particular, posing as a revolutionary. My work has been fruitful."

Now the Superior looked to her left, where a strapping male stood, his hands folded in front of him. He had a lionlike face, prominent brows, and deep dark eyes that darted briefly to Polyvox, who did not meet them. He then inclined his head slightly at the Superior, whispering in her ear. This was Polyvox's eldest brother, Sarcovox, the consort and first deputy to the Superior. He was an unsympathetic man; between him and Polyvox there was loyalty, but little affection. The Superior turned away from him, looking back at Polyvox.

"We have been following your reports and are grateful for your diligence," she said perfunctorily. "But can you give us any word about our Queen and her situation?"

"I hope to be able to tell you something soon, my lady. The Ape faction with which I am aligned has recently come across valuable intelligence that is currently being analyzed. This intelligence should lead us to the identity of the Evil One who holds our Queen hostage, and who threatens to harness the Abominables for the purpose of becoming a kind of Autocrat of All the Apes."

"But who is this fiendish alpha ape?" asked the Superior. "You have been on the surface a long time, Sister Polyvox, and yet you still have not determined its identity."

"It will happen soon, my lady. I promise you. And then we can finish what we started so long ago."

The Superior stroked her chin, pondering. "Do any of the Human Apes suspect you?"

"None."

"Who is the human you are traveling with? Our Surface Sentries noticed him. A servant, I presume?"

"He is the one who provided the intelligence that will, hopefully, reveal the true identity of the Alpha Ape who holds our Queen in captivity."

"The Surface Sentries tell me he accompanied you all the way from the metropolis in the Continental Empire to the south. Why did you bring him so close to our motherhouse? Was that not imprudent?"

"The corporate rulers of the Continental Empire and their lapdog government officials have dispatched Plutocroid mutants to capture him, my lady. It was necessary to get him out of the Empire for his own safety."

"Have these detestable Plutocroids followed you here?"

"No."

"Can you be sure of that?"

"As sure as is statistically possible, my lady. As we know, there are no sureties in the world of Apes."

The Superior nodded. "You have done well, Sister Polyvox. Your understanding of the cultures and psychology of the Human Apes surpasses that of any of us, and you are to be commended. We trust that your operations will continue to yield fruit. Sisters and brothers, we know that humans are in some ways even lower than the Araknoids themselves. It was only an evolutionary accident that allowed their flatulent, hirsute, leaf-munching forebears to stumble into the rudiments of civilization during our Long Slumber. But do not underestimate them: this ethically bungling species has within it the power to awaken the Araknoids. Our sister Polyvox has taken great risks on the surface, masquerading as a Human Ape and collecting intelligence on their various factions in order to complete our mission. We will give her refreshment before she returns to that sordid world where she now works as our primary agent. But before we do so, I wish to ask our sister Polyvox if she has any requests of us."

"I do request one thing, my lady: that the Order lend me one of its vehicles. Ape cars are unreliable. The Teutonic Apes and the Ingenious Apes make serviceable vehicles, but even these cannot begin to surpass ours in quality and technology."

"This shall be granted. Which vehicle would you prefer? And where do you wish it to be delivered?"

"One of the new sedans, please. It would be better not to park it anywhere near the secret entrance to our motherhouse, or in the Old City. Rather, please park it on the Rue St. Jean, just outside the gate. Before we depart from the city, I will return here to give you the word."

"Very well. Now let us feast."

The floor of the chamber opened up, and a long refectory table emerged, set with heaping plates, overflowing bowls, and full decanters. The sisters and brothers sat at the table and plied Polyvox with food and wine. They spoke lovingly of their Queen, longingly of their captive kinsfolk. They recalled the surprise arrival of the Araknoids so long ago, the final battle, the Time Bomb, the dismal result. They lamented their current predicament, and looked hopefully toward the imminent reversal of their sorrows.

From the shadows at the entrance to the chamber, Jack watched these strange people as they conversed in their incomprehensible language. They were a race unto themselves, unlike any that existed on the surface of the earth. Their towering height and their obvious physical strength set them apart as superior beings. But what could possibly be their connection to the plot his parents had uncovered? Was there, in fact, any connection? Or was Polyvox merely leading him deeper and deeper into the rabbit warrens of madness?

Could he even trust Polyvox? Who was she, really?

The old poem was right—it was indeed a mad world, but one with many unfamiliar faces.

19

Jack's ruminations threatened to overwhelm him. He sat back against the wall in the dark, just behind the chamber, his head still throbbing from the effects of the alcohol he had consumed at the festival. He could hardly believe he was here, or that he had dared to follow Polyvox to her meeting with the members of her order.

He had never intended to do so, and had fallen asleep immediately after returning to the hotel. But upon awakening, he sensed that Polyvox was watching him. Acting on a whim, he pretended to be asleep. When he heard the hotel door close behind her, he followed her onto the street, down the alleyway, and—deep, deep below the surface of the city—to an abandoned sewer tunnel that at first appeared to end in a rock wall. At Polyvox's touch, the rock slid away, revealing a door, which she also opened. Perhaps she had been preoccupied with her task, because she had left the door partly open. He had managed to slip in a few seconds behind her, before both the false rock wall and the heavy door had thudded shut.

Even now he was incredulous that she had not noticed him tagging along behind her. But he had become tired of mysteries, innuendoes, and evasions. And so he was here, and rather proud of himself for having had the courage to pull it off. Presumably, Andronicus knew that Polyvox was meeting with her brothers and sisters in the Order. But did Andronicus really understand the Order itself?

Jack felt a chill coming on, and then a sneeze.

He pinched his upper lip, without success. His sneeze echoed like a gunshot in the chamber beyond.

Instantly he was seized by strong arms and dragged across the floor to the tall woman who was their leader. He looked up and found himself surrounded by the strapping warrior men and women, many of them brandishing battle staves. The Superior's eyes flashed in anger, and she spoke harshly to Polyvox, who was looking down at Jack in chagrin. Another woman came forward. She was taller than Polyvox, square-shouldered and muscular. She had a sibling's resemblance to Polyvox, though her chin was sharper, her face more harsh in its angularity, her expression much harder. She pointed at Jack, speaking angrily, gesturing emphatically with her other hand. The other brothers and sisters responded, glaring at Jack with eyes that glowed unnaturally in the dim light of the chamber.

Jack saw the fierceness in those eyes, the curiously primeval passions—he saw it even in the faces of the adolescents, who were nearly as tall as Jack was, and as well-formed as young gods. To his right, a boy and a girl looked down on him with wide-eyed amazement and horror. To his left a man as hulking as a Dark Age knight glared at him. The speaking woman continued her angry tirade. Jack began to feel lightheaded.

Polyvox, however, remained composed. At last she stepped forward and spoke calmly in her own language, gesturing to Jack.

"This Ape is essential to our plans," she said to the Superior. "He is the key to information that will help us locate and rescue our queen. I intentionally let him follow me. I wanted him to see that we are real, that we have power. He is inherently suspicious, like all apes. But seeing us here will elevate our status in his eyes, because he will not be entirely sure about what he is seeing. It is Ape nature to have reverence for the unknown and the mysterious."

"As always, Polyvox, you state your case cleverly and leave little room for disagreement. Still, you should not have allowed him access to our inner sanctuary. Your siblings Sarcovox and Monovox are correct. You have committed a great violation. Never before has a Human Ape been admitted to the Chamber of Gathering. And I am still not convinced that this Ape is essential to our objectives. What can he possibly know that we cannot find out for ourselves?"

"He risked his own life acquiring information for us, using his official access to highly secret Ape computers. He is now an enemy of his own state. He shared classified electronic documents with us—containing data that other trustworthy Human Apes are now analyzing, as they understand the implications better than we do. We are dependent upon the cooperation of a select group of Apes. Sarcovox and Monovox can posture and threaten, but honor requires that I defend this Ape. Just so they know. If necessary, their disagreement with me on this matter can be resolved through trial by combat."

The Superior shook her head. "There will be no fighting here. I do not forgive your transgression, Polyvox, but I will give you time to redeem yourself by following through with your plan to rescue our queen. Now go, and take your Ape with you. Never bring him back to the Chamber."

Of course, Jack did not understand a word of this. He could perceive that the tall female and the gigantic male wanted to harm him in some way. He intuited that the leader had ordered them to let Polyvox explain the situation. But he could only watch as Polyvox spoke, hopefully defending him, while the others watched him with their feral eyes simmering with suspicion.

Polyvox grasped his arm. "It's time to go, Jack," she said. "My brothers and sisters are not in a good humor right now because of your sneakiness. Never before has an outsider entered this place. Technically, the punishment for trespassing is death, but the Superior has absolved you. Let's get out before they change their minds."

F9

Jack remained silent as he followed her out of the chamber, through the labyrinth to the steep stone stairway, and through the grate into the alleyway. It was snowing again on the street. Polyvox carefully replaced and secured the grate. Then she turned to Jack and said, "You must be hungry after your misadventure."

"Who were those...*people?*" asked Jack quietly, aware that he had barely escaped a terrible fate. He also felt shame that he had, perhaps, jeopardized Polyvox's position. But his curiosity about the Order still gnawed at him.

"They are merely the brothers and sisters of my order. Of course, they follow world events closely, but they cherish their secrecy. Never are outsiders permitted in the Chamber of Gathering, so you violated a sacred taboo. But I argued on your behalf, and all is forgiven. Are you hungry?"

But Jack was in no mood to move on so easily. "Let's not get off the subject, Polyvox. What kind of order is it? A religious order?"

Polyvox lifted her shoulders. "A political order, you might say."

"A political order of people who gather in underground chambers and carry battle staves?"

"Every political order has its peculiarities."

"What language were they speaking? What country are they from?"

"This interrogation grows tedious, Jack," sighed Polyvox. "They are from no country that you know of, and they speak no language that you've ever heard of. As for their 'ethnicity,' this is a human construct. In our order, there is no such thing. I don't know about you, but I'm famished. I could eat a mastodon, and I'm a vegetarian."

To Jack, Polyvox seemed oddly evasive about the whole matter. Then the truth occurred to him. "Did you let me follow you?"

"Let you follow me?" Polyvox laughed. "Now why would I have done that?"

"I think you did. You are trained in the art of stealth. How could you not have heard me blundering along behind you in the labyrinth? If I hadn't been drunk, I wouldn't even have attempted it. You mean to tell me you didn't hear my gasping as I tried to keep up with you?"

"You underestimate your own cunning, Jack. I was so intent on getting to our meeting on time, I simply didn't notice you."

"I don't believe you."

"Very well, I let you follow me."

"I knew it," grumbled Jack. "And the other members of your tribe almost killed me. Thanks."

"You were never in any danger—I was always in complete control. It was risky, of course, but I thought it was important for you to see what no human has ever seen. My order is a good ally to have, and now they see you as an ally as well."

Jack nodded, stroking his chin. "Who was the woman who looked like she wanted to dash me to pieces?"

"She did not want to dash you to pieces, she wanted to frighten you. That woman was my blood sister Monovox, the daughter of my mother."

"And the man?"

"My brother Sarcovox, consort of the Superior. He probably did want to slay you, but I would not have suffered that to happen."

"Now we're getting somewhere! Again I'll ask, what language were you speaking?"

"What a tenacious, prying Security Agent you are! When the New Global Order is established, Jack, you will have to relearn the virtue of minding your own damn business. But I'll tell you this: the language of our order is thousands of years old, with roots that go back before ancient Egypt and Sumer. We speak among ourselves a language isolate. Like ancient Sumerian, it is unrelated to any living tongue. And that's all I'm going to say for now."

For the time being, Jack had to be satisfied with these answers. Together, they returned to the hotel and went to bed. They slept late the next morning, and only went out to get something to eat in the afternoon. They consumed maple taffy and dark French-Canadian ale. And then they wandered home, through the merry mobs.

"I have a present for you," said Polyvox. She removed a small, gift-wrapped package from her coat and handed it to him. The wrapping paper was blue with a white *fleur-de-lis* pattern. The ribbon and bow bore the red maple leaf.

"Why did you buy me a present?" asked Jack suspiciously.

"You've been under stress from all these life disruptions, Jack. This is for your troubles."

Jack impatiently tore off the bow and wrapping paper, casting them onto the floor. He flipped off the lid of the box. There, resting on a bed of cotton, was a five-inch saxophone.

"What's this?"

"What do you think? A saxophone. Carry it with you at all times. As protection."

Jack looked at it dubiously. "You mean as some kind of charm?"

"Of course not. It's completely functional. It was crafted by members of my order."

Jack gave a dry laugh. "You must be *joking*. This looks like a toy saxophone. Or a saxophone for a gnome."

"Try it. Play something simple. Johnny Kenwood's 'Moonlight and Thou.'"

"I can't play this puny toy…" Jack glared at her. "You're making fun of me, aren't you? My father taught me to play the saxophone. You may think it's stupid, but—"

He stopped. Polyvox was regarding him with her chilly gray eyes, her dark eyebrows slightly lifted.

"I'm not mocking you, Jack. In any case, my sense of humor only comes out in moments of extreme stress or aggravation. I'm perfectly rational now, and I assure you that this device will protect you from Plutocroids. You don't even have to blow into it, just lift it to your lips and press the keys. It's powered by a battery that will last a hundred years, and it generates precisely the same sonic wavelengths that Plutocroids find intolerable. It's simple neurophysics. To Plutocroids, any harmony played on that little saxophone is like a metal claw scraping across a slate surface—only a thousand times more horrid. Will you play?"

Jack put the tiny instrument to his lips and generated the first few bars of "Moonlight and Thou." To Jack, the resulting sound was like high-pitched, eerie space music, but Polyvox, her expression inscrutable as always, gave an affirmative nod.

"Carry it with you always."

F9

Within a week, they had both become fatigued by the constant commotion of the Winter Fest. They remained in their room, venturing out only around three or four in the morning, when most of the intoxicated revelers had returned to their homes, hotels, and youth hostels. Each day, Jack bided his time playing his mini-saxophone for a few hours until Polyvox would ask him to stop. Finally she decided it was time for them to leave Quebec City.

Before that, however, she had to make one last visit to her sisters in the Order.

"You stay here, Jack. I'll be back in a few hours. I have a plan for getting us back across the border, which I will explain."

She left him alone. A few hours later, he heard footsteps outside the door and assumed she had returned.

The knob rattled for a few seconds. The door opened, and in glided a gangly figure in a dark suit and a broad-brimmed hat.

"*Bonsoir, Monsieur Tone,*" hissed the Plutocroid. "So nice to finally see you again, so many weeks after our abortive little encounter in that lovely cemetery where your traitor parents lie rotting…"

CHAPTER EIGHT

A Plutocroid Drops
by for a Chat

Jack had been sitting in a chair perusing the latest edition of *Le Soleil* on the somewhat old-fashioned reader that the hotel provided. His saxophone was on the nightstand across the room. His eyes darted towards it.

The Plutocroid followed his gaze and scowled. He held up a long warning finger and sat down across from Jack, placing himself between Jack and the instrument. With one hand the intruder took out a wide, serrated bowie knife. He held the other hand up before his sickly red eyes, examining his own branchlike fingers and long, grotesque nails.

Jack did not move. He sat and stared at this repulsive thing, this abomination of humanity. In a way it was a relief. These creatures had been stalking him for so long that to have one of them simply introduce itself helped dispel some tension.

"What do you want from me?"

The Plutocroid's free hand dropped to his lap. He looked directly at Jack. "People want to talk to you, people who consider you an enemy of the State, a traitor to the American Way. They'll be here shortly."

Jack's hand crept up to the button that hung around his neck.

The Plutocroid sat up straight and alert, like a praying mantis positioning itself for the kill. "No touchy-touchy!" he hissed with a leering grin. He spun the knife in his hand so quickly that the blade became a blur.

Jack moved his hand from the lanyard. "How did you find me?" he asked, gulping. "If you don't mind my asking."

The Plutocroid made a sound like steam escaping a cracked radiator. Jack realized it was a giggle. He decided to venture another question.

"Do you want me to go with you somewhere, or do you want me to just sit here?"

The Plutocroid leaned forward and snarled at him like a dog, baring his narrow, yellow teeth, saliva dripping from his leprous white chin. Then he closed his eyes and began to mutter something in slobbering gibberish. He shook his head with manic intensity, and suddenly went stock still, neither moving nor breathing—like a waxwork statue of a Plutocroid. He maintained this motionless, unblinking posture for ten minutes, until Jack could stand it no more.

Jack moved his leg slightly, and the Plutocroid leapt to his feet, shrieking and brandishing his knife. At that instant the door opened, and the Plutocroid spun around. Polyvox struck out with her glaive, slicing off his head at the neck. A fountain of red blood gushed up onto the ceiling, while the head and hat rolled across the floor as if they were racing each other towards the wall. The head won and bounced off the baseboard, coming to a rest with its eyes open, its tongue lolling out, its scowl intact. The body collapsed in a heap—a jumble of cloth, flesh, and bone in a pond of blood.

In her free hand Polyvox was holding a pizza box. She placed it on the table and stared down at the gory remains of the Plutocroid.

Her eyes lifted to meet Jack's.

"A *foutre* for the world and these nasty things," she said in a subdued but deadly serious voice. "We've got to get out of here now!"

F9

Polyvox searched the Plutocroid's suit and found various altered photographs of Jack, including one with a beard. The monster was also wearing a watch. While Jack looked on, wincing, she stripped the Plutocroid of his clothing. Beneath his suit he wore a sleeveless undershirt, a hexagonal dog tag with a four-digit number on it, and cotton boxers decorated with little green percentage signs. His skin was sallow green, his musculature thin and wiry, but Jack could see that the thing was essentially human. With revulsion, he noted that it completely lacked genitalia. Instead there was what appeared to be a trademark symbol on its groin.

"To think this was once a man," he muttered. "What kind of sick minds would do this to a person?"

"Human minds," answered Polyvox. "Human beings have been exploiting, mutilating, and manipulating each other since the dawn of history. And trust me, the way human culture is moving, this is just a taste of things to come. This is why we must stop them, Jack."

"Do you think he was acting alone?"

"I think he was just a scout, possibly a Type III, of moderate intelligence. He must have seen you at some point and made a visual identification. How long ago did it come in?"

"About a half hour."

"And your saxophone?"

"I couldn't reach it in time."

"If this one had been working with a team, they would have arrived by now. The question is, *did he communicate with any others?*"

"Maybe through the watch."

Polyvox pried open the watch and carefully studied its inner workings. "No, this is just a conventional watch. There could be some kind of biotransponder embedded in the Plutocroid itself. But I'm not about to perform a dissection. We have to get out of here now."

Jack grabbed his coat and backpack, slipping the saxophone into his pocket. They fled down the stairs, where Polyvox paused at the doorway, searching the darkness. A few late-night partiers staggered down the street, but that was all.

"We have to make a dash for the car," whispered Polyvox.

"What car?"

"Just follow—and don't fall behind, unless you want to be taken by the mutant freaks of the U.S. Defense Department, which can apparently penetrate deep into sovereign countries and operate with impunity."

Jack tried to keep up as she ran in a seemingly helter-skelter fashion through the narrow streets of the Old City. At first they were alone, but presently Jack heard the patter of feet on the cobblestones behind him. Looking over his shoulder, he saw one Plutocroid, and then another. Soon five were giving chase, then ten, pursuing them with their weird loping gait, their arms flopping like rubber cables, their eyes yellow, their faces fixed with crazy leers like fratboys having perverse fun.

Ahead was a gate in the wall of the Old City. Polyvox, fifty feet ahead of him, turned and shouted, "Faster, you fool!"

Jack was running as hard as he could. He was not out of shape, and in fact was an excellent runner, but he could hardly keep up with her. His chest ached in the cold air, and his breath had a metallic taste and came in gasping bursts. Behind him the Plutocroids were closing in from several directions.

One leaped out at Polyvox, who swung her arm and punched it square in the face, sending it flying back, its rangy arms and legs thrashing in the air. She ran through the gate. Jack followed. Behind him came the hisses and jeers of the other Plutocroids. Then he slipped on a patch of ice and fell on his side. Looking up he saw the gang nearly on top of him—seconds away. Polyvox was already far ahead.

He pulled out his mini-saxophone, put it to his lips, and played the first song that came into his head, an elevator favorite: Johnny Kenwood's "Cruzin' with the Blooze."

The Plutocroid pack stopped just ten feet away, like vampires detecting the first light of dawn. They covered their ears with their hands and spindly fingers, howling in misery. Such was the existential depth of their agony that Jack felt a terrible remorse, a burning shame. What was he doing to these abominable creatures? Music was for healing, not for torment. What had he become?

He paused in his playing.

Immediately they recovered, this time with tenfold savagery in their red eyes.

They started for him.

There was a bright glare of headlights and a screech of tires. A long, streamlined black car with high sides and narrow windows plowed into the mob of Plutocroids, crunching into them, knocking them down like ninepins. The passenger door opened and Jack jumped in.

"Your ancestors were faster runners than you are," observed Polyvox, scowling behind the wheel. She went into reverse, turned the car around, and shot through the gate. Something was pounding on the roof of the car. She slammed on the brakes, and a Plutocroid went tumbling over the hood and onto the street.

Polyvox ran over it, and the car bumped sickeningly.

"Did you have to do that?" Jack winced. "My God, you just callously crushed that guy...."

"Guy? *Guy?*" scoffed Polyvox. "These are monsters, Tone! They eviscerate men, women, and children. They are like a hybrid of zombies, vampires, Klansmen, serial killers, the Khmer Rouge, Southern slavers, cannibals, NKVD torturers, Einsatzgruppen, Janissaries, Teutonic knights, Grand Inquisitors, headhunters, Belgian Congo officials, survivalists, Islamic State fighters, Boko Haram fanatics, redcoats, werewolves, wicker-man druids, criminal abortionists, quack surgeons, pedophile priests, Republicans, and Wall Street hedge-fund managers! Do you really want to go back and render first aid to *that?*"

He said nothing, and Polyvox kept driving fast, until they were south of the city and cruising through the Quebec countryside.

F9

The moon illuminated snow-covered fields and the occasional church steeple as the car raced soundlessly along the highway. Jack was irked that Polyvox had lost her temper with him; he had grown thoroughly sick of her company. He longed to speak to Andronicus and get some answers.

"Where are we going?" he asked her after an hour of driving.

"Back to the City of Brotherly Love," she replied cheerfully. Her tone gave no hint of her previous aggravation.

"How long will that take?"

"Longer than normal, because we are not going there directly, but crossing into Maine first. When traveling on the lam, it's always best to take the least predictable route."

The car was very spacious on the inside, with a dashboard that looked more like the console of an airplane—a patterned network of lights and switches. Polyvox had pushed her seat back and placed her hands behind her head, letting the car drive itself. After a while, she assumed an even more relaxed position, pushing her seat all the way back and crossing her legs slantwise over the dashboard.

After a few hours, they came to the border crossing, and she assumed a normal driving posture. They stopped, rolling down their windows. Border Patrol officers approached on both sides.

"Passports, please."

Polyvox handed the guard their passports. He looked at them, then shined a flashlight in their faces. Other guards were looking under the car with flashlights and mirrors.

"Please state your full names and citizenship," said the guard at the window.

"Mary Custis Payne, United States."

"Thomas Darwin Payne, United States."

The guard was looking at Jack intently, and Jack felt his throat go dry.

"Thomas Darwin Payne?"

Jack cleared his throat. "Yes."

The guard handed their passports back. "Welcome home, citizens. God bless you, and God Bless America."

"God Bless America to you as well, sir," said Polyvox. "And God bless us, every one."

The officer nodded. "God bless you, ma'am."

"Thomas?" prompted Polyvox.

"Oh…God bless you, Officer," said Jack quickly.

"God bless *you*, Mr. Payne," smiled the Border Officer, looking at him with a strange, almost bemused, intensity.

The officer waved them on. They passed through the checkpoint and back into the Empire.

F9

They drove for an hour along a road that wended its way through the dark, cold, impenetrable forests of Maine. Finally they came to the small hamlet of Breckenridge and the Moose Motel, where a bright red "Vacancy" sign crackled and sputtered in the window. Adjoining the motel was a tavern with a neon sign for "Kohrs Beer: America's Original Premium Lager."

Polyvox pulled into the gravel parking lot. Before they got out of the car, she said to Jack, "There are some minor, loosely organized factions operating in this area. They tend to be antigovernment, but more of the rural survivalist or libertarian kind. They don't acknowledge the authority of Number One, and they might be hostile if they find out who we are. So take care."

"Should we even stop here, then?"

"We'll be fine. In a way, they are fellow travelers. Just mind your own business and don't be too chatty. Not that you're very chatty."

They exited the car. Though it was close to two in the morning, there were several beat-up old pickups in the lot, compared to which Polyvox's car seemed oddly long, large, and sleek.

They entered the tavern. At various places in the bar sat men and women, country types wearing bomber hats and woolen watch caps. Country music from the 1950s played on an antique Rock-Ola jukebox. Jack and Polyvox took off their coats and sat at the bar.

"What will you have?" asked the bartender, a woman with flinty, unfriendly eyes.

"What kind of beer do you have?" asked Jack.

"Kohrs."

"Do you have High Nevada?"

"No hoity-toity foreign beers. Just Kohrs." The bartender jerked her thumb at a faded, turn-of-the-century poster of Anton Kohrs holding out an old-fashioned screw-top can of Kohrs. "We have Kohrs Premium, Kohrs Light, Kohrs Ice, Kohrs Draft in bottles, and Spring Break, which is brewed by Kohrs. American beer only."

"High Nevada is actually American," said Jack, endeavoring to sound helpful. "And I'm pretty sure Kohrs is now owned by a big European conglomerate."

The bartender, unimpressed, pursed her lips. "Did you come here to *order* a beer, or did you come here to lecture me about beer?"

Jack felt the toe of Polyvox's boot knock once against his calf.

"Sorry…I'll have a Kohrs Premium."

"Make that two," said Polyvox. "Can we see menus?"

"No menus. We've got Mooseburgers and Freedom Fries."

"I'll take a plate of fries," said Polyvox.

"Freedom Fries?"

"What other kinds do you have?"

The bartender shook her head. "Just Freedom Fries."

"Well, then," said Polyvox, enunciating carefully, "I will take the Freedom Fries."

"And I'll take a Mooseburger," said Jack. "Well-done, with cheddar."

"We have Cheez Chizz, no cheddar."

"You don't have cheddar?"

"Nope."

"Provolone?"

The bartender sighed heavily. "Only American cheese—Cheez Chizz."

"That's strange you don't have cheddar. I mean, you share a border with Vermont."

"We actually *don't* share a border with Vermont, we share a border with New Hampshire. Do you want Cheez Chizz or not?"

"Sure, I'll take Cheez Chizz on that Mooseburger."

She brought them their beers, then their food. The Freedom Fries exuded copious amounts of browned grease; the Mooseburgers were rubbery and dry; the Cheez Chizz was a vulgar fluorescent orange. As they were eating, a tall man with an eighteen-gallon hat and a bolo tie sat down at the bar. The bartender set a bottle of Kohrs Draft down in front of him without saying anything. Her eyes darted towards Polyvox and Jack.

The man turned to them. "You folks from out of town?"

"Yes," said Jack. "We're from New York."

"Wall Street," said the man with a grim smile, taking a long swig of his Kohrs. "This town used to be something, till the Wall Street Jew bankers shut everything down."

Polyvox dabbed her lips with her napkin and, smiling coolly, turned on her stool to face the man.

"What's your name, sir? I'm Mary Payne, and this is my husband Thomas."

"Breckenridge," he said, holding out his hand. "Earl Breckenridge. My great-great-grandfather helped found this town." He looked at her quizzically. "Aren't you a bit cold in that outfit, young lady? I ain't never heard of someone wearing a sleeveless vest in the middle of winter. Some New York thing, I reckon."

Polyvox laughed lightly. "Mr. Breckenridge, you're right to blame Wall Street on your woes, but I can assure you that blaming the Jews is inaccurate and unhelpful. Wall Street cares only about one thing: money. The Greedheads come from all kinds of backgrounds."

"The *He-Brews* and the *Nee-Grows*," said Breckenridge musingly, as he stroked the graying stubble on his chin, "are in cahoots." He kept staring at her.

"It's important that people like you and me don't get caught up in blaming each other," continued Polyvox, "because that's exactly what the Greedheads want. See, if you're blaming the Jews or African Americans, or anybody on the basis of ancestry, you're not blaming the real enemy: the venal, multinational plutocrats who rule the world. Their policy is to divide and conquer."

Breckenridge jabbed his finger in the air at Polyvox. "Listen, young lady, that banker who walked so big and proud and cocksure into this town twenty years ago, with his team of lawyers and other vipers, and shut down our saw mill—he was for sure a goddamn Jew, so don't tell me otherwise."

"But how do you know he was a Jew?"

"What else could he have been?"

"I mean," Polyvox said reasonably, "you have to have some empirical evidence to support this conclusion. Not that his ancestry matters, in any case."

"All those bankers are Jews. Afro-Asiatic Jews. And I'll never forget the name of that goddamn Jew as long as I live." Breckenridge's face twisted into a mask of loathing and contempt. "Patrick Doyle Cohan. That scheming, money-grubbing Jew destroyed this town."

"That's not really a Jewish name," ventured Tone. "Co*han* is Irish. Co*hen* is Jewish."

"Irish? Well now I've heard everything, you goddamn punk fool from Jew York Shitty. Cohan is a Jew name, not a Mick name. It's Afro-Asiatic Jew for 'slayer of animals.' I read it on fucking *Stormfront*. Besides, what do you know about Irish?"

"I have some Irish ancestry...."

"Oh, you do, do you?" Breckenridge slapped his hand on the bar, and the bartender instantly poured him a shot of bourbon. He peered menacingly at Jack. "You don't look so Irish to me...there's something of the *mischling* about you. But no matter. Let me ask you something, New York Irish Boy. If a goddamn big black bear came into this bar right now, and he was wearing a green hat on his head, with a shiny gold buckle on it, and he reeked of Guinness, and he was singing 'Molly Malone,' would you say, 'Now that's an Irishman,' or would you say, 'Now that's a bear'?"

"I'm not sure what your point is?..."

"An Irishman or a bear? Answer the question!"

"Are you talking about an actual bear, or some person in a bear suit?"

"I'm talking about a goddamn bear!" growled Breckenridge. "Shits in the woods, has black fur, eats honey, builds himself a burrow in the winter and sleeps for five lazy months until spring, when he finally emerges and farts and bonks his she-bear. That's what I'm talking about."

"Well, then," said Jack, swallowing hard, "I would say that's a bear."

"Thank you!" Breckenridge downed his shot and slapped for another.

"But I don't get the connection…"

"Because the Jew is the bear!" replied Breckenridge, nearly shouting. "Like the bear, the Jew is a master of disguise and deception."

"Huh?"

Breckenridge held his hands apart, like a man trying to explain something to an imbecile. "So this guy Patrick Doyle Cohan comes in here, with his red hair, and his pale complexion, and his brogue so thick you could cut it with a knife, working for some goddamn Dublin-based company, and he buys our sawmill for pennies. And then he and his bog-wog hooligans actually have the…the what do they call it…the *hootspah* to sit in this bar, eating our food, and drinking all the whiskey in the house, saying their *Jesus and Mary and Josephs* and their *Mother Machrees*, singing 'Molly Malone,' and 'I'll Take You Home Again, Kathleen,' and 'Danny Boy,' thinking they're playing us all for fools, before they finally get their socialist Jew asses back on their airplane for Ireland. And in the end, a hundred and fifty white people are out of a job, thanks to the eternal scheming of the faithless Jews."

Breckenridge concluded his oration by shooting back his bourbon and slapping for a third, which was immediately delivered.

"Sir," said Jack, "surely you are not saying this fellow was faking being Irish? That strikes me as utterly implausible."

Breckenridge stared at Jack wide-eyed, as if at a thick-skulled moron. Behind him other patrons had gathered round and were glaring at Jack and Polyvox with undisguised hatred. Jack felt Polyvox's hand on his arm. "We should go," she said softly.

"But I haven't finished my Mooseburger…"

Polyvox gave her head a quick, urgent jerk towards the door and placed money on the counter. "Forget the Mooseburger," she muttered, "unless you want it to be your final meal."

Jack put it down and wiped his lips with a paper napkin.

They stood up. "Good night to all of you," Polyvox said pleasantly.

They headed for the exit. As they went, they were followed by twenty pairs of searing, unblinking eyes. Even the moose head mounted above the door seemed angry. They walked briskly to the car.

In the trees beyond the tavern, the wolf-coyote hybrids howled.

Polyvox, her tires rumbling against the icy gravel, drove out slowly, trying not to give the impression of panic. The last thing she wanted to do was provoke the predatory chase instinct of this peculiar community of embittered Apes. From the windows and in the doorway, the patrons of the Moose Tavern stood and stared. Polyvox and Jack did not make eye contact with them. They did not even dare to exhale until they were again speeding down the narrow, winding road through the pitch-black Maine forest.

"Why did you have to start a discussion with that cretin?" asked Jack. "*Mind your own business and don't be too chatty*, you said to me. And then you go ahead and single-handedly try to cure him of his anti-Semitism."

"Well, I wasn't the one who was trying to disabuse the bartender of her faith in the essential Americanism of her favorite crappy pisswater beer."

"Oh no?"

"No. Nor did I engage a local ruffian in a completely bizarre conversation about…about…hell, I didn't even know *what* you two were talking about, and I couldn't believe I was hearing what I was hearing—as soon as he started talking about the bear and the Irishman, I realized his neurological wiring was completely crisscrossed. At that point any reasonable person would have politely terminated the conversation, even agreed with him to keep him from going ballistic. But you kept on encouraging him."

Jack looked away from her, out the window and into the darkness, shaking his head. "I thought we were supposed to be changing the world for the better, educating people, confronting wrongheaded attitudes with reason. Instead we scrammed like a couple of chickens out of a boondock bar when the talk got too hot. A fine couple of revolutionaries *we* are."

"Maybe you didn't notice it, Tone, but every one of those people in that bar was carrying."

"What do you mean?"

"Weapons. Some in their pockets, some in their coats, some strapped to their ankles—and by the nervous twitching of their thumbs, they were getting ready to use them."

"Oh, come on, Polyvox. Don't be ridiculous. They weren't going to *shoot* us."

"You think you're still in Canada? This is America, Jack. The whole goddamn country is a shooting gallery, which is exactly what the corporate powers want it to be. Rule by fear. Keep the peasants at each other's throats, and you can laugh your fat, pimply, plutocratic ass all the way to the bank. That's exactly what was going on in there, and what's been going on across this failed republic for generations."

For ten minutes, they continued driving in tense silence.

"Look," said Polyvox presently, "we mustn't be too hard on ourselves. We each tried. If we can't win the common people to The Cause, then there can be no hope of victory."

"If the 'common people' all think like those clowns," replied Jack bitterly, "then there will be no 'victory.'"

"Most people do not think the way those oddballs think. Some do, only because they have been brainwashed by the Corporate Elites. It's the same old story, and it hasn't changed for ten thousand years. But it's about to change soon, Jack, and you'll be there to see it."

They found another motel fifty miles down the road. Here Polyvox and Jack avoided political discussions. They stayed the night and rose early in the morning, driving all day, and reaching the Trappist Tavern in Philadelphia by evening.

Polyvox parked the car out front and they went inside.

Andronicus was in the back room, with Max Blackshield, Emily Bombsinger, Doctor Krypton, and the Professor. As soon as Jack and Polyvox entered the room, all five of them stood up, smiling broadly.

"My good friends, welcome back!" said Andronicus. "How was your trip?"

"There were ups," said Polyvox, "and there were downs."

"To be sure, to be sure," said Andronicus. He seemed to have something on his mind.

"And do you have news for us?" asked Polyvox.

"Great news…wonderful news. We have thoroughly crunched the PISIBANK data, and we now know who Senator Lance Boyler is working for. We now have the ringleader of the Plot. A notorious man—one of the richest and greediest, most ruthless and dangerous men in the world."

"Who?" cried Polyvox with sudden energy. "Who is it?"

Andronicus smiled and raised a finger. "Listen," he said softly, "and I will tell you."

Phase Two

Assassination Street

CHAPTER NINE

In the Tower of the Mad King

Sixty-eight-year-old Senator Lance Boyler of Pennsylvania—tall, gray-fringed, with a polished dome of a crown—sat in his spacious office in the Russell Senate Office Building on Constitution Avenue in Washington, DC. He held an 1864 Manhattan Arms Company cavalry pistol, fully cleaned and loaded—luxuriating in its heft, revering its gleam, imagining it blazing away in the hot smoke of battle.

As he admired his gun, he was speaking on the phone. "I don't care who he is, he must sell now. His damned Constitutional rights are immaterial. You make it clear to this Nabot or whatever his name is that he has no choice in the matter…what?" Boyler cackled cynically. "Let him try to sue if he wants to. Does he really think any court in the land would cross me, that he has any rights worth a fiddler's fart? What does he think this is—a democracy?" Boyler was silent for a while, listening. Finally his patience was at an end. "Does he have family? Yes? Young children, very good. You make it known to him, through intermediaries, that all Senator Lance Boyler has to do is sign a *lettre de cachet*, and his children will be taken away from him and his wife sent to a madhouse of my choice. Meanwhile, he will spend the rest of his days rotting in my private prison. You ask this impudent creep if he values his so-called rights more than he loves his family, and then ask him to choose accordingly. This will be my last warning."

Boyler hung up and smiled to himself, still holding the pistol.

His office door opened and in came Mark Boner, his chief of staff. Boner bowed low in front of Boyler's massive mahogany desk, averting his eyes. "Your Senatorship, I have to speak with you. I'm afraid it's rather urgent."

Boyler did not look at him, but continued to admire his percussion pistol. "Have I ever shown you this one, Boner? It's a real beauty. Thirty-six caliber, six-and-a-half-inch barrel. A five-shooter. They called it a Navy revolver, but the cavalry used it, too. A beautiful handheld killing machine of deadly accuracy…so long and hard and explosive." Boyler sighted down the barrel at the wall and made a firing sound with his lips, then imitated the gurgling sound of a dying victim.

Boner wiped his brow with a handkerchief. "Your Senatorship, the Director of the U.S. Security Agency is here to see you."

Boyler put down the gun. "Eh? What the devil does that little toady want?"

"He says it's highest priority, and he must speak with you."

"Can't you see I'm busy, Boner? Have him make an appointment."

"Sir, there's been a security breach."

Boyler suddenly forgot about his pistol. "Send him in."

The SA Director came in with two aides on either side of him. He bowed crisply. "Good afternoon, Your Senatorship. I'm afraid I have a matter of the greatest sensitivity to discuss with you." The Director looked questioningly at Boner.

"Boner can be trusted. Get on with it, Director."

The SA Director cleared his throat and held out a one hundred-page report, as if it were an offering to Boyler. "It appears that there has been a security breach and that…"—he cleared his throat again while his two aides stood on either side of him, their heads joggling like two bobblehead dolls—"…and that some information about you has been compromised."

Boyler's thin lips pursed, his brow furrowed, and the network of wrinkles around his dark eyes contracted. "What has been compromised?"

"It has to do with the PISIBANK program."

"Explain. I don't understand your accursed bureaucratic acronyms."

"The Personal Identification System Information Bank. This is a top-secret database containing detailed personal information on all citizens, legal residents, and non-residents in the United States. It looks as if a rogue Security Officer downloaded a full report on you and absconded with a hard copy of it."

Boyler shot up from his chair to his full six feet and three inches. "What?"

The Director held out his hands. "I want you to know that everything is under control and that we fully expect that the breach will be contained shortly."

"Shortly? When did the breach take place?"

"Several weeks ago."

"Several weeks ago?" thundered Boyler, his face turning red. "The hell you say! Why was I not informed immediately?"

"Protocols required—"

"Damn your protocols, man! Damn all of you degenerate bureaucrats to the maggot-infested pits of hell!"

Boner was shaking uncontrollably, like a cornstalk in a gusty wind. The two aides were quivering like aspens. Boyler marched around the table and seized the Director by the collar, lifting him up Darth Vader-style. The hundred-page report fell onto the floor.

"What is the name of this rogue agent?"

The Director's face was beet red as he sputtered and choked.

"The name, knave!"

Boner, arms flapping like goose wings, said, "Senator, you are strangling him!"

Boyler lowered him to the floor. The Director, massaging his neck, said in a rasping voice, "His name is Jack Tone."

"Where is he? Have you apprehended him?"

"No. We have dispatched all our agents to track him down. The FBI, CIA, and the Wall Street Espionage Consortium are on the job. NSA supercomputers are monitoring every phone call in the country. Interpol has been informed, as well as MI5 and MI6, Mossad, the Canadians, and the Australians. The French, Germans, and Japanese are cooperating, along with the Saudis, the Egyptians, the Indians, the Pakistanis, the Cubans, and our 'Allies of Convenience' among the Islamist networks. The Russians and Chinese have their eye out for him. The Sinaloa Cartel, Cosa Nostra, the 'Ndrangheta, the Five Families, the Yakuza, and the various Tongs have been paid appropriate headhunter fees. A team of private global contractors has also been engaged. Agents, hit men, terrorists, and contractors have fanned out across the globe in search of him."

"What, is he so microscopic that none of these organizations have found him yet?"

"He appears to have disappeared."

"Do we at least know something about this miscreant? For example, who he is working for?"

"We don't know. Possibly one of the revolutionary factions, but, as you know, there are so many, and they are only loosely aligned. We haven't even been able to determine whether or not their paramount leader, Number One, actually exists, or is merely a fiction designed to throw us off."

"Target Tone's family," said Boyler, shrugging. "And be done with it. Forget about trying to get these useless criminal and national security organizations to find him. What a bunch of pathetic Keystone Kops they are. The Bible tells us that when you want to stop evil, you have to slash away at the roots of the vine, you have to slaughter the runaway lamb where you find it, you have to seize the pot from the potter's wheel and smash it without hesitation, you have to pin the evildoer to a tree with nine-inch nails and shove a spear into his side. Interrogate his family, starting with his oldest family members, and working down to the youngest, to the children. Supreme Court Secret Security Authorization HL666 gives us the authority. Use waterboarding—at first. If that does not work, then progress, as Torquemada instructed, to more *persuasive* methods. And make sure you record the interrogations so that I may review them. This is America, goddamn it. Get on the stick, Director. Do your patriotic duty."

"But, Your Senatorship," said the Director in a bleating voice, "he is unmarried, he has no family members—none that we can find. He has no friends. He is an *isolate*."

"What, no parents, brothers, sisters, aunts, uncles, nephews, nieces, grandparents? Nothing? How can that be?"

The Director took a deep breath. "His parents were Robert and Rebecca Tone."

Boyler visibly paled. "So it must be revenge…" he whispered. Then, with renewed fury: "The brat should have been liquidated!"

Boyler dropped back into his chair and cradled his head in his hands. Looking up, eyes already bloodshot, he said to the Director, "Keep me apprised of developments. Now, begone! You have angered me, and I weary of your presence."

The Director and his aides bowed low. "Yes, Your Senatorship," they said, maintaining their bowed posture and retreating backwards all the way to the door.

When they were gone, Boyler said, "I suppose we must go speak with *him*. The sooner we get this over with, the better."

"I agree, Your Senatorship."

Suddenly overcome with anger and frustration, Boyler grabbed his cavalry pistol, stood up, and discharged five rounds at the bust of Benjamin Franklin on his mantel, blasting it to smithereens.

He set the gun down and opened a drawer in his desk, lifting up the green handset of an old-fashioned phone.

"Boyler here. Please send a helicopter…I have an urgent matter to discuss with Mr. Reid."

F9

The green helicopter landed on the roof of the braided, twisting skyscraper that New Yorkers called the Gazillionaire's Tower, the Corkscrew, and, sometimes, the Pig's Cock. Boyler and Boner stepped out, bending against the powerful downdraft. Security personnel frisked them and took them down into the top floor. Boner was given a seat and a cup of tea in the drawing room, while Boyler was escorted into a large anteroom with a lofty, glass-plated cathedral ceiling through which the blue and cloudless winter sky was visible. The guards departed, and Boyler stood meekly before a pair of three-story doors, each emblazoned with a gold Percentage Sign. At length the doors swung open silently.

This was the Senator's cue. He fell to his hands and knees and slowly entered the room beyond, crawling like a dog. Keeping his head down, he advanced until he came to the pentagram shape in the carpet; then he stopped. The towering doors closed behind him.

"You may lift your head."

Boyler looked up fearfully, his eyes now watery and wide. This was always the most dangerous part of his meetings with his Wall Street overlord. He knew that beneath the pentagram was a trapdoor that could open up at any moment, sending him into a modern-day *oubliette*.

In front of him was an enormous desk—a ten-foot-high wall of pure granite— decorated with skulls plundered from ancient mass burial and massacre sites from around the world. On the wall behind the desk, in a gold shrine with candles and incense burners, was a framed MBA diploma. Around the room were electro-tapestries and electro-frescoes vividly depicting savage battles, scenes of mass murder and genocide, both ancient and contemporary—executions, and tortures, and rivers of blood in which corpses bobbed. The scenes changed constantly, sometimes morphing into images of tropical islands with bone-white beaches, snow-draped alpine chateaux, and fleets of yachts.

Behind the desk sat Gregory Randolph Reid, a brown-haired, ruggedly handsome man of middle age. His eyes had the dreamy clarity of a lost boy who does not know he is lost; his face was strikingly weathered. His shoulders were broad, his $500,000 sharkskin suit tailored perfectly—a second epidermal layer of paneled silk that shimmered like schist. A pungent aroma of over-applied rare cologne wafted from him, and his fingers were encrusted with scintillating scutes of diamonds and gold.

"Rise, my dear and faithful servitor," he said.

The Senator climbed to his feet and stood, tense with apprehension.

The first several minutes of an audience with Gregory Reid dragged on like hours. No miserable royal official summoned into the Star Chamber of Henry VIII had been as burdened by the fear of personal extermination as the U.S. Senator upon entering Reid's lofty holy of holies.

"I had a meditative dream," said Reid, affecting a breathy, lisping accent that creepily reminded Boyler of Marlon Brando in *Apocalypse Now*. "In this dream I sailed as a voyager down my own alimentary canal—an explorer of forbidden things. I entered into a Dimension of Perversions, where there was no right or wrong, and there I finally found God. I woke from this dream like a turd expelled from a divine ass, and I knew that I was good, and that Good was Horror. Do you believe in God, dear friend? Do you believe in Horror?"

"I believe in God, Mr. Reid."

"Who is God, Boyler?"

"God is the Creator, the Judge, Mr. Reid. The Lawgiver."

"Am I God, Boyler?"

"Excuse me, Mr. Reid?"

"Because if I am God, then you don't have to tell me what you have come to tell me, as I already know it." Reid descended the steps from his giant granite desk and slapped Boyler hard across the face. The U.S. Senator crumpled. "Mercy, my lord!" he whimpered. "Mercy!"

"How could you have allowed such a breach to happen?" shouted Reid, assuming his natural manner of speaking, which was loud and brash.

"I assure you, it was not me, it was the Security Agency...they're a bunch of idiotic bureaucrats. Here is the report on the breach."

Boyler held out the thick sheaf of papers, but Reid swatted them away, causing sheets to flutter all around the room.

"The problem is precisely all this endless paperage! Do you think a successful multibillion-dollar business is built on paper? Do you think progress is made through paper? May geese defecate all over your bureaucracy, all over your detestable paper!" Reid punched Boyler, then tackled him. The two men rolled on the floor and wrestled, kicking and pummeling. They grappled; they tried to garrote each other. Their faces turned red and animalistic, their teeth flashed like fangs, their saliva flowing copiously.

Reid won the upper hand, picking up Boyler bodily and holding him over his head: a struggling Hercules in a suit. Under the weight he wobbled slightly, while Boyler thrashed his arms and legs like an upturned beetle. Reid's face was as strained as a constipated bulldog's. Summoning all of his power, he tried to heave Boyler across the room. But Boyler hit the ground only three feet away, landing with a crunch. Boyler wrapped his arms around his rib cage, unleashing a vile effluvia of the most degrading personal slurs upon Reid.

The Wall Street mogul staggered over to him, panting. "Triumph of the will, my friend," he said, kicking Boyler twice before falling into an armchair. "It's what separates leaders from followers, rulers from slaves. Come now. Let's sit down and discuss this like civilized men."

Groaning, Boyler got to his feet and sat across from Reid, who poured him a Scotch. Boyler drank it, grunting.

"Do you remember that time," said Reid nostalgically, "when we were at school together, and we took that trip to Thailand to have sex with underage prostitutes?"

Boyler, grunting again, nodded. He was twenty-five years older than Reid, and it was Reid's father who had been Boyler's brother in Skull and Bones—not Reid himself. Reid had long ago slain his father in a private duel with medieval swords that Boyler had helped to organize. Nevertheless, the Senator generally humored Reid during his reveries and fantasies, which Reid often confused with those of his dead father.

Reid continued. "And, of course you remember how we had to kill them all, how we had to cut them up, like Herod in Bethlehem—"

"Let me interrupt you right there, GR," said Boyler, tossing back the contents of his glass. "I know you are upset about the breach, and that you think it will jeopardize Project Autocrat." Boyler wagged a long finger reassuringly. "But you need not have any fear on that account. So long as you control *her*, you have power. Nothing, no one, can do anything to stop you."

Reid considered this, kneading his lantern hard jaw. "What an American woman likes in her man is a brute. That's why I love American women, and why they love me."

"Sooner or later we will track down Jack Tone," said Boyler.

"Did you know, Boyler, that fully 25 percent of a man's brain is dedicated to the regulation and proper functioning of the man-rod?"

"The 'man-rod,' GR?"

"The pego, the wand, the scepter, the battering ram, the pole, the johnson, the rooster that crows at dawn, the worm that makes the rose sick, the serpent that gave the lady an apple."

"GR, with all due respect, have you taken your meds today?"

Reid sat back, crossing his arms. "Only the court jester gets to speak to me that way."

"I'm serious."

"Yes, I have taken my meds. But as I was saying, the typical American woman desires the quarterback, the jock, the cocky thug. But *this one* is not a typical American woman, is she?"

"No, GR, she is not."

"Sometimes she goes into this catatonic state, and I can't even communicate with her..." Reid looked worried, distant.

"Whether she speaks to you or not doesn't matter," said Boyler. "That everyone knows you have her is all that counts."

"And suppose they try to take her from me?" retorted Reid. "Every corporate bloodsucker in the world covets what I have. But I am the Supreme Bloodsucker...I am the Bloodsucker of Bloodsuckers!"

"You are, GR."

Reid gazed up at his wall, where an image of a magnificent nuclear-powered helicopter yacht was cruising the open skies. The name of the yacht was *Never Enough*.

"Did I ever tell you, Boyler, that my father cuckolded the Devil?"

"Excuse me, sir?"

"He used necromancy to summon the bride of the Devil, and then he committed adultery with her. It was she who gave birth to me, and I was conveyed to the surface of the Earth on the backs of three jackals named Beelzebub, Pazuzu, and Mephistopheles. But the Devil's bride was also his daughter, the offspring of the Devil and Tiamat, the primordial Sea Dragon who was slain by Marduk, so I am both the grandson and the son of Satan."

He was clearly off his meds, Boyler concluded dourly.

"Your mother was killed by your father in a drunken rage, GR. That's why you killed him in a duel."

"No. That is a false memory implanted in me. I am the son of the Devil's daughter. I think *she* is the Devil's daughter, Boyler. She is both my mother and my sister, and she must become my lover in order for the prophecy to be fulfilled." Reid's eyes were smoldering.

"What prophecy?"

"There must be one. There must."

Boyler had endured enough. It was time to take the rod to this boy. He gingerly placed his crystal snifter on the floor. "GR, listen to me. We must capture this Jack Tone before anyone else does. Do you understand? Operation Autocrat is in jeopardy. Our discoveries may be revealed."

Suddenly clear-eyed and lucid, Reid gazed at Boyler. "Do you think, old man, that I am not aware of the situation? Oh, I fully intend to capture this Tone, make no mistake. Is your peon out there?"

"Boner? Yes, why?"

Reid produced a small pistol from his pocket. "Shoot him."

"Shoot Boner? Why?"

"As a sign of loyalty to me. To prove to me that you have not betrayed me, and that you are not at the root of this evil breach."

"But Boner is the best chief of staff I've ever had. He's at once intelligent and totally docile. He understands my operation better than I do. He may seem worthless, but he's my Eichmann. I cannot function without my Eichmann."

"I understand, Boyler. You are *my* Eichmann. We all have our Eichmanns. Eichmanns are a dime a dozen. You can probably order a new one on the Internet. Shoot him."

Boyler sighed heavily. "Very well." He took the gun and rose. Reid followed him through the anteroom and into the drawing room, where Boner was sipping his third cup of tea.

Boner looked up just as Boyler raised the gun to shoot him.

"Senator?"

Boyler cocked the gun and Boner's jaw dropped in horrid realization.

"Abraham, Abraham, do not harm the boy!" cried Reid. "Do not lay a finger upon him!" He rushed forward and punched Boyler hard.

"Ach, you swine!" cried Boyler. He dropped the gun and clutched his side, which, still hurting from where Reid had kicked him, exploded with fresh pain.

Calmly, Reid picked up the pistol and slipped it back in his pocket. "Note well, Boner, that Senator Boyler of Pennsylvania was perfectly willing to kill you upon my command. I want you to listen to him in all things, and to obey him as a son obeys his father. However, never forget that I am your master."

"Yes, Your Excellency," said Boner, his lips trembling.

A few minutes later, Boyler and Boner stepped into the green helicopter. As it took off from the Gazillionaire's Tower, Boyler said, "Sorry about that, Boner. Of course you know that the whole thing was a setup. Reid was trying to prove some kind of point, I suppose. That gun wasn't even loaded. He's off his meds. Not that they would help. He's too far gone for meds."

"I understand, Your Senatorship."

"So we're square again?"

"Yes, Your Senatorship."

"Excellent. When we get back to the office, remind me to give you that 1864 Manhattan Arms Company Navy pistol as a token of appreciation from me."

CHAPTER TEN

Stephany Miscellany

After Boyler and Boner had departed, Reid returned to his office and stood on the pentagram, scratching his chin reflectively. Silently, a towering Plutocroid stepped out of the shadows behind him, and Reid looked up, apparently surprised to see him.

"What did you think of that exchange, Mr. Ichabod?"

"Senator Boyler is a useful idiot, sir," said the Plutocroid. "A very useful idiot, like most politicians. It is useful, too, that he thinks you are the idiot."

"You mean, he thinks I'm an idiot and doesn't realize I'm mad."

"Precisely, sir. Though I think he does realize you are mad."

"And what of this Tone, Mr. Ichabod?

"We continue to search for him, sir. There is no place on the planet he can hide forever."

"I am not so worried about that, Mr. Ichabod. What damage can he do that he has not already done?"

"That is not the issue, sir. There is no doubt he is part of a larger organization. I venture to say that this organization can do a lot of damage if it learns about Operation Autocrat. Whoever they are, they did manage to kill Agent 4940 in Quebec City before he could make a full report. Cut his head clean off. Agent 4940 was a Type III—perhaps not the strongest and fastest of Plutocroids, but certainly a match for any human."

"What are you saying, Mr. Ichabod?"

"I'm not sure, sir. It requires further thought. I shall be opening up a can of sardines and pondering the matter some more."

"As you said, you will find him. I think I will visit my family now, Mr. Ichabod."

"Very good, sir. I assume you mean your *special* family, and not the twins."

"Of course."

Mr. Ichabod walked over to the wall and pressed a button. A door swung open, and Reid entered. The door automatically closed behind him. Reid was suddenly in an upper middle-class house in the suburbs, with sunlight shining in the windows. He went into the living room.

"Daddy, Daddy!" cried a little girl, jumping up from her coloring book and hugging him. "Come see the pictures I've been drawing! I drew a pony and an angel and a most lovely little flower!" A boy, a few years younger than the girl, was sitting on the floor playing. "Daddy, see what a swell crane I've built with my erector set! Come see, come see!"

"Excellent, my children, excellent," said Reid distractedly. "Where is your mother?"

"She's in the kitchen, Father," said the boy. "Father, Mother is most exceedingly lovely, isn't she?"

"Yes she is, son. Your mother is quite lovely."

"And she is very clever, isn't she, Daddy?" said the little girl.

"Your mother is the cleverest woman in the whole wide world. That's what makes her so dangerous."

Now a tall woman in black boots walked into the room. She wore a formfitting coatdress with a high, open collar; around her neck was a diamond choker.

"Ah, my love," said Reid, going up to her and trying to take her in his arms.

She pushed him away and dropped into a chair, glancing out the window. Some birds had settled on a branch and were tweeting joyfully. The sun was radiant. A bunny hopped past, and a deer nibbled on the grass. Across the street, a neighbor mowed his lawn.

"What's the matter with you?" Reid demanded.

"Leave me alone, you bastard," she said.

"Do you want a drink?" asked Reid, going over to the bar and dropping ice cubes in a glass.

"You know what I like," she said.

He fixed her a drink, while the boy and the girl continued to clamor around him, fighting for his attention.

"Children, I said be silent!" he barked.

That only increased their exhortations for him to look at the coloring book, to play with the crane. Exasperated, Reid took a remote control device from his pocket and aimed it at the children, shutting them off. They stood still, frozen in time.

"God, those damn things make so much noise..." he muttered, bringing the woman her drink.

She crossed her legs and looked at him severely. "What kind of sick sociopath keeps animatronic children? Especially when he has real children, not to mention a nephew and a niece?"

"My real children vex me, along with my real wife. That's why I sent them to Davos. They are happy and I am happy. As for Fritz and Clara, they are the swarthy products of my deceased brother's miscegenation, and as such they can never be considered genuine Reids. You know why they are here."

"Yes," she replied with no expression, "in case you need to harvest their organs."

Reid shrugged. "There are many who would like to see me dead, many superrich schemers who envy my ultimate power, my cosmological portfolio, and my flawless network. They will stop at nothing, including poisons and bombs. My personal worth has far more value than the sum of my physical organs; therefore I must have spares, since the whole should not be destroyed on account of the part, the hero must not be brought down because of the heel." Derisively, he looked down at her coatdress. "Why are you wearing that boring outfit again? Why don't you ever wear any of the elegant gowns and dresses I've given you?"

"Because I am not now, and never will be, your whore. I came to you in good faith, Gregory, and you made me your captive."

Reid gestured around the room. "I've built all this for you. I've given you a home and a family. Two adoring children. And yet you refuse to return my love." In disgust, he pressed a button on the remote control, and the suburban house interior was replaced by a series of empty rooms with bare metal walls scored vertically and horizontally with an illuminated gridwork.

"I've tried to have conversations with the children, Gregory," she said. "But they don't have souls or true consciousness, and so after a while their literally mindless prattling, and their penchant for non sequiturs, becomes tedious."

"How do you know they don't have souls or consciousness? Do you know how much I paid for those units? That's state-of-the-art artificial intelligence right there. I paid enough money to feed, clothe, and educate ten thousand starving Third World children. Ten thousand children perished so I could provide you with those units, and you complain that they don't have souls."

"If you can't tell that they don't have souls, that's probably because you don't either, you depraved animal."

"What can I do to make you love me, Stephany?" pleaded Reid. "What can I do to win your love, to buy your love?"

The woman stood up and regarded him with a withering, imperious stare; he felt yet again what he had felt so many times before when in her presence: abject fear. He gripped the remote control in his pocket.

"Take this thing off of my neck," she said. "This deathtrap."

"Oh, no," he replied with a jittery chuckle. "That I cannot do."

She bared her teeth, reached down, and grabbed him by the collar, lifting him up and slamming him against the wall. "Take this thing off me, you damn dirty Ape!"

Mr. Ichabod slipped silently into the room—a gentleman's gentleman from hell, a demonic Jeeves. "Is there a problem, sir?"

Stephany eyed the Plutocroid with barely repressed revulsion, then let go of Reid.

"No, Mr. Ichabod," he said, rubbing his neck. "The lady of the household and I are just having a little disagreement."

Stephany was calm again. She smiled and assumed a more dignified pose, picking a fleck of lint off Reid's shoulder. "I'm sorry, my love. You know my temper. Turn on the children again, if you like."

"Forget it. They're more tolerable the way they are." Reid reached for his drink with a shaking hand and sloshed it back. "Will you come to the Save the Children Charity Gala?"

"Of course."

"Will you wear the black evening gown I purchased for you?"

She paused and then said, "Of course, my love."

Mr. Ichabod, satisfied that the domestic turbulence had subsided for the moment, quietly slipped away.

CHAPTER ELEVEN

American History Zero

Polyvox looked questioningly at Andronicus. "Gregory Randolph Reid? Who is he?"

"One of the richest men on Earth," said Andronicus. "Not only that, but the Reids have been rich for generations, which no doubt accounts for Gregory Reid's peculiar psychological tendencies."

Andronicus turned off the light. An image of Reid appeared on the wall screen.

"The Reids are an old family," he explained. "The original Reid, Angus the Immigrant, was transplanted to the American Colonies in the 1600s. He was the youngest son of a Scottish highland laird and had been condemned by his own family for what we today would call serial murder."

The next image showed a young man in highland garb. He had pallid skin, scarlet lips, and dull but hungry eyes.

"It was said that at least seven women, all commoners, were victims of his sociopathic compulsion for rape and mutilation. While his clan deliberated on whether to burn him, behead him, or exile him to an isolated island crag where the elements and God would mete out justice, his mother smuggled him onto a ship for America. Though he arrived penniless, he prospered in that lawless, violent, and blood-drenched era—first as a hunter of fugitive slaves, then as an overseer on a plantation, then as a landowner in his own right. His sons made their fortune in the slave and cotton trade. His grandson Ahab 'Red Cock' Reid built a slave ship with special chutes through which sick African men, women, and children could simply be discharged into the ocean when their ailments threatened the still healthy slaves. These ships plied back and forth across the Atlantic for decades, and were responsible for an unbroken flow of gold into the coffers of the Reids. After the Civil War, the Reids reinvested their wealth in the railroads, and by the beginning of the twentieth century, they had become prominent in oil, chemicals, and armaments."

The next set of images was of a sprawling factory with belching smokestacks, followed by colorized hi-res footage of soldiers on the battlefield.

"World War I was a great boon for the Reids; their factories produced a very profitable line of war products—sold to both sides—whose purpose was to demoralize the enemy by grievously maiming, but not killing, combatants. World War II brought in similar riches. Reid's great-great-grandfather Cavendish Reid, who married a fabulously wealthy Japanese princess, extended the family interests into entertainment pharmaceuticals, genetic engineering, and the devising of ingenious new financial instruments that increased the Reid family's wealth like a quickly growing malignant mass."

The factory and battle images were replaced by those of gleaming labs, state dinners, and a sixteenth-century two-handed sword.

"Fauntleroy Reid entered politics and was Secretary of State during the Drumpf Administration. In succeeding generations, the family split into several branches. Gregory Reid's branch is the most powerful. His grandfather Kaiser and his father Ivan were instrumental in initiating the Wars of Betrayal. Gregory Reid, a diagnosed psychotic who underwent significant genetic therapy as a boy, is alleged to have killed his father in a bizarre duel involving bastard swords. Purportedly, he retains the head. He is a scion of devilry, the perfected, purified distillation of generations of American-style corporate rapaciousness. He is an American Original."

"And what specifically do we now know about his connection with Senator Lance Boyler?" asked Polyvox.

"Boyler is Reid's servitor. He is, if you'll excuse the expression, Reid's Senatorial Bitch."

"I'll excuse the expression this one time. Go on."

"Boyler is the fanatical but capable henchman of Reid. It is Boyler who makes regular visits to the Pit, where scientists of Reid's Grombex Corporation are working tirelessly to effectuate the Plot. So far, they have had no success."

"Where does Reid reside?"

"He's a recluse," said Andronicus. "He spends most of his time on the top several floors of the so-called Gazillionaire's Tower in Manhattan. Sometimes he travels on his nuclear-powered, auto-piloted helicopter yacht *Never Enough*. He also attends Charity Galas hosted by other global money moguls, but these are intensely secret affairs, heavily guarded by armies of security personnel."

"But who lives there with him?" pressed Polyvox, betraying a sudden, intense interest in Reid. "Does he live there alone? Is he married, does he have a family?"

It was Max Blackshield who answered now. He was of average height and slender, with wavy black hair and deep, penetrating blue eyes. "His wife Helene Lemercier and their two children, Sultan Selim Reid and Elizabeth Báthory Reid, are in Davos. She is reputedly a chemist, of French and Vietnamese ancestry. Reid never sees them, and it is said they are estranged. He lives with his twin nephew and niece, the young children of his brother Anton, who died with his wife under mysterious circumstances years ago. There are also strange rumors that he purchased a pair of animatronic children and makes use of a 'dry' sensory hologram deck to recreate scenes of settled, middle-class domesticity. God only knows why. With Reid, even the most exaggerated speculations often fall short of the demented truth."

"And so that's it," concluded Polyvox. "He lives with two robots, a nephew, and a niece in a New York City plutocrat tower."

"Of course he and his household are waited on by a full staff of servants," said Blackshield, "and surrounded by multilayered organizational ramparts of security personnel. We believe these may include some of the higher-level Plutocroids. So if you are wondering if we could ever get into his fortress, Polyvox, I can promise you it would be impossible."

"That's not what I'm getting at. I was wondering if anyone else resided with him."

"Well," said Blackshield, "he is said to have a mistress."

Polyvox's eyes narrowed. "A mistress?"

"A captive woman, as it were. It is said that she appears at Charity Galas occasionally."

"What is her name?"

Andronicus said, "We don't know. Even her existence could just be a rumor. Let's not draw any conclusions just yet, Polyvox."

"There is no need to draw a conclusion when you have documented facts to work with," said Polyvox.

Jack noticed that Polyvox had fallen into a curiously reflective, even morose, mood. She moved away from the others, sat down in a chair, and poured herself a large glass of rust red Belgian ale. Crossing her legs, she stared at the wall, tapped her jaw, and pondered. Andronicus watched her, and Max Blackshield, standing with his hands behind his back, coughed slightly.

"Ah, yes," said Andronicus. "Tone, you've never been properly introduced to the inner circle of our political discussion group. This is Max Blackshield, our Director of Intelligence and Spymaster. Max is a veteran of the wars."

Blackshield held out his hand. "Mr. Tone. I commend you for your work."

They shook hands.

"And this is Emily Bombsinger, Director of Propaganda and Liaison to Other Factions. She oversees communication to and from Number One. The Trappist Tavern is her establishment."

Jack remembered Bombsinger from before. She was very pretty, with violet eyes and chrome-green hair. She was in her twenties and so had probably been born with these particular features—the result of prenatal genetic modifications. Bombsinger went up to Jack, took her hand in his, and shook it warmly, all the while staring curiously at him with her violet eyes, her mouth turned in a semi-smile.

Though Jack was in his thirties, the younger generation had always been an enigma to him. He attributed their weird behavioral patterns to all the gene-mods, which were especially common among upper-class urban dwellers.

"Hello there, Jackie," she said. "Do you mind if I call you Jackie?"

"I prefer Jack, but if you want to call me Jackie, very well."

"Jackie it is then." She gave his hand a squeeze and let go.

"Emily has a wonderful voice," added Andronicus with a chuckle. "You should hear her sing. It's explosive!"

Jack detected flickering smiles on the faces of the others, but he resisted the impulse to ask for an explanation of what seemed an inside joke. He was too impatient, too eager to continue unwinding the complex conspiracy that had originated with his parents' murders.

"Professor Abdullah is our cryptologist," continued Andronicus. "And Doctor Krypton, a former track and field Olympian whose actual name you might even recall were she to tell you, which she cannot, is our resident physician and psychologist. Both teach at local universities, where they are known for their rather pedestrian and conservative views defending the economic and political status quo."

Both the Professor and Doctor Krypton were in their mid to late sixties, but neither appeared in any way frail. The Professor was athletic beneath his tweed waistcoat, while Doctor Krypton displayed the quiet, smiling dignity of a matriarch. It was she, Jack realized, who had driven the car into which he had tossed his backpack with the PISIBANK report.

They both shook hands with Jack, their grips strong.

"Paul Bunyan, our engineer, Taras Petriv, our Security Specialist, and Father Daniel Doublecross, our Jesuitical heretic and in-house philosopher, are out conducting business for our political discussion group," concluded Andronicus. "You will meet them again shortly."

Throughout these introductions, Polyvox had remained quiet.

"Now what do you plan to do?" asked Jack.

"To do? What do you mean?" asked Andronicus.

"Thanks to the information I provided you, and on account of which I'm being hunted everywhere by things called Plutocroids—which, to be honest, I can still barely convince myself are real—you know that this Gregory Reid is behind the plot that my parents discovered. So what do you intend to do with the intelligence that has come at such a high price?"

"What do you suggest we do, Jack?"

"Since I don't even know what the Plot is, I'm not in a position to make any suggestions. Maybe you could enlighten me on that score."

"There's no point in explaining it to you," shrugged Andronicus. The other members of the discussion group—except for Polyvox—all nodded their heads.

Jack felt his anger rising. "What do you mean? After all I've gone through on your behalf, after all I've sacrificed, you still refuse to tell me what's at the heart of this conspiracy?"

It was now Emily Bombsinger who spoke, her voice soft and clear, like a winter wind sighing across a snowfield. "The Plot cannot be explained, Jack. It can only be seen to be believed."

"Yes, Jack," said Doctor Krypton, "we must take into account your predicted reactions based on our personality profile of you. You have a tendency to deny the reality of things when that reality pushes the limits of acceptable norms. And having worked as a bureaucrat for so long, you are now inclined to become emotionally disoriented and incredulous when confronted by what appears to be the warping of reality as you understand it and as your subconscious expects it to be. So no amount of verbal explanation will help to prepare you for something that you will simply have to see for yourself."

Jack listened to this brief psychoanalysis patiently, and then said, "I have a right to know all the details of the Plot, and you have an obligation to tell me. You can't just withhold the information indefinitely."

"We fully intend to enlighten you on the matter," said Andronicus. "And very soon. Tomorrow, perhaps. However, bear in mind that the place we will take you is very dangerous, and after you see what is there, you will never be the same man again." Andronicus's expression was inscrutable.

"And what does that mean?"

Jack noticed that Polyvox was standing right next to him, offering him a glass of Belgian ale. "It means nothing, Jack. Andronicus is a manipulator, a puppeteer of souls. Relax, for all will be well."

Far from taking offense at this comment, Andronicus smiled. He seemed very pleased with himself—a man totally in control of his revolutionary game.

F9

"I wish to invite all the members of the Faction Nine political discussion group to the front room of the Trappist Tavern for a meal of steamed mussels," said Emily Bombsinger.

When everyone had left the meeting room but Jack, Andronicus took him aside.

"Was everything okay in Canada, Jack?"

"Yes."

"How was the Winter Festival?"

"Entertaining."

"And you felt secure the entire time?"

"I suppose so. There were a few close calls, but we're alive. One of those Plutocroids did find us up there, but Polyvox…" Jack paused. "…chopped its head off."

"Regarding Polyvox—did you notice anything unusual?"

Jack wondered what Andronicus was getting at. "You mean apart from the fact that she's a member of an order of secretive, seven-foot-tall oddballs who carry telescoping blade weapons?"

"It seems you met other members of the Order."

"I briefly met her sister—her biological sister, that is."

Andronicus was intrigued. "You did? What was her name?"

"I never got the name. It was an unexpected meeting, and very brief."

"What did she look like?"

"Taller and more muscular than Polyvox. Why? What is it with this order, anyway? She has avoided explaining it, other than to claim that it is older than Ancient Sumer and Egypt."

Andronicus chuckled dryly. "It's human nature to form cultic organizations—religions, political parties, social groups, fraternal clubs, hereditary societies, even political discussion groups like ours—for we are a tribal and clannish species, and to belong to such groups satisfies a fundamental need for meaning and community. Many groups create legendary histories for themselves. Hers is no different."

"So her order is not ten thousand years old?"

"Hardly. Did you happen to meet the Superior of the Order?"

"No." Jack fidgeted slightly and looked down.

Andronicus lowered his voice. "I want you to do me a favor, Jack, and keep an eye on Polyvox."

This was a surprising request. "You don't trust her?"

"I trust her implicitly," Andronicus replied quickly. "Her order, on the other hand, is a bit of an enigma, and I would not want her to feel too pressured by them in a way that might compromise her work for us. I mean emotionally or cognitively taxed, you understand. As you shall see, we're involved in a dangerous exploit here, and it is not unreasonable to surmise that our objectives, and those of her order, might diverge, however slightly."

"You are worried about divided loyalties."

"In a way, yes. But serving more than one master is part of the human condition. You are gifted in observation, Jack. You are trained in piecing together patterns of behavior. If you observe anything unusual, no matter how insignificant, let me know."

"It sounds like you want me to spy on her."

Andronicus picked up a half-empty beer glass from the table and studied it as if its liquid black contents were suddenly of great interest. "Jack, in this business, we're always spying on each other, always looking through the glass, always trying to see what's on the inside. There is an expectation, even a duty, for us to observe each other for any signs of mental breakdown. Every once in a while, leaders of factions recommend that members of their discussion groups be sent for a few weeks or months of Rest and Relaxation. There are facilities for this, hidden away in remote corners of the world. Pleasant places where revolutionaries can sit and chat about the deplorable state of the world, or just take long hikes along the seashore or through the forest primeval. This is the normal course of affairs and has been standard since the social revolutionary movements of the nineteenth century."

"Very well, Andronicus. But why me? You all know Polyvox better than I do, and have known her longer. Any one of you is more likely than me to notice if her behavior becomes aberrant."

"Because you will be staying with her, in her apartment, for the time being. She has agreed to this arrangement."

Jack raised both eyebrows. "Excuse me? Staying with Polyvox?"

"You object?"

"I would prefer my own place," Jack said firmly.

"And where do you think you might stay, now that you've gone underground?"

Jack locked his hands behind his back. "I hadn't really given the matter much consideration, but I imagined I would rent an apartment or something like that right here in Philadelphia or its environs."

Andronicus seemed bemused. "Rent an apartment. And how would you pay for it?"

"I have substantial savings in private accounts, including money I inherited from my parents."

Now Andronicus made a pretense of being startled. "Of course you know that these funds are essentially frozen, like mammoths in the tundra."

"On the contrary, even before this whole affair began, I took great care to conceal my funds. I'm a Security Officer, after all. I know how to bury my treasure, because I know how the other pirates go about looking for it."

"My dear Tone, I have no desire to impugn your cleverness, but the instant you attempt to transfer any money from one account to another, or to your wallet, you will be seized and transported to a federal torture chamber. And that will be the end of you. We can do many things. Penetrating governmental or corporationist interrogation dungeons is not one of them."

Jack felt his exasperation growing. "And can't the faction help me get access to that money?"

Andronicus put the beer glass down, faced Jack, and gestured with both hands, like a professor delivering a lecture. "Listen to me. This is how we have made use of your accounts. We have periodically initiated account activity in cities across the world, falsely alerting bevies of state agents and mercenary investigators to your alleged whereabouts, only to leave them frustrated and flummoxed when it turns out you're not there. As for the money itself, you will never, ever see a single cent of it again. I'm sorry, but these are the sacrifices we must make for The Cause. Remember, your parents made an even greater sacrifice, and by making this one, you honor them." Andronicus gave Jack an avuncular slap on the back. "Come now, let's have some mussels and a glass of Rochefort ale."

F9

Jack went out with Andronicus and sat at the table. Andronicus took his seat right away, leaving only one place: between Polyvox and Emily Bombsinger. As soon as Jack sat down, Bombsinger scooped out a bowl of mussels for him and ordered an ale from one of the waiters. She herself was drinking mineral water from a bottle.

"Do you like mussels, Jackie?" she asked.

"Sure."

"These are really good," said Bombsinger, digging one out and popping it into her mouth. "They're only slightly above the federal government safety limits for mercury."

He nodded and unenthusiastically chewed on a mussel. When his ale came, he nursed it, taking meager sips.

Jack was not really in the mood for mussels, or for talk, or for ale. He had other preoccupations. Until now, he had comforted himself with the idea that Faction Nine was unified in its opposition to the government, but now he was beginning to wonder if the faction itself was fractious. He was not satisfied with Andronicus's explanation of why it might be necessary to spy on Polyvox, and he suspected that Andronicus was subjecting him to some kind of loyalty test. With such internal divisions, could Faction Nine effectively confront the leviathan of the State? More than any of his new revolutionary compatriots, he knew that the government, though often bumbling, made up for its inherent idiocy by its sheer size. All the great non-democratic governments of the world, whether American, Russian, or Chinese, were perfectly capable of crushing dissent.

The other members of the political discussion group were sitting around a circular table near a bay window, drinking their ale and feasting on mussels, bread, and cheese. Andronicus and Jack joined them. The discussion was rambling and interesting, but any political observations they made were conventional and leaned heavily towards reaffirming the establishment. Jack was tired from his travels and made only a few contributions, but he admired their ability to camouflage forbidden speech beneath a superstrate of shallow American banter.

One by one, the discussion group members left the table and headed home, until only Andronicus, Polyvox, Bombsinger, and Jack remained. Giving Jack one final curious and slightly baleful look, Bombsinger excused herself to attend to business in the back office of the Trappist Tavern.

"Now," said Andronicus, rubbing his hands expectantly, "let's see this wonderful car that your order has lent you, Polyvox. What kind of car is it again?"

"A prototype, tentatively called the *Argo* Cruiser. The manufacture is German and Japanese."

They exited the Trappist Tavern and walked down a block to where Polyvox had parked the car, which because of its extraordinary length had essentially been hemmed in by vehicles in front of and behind it.

Andronicus's eyes smoldered when he saw it. "It evokes a big, spaceship-style 1948 Tucker," he said, running his hand along the fuselage. "The specifications?"

"It has an environmentally friendly plasma pulse engine, a virtually indestructible plasto-metallic body with full color-shifting capability, an autopilot, a radar scrambler, a smart defensive system, submarine function, a wet bar, hygienic accoutrements, a water processor, and sleeping accommodations for four," boasted Polyvox, who was by now a bit tipsy, as was Andronicus.

Andronicus laughed—whether in response to Polyvox's seeming hyperbole or out of genuine wonder, Jack could not say, because he had no idea if her over-the-top description was in any way rooted in reality. She had not mentioned any of these alleged capabilities to him during their journey from Quebec. On the other hand, they had not once stopped to refill the tank with gas.

"It will be our battleship *Potemkin*," said Andronicus, "our flagship of the revolution."

"Our *Constitution*, our Old Ironsides."

Polyvox and Andronicus laughed joyfully.

"Can we take it for a spin?" asked Andronicus, sounding like an eager little boy.

"I'm tired, Andronicus, and want to go to bed."

"Just a short trip. It's late on a Sunday night and there's no traffic in Philadelphia."

"Very well—prepare to be astonished, my friend."

"Perhaps this isn't a good idea," interjected Jack soberly, "since between the two of you tonight, half the world's store of Trappist ale has been depleted."

"We may be drunk, but the car isn't," replied Polyvox.

She opened the driver-side door and slipped behind the wheel. Andronicus offered Jack the passenger side, but he shook his head and sat in the back.

Their doors thudded closed around them. The dashboard lit up like a console on the *Enterprise*.

"Drive randomly around the city," said Polyvox, keeping her hands behind her head, "and at a safe and considerate speed."

The *Argo* slipped laterally out of its parking space and proceeded to roll at slow cruising velocity down the street.

It took them down the Benjamin Franklin Parkway, turning around at the Philadelphia Museum of Art and heading back again. Jack—weary of the car, weary of travel—dropped off into a doze. When he opened his eyes again, the *Argo* had stopped and the engine was off. Andronicus and Polyvox were looking tensely towards Independence Hall—Andronicus through a pair of field glasses, even though they were less than a block away.

"Here comes the devil," said Andronicus softly.

CHAPTER TWELVE

Polyvox in Light and Gloom

"**W**hat are you looking at?" asked Jack.

They didn't answer, so he peered through his window. A tall man with a large head—bald except for a fringe of gray hair—lurched from behind the arches in the eastern arcade of the building. Jack could see by the bright moonlight that he was imposing but ugly. His legs and arms were overlong in proportion to his body; his eyes too small; his gait, while resolute, completely lacking in grace. His jaw was heavy and jutted forward, the lower jawbone beyond the upper one, which was almost even with the tip of his nose—wolfish and aristocratic. The moonlight glinted sharply off the massive, bulb-shaped cupola of his head. His appearance was something that a children's illustrator might draw to convey a sadistic reform school headmaster. He looked furtively to his right and his left and then folded his long frame into the backseat of a waiting car, which immediately sped off.

"That was Senator Lance Boyler," said Andronicus. "Of Pennsylvania."

"What was he doing coming out of Independence Hall at three o'clock in the morning?"

"Soon you shall learn. But not tonight."

Polyvox, who now seemed completely sober, ordered the *Argo* to drive a few blocks away, where they dropped Andronicus off. She then continued driving until coming to the entrance of an underground parking garage, where she tapped out a code on the dashboard. A solid metal gate lifted, admitting them. Polyvox and Jack exited the car. He followed her past other parked vehicles to an elevator, which they took to the top of the building: the 40th floor.

They entered a large and—to Jack's mind—surprisingly lavish apartment with a peculiar and darkly gothic interior. Against one wall was a cathedral organ with a staggered pyramid of pipes. Opposite this was a stone fireplace where, to his surprise, a heavy log was already burning. Above the fireplace was a very large painting of a high-walled fantasy city. An adjacent room had a window looking out onto the wide, dark sweep of the Delaware River and the full span of a blue suspension bridge. There were still more rooms, all of them with tall doors and tapestry-covered walls.

"This is where you live?"

"For now."

"This hardly seems the dwelling place of a social revolutionary."

"It does not belong to me but to the Order, and we only use it when we are conducting business. Your room is over there," she said, pointing. "Now, if you don't mind, my thoughts and heart are in a turmoil. I have many things to reflect upon, and so I will play the organ."

Polyvox unbuttoned her coat and threw it over the back of a high wooden chair. She took long-legged strides to the organ, her boot heels striking loudly against the cold flagstone floor, and seated herself on the bench. Her posture was ramrod erect, and for a moment she appeared to pray or meditate. It appeared to Jack as if the runes on her skin flushed a deep blue color. Then she lifted her hands in claw formation and brought them crashing down upon the keys, generating a vibrating, thunderous opening chord that so startled Jack he almost flew back and hit the wall. This was merely the introduction to a tempestuous fugue that channeled all of the darkest and most hyperborean aspirations of the soul. So loud was this alien music that Jack couldn't help wondering how long it would be until the downstairs neighbors began thrashing at their ceilings with broomsticks.

He turned to enter his bedroom and closed the door. Instantly there was silence. The room was perfectly soundproofed.

F9

For an hour or two, he tossed and turned in the large bed. Then he fell into a deep slumber. Weird dreams and visions partially awakened him, but again he drifted off. Eventually, cold morning light filtered softly through the curtains and he sat up.

After showering and dressing, he left the bedroom. The organ room was filled with light and the fireplace was cold. He studied the painting. The fantastic city had many towers and garden terraces, and was located on a sloping hill. Around the city, the landscape was of forest and meadow, with grazing herds of archaic mammals. Among them were apelike creatures with benevolent, contented faces. They squatted in family groups, grooming each other peaceably, chewing on leaves and fruits.

"A lost world," sighed Polyvox.

He turned around, not having heard her creep up on him. She lifted a large coffee mug to her lips and slurped it noisily, her eyes still fixed on the painting.

"Who is the painter?" he asked.

"The painter belongs to the ages." She pointed at one of the apelike creatures sitting apart from the others, looking directly at the viewer with a surprised expression, as if he could somehow see the world beyond the painting and wasn't entirely sure he liked what he saw. "This one looks like you."

For a few seconds, Jack and the ape regarded each other. The painting was remarkably detailed, and in the ape's large watery eyes Jack perceived a sad thoughtfulness, as one might see in the daguerreotype of a long-dead forebear.

"Come, my friend, there's no need to dwell on past glories and present sorrows. There is work to be done. But first, breakfast is ready."

They sat in the dining room, drinking coffee and eating bread and cheese.

"Tonight," said Polyvox, dabbing a napkin to her lips, "you shall be taken to the Pit."

"Finally. And now you can tell me what it is."

"It is that which your parents discovered during their geophysical investigations."

"And what's in this pit?"

Polyvox poured herself another full mug of coffee. Before drinking any, she picked up a piece of bread and examined it indifferently. She was not particularly hungry. After chewing and swallowing, she looked at him. "You shall see. Before we go down, we will conduct this day as any other—a stroll about town, perhaps stopping off at a museum, then lunch."

To Jack, impatient for knowledge, it sounded dreary.

After breakfast, they took the elevator down to the lobby of the building. It was cold as they walked along the cobblestone colonial streets—some too narrow for cars, like medieval alleys. Philadelphians of all ethnicities and classes passed them—merchants in business suits, their teeth bared; burly workers chugging cups of scalding coffee and gnawing on cold soft pretzels; old bluebloods with parchment skin and gunmetal eyes; aimless recent college graduates, underemployed and plotting their futures; homeless people with wizened faces; artistic types gesticulating amongst themselves; and little knots of people whispering conspiratorially and looking fearfully over their shoulders, then breaking into peals of irrational laughter.

There was a quiet domestic madness to this city that New York, for all its arrogant hustle and bustle, completely lacked: a colorful, slow-baking insanity, a universal feeling emanating from all of its subcultures that something momentous was About to Happen, or Had Happened, or Might Possibly Happen in the dark and unpredictable Future. But then again, Maybe Not. This was a city that did not proclaim itself the Center of Civilization, that did not regard itself as a Galactic Core, but as a fiercely defensive satellite planet, a dwelling place where every cobblestone, every broken granite curb, every half-squashed pretzel being peddled by grubby hands, every spruce-flavored ale, every slanting ray of icy sunshine that caused a cry of distress to hung-over students, every infuriated green-faced sports fan venting his frustrations like a gladiator at the arena, every feathered mummer and drunkenly prancing comic in gold spray-painted shoes, every priest, every rabbi, every imam, and every potential mugger had no real idea who—exactly—they really were. But at least they knew *where* they were.

This was the City of Brotherly Love, the first and now forgotten capital of the United States of America, the signatory house of its revered freedom document (long since transferred to shrines in more esteemed cities), the first seat of its federal government, the home of its first national bank.

This was the mad attic of America, a city most Americans chose to ignore.

But like Rumpelstiltskin in his cave, it had not forgotten about them, and perhaps—even now—it was plotting its revenge.

Polyvox and Jack meandered for several hours, finally coming to the Mütter Museum of medical pathologies, which contained a gruesome collection of deformed skeletons, preserved tumors, floating fetal abominations, body parts of murderers and sociopaths, corpses disfigured by nightmarish diseases, and assorted wax renderings of people afflicted by various shocking maladies of congenital origin. Revolted and alarmed by these gratuitous displays, Jack retreated and found himself in a gallery that contained a panoply of archaic medical instruments, many of which resembled implements of torture.

"I insist we leave," he said to Polyvox as she studied a long pair of medieval brass tongs used for removing arrowheads from warriors. "I've had enough."

"But you haven't yet seen the thorax of John Wilkes Booth."

"I don't give a farthing about his thorax. I want to get out of this house of horrors."

Polyvox shrugged, then glanced at her timepiece. On the street, they leaned against the cold wind as they walked, passing three National Police officers who had detained an intoxicated homeless man and were angrily demanding that he produce his Identity Documents. Jack and Polyvox followed Chestnut until they came to a small, darkly lit café located below street level.

"Why did you take me to that museum?" asked Jack as they sat at a corner table, away from the door.

"I thought you might be interested in the medical history of the species."

"I am not so easily deceived, Polyvox. You are a calculating person, and everything you do is for a reason. There is nothing random about you." Jack was still agitated by the things he had seen at the Mütter Museum. After glancing at the menu disinterestedly, he continued, "Sometimes I wonder if you yourself don't have sociopathic tendencies, like the enemy you have dedicated yourself to hunting down."

"Are you now a psychologist?"

"I am a Security Officer trained in making judgments about human beings. The enemies of America are often sociopaths, so I must be able to identify them."

"A sociopath is completely lacking in empathy. If I am incapable of empathy, none of my lifelong friends, colleagues, and associates have ever made me aware of it. On the contrary, I deeply feel the pain of human beings, and I pity them and their wretched state. If you want sociopaths, look no further than your own elected officials in Congress, and beyond them to the ghouls of Wall Street, any one of whom could easily pass muster for the Waffen-SS. The reason I took you to that museum was not so that we could revel in human suffering, but so we could both pass a few hours contemplating medical oddities before going down into the Pit, where you're in store for something far stranger, if not quite as horrible."

"Tell me now what's down there. I promise I won't say anything to Andronicus."

Polyvox considered this. She leaned forward, and whispered, "Very well. You have a right to know. In that Pit—"

The waiter wafted over.

"Hi. I'll be taking care of you this afternoon. Have you made up your minds?"

They ordered, and as soon as the waiter left, Andronicus himself came into the café and sat down next to them. For the first time, Jack realized that there were no other patrons.

Andronicus seemed pensive. "Doctor Krypton has arranged everything," he whispered. "Jack must be prepped."

F9

After the waiter returned he watched them eat, impatiently drumming his fingers on the table. As soon as the plates were taken away, he instructed them to follow him to the back of the café. They went through a door, down a flight of steps, and into a small room with several chairs and a large mirror. It looked like the interior of a dingy hair salon.

"Have a seat, Jack," said Andronicus. "Do not ask questions if you wish to learn the truth."

Once Jack had seated himself, two cosmeticians entered and began to work on his hair and face, applying makeup, combing, coloring. By the time they were finished with him two hours later, he felt as if his face was covered with a thin coat of flexible plaster, and he looked like Harpo Marx.

He stood up from the chair. "Explain all this, for God's sake!" he demanded.

Andronicus, Polyvox, and Doctor Krypton were there, wearing white lab coats. Jack was instructed to put one on, as well as a pair of eyeglasses with heavy plastic frames.

"Listen carefully, Jack," said Andronicus. "I am Doctor Sanders, and Polyvox is Doctor Karon. You are Doctor Metron. Doctor Krypton is Doctor Abraham. We are going to visit the Pit. Doctor Abraham is employed there as a consulting theoretical neurologist, and we are visitors from her private lab. Do you understand?"

"Yes."

"Who am I?" asked Andronicus.

"You are Doctor Sanders."

"And who is that?" Andronicus pointed to Polyvox.

"That is Doctor Karon."

"And who are you?"

"Doctor Metron."

"What are we doing?" asked Andronicus.

"We are visiting the Pit with Doctor Abraham. We work in her private lab."

"And what are you going to say when we get to the Pit?"

"You didn't tell me that."

"I'm telling you now—you say nothing, nothing at all. If someone addresses you, one of us will answer."

Beyond the dressing room was an underground chamber with a little vehicle that resembled a mine cart or a roller-coaster car. Andronicus sat in the front with Doctor Krypton; Polyvox and Jack sat in the back. Andronicus pulled a lever, and the cart rattled forward along a track. For the most part the tunnel was straight, and illuminated by lightbulbs in little metal cages. Here and there the track intersected with others, their own tunnels curving away into darkness.

Jack leaned over to Polyvox and very softly whispered: "Where the devil are we? Will this take us to the Pit?"

"No. This is just a secret transportation network beneath the city. Only faction members are permitted to use it, and they have to get clearance from the High Revolutionary Council and Number One."

After fifteen minutes, the mine cart lurched to a stop. They got out and descended a circular stone stairway that led to a basement. Stairs from the basement took them to an old kitchen. They were in a colonial row house that faced one of the narrow streets of the Old City. By now it was dark. From here they walked north on 6th Street until they came to the west wing of Independence Hall, entering through a side door. Doctor Krypton placed her hand on a scanner and two elevator doors opened for them. They entered and took the elevator down.

When it opened again, they were on a wide circular catwalk overlooking the Pit.

CHAPTER THIRTEEN

A Pit, a Horror, and a Chase

Jack had not known what to expect. Too long had he been presented only with suggestion and innuendo. Too long had the Faction Nine members refused to divulge a single thing about the secret that his parents had helped discover, and for which they had been murdered. To fill this information gap, his mind had reached out in a thousand different directions, presenting, one after another, a continuous stream of ever more extraordinary possibilities, most of which he had immediately rejected as implausible. He had ultimately decided that they were going to show him some kind of secret plant for the illegal manufacture of weapons of mass destruction.

The reality was altogether different. There were no nuclear weapons or deadly chemicals—at least that he could see.

The Pit was a massive well, hundreds of feet deep and illuminated by rows of halogen lamps. The catwalk spiraled down along the wall of the well, which appeared to be hewn from solid granite. Here and there were men and women in white lab coats, sitting at terminals, typing, but overall the place was quiet. As Doctor Krypton led them down the spiral catwalk, Jack began to make out something at the bottom of the Pit—something very large. It appeared to be reddish orange and to be made of metal, but its structure was unusual and did not resemble a building.

Finally they reached the bottom.

Jack blinked. In front of him was something like an industrial sculpture produced by a brilliant but schizophrenic artistic mind. It had legs like a crustacean's and tubes connected to shiny metallic bladders. From its spine—if it could be called a spine—jutted rows of spikes or bristles. Four very long, segmented, whiplike antennae reached out in front, and two smaller ones protruded from behind. In front of this thing was a company (Jack could think of no other word) of smallish bipeds in an unmoving phalanx. There were about fifty of them altogether—fifty upright crustaceans with reticulated exoskeletons, cumbersome claws, lashing antennae, and faceted spheroid clusters that might have been eyes. Their barbed tails resembled those of scorpions. Each one was only about four feet tall—an invertebrate with razor-sharp armor.

Jack remembered being warned by Andronicus to say nothing, and so kept his mouth shut. But the sight of these abominations profoundly disconcerted him; they were like something that had crawled up out of the bilges of his own subconscious and assumed material form in the real world. Though they were not moving—apparently not even alive—there was something about them that induced primal turmoil in the very depths of his soul. They were there in front of him, but they were *impossible*.

A skinny, bespectacled man in a white lab coat cleared his throat diffidently. "Good evening, Doctor Abraham."

"Good evening, Doctor Carr. You know my associates, Doctors Sanders and Karon. Doctor Metron here has newly joined my team. All are theoretical neurologists currently working on speculative mathematical models to test Hypothesis Three. All their clearances are in order. I have the documents, if you wish to see them."

"That won't be necessary, thanks to our new, state-of-the-art security installations," said Doctor Carr without explaining. "Welcome, friends. I'm afraid His Senatorship has not scheduled a visit for today. In fact, he was here only yesterday for an inspection. We were all so pleased to see His Senatorship, and he, in turn, conveyed to us the gratitude of Our Benefactor, which as you can imagine pleased us greatly. His Senatorship also informed us that Our Benefactor will be hosting another clandestine Charity Gala, which always provides an abundance of research funds. We truly must be grateful to Our Benefactor, though we have no idea who he is."

"Excellent news," said Krypton. "We won't stay long, Doctor Carr. I simply wished to show Doctor Metron the specimens."

"Oh yes, of course. Go right ahead." Carr turned to Jack. "I've read some of your work, young man. You show great promise. The State rewards her loyal sons and daughters with great riches and exquisite privileges. Now if you'll excuse me, I have a meeting with Major Studdguard, who has just arrived."

Carr walked away from them, towards a bearish military man with a half-chewed cigar projecting over the anvil of his lower jaw. The major grabbed Carr's hand, shaking it violently. Soldier and scientist disappeared behind a door.

"Come," said Doctor Krypton, taking Jack over to one of the bipedal creatures, "let's examine the specimens. Here we see the basic elements of an arthropod—the head, thorax, and abdomen. The tail is equipped with a barbed structure that is probably a stinger. The sensory whips are probably used for communication, but it is also possible that they can deliver a mortal neuro-shock. The cerebral ganglion is mostly likely located here, beneath the cranial shell. If it is like other arthropods, it will have several hearts located at intervals along the dorsal blood vessel. The mandibles appear to have evolved from a pair of forelegs at some point in its evolution. It probably breathes through these spiracles, right here, and given their size and structure, these pincers could be capable of shearing through a six-inch rod of pure steel."

"I don't understand," said Jack quietly. "What exactly am I looking at? Is this the result of some genetic experiment?"

"Quite the contrary," said Doctor Krypton. "We think these things have been here for millions of years. We call them the Araknoids."

"But where did they come from?"

"We will discuss our theories on that subject in a briefing later today, Doctor Metron. For now, I would like you to notice how the creatures are completely immobile, impossibly hard. You could swing a monkey wrench against the delicate, tapered end of one of the antennae, and it will not crack, not so much as budge. Nothing, not even lasers, can cut into their shells. We have not even been able to dissect them. Scanners generate only empty ghost images. Our hypothesis is that they are somehow frozen in time, and so information cannot be transferred from them to us, other than their superficial appearance."

Jack looked around circumspectly. "Is it safe to talk here?"

"Yes, but not too loudly," said Krypton.

He lowered his voice to a whisper. "So *this* is what my parents discovered?"

Krypton nodded imperceptibly. "First they seismically detected the cavern, deep beneath the city of Philadelphia, directly below Independence Hall. Later they gained access to the cavern and discovered the Araknoids."

Jack's heart was pounding—finally, he was getting some answers. But he needed more answers, more resolution. "And what do Senator Lance Boyler and Gregory Randolph Reid have to do with all of this?"

"Reid wants to revive the Araknoids—to create his own personal army, unleash them upon humanity and become Sole Ruler," said Andronicus.

"That's…that's absurd…" stammered Jack.

"Is it really? Stalin dreamed of creating an army of gorilla-human hybrids. Hitler succeeded in building an army of meth-crazed psychopath soldiers. Pol Pot raised an army of children that murdered millions. The list goes on. Don't underestimate the capacity of mad humans to create Armies of Darkness."

"But an army of bugs?"

"Perhaps the most ambitious Army of Darkness yet," said Andronicus. "That's why Reid has invested billions of his own funds, and raised hundreds of millions more in bogus charities. He is one of the richest men in the world, and he fancies himself a prophet. This is not simply a question of wanting to rule the world, which many people have dreamed about—including, I admit, myself and probably everybody in this Pit. But no, for Reid, this is a matter of advancing social evolution into its next evolutionary stage. He has taken corporate capitalism as far as he can possibly take it. Now he must move to the next level, where he resides at the pinnacle of a machinelike organization of violence and repression. These warrior arthropods are his salvation. They will help him to subdue and then reshape the very flesh of humanity. He calls the project 'Operation Autocrat,' and he sees his own mind as the germ of a new metaconsciousness. In this he will fulfill the promise that corporate capitalism holds out to all who submit to its seductions—he will become an Immortal, a God."

Jack was unmoved. "I'm sorry, but if this is the big secret, the nefarious Plot, that everybody has been angsting over, then I have to admit to being underwhelmed. Even if Reid were to revive these things, how far could he get? He's going to take over the world with a gang of fifty oversized lobsters? Even if they ever were reactivated, they could be taken out with a single conventional bomb."

"You've made the classic mistake of underestimating your enemy," said Polyvox dismissively. "Both human and otherwise."

"There is something else you should see," said Andronicus.

They led him to the very end of the catwalk, and through a door. Beyond was a hundred feet of crooked, cavelike tunnel. And beyond that an interior cavern whose vastness boggled Jack's mind. It was a kind of roadway, several miles wide, slanting down into subterranean shadow.

On the surface of the roadway, in good marching formation, was an army of Araknoids, lined up in ranks and files, their multifaceted eyes bulbous and unblinking. Each unit of fifty bipeds was accompanied by one of the larger multilegged specimens. The army stretched to the right and left, disappearing into darkness. The column of warriors was far longer than the eye could make out. It was like an immense terracotta army of warrior insects that had been buried for eons in the depths of the earth.

"We estimate that there are several tens of millions of them," said Doctor Krypton, "and that they were massing for an invasion from below. Something stopped them in their tracks."

Jack gazed silently into the darkness. He tried to get his mind around the image of an organized swarm of Araknoids, millions strong, heading for the surface of the Earth.

"Whatever stopped them must have been far more powerful than they were," said Krypton. "Maybe it was some plague, or maybe they perished as they neared the surface."

"Maybe," said Polyvox flatly. "And maybe it was something else."

"But you admit that something stopped them," said Jack, recovering slightly. "And that for millions of years they've been dormant or dead. How could Gregory Reid, with all his money, undo whatever that force did?"

"And yet," said Polyvox cryptically, "he may be far closer to a solution than you think."

Before Jack could request an explanation, a siren sounded loudly, and caged red lights fixed into the rocks began to flare.

"Security Alert," said Doctor Krypton. "Most curious."

19

They followed Doctor Krypton along the tunnel to the Pit, where Major Studdguard, still masticating his cigar, was barking orders. Doctor Carr stood nearby, his hands twitching like spiders in his labcoat pockets. A squad of ten Security Soldiers in black-and-gold uniforms was advancing quickly from the top of the Pit, their heavy boots ringing against the metal catwalk. Another group of five soldiers was taking the cage-elevator.

"What appears to be the problem, Doctor Carr?" asked Doctor Krypton.

"Newly installed DNA detectors indicate the presence of unregistered human DNA in the Pit. It could be random street DNA, or DNA of an employee's family member. Or it could be an intruder. Everyone will have to be checked."

Major Studdguard turned to Carr, scowling, his breath redolent of wet tobacco. "How many eggheads are on duty tonight, Doctor?"

"Twenty-five, including Doctor Abraham and her three assistants."

"Right. We'll need samples of everyone's bodily fluids in order to conduct Secondary Analysis and verify the identity of everyone in this pit. Muster your eggheads and distribute their spit cups."

The scientists in white lab coats gathered nervously while Doctor Carr handed out the plastic cups, each of which had a surname and serial number on it. The Security Soldiers surrounded them, guns at the ready.

Very softly, Polyvox whispered to Jack, "Unfortunately, you have not been provided with a jaw bladder. But don't panic. I'm thinking."

"What is a jaw bladder?" he muttered back.

"A small device containing artificial saliva, retained in the mouth and positioned so it can be crushed between the teeth, discharging fluid with decoy DNA into a cup or scanner."

"I can confirm I have no such thing in my mouth at the moment."

Polyvox leaned towards Andronicus and whispered, "Unfortunately, our mutual friend has not been provided with a jaw bladder."

"Didn't Krypton supply him with one?"

"I did not ask her to. Arrangements for Jack's visit to the Pit were arranged hastily, as you know—"

"What's all this whispering there, scientists?" growled Major Studdguard. "We've had a possible security breach. There will be silence until I give the all-clear. Doctor Carr, I want all oral bodily fluids collected and analyzed immediately."

"Yes, Major." Carr was already busy collecting the filled spit cups and lining them up on a cart.

"I'll run the samples through the Secondary Analyzer," said Doctor Carr.

"And I will watch you," said Studdguard. "Like a bald eagle from his aerie."

"Your soldiers have not provided samples, Major," said Krypton.

"Excuse me, Doctor?" The Major snorted rudely. "My soldiers are all cleared for service and, in any case, they were in their barracks when the alarm sounded. There is no need for them to give samples. I will personally vouch for their bodily fluids."

"On the contrary, Major," said Krypton, "security protocols require that all human beings in the Pit provide saliva samples in the event of a DNA alarm. I don't need to remind you what a stickler for security His Senatorship is."

Major Studdguard cursed and threw down his cigar, grinding it into the ground with his boot. "Very well—soldiers, prepare to spit." He took a fresh cigar from his pocket, ignited it, and drew out a foul-smelling cloud.

"I will collect their samples, Major," said Krypton.

Carr maintained a meek and respectful silence. He seemed more than happy to let someone else confront Studdguard on this matter.

Krypton took the samples from the soldiers and then placed them on the cart.

As she started to trundle the cart to the Secondary Analyzer, a red phone on the wall flashed and rang. Studdguard picked it up and listened. "Yes, sir!" he said, hanging up. He pointed to Jack.

"Arrest that man, Master Sergeant. He is an Enemy of the State."

F9

"Major Studdguard," replied Krypton. "Whatever do you mean?"

"This man is an imposter, Doctor Abraham. He is a rogue Security Agent who has eluded the authorities for the last month. An administrative Security Agency court has sentenced him, in absentia, to be waterboarded."

"But Major, there must be some mistake," said Krypton. "Doctor Metron has been on my staff for several years now and has passed all required governmental and commercial background clearances. He has a Five Star rating from the Security Corporation of America—a Fortune 500 Company. I suggest to you that the DNA detector is in error. It's given you a false positive."

"DNA doesn't lie, Doctor Abraham. The Acme Gene Reader is programmed to pick up any unregistered human DNA in the Pit and to disregard the DNA of any animals. It picked up one human individual, a male, whose DNA also happens to match that of a known traitor. As every other person has been in the Pit before, a process of deduction leads to the conclusion that the odd man out must be this man, as he is the only newcomer. Therefore, he is a traitor and a spy."

"DNA doesn't lie, Major, but the machines that detect it can be faulty. I earnestly entreat you to let me confirm the results through

Secondary Analysis using Doctor Metron's spittle. You will then see this is all just a nucleotide-base misunderstanding."

"No Secondary Analysis is required. The Acme Double-Helix Gene Reader XIII is the best on the market. The only thing I trust more is the Lord of Hosts."

Krypton persisted: "Major, please recall that case in the Republic of Texas a few years ago, where a sixteen-year-old boy from a troubled family was convicted of murdering an oil tycoon on the basis of results from the Acme Double-Helix Gene Reader XII. He was executed through lethal injection with carbolic acid, while his parents and siblings were declared anathema, stripped of their property, and expelled from the Republic of Texas. Only later was it learned that the tycoon was killed by his wife's lover, a prominent attorney, who was then sentenced to ten years of house arrest, with leave on weekends. Certainly we wish to avoid a similar embarrassment in this case."

"I don't know what you're jabbering on about, science woman," grumbled Studdguard, waving his wet cigar stub at her. "This isn't some goddamn seminar with your pie-in-the-sky undergrads. We are at war! For now, this 'Metron' will be detained and turned over to the U.S. Security Agency. I have my orders. Master Sergeant, arrest this traitor." Studdguard's jaw muscles twitched spasmodically as he chomped on his cigar. "I find it curious, Doctor Abraham, that you would so doggedly defend your assistant, whose DNA appears to condemn him as a traitor. Master Sergeant, arrest this woman as well. She will be questioned."

The iron-jawed Master Sergeant approached with his hulking soldiers on either side of him. Before any of them could react, Polyvox withdrew her baton, expanded it, and spun it around, generating a wide, blinding flash beam that caused some of the soldiers to fall back, others to cover their eyes and yell.

The members of the Faction Nine political discussion group ran back down the twisting passageway that led to the Araknoid horde. A flight of roughly hewn stone steps took them down to the level of the Araknoids themselves. They fled through the petrified monster statues, trying to avoid cutting themselves on their bladelike carapaces or jabbing their eyes out on the rigid antennae.

From behind they heard gunfire. Bullets sparked and ricocheted off the motionless Araknoids. The soldiers started hurling stun grenades. Holding her baton like a torch, Polyvox led her comrades away from the Araknoids and into another cave tunnel. They kept on going until, behind them, there was silence.

At a fork in the tunnel, they waited and listened. The silence was broken by a distant whining accompanied by shrill sonic pulses.

"They're sending down sniffer drones," said Andronicus. "We should split up. Polyvox and Jack, take the Schuylkill Expressway. It is more dangerous, but you are less likely to be followed by drones. Krypton and I will take the Blue Route. We have our flashlights. If we make it out, we should all reassemble at Reconnoitering Point Green."

Without any more discussion they went their separate ways. Polyvox and Jack ran, climbed, and crawled through the cave. At one point, they thought they heard the echo of gunshots.

"Keep going," she said, "or we'll be next. If the sniffer drones catch up to us, we're finished. Doomed. Dead meat."

They waded across a cold subterranean stream, then followed it until again they entered a tunnel. By now Jack was feeling claustrophobic and panicky. He had the dreadful suspicion Andronicus and Krypton had come to a bad end with the sniffer drones.

"Where are we going?" He was holding a small, bright flashlight that Polyvox had given him. He was sweltering even though the caves were cool and dank. His hands were chafed and scraped from scrabbling over rocks. He flung off the fake eyeglasses, discarded his white lab coat, and peeled away the false facial skin that had been applied to conceal his identity.

Polyvox took off her own lab coat, dropping it on the ground. Underneath was the black coat she normally wore, which she now unbuttoned. She, too, was perspiring and gasping from the flight through the caves. She put a finger to her lips, signaling for silence. Her face was as tense as a stalking tiger's. "Do you hear that?" she whispered.

"No." Jack strained to listen.

She pointed. Ahead of them, a pallid form jumped soundlessly across the passageway and disappeared.

"What the hell was that?"

"A Trog."

"Please explain."

"Primates like you, probably descended from australopithecines that migrated underground and evolved accordingly. They are blind, but nimble and fiercely territorial. Take care that we don't get separated. They share one characteristic with your own species: an appetite for flesh."

"Can we just keep taking the 'Schuylkill Expressway,' whatever that is, until we get out of here?"

"What do you think we're doing?" She started walking again. "It was imbecilic for us to come down to the Pit. Now, everything is in jeopardy. Andronicus and Krypton are in terrible danger of being tracked down by sniffers, and the DNA detectors surely identified you. The Enemy now knows you are skulking about Philadelphia.

When we get out of here, you'll have to be extra careful. The whole city will be swarming with Plutocroids. We may have to completely change our plans. Everything we've worked for all these years is now in jeopardy."

"And what exactly was the plan?"

"The plan was to assassinate Gregory Reid and rescue his mistress."

"Why his mistress?"

Polyvox turned and looked at him intensely. "Because she is my mother."

"Your *mother*?" For an instant, Jack forgot his terror and physical discomfort. "What is Gregory Reid doing with your mother?"

They heard a sound nearby—a foot splashing in a puddle? A few yards away, a monkey-like human with fish-belly-white skin was crouching, clutching their discarded lab coats in its black-nailed hands. Irked, Polyvox picked up a stone and hurled it. It squealed angrily and scampered away.

Jack shuddered. Under other circumstances, his first glimpse of a "Trog" would have left him speechless. But Polyvox's last statement had left him urgently wanting to know more. "Polyvox," he repeated, "what is Gregory Reid doing with your *mother*?"

Polyvox nodded reflectively; her nickel gray eyes flickered. Something, some recollection, was transporting her mind away from this cave, from this reality. She answered, speaking mainly to herself: "'Tis a strange world, is it not?"

"It is especially strange without explanations."

"Somehow, Reid captured her."

"But why, how?"

"Your endless questions fatigue me," she sighed, starting again down the cave tunnel. She had expanded her baton to half length.

From one end, the light orb glowed brightly, while on the other was a smooth knob, like a mace, presumably for smashing attackers.

Jack followed her as she stepped over rocky outcroppings in the increasingly narrow passageway. "So Gregory Reid has your mother in captivity. That makes no sense. None of this makes any sense at all. Just when something gets clarified, it becomes more confusing. I kind of thought I had figured it out at last: a mad, depraved billionaire decides he will try to revive an army of fossilized gigantic brine shrimp to take over the world, and Faction Nine is resolved to stop him. Okay, I'm willing to accept that. Sure, it sounds like something from a graphic novel, but I can make myself believe it if I pull my credulousness in both directions like an overstretched rubber band."

Jack paused to give Polyvox a chance to respond, but she didn't, only glancing over her shoulder at him with what he interpreted as pensive irritation.

He continued: "But then you throw in your mother, and I have to wonder how this is connected with your order, and why you all use fake names, even though I use my real name. And then there are the Plutocroids, and nothing actually does make sense in the end, and I feel like someone has injected me with LSD and is now making me watch a David Lynch movie."

"You mean like *Eraserhead*?"

"I was thinking more along the lines of *Lost Highway*, which thoroughly perplexed me. At least *Eraserhead* sort of made sense."

"Personally, the current situation is like watching a Guy Maddin movie in a David Lynch world. We need not even mention Kafka. If you believe the philosophers who say all of reality is a simulation, your conclusions may not be too far off the mark. But there can be no harm in revealing everything to you at this point, since doom stalks us now like darkness stalks the setting sun. So I'll do so. What I'm about to tell you, only Andronicus knows. You must not divulge these secrets to anyone, including the other members of Faction Nine. Do you promise?"

"I swear upon my honor as a public servant."

The minutes dragged on as Polyvox kept her fingers on her chin, apparently considering his oath of confidentiality from every angle. Water dripped, echoing softly throughout the caverns. "Your honor as a public servant," she repeated. "For now, that will have to do."

CHAPTER FOURTEEN

Jack Learns the Truth
about Polyvox—Maybe

Polyvox paused again to listen for any sounds that they were still being pursued through the caverns.

"Nothing," she concluded. "I imagine the sniffer drones are loathe to come in this far. The treacherous twists and turns of the Schuylkill Expressway confound their sonar systems, so they've almost certainly turned back. But then again, they're sneaky little mechanoids. They could be planning an ambush. Don't let your guard drop."

She started again through the cave tunnel. "Back there, in the Pit, our visit was disrupted because, in our hubris, we made a critical error. We forgot to take into account the possibility that the Pit might be newly outfitted with hypersensitive DNA detectors."

"It would seem so."

"These DNA detectors would be designed to screen for the DNA of any humans who have not been registered to work in the Pit. That means their alarms will not be set off if they detect, for example, a squirrel or a rat or some other animal that has somehow wandered into the Pit. But they will detect the presence of unauthorized humans. Do you follow me?"

"Go on."

"Now, Doctor Krypton long ago infiltrated her way into the Pit and was cleared to work there as a scientist. She is our mole—or was. She also previously registered Andronicus's DNA, naming him as one of her lab assistants. She did not register your DNA, because you are a wanted man. She wanted to register someone else's DNA under the name of Dr. Metron and then give you a jaw bladder and a decoy-DNA-emitting device. That would have been standard procedure, but it would have taken several weeks to arrange, and I wanted you to see the Pit as soon as possible. Honestly, I didn't think you would be detected, since the current generation of DNA detectors has been very unreliable when it comes to large spaces like the Pit. However, like all machines, DNA detectors mature quickly. This was a grievous error on my part, the kind of stupid oversight that might just have cost us the mission, and our own necks."

"But what are the actual implications for us—for me?" said Jack, the panic rising in his voice. "What does all this mean, practically speaking?"

"It means, Jack, that the detector did notice your DNA, and that government security computators made the identification. Krypton, Andronicus, you—all of you are now in a more perilous situation, because of my carelessness. *They* are now on a DNA wanted list. *You* are slated for torture and death."

Polyvox stared at the rock wall, clenching her fists and gritting her teeth in self-reproach.

"And you," said Jack gloomily, "you are also in danger, I suppose."

"Ironically, no. These same DNA detectors would not have been at all alarmed by my presence, any more than they would have been alarmed at the presence of a ferret."

"Why not?"

She looked at him, smiling coldly. "Because I don't have human DNA."

"Right. You don't have human DNA. What kind of DNA do you have?"

"My DNA would be more like that of a cat, or a bear. Or a lynx."

Jack looked at her, his arms hanging limply at his sides. "Why would you have *cat* DNA?"

"My DNA is not *precisely* that of a cat. I have Carnivoran DNA. *Carnivora* is a taxonomic order that includes cats, bears, lynxes, even pandas. Also, ferrets and seals. It even includes otters—those charming, playful creatures that frolic in stream and sea for whom I've always felt a certain kinship and fondness. I am more closely related to all of these creatures than I am to humans. Humans belong to the Primate Order. You are more closely related to monkeys and apes. In fact, you *are* an Ape. You are a Primate, and I am a Carnivoran."

"But, Polyvox, you're a vegetarian—you don't eat meat. How can you be a Carnivoran?"

"I said 'Carnivoran,' not 'carnivore.' Even if I ate meat, the fact would be immaterial. Your primate cousins subsist primarily on nuts, roots, fruits, shoots, and leaves, with just a little animal protein tossed in here and there. Human Apes, on the other hand, enjoy grilled steaks, juicy hamburgers, and greasy sausages—foods that would make most other primates vomit. Times change, people change: it's called Evolution, Jack."

"Very well, so you're a Carnivoran," said Jack, though he was not sure if he really believed that, remembering what Andronicus had told him about Polyvox's weird order and its invented pseudo-history. "What kind of Carnivoran are you? A cat, a dog, or a panda?"

"None of those. According to our most ancient mythology we are *The People of the Time Goddess Chrona*. You could call us *Chronasians*. From a less mythological and more rational perspective, we are descended from a line that branched off from the earliest Carnivorans, perhaps during the Eocene Epoch, before the order split into the catlike and doglike subgroups. That was forty million years ago. My line evolved independently, into the form you see before you. We are hairless bipeds, like you, with keen intelligence. The physical similarities between Human Apes and my people are mostly due to chance, to convergent evolution. But there are significant physiological differences between us. Our eyesight is better than yours, as is our sense of taste and smell. We're faster, stronger, and have superior muscular-skeletal architecture. We live much longer. We're less prone to irrationality and madness, and our technology was superior to yours in every way. We used our technology to perfect and prolong life, to eradicate disease, to promote the good. For this reason, we never developed the atomic bomb."

"You're smarter than us but never developed the bomb?"

"Had we wanted to, we could have. But the Chronasians never felt the need to create weapons of total annihilation, unlike you Human Apes. There were never that many of us to begin with—even at the peak of our civilization, perhaps several million—and though there had been a few wars and violent conflicts in our past history, they never compared to the global wars and genocides that are part and parcel of Ape Nature. In fact, it was difficult for us to conceive of such wars, such mass violence, and this was what handicapped us when, ten million years ago, the Invasion began. We were simply unprepared for megawar."

"I'm assuming the Araknoids were the invaders."

"Correct."

"And that they came from outer space."

"Yes and no. They arrived, we think, some time in the late Jurassic, and then burrowed deep into the earth. Perhaps they would have emerged sooner, but the Cretaceous-Paleogene extinction event of sixty-odd million years ago made the Earth an inhospitable place, a poor hunting ground. They remained dormant for tens of millions more years, and then began to stir deep within the earth, like a teeming brood of giant cicadas. They burrowed a huge channel in the rock and began their march to the surface. We Chronasians were unprepared for it. We had no idea how to defend ourselves. We sent small groups into the earth to reconnoiter, and most of them were savaged. The Araknoids advanced. Our Queen summoned the High Council, which had not convened in hundreds of years. A decision was made to relocate most of the Chronasians into mountain refugia, where they were placed in an induced slumber: a kind of coma. When this was done, our Queen led a mission with a band of two hundred warriors. We confronted the advance guard of the Araknoids just a mile beneath the earth, and we hit it with a Time Bomb."

"A *time bomb*—against an army of tens of millions?"

Polyvox nodded, noting his incredulity. "You see, Jack, just as Human Apes some generations ago began to probe the mysteries of the subatomic world, the quantum world, we Chronasians had, ten million years ago, begun to investigate the mysteries of Time. And just as Human Apes managed to achieve some crude control over the power of nuclear forces, we Chronasians had actually begun to manipulate Time, in a very rudimentary way. We could not travel in time, we could not go forward or back, but we were beginning to glimpse something of its profound nature and its vast connection with other things, including consciousness and philosophical self-reflection. And so at the time of our great crisis, we were able to cobble together a kind of weapon that we unleashed upon the advancing Araknoid horde, freezing them into a state of unbreakable temporal stasis. I was there when my mother the Queen instructed our scientists to activate the Time Bomb. Our ambitious objective was to send the Araknoids *back* in time. Our understanding of Time was no doubt faulty and incomplete, however."

Polyvox frowned, a hint of regret passing over her expression.

"And there may have been other factors as well. Perhaps we were uncomfortable with the ramifications of such a weapon; perhaps we were too frightened by the approach of the Enemy, whose feet were stomping deafeningly against the rock as they moved ever closer to the surface. All I know was that there was some warp, some rupture. Our thoughts became mangled; we lost consciousness. We accomplished our goal and stopped the Araknoids, but we ourselves were scattered throughout space and time and each one of us was plunged into her own abyss of dreamless stasis. The earth covered our bodies. The stars continued to spin quietly in the sky over this planet, glaciers came and went, the continents continued their movements, generations of species evolved, achieved primacy, and then died away or became insignificant. And during these millions of years, the peaceable proto-apes that once lounged near our cities, the lethargic reddish brown beasts that we'd occasionally domesticated as pets, followed the evolutionary path that had been cleared for them. They stood upright, they made sticks and bones into weapons, they mastered fire, they branched into subgroups, they competed for resources. And in the end, every line of your genus died out but two. Your own species, and the one that dwells in darkness beneath the earth: the Trogs. You even edged out your Neanderthal cousins, though I suspect they would have ultimately been more civilized than you, had they won the survival game."

"You do?"

"Yes, though I admit that conclusion is based on *The Clan of the Cave Bear*, my favorite human novel in the Ice Age soap opera genre. As for the Trogs, they are technologically insignificant. But the Human Apes have accomplished great and terrible things, and now you are on the verge of your own extinction."

Though Polyvox was holding her light-orb fairly steadily, the rock formations around them shivered and leapt in weird dancing shadows. Her own shadow rose up against the craggy, dripping wall of the cavern, like a spectral interloper from another world.

"But how did you survive through all these millions of years?" asked Jack.

"None of my brothers and sisters in the Order knows exactly how we survived. All we know is that we awoke, one by one, scattered all across the world. Not all of us did survive, apparently. These are mysteries that we have not been able to explain. It seems inconceivable that we lay dormant in the earth for ten million years, and so we think it more likely that the Time Bomb deposited each of us far into the future. In fact, it is quite possible that we were deposited into an alternative future."

"What does that mean?"

"At any given, fleeting instant, you inhabit the present. But that present which you inhabit is merely one of a multitude of possible presents that could have been, or that exist simultaneously at the tips of an infinite number of branches. It's kind of like…" Polyvox narrowed her eyes and bit her lower lip. "It's kind of like an author who writes a novel about an alternative present. Or a novel about the future that is really about the present. Or a novel about the past that is really about what could have been, not so much what was. When you travel along the strands of time, all bets are off."

"So you just sat up one day, after the Time Bomb went off, and here you were, in the future, or an alternative future, or whatever?"

"No. The superior of our order was the first to awaken after the Catastrophe—over five thousand years ago, during the Middle Kingdom of ancient Egypt. She realized she was in a New Age, and that the Human Apes now ruled the planet. She was dazzled by what she saw, but also fearful. For a thousand years she was alone, wandering the Earth among the Human Apes, observing them. In the millennia after her Awakening, others revived. In time, they found each other and formed our order. I myself crawled out of a bog in England on October 14, 1066, just in time to see William the Bastard annihilate the exhausted forces of King Harold Godwinson at the Battle of Hastings."

Polyvox gazed back in time, reliving her own confusion and perplexity from so many centuries ago.

"I had no idea what I was seeing, no comprehension of the meaning of this battle. Even the humans were ghastly to me—like short, ugly versions of the Chronasians, with hair on their faces and a most intolerable stench. Terrified, I fled into the forest. I had nothing but my boots, my cloak, and my baton. Someday I will tell you about my adventures."

"But how long did you stay in England?"

"For a century I traveled in Europe, Africa, and Asia. The various dialects of Ape-speak are not difficult for Chronasians. I mastered them pretty easily. I was much taller than most Human Apes, but I could usually manage to blend in. In the beginning, I killed many in self-defense. Some accused me of witchcraft and tried to burn me. Often I was set upon by brigands, and had to dispatch them all. It was a harsh life, and despite myself, I frequently reverted to a kind of primal savagery."

She shook her head, and then looked at Jack accusingly, as if he shared some kind of responsibility for her past miseries. "There is something about your species that provokes the worst in everybody. You know that, Jack? It's fortunate that the Araknoids encountered the Chronasians, and not fully evolved human beings. Who knows what kind of mischief the two of you would have hatched together."

Jack felt guilty somehow, but Polyvox sighed. "I'm not blaming you, of course. The loneliness of my existence was very painful. At the time I had no idea that there were others like me in the world. I believed I was the sole survivor of the Chronasians. I was forced to certain conclusions about the Human Apes, namely that most were cunning and brutish, while a few were kind and compassionate, and that the former generally succeeded in exterminating the latter. And so I wandered and observed. At last I met one of my own people in Byzantium, where I had been making a quiet living selling alchemical remedies."

Polyvox's gray eyes appeared to brighten.

"It was the most joyful day of my life. That was around the year 1400; the exact date is unimportant. I joined the small community of survivors, including my older sister, who had formed an order. And so now you know the history of my sorrows, the sad biography of the ruined daughter of a once-noble dynastic house."

She unbuttoned her vest and showed Jack a vivid tattoo, on her right breast, of a gold shield with a black oak tree and a blood-red heart.

"That is your family coat of arms?" he asked.

"Yes," she said, buttoning her vest again and briefly checking her watch. "And now I am a socialist, without a pot to piss in, committed to the eradication of evil from your world, and to the personal destruction of Gregory Reid, who holds my mother as a thrall."

"Your account makes the course of human civilization seem rather insignificant, a mere footnote in the planet's history."

"That is precisely what it is."

"And the history of the United States is just the period at the end of the footnote."

"It is barely that, Jack." She gestured to the caverns all around them. "In one inch of these rocks there resides a billion times more history than in all the chapters of the United States, than in all the epochs of humanity."

Jack was still not certain if he could believe any of this. "If you've been around since the eleventh century, you've obviously known many generations of humans."

"True."

"Compared to you, I've got the lifespan of a housefly," Jack remarked dejectedly. "A single human life must be incredibly insignificant to you."

"Judged only by the measure of time, perhaps. But time is not everything, Jack. A brilliant philosophical intuition might last just an instant, a useless idea can linger for years. But to be honest, my people tend not to associate with your kind on an individual basis very much. We keep to ourselves and, when we observe you, we do so from the outside. We also periodically engage in extended spells of sleep—a form of hibernation—which helps stave off the emotional strain of being long-lived. We form strong bonds among ourselves, while history rushes by us. Few of us have ever had very deep friendships with any of you. The great taboo is to fall in love."

🕈9

Jack asked no more questions, and Polyvox fell into a brooding silence. For several hours they picked their way through the dripping cave tunnels, over the damp and slippery rocks, following the Schuylkill Expressway. Now and then they saw a flash of white skin in the shadows, but the Trogs did not bother them. From the popping in his ears, Jack knew they were ascending. Finally the temperature dropped and he tasted cold, fresh air. They emerged from the caves at the bottom of a creek gorge.

On either side were steep rocky hills with towering trees so wide and ancient that their leafless branches extended over the creek from either side, creating an icy arch. It had been snowing for hours. The snow was six inches deep on the ground, the trees frosted with white. The creek gurgled along its narrow, twisted course, and as branches succumbed to the weight of the snow and fell, the gorge echoed with the sound of cracking wood. From the wooded fastness came the eerie howls of coyote-wolf hybrids.

"We must be far from the city," concluded Jack, as they stood at the edge of the water. He wrapped his arms around himself.

"Actually, we only went a few miles. We're still in Philadelphia. The park that surrounds this gorge is centrally located in the city. Various factions have portals to their subterranean hideaways here."

It seemed farfetched that a city could have a gorge in the middle of it, but as they climbed to the top, he saw the tips of skyscrapers not too far away, peeking up over the crystallized white branches.

"Now we must head to one of our emergency meeting points and hope for the best," said Polyvox.

They followed a path that took them over several stone bridges until they finally came to a rambling old, two-story inn. An elderly proprietor wearing eighteenth-century knee breeches and waistcoat, along with a pair of contemporary ergonomic walking shoes, opened the door for them, nodding at Polyvox. She entered first and led Jack straight upstairs, to a modest private dining room with a fireplace.

At a table by a fireplace, sat Andronicus, Krypton, and Max Blackshield, who had apparently joined the others after they had escaped from the Pit. Andronicus was hunched behind a heavy mug of dark beer. Krypton was sipping from a glass of red wine, while Blackshield sat upright behind an untouched glass of ice water.

"So you're both alive," said Polyvox without showing much emotion.

"And we will remain so," replied Andronicus, whose woozy manner betrayed that this was not his first mug of beer, and most likely not even his second. "The Good Lord willing and the creek don't rise."

"How did you elude the drones?" asked Jack.

"They were closing in when we heard them crash and explode. They were manufactured by the lowest bidder, after all." Andronicus took a long drink of his beer. "We've been discussing the debacle with Blackshield. We have to figure out what to do next. To say that we've been dealt a setback is an understatement. We could very well be screwed."

"Here's what we have concluded," said Blackshield, his eyes bright and alert. "Our Enemies will now know that Jack is in this city. They will know that we know, and they will expect us to send him elsewhere. So he will stay here, and we will continue manipulating his bank accounts to keep the Enemy distracted, making them think he has fled to other places. They will already suspect we are doing this and will therefore assume that he may still be here, so we will have to take care that he does not overexpose himself. Luckily, we've not yet reached the point in the technological and political evolution of the United States where entire cities have been outfitted with Security Agency DNA detectors. Also, Doctor Krypton has now been revealed to be an Enemy of the State, so she will have to go completely underground like the rest of us."

Krypton took a resigned sip from her glass. "I had already made arrangements with my family in case this happened."

"As of this point," said Blackshield, his deep blue eyes connecting with hers, "the pressure the enemy bears down upon us will only increase. It is now more urgent than ever that we initiate Operation Moneybags. Andronicus, it's up to you whether you think it prudent to discuss the details of this with Jack."

Andronicus nodded gloomily.

Jack looked to Andronicus for clarification, but he merely gestured to the old man to bring him another dark ale.

"It's late," said Blackshield, looking at his watch. "I suggest we spend the night at our quarters in this inn, and then in the morning perhaps Polyvox can summon the *Argo* to take us home."

Blackshield, Polyvox, and Krypton got up and exited the room, leaving Jack alone with Andronicus.

"What is Operation Moneybags?"

"A plan to liquidate Gregory Reid at one of his upcoming charity dinners."

"And, I assume, to free Polyvox's mother, the Queen of the Chronasians, whom he has taken by force as his mistress."

Andronicus glared in surprise. He then broke into loud laughter. "I see you've been chatting with Polyvox while down in the caves."

"She told me the whole story. It's quite incredible."

"It is incredible. Because for something to be believable, it has to be real. I told you before that Polyvox is a fantasist. I had hoped she might spare you the more outrageous plot elements of her delusional religious history."

"You mean she's not—"

"No, she is not a Carnivoran descended from some humanoid civilization that existed ten million years before *Homo sapiens*!" snapped Andronicus, slapping his hand down heavily upon the table. "It's a ridiculous story, a crypto-feminist-revolutionary fable."

"But maybe it is true…"

"If it were true, there would be archeological evidence, wouldn't there? If they really did build these great cities and have these amazing technologies, then where are the ruins? Where are the fossils of their culture? We're talking ten million years ago. That's not so long. We have fossils of animals that lived further back than that, in the Mesozoic. How far back was the Mesozoic, Son of the Geologists?"

Jack sat still, his hands flat on the table. "At last count, sixty-five to two hundred and twenty million years ago."

"Right. So we can dig up the femur of some pissant little mammal that lived *sixty-five million years ago*, we can fill museums with all those little femurs, but we can't find a single shred of evidence of this 'Chronasian' civilization that allegedly lived ten million years ago. Polyvox, you see..."—Andronicus nodded his head—"...I have great respect for Polyvox. I have met few people like her. She transcends all boundaries of culture and gender and spirituality. But Jack, she is functionally insane. She and all of the members of her religious 'order.'"

✝9

Andronicus raised his large, angular frame and walked across the room to draw himself another mug of beer from the tap, the old floorboards creaking underfoot. Jack was tired, but he was also alert. "If she is so insane," he retorted, surprised by his offense at this accusation against Polyvox, "then why do you even tolerate her within the inner circle? It seems like having such a person would be a disadvantage."

Andronicus turned around, holding the bottle in one hand, the mug in the other. "Ah! Because as should be apparent, I greatly admire her. And second, I will admit, because her order is generous, and they are determined to overthrow the hegemonies of contemporary human civilization. Where do you think our operational budget comes from? The other factions have to scrabble and scrape for money—some even engaging in borderline criminal activity. Not so the Friendly Neighborhood Political Discussion Group! Polyvox's order is fantastically rich and gives us what we need. A few radically minded members of the upper classes help us out as well—old money, patrician types who fear and despise warlocks like Reid. My mother is one of them. But it is primarily thanks to Polyvox that we are able to pay for our operations and our fancy gadgetry. Also, she is cunning, clever, devious, and insightful."

"I see."

"So when she tells you that her first cousins are saber-toothed cats and dire wolves, just humor her. That's what I do."

"It seems kind of patronizing."

"Sometimes we have to patronize people, Jack."

"Yes, but—"

"There are no 'buts.' This is a 'but'-free paradigm. The overthrowing of entire political orders is a dirty game. We strive to do it peacefully, and for the most part nonviolently. The other factions are far less scrupulous than we are, and some of them are downright crazy. Take the Anarchists of Faction Six, for example, and their leader Bluebeard, who's part professor, part preacher, part pirate, part dissident political theorist. They think you can solve all the world's problems by running around throwing jars of red paint at statues of George Washington and Andrew Carnegie. That's probably why Polyvox left them. They were too crazy even for her. Personally, though, I think they are all talk and no action."

"Polyvox was in their faction?"

"That's what I said."

"Exactly how many of these factions are there, anyway?"

"Too many to count, including some really scary ones, like the New Crusaders, the Geniacs, the Gender Reorganizers, the Neo-Bolsheviks, the Neo-Mensheviks—the list goes on. Occasionally there are secret conventions of factions, grand underground gatherings where you can see how disorganized and crazy everyone is. The only thing we can all agree on is that the Greedhead Fascists must be eradicated, but they're all willing to destroy each other for a chance to get at the enemy. The state of most revolutionary organizations operating in the U.S. today is pretty pathetic, even laughable. I'll take a religious order comprised of relatively sober-minded feminist martial arts types over the rest of them any day."

"Polyvox says that Reid is holding her mother captive."

"Well, he is."

"But you just said her story wasn't true."

"That part is true, the rest is fantasy."

"Then maybe you can explain to me who her mother is and why Reid is holding her captive?"

Andronicus crossed his arms and looked beyond Jack. "I'll tell you another day."

"I'd rather know now, if you don't mind. I'm wide awake."

"What is there to tell? Her mother is something of a rogue physicist, an expert in the fields of time, quantum information theory, entanglement, quantum teleportation, and other obscure matters that I can't even pretend to understand." Andronicus hissed through gritted teeth and stared down at his beer, as if expecting to read the solution to human hypocrisy in its foam lace. To Jack, he was showing uncharacteristic signs of tipsiness, and Jack himself was not feeling so well. He pushed his beer mug away and sat back in the chair. The shades were drawn over the two windows in the room and Jack wondered what time it was.

"The important thing," continued Andronicus, still staring into his mug, "is that Reid believes she has the key to unfreezing the Araknoid army from its temporal stasis."

"It seems as if the academic world would notice the disappearance of such a prominent figure," Jack observed.

"She was considered a crackpot by the establishment and had no lasting academic appointments. No one has noticed her absence at all. Except for her order, of course, and they've been plotting to get her back for some time now."

"What is her name?"

"Her *nom de guerre* is Stephany Miscellany." Andronicus finished off his ale and shrugged apologetically. "What her real name is, God only knows. I've been in this revolutionary game so long sometimes I can't even remember my own real name. I guess you could say we live in strange times. Would you like another beer?"

"No, I've had enough. I think maybe you have, too."

Andronicus took obvious umbrage with his remark. "I'll have you know that I come from a long line of men, and a few women, known for their prodigious capacity to consume hard drink under a variety of taxing conditions. To be sure, they weren't always successful. Some day I'll take you to the exact location where, tradition has it, one of my mother's ancestors, during the Battle of Germantown, dropped dead of apoplexy thanks to a surfeit of rum."

Until now, Andronicus had said little about himself and his origins. Jack felt curious. He might have gone rogue on his government, but he was still, in some ways, the introverted, prying bureaucrat he had been with the Security Agency. "In that case, do you want another beer?" he asked.

Andronicus shook his head. "No, I've had enough."

"So your ancestor fought in the American Revolution?"

"My ancestors on both sides fought their enemies on land and sea, in mountains, forests, and swamps, leading entire armies and fleets to victory. They fought the Japanese and the Chinese. They fought the British. They were officers, sailors, drummer boys, and rum-swilling privates in the Continental Line. They fought—and they died. I myself fought in the Wars of Betrayal. Don't let anyone say I am not a patriot." Despite his boast, he was starting to slur his words. He jabbed his chest with his thumb. "I am an American Patriot. I am a Korean Patriot. But most importantly, I am a *World Patriot*. Because in the long run, my friend, nations are nothing and humanity is everything."

He tried to get up but stumbled, falling against the wall. The old proprietor drifted into the room and said, "Mr. Andronicus, your bed is ready."

Andronicus grunted. He started to lurch away from the wall, but almost fell again. As Jack tried to help him, Andronicus shoved him away. "Don't patronize me, pal."

"You can barely stand, Andronicus."

The waiter quietly withdrew, leaving Jack and Andronicus alone again.

Andronicus looked at Jack, an irrational glint in his eyes. "What are you implying, Security Officer Tone? That I am a weak man? A man who is not in control of his destiny? Who are you to imply such things about me, to even contemplate them in the deepest recesses of your shallow soul? What do you have to say to that, bureaucrat boy?"

"I'm not implying anything, Andronicus. And don't call me 'boy.'"

Andronicus squared his shoulders. "And what are you going to do about it, Jack-boy?"

Andronicus loomed over Jack, and then took a lazy, irregular swing at him.

Jack deflected it with his forearm, but he felt the power of the blow, sloppy as it was. Andronicus stepped back and laughed. "So,

Jack's a tough guy, after all. Jack is Elliot Ness. Tell me, Agent Ness, what's the difference between a Security Agency bureaucrat and a blithering idiot?"

Jack said nothing, stroking his smarting forearm.

"A blithering idiot has brainwaves," said Andronicus. "What do you call two Security Agency bureaucrats in a very large building?"

"I'm not a Security Agency bureaucrat anymore, Andronicus. You saw to that."

"An *infestation*."

A door opened and Polyvox entered, much to Jack's relief. She surveyed the scene. "As I suspected from all the obnoxious noise. Inebriation." She faced Andronicus with a rock-hard, unwavering stare. "Perhaps you imbibe too much."

"I've got it under control, baby." He placed his communicator on the table, and tapped it until it began to play the Beatles' *Abbey Road*. "This is the music that got my great-grandfather through his tour of duty in Vietnam, in the White Horse Division, before his legs were blown off. Do you know how many Koreans fought in Vietnam, Jack? To keep the Reds out of your backyard?"

"I wasn't aware the Vietnamese were threatening to come into my backyard."

"Smart-ass. How many Security Bureaucrats does it take to screw in a lightbulb, Jack?"

"Go jump in the lake."

Andronicus snorted and turned to Polyvox. But her face was impassive, as if his drunken passion bored her. "I have no idea," she said.

"Three hundred fucking thousand."

"It takes three hundred thousand Security Bureaucrats to screw in a lightbulb?" Polyvox cocked a quizzical eyebrow.

"No…" Andronicus shook his head. "Three hundred thousand soldiers from the Republic of Korea served in Vietnam, at the behest of their American allies. And for what, I ask you? For what? So that a path could be paved for an enemy equally as vicious but a hundred times as insidious to ooze into global power, like some bubonic plague."

"Come to bed, Andronicus."

Andronicus took Polyvox in his arms and began to dance with her, somehow managing to keep control over his own movements despite the alcohol that was coursing through the subterranean channels of his brain. Jack watched them as they danced. With a certain despondency, he concluded that there was no way in hell that these people—these crazy, idealistic dreamers—could ever change the world order, could ever disrupt the global congress of capital, let alone thwart the schemes of a ruthless would-be dictator like Gregory Randolph Reid.

And yet, somehow, they danced together very gracefully, in a way that made Jack jealous.

Until the drink finally conquered Andronicus, that was, and he began to flounder like a punch-drunk boxer.

He did not object as Polyvox slung his arm over her shoulder and, with Jack following, helped him stagger down the second-floor hallway, past several closed doors, and into a bedroom with a wood stove, two chairs, a lamp stand, and a bed. Polyvox was nearly as tall as Andronicus, and from what Jack could determine, stronger than any human being. Yet even though there was no fat on Andronicus, he was heavily boned and not easy to carry. Polyvox made no attempt to be gentle, but unhooked his arm from her shoulder, sending his large frame crashing onto the mattress, where he lay half sprawled. "Help me turn him over onto his stomach, Tone," she said, "lest he regurgitate."

Together, they flipped him over bodily.

For a moment Polyvox looked down on him, her gray eyes unblinking.

"I'll show you to your room now, Jack. Then I'll come back here and watch over him in his Gethsemane of self-inflicted miseries."

"Are you sure? I've never seen him like this."

"I have."

Polyvox took Jack down to the very end of the second-floor hallway, to another small bedroom, identical to the one Andronicus was in. When she had gone, he undressed to his underwear and stretched out on the bed. He lay in the dark, beneath his blanket, wondering what side he had chosen—wondering if choosing any side made any sense at all, or if they were all, the whole pathetic lot of them—the rebels, the plutocrats, the entertainment-drunk global *lumpenproletariat*, the demons beneath the earth, and the angels above it—if they were all just pawns in some cosmic chess game over which they had absolutely no control whatsoever.

He would have fled that place, run as far away as he could—but he was just too damn tired, and soon sleep overcame him.

🯅9

Andronicus groaned and rolled over onto his back. He sat up in the bed. Polyvox was sitting in a chair, looking at him. She had taken off her coat and crossed her booted legs. She was twirling her weapon, which in its collapsed form resembled a shiny chrome flashlight shaft.

"How long have you been sitting there, spying on me?" asked Andronicus, rubbing his blurry eyes.

"Two hours."

His head hurt and his throat was parched. "Why are you gawking at me like that? Why are you holding that infernal zap-stick? Turn out the light, leave, and let me sleep."

"I simply wanted to make sure you didn't choke to death on your own vomit," she said. "Is that so terrible?"

"Vomit?"

"I understand that this sometimes happens to your kind. I know it for a fact, actually."

Andronicus slowly swung himself around and sat on the edge of the bed. "Your concern is touching, Polyvox. But I'm perfectly capable of sleeping off a bender by myself. Go."

"My concern is not personal, Andronicus. You are critical to the Movement and your loss would be a serious setback."

"Thanks. You don't have to wear your utilitarian cold-heartedness on your sleeve. Can you get me a glass of water, please?"

A subtle twitch of annoyance played at the edges of Polyvox's mouth. She placed her weapon on the floor by the chair, stood up, poured a cup at the sink, and brought it back to him.

He drank it down. "Ah, that's better. The Schuylkill River refreshes."

She sat down next to him on the bed. "My friend, of course I have personal affection for you, but the exigencies of The Cause must be primary in both of our minds."

"You should write sonnets, you have such a gift for eloquence. But I have a serious matter I wish to bring up with you, Polyvox."

"Oh." Polyvox seemed uninterested. She brushed his scraggly, unkempt hair out of his eyes.

"Why," he continued, trying to ignore this, "did you reveal your origins to Jack, down there in the caves? What on earth came over you? He's barely a novice in the Movement and should not be trusted with such sensitive facts."

"Jack spoke to you about our conversation, did he? No matter. We've entrusted him with more sensitive information already. He may be a novice, but he is already in very deep."

"Your origins are none of his business. Too many people in our group already know about you. Krypton, Blackshield, and now Jack. Why don't you just write an autobiography?"

"Let's stop talking about this. You're pale and you reek of alcohol. You have a slight tremor which you yourself may not have even noticed. I will lie here with you for the rest of the night to assist in your recovery."

Andronicus knew what that would entail, and he was suddenly cautious. As a man of the revolution, he prided himself on being a master of his own passions. The unbridled lust of the old American playboy tradition repelled him, partly because of his confused WASP-Korean-Quaker-Catholic upbringing, but mostly because he saw commercialized sexuality for what it was, for what it had been for generations: a tactic by which the Corporate Powers seduced and ruined human beings—all for their own profit. Many men and women in the Movement embraced a lifestyle of virtual celibacy or radical monogamy, as a personal repudiation of the porn-glam filth that continuously erupted from Wall Street's sewer portals and into the slums of global serfdom.

On the other hand, Andronicus was a man like any other, and he could not fully suppress his attraction to this woman. He was not sure how she felt about him, because the passions of her species appeared—so far as he could tell—to be differently ordered than those of human beings. In this respect, her Carnivoran nature was more catlike than doglike; overt expression of emotion was alien to her, and any inkling of affection tended to be manifested through wordless and at times weirdly intimate physicality. He had been surprised when she told him she had kissed Jack—surprised and a little jealous—for kissing in the manner of humans was not characteristic of her species. The two of them had never kissed. Andronicus was not even sure if she had ever made love to a human being, though she had been around for so long it seemed probable. A few times before, when they were alone, she had tried to compel him to lie alongside her in a warm and nuzzling embrace. Andronicus had been unnerved by this; it was like lying next to a panther in humanoid form. On a subconscious level, he was vividly aware that *she was not human*. He had moved away from her, not from want of desire but just the opposite: because she stirred something in him that made him afraid. She had not taken offense.

Now she was more insistently pulling him towards herself.

"Polyvox, listen to me. You confused Jack with all that talk about your origins. I told him that what you said was religious, quasi-mythic nonsense, and that you were partly insane."

"Perhaps I am insane," she said. "But that's because I'm fatigued. You have to rest, Andronicus, and I will rest with you. Your alcoholic indulgence has weakened you…." She sat even closer to him.

They lay back on the bed together, but they did not make love. She stretched an arm over him, then one of her booted legs, pressing her face against his. He felt her breath against his neck, her warm skin against his own, which he imagined must be clammy given how ill he felt. But sleep again was overcoming him. As soon as he had closed his eyes—just for a second—the winter sun's rays were streaming through the window, warming his face.

Polyvox sat up. "Awake, my friend. Night has withdrawn its comforting dark mantle, and the harsh light of reality is again upon us."

"That's exactly what I was thinking," said Andronicus, before he wearily climbed out of bed.

CHAPTER FIFTEEN

The Death Sentence

Taras Petriv, Faction Nine's security specialist and manager of the Trappist Tavern, pulled up to the tavern in the *Argo*; he stepped out, wearing a faux fur *ushanka* hat, and entered. His fellow faction members, the only guests, were sitting at a table, hurriedly slurping down coffee and munching away ravenously on bagels and cream cheese.

"Can I have some?" he asked.

Andronicus nodded quickly, crumbs falling from his mouth. Petriv sat down and helped himself. For the next ten minutes, the revolutionaries hardly said anything to each other, until the food was gone and the old man in colonial knee breeches took the plates away.

"You brought Polyvox's car, I assume?" asked Blackshield.

"I did," said Petriv.

"Good. Because I want to give you a briefing on Operation Moneybags. Last night I received information from some of our field sources that has led me to believe we must act as soon as possible."

Their chairs scraped on the old hardwood floorboards as they stood up, dropping their napkins on the table and trooping out the door, down the stairs, to the *Argo*. Krypton sat in the front passenger seat, next to Petriv. Jack sat in the back, next to Blackshield, across from Andronicus and Polyvox.

As Petriv piloted the *Argo* back to the center of the city, Blackshield handed Andronicus and Polyvox files printed on paper and bound in old-fashioned sheet protectors.

"What's this?" asked Polyvox.

"Your mission dossiers. I spent all night preparing them. This information is too sensitive to be conveyed through the Metanets."

Andronicus and Polyvox flipped through their files.

"In one week," Blackshield said, "Gregory Reid will be attending the annual Children First Charity Gala at the Freedom Fortress Maximum Security Prison in Calhoun, West Virginia. Freedom Fortress is built on the plateau of a mountain that was decapitated for coal-mining purposes. It's the flagship private prison of Incarso Corp—the corrections conglomerate run by Reid's old school chum Frake Inyards, who holds the Charity Gala every year at Freedom Fortress's luxury hotel. This year the dinner will be held in the Golden Manacles Ballroom, which is surrounded by bulletproof two-way mirrors so that the guests can see the prisoners in their cages."

"I suppose we're just supposed to walk into this place unannounced?" asked Andronicus skeptically.

"We've made careful arrangements for you to go as Robert Park, the prominent owner of a global interrogation firm based in Seoul. Your American wife and business partner is Lizzie Borden Park, MD, a psychiatric torture specialist with an Ivy League degree."

"A torture specialist?" frowned Polyvox. "I don't like that."

"That's better than your husband Robert," said Blackshield, "who is highly active in the most loathsome and vile form of sex tourism."

Andronicus, who was still hung over, suddenly lifted his head in anger. He threw his mission dossier at Blackshield's feet. "I refuse to play the role of some depraved exploiter. What do you think I am? How can I fake that? I already want to strangle this bastard Robert Park to death even though he's fictional."

"I demand a new persona, too," said Polyvox. "Not a torturer. Make me a dealer in stolen art or something."

"Listen to me, both of you," said Blackshield sharply. "You are infiltrating the filthy world of the global superrich. You cannot go in as angels, and you can't even go in as mere evil criminals. The superrich inhabit a cultural zone analogous to the diabolical alternative dimension that mangled the crew in that old cult classic film *Event Horizon*. Have either of you seen it?"

"I have," said Jack. "In a college course I took called The Psychology of American Horror. The course was later banned and the professor sent for reeducation."

"Is that the movie where the guy goes around hunting replicants, and it turns out he's one, too?" asked Andronicus.

"No, that's *Blade Runner*," said Polyvox. "Loosely based on the novel *Do Androids Dream of Electric Sheep?* by Philip K. Dick, whom I met once, many decades ago. In the movie *Event Horizon*, a fanciful warp-drive gadget sends the crew into a realm of horrors. It began promisingly enough, but ended up descending into a disappointing slasher flick."

Andronicus rubbed his aching temples. "Are we discussing fiction and film here, or are we discussing a mission?"

"My point is this," said Blackshield. "The only way you'll be able to attend this Charity Dinner is if you have pus-oozing scabs on your souls, just like the other attendees do. In this evil dimension of wealth and power, everybody knows everybody else's inner demons, and that's how the balance of power is maintained. So, Polyvox, you are a professional torturer. And you, Andronicus, are even worse. That's because Frake Inyards shares your depraved appetites, and knows as much about you as you do about him, even though you have never met in person."

"How am I supposed to have a conversation about underage sex tourism with this animal Inyards? I find the very subject repellant. I couldn't even pretend to talk about it with him."

Jack turned to look out the window, still listening, but also thinking about the professor who had taught that course. He'd returned from the Federal Reeducation Center the next year a much more cheerful man—and a much more boring lecturer. For a while, as Petriv drove the *Argo* through Fairmount Park, it was as if they were far from any urban centers, deep in the heart of a forest. Now, abruptly, the city appeared again.

"It is sufficient that Inyards knows," Blackshield was saying, "—or thinks he knows—your personal demons, and that you know his. You will not even allude to each other's abominable predilections at the Children First Charity Gala. You are there to give lip service to this charade of a charity, and then to get down to the real business of making more and more money. This is how the elites keep each other in check. What you will discuss with Frake is a possible contract in which you install state-of-the-art interrogation chambers in his archipelago of private prisons across the U.S. The financial details are all there in the dossier, and they've been vetted to the fourth decimal point by the Professor. Your people and Inyards' people have already been discussing the matter. Gregory Reid has significant investments in Inyards' prisons, so through Inyards, you and your wife Lizzie will gain access to the personal quarters of Reid and his mistress. There you will inject neurotoxin into Reid's neck using a fountain pen pocket syringe. Since you've both been DNA-tagged in the Pit, you will have to wear DNA-decoy watches at all times. It's almost a certainty the hotel will be outfitted with the new Acme Double-Helix Gene Reader."

Andronicus picked up his dossier from the floor and unenthusiastically leafed through it. He kneaded his throbbing temples with his fingers. "Does the *Argo* contain a stock of spirits?" he asked Polyvox. "I require some hair of the dog."

"Not for you. Go home and sleep it off. If you want, I can fix you a pick-me-up. Be forewarned, it contains a raw egg, crushed ginger, beet juice, liquefied kale, brewer's yeast, and a splash of bitters."

"Make it so," said Andronicus, closing his eyes.

Polyvox stood up and slid aside her chair, disappearing through a small doorway into the cabin at the back of the *Argo*. They heard the clatter of kitchen implements; shortly she returned holding a glass of dark green liquid and resumed her seat.

"Cheers." Andronicus tossed the concoction back in one gulp, grimacing and shaking his head.

"Damn it, Blackshield, why must I play the role of a monster?" he asked desolately.

"Unfortunately, in our business, we must sometimes construct these foul backstories," said Blackshield. "We must create narratives of disinformation to feed into the intelligence databases of the Enemy. In the end, as in all wars, information determines who wins or loses. But no one would ever mistake you for a monster, Andronicus. You are a man of honor. A righteous man."

Turning away from the window, Jack noticed again the fathomless iciness in Blackshield's blue eyes. And he wondered what had motivated this slender, dangerous man to join a revolutionary movement. Was it a passion for justice, as with Andronicus? Was it some mysterious yearning to correct the trajectory of history, as with Polyvox? Jack suspected that for Blackshield it was something else, an imperative to eradicate evil—one so deeply ingrained within him that it resided beyond the domains of passion and reason, maybe even beyond good and evil, at least as these categories were judged by human beings.

Polyvox was also looking at Blackshield, her arms crossed. "And what is your role?" she asked him.

"I will go as your chauffeur and valet. If it's any consolation, the actual termination of Reid will be effected by me."

"Do we get to assassinate Frake Inyards as well?" asked Andronicus.

"I'm afraid not. Only Reid. We will have to arrange to meet privately with Reid. At that point the kill will take place. You have a week to memorize your backstories. And remember to speak a mixture of English and Korean to each other when you are in public spaces at the Freedom Fortress. This will add an essential element of realism. I will accompany you as your manservant."

Andronicus asked, "Once we kill Reid and rescue Stephany Miscellany, how do we get out?"

"That's my part of the operation. Don't worry about it. I will lead you out."

"And what about Jack and Krypton? Will they participate?"

"No," said Blackshield. "Jack can stay at Polyvox's apartment. Krypton will lodge with Bombsinger at the Trappist Tavern. Petriv and Bunyan will drop in on them regularly to make sure they are okay. Because of recent events, they will have to lay low for an extended period of time."

"I want to go along on this mission," said Jack, surprising himself. Up until this moment, still stung by Andronicus's drunken condescension from the night before, he had been considering how he might slip away from these people. But something had changed. "I want to see the people who arranged my parents' deaths," he added quietly.

Blackshield shook his head. "Impossible."

"I concur," said Andronicus tersely. "Your participation is not even a point of debate."

With a touch of cunning, Polyvox gave her cryptic half-smile. "On the contrary, I think Jack should come along."

For a few seconds, Andronicus and Polyvox exchanged severe and defiant looks, then Andronicus said, "What are you talking about? Jack is now a registered known traitor. His genes are on wanted databases all across the globe."

"There are technologies that can disguise his genes, as you know," said Polyvox. "As well as ones that can disguise his appearance. Blackshield can easily write a role for him into the mission."

Andronicus kneaded his fingers into his throbbing temples. "Your idea is so reckless that I can't help but wonder, Polyvox, if you have some ulterior motive here."

Petriv had now pulled the *Argo* into the underground parking lot at Polyvox's building. He turned around. "We are arriving. Are we continuing to argue in here, or inside?"

"There is no need for further discussion," said Polyvox. "Unlike Andronicus, I am not encumbered by a hangover; I am confident that my suggestion that Jack accompany us on Operation Moneybags is the correct one. I have already come up with his role: he will be my body servant, an extremely low-status, unfree manservant, outfitted with an indentured servant's face visor—one equipped with a genetic disruptor. This will hide both his physical appearance and his essence. Trust me, friends, I have accounted for everything. Even his mission name, which will be Boichik."

Andronicus seemed about to argue. Then he waved his hand and quickly exited the car.

F9

Senator Lance Boyler sat on a gold-plated toilet seat in his lavishly appointed bathroom at the Russell Senate Office Building. His neck muscles stood out as he strained to achieve colonic climax. The hollow wet report of his evacuation sounded loudly in the bowl, and he sighed with blissful relief. He slapped the roll of toilet paper, which had a parchment texture and was printed with the words of the Constitution, and tore off a thick wad.

The intercom next to the toilet buzzed. It was his chief of staff.

"What do you want, peon? I'm busy."

"Sir," said Mark Boner, "there's a Ronald Hedrick here to see you. He says it's urgent."

"Bison shit. Everybody who wants to see me says it's urgent. Tell him to wait while I finish purifying my backside after a most prodigious crap."

Boner spoke more softly. "Sir, he says he's with the FBI."

"Do you think he is?"

"Um, I suppose so, Your Senatorship."

"Well, does he look like a manly white man, or a poofter?"

"I don't know what a poofter is, sir..."

"Send him in," barked Boyler. He finished wiping himself with the Constitution toilet paper, pulled up his trousers, tucked in his shirt, and buckled his belt. At the sink, he furiously washed his hands with scalding water and antibacterial soap, making strange faces in the mirror.

He opened the bathroom door and strode over to where Boner and the visitor were standing.

"Sir," said Boner, "this is Special Agent Ronald Hedrick."

Hedrick was tall and blond, with a long face that was strikingly horselike and not particularly handsome.

The senator and the FBI agent shook hands.

"Have a seat, Hedrick," said Boyler. "You're from the FBI?"

"The Warforce FBI, my lord Senator—the military wing."

"I see, yes."

"In fact, I'm a captain in the Warforce FBI, but because of the seriousness of this mission I have been temporarily posted to the Investigatory FBI."

"Right. I see. Oh, that will be all, Boner."

Boner bowed and left the room, and Hedrick looked up at a row of pictures on the wall behind Boyler. They showed wide, fenced-in campuses dotted with circular pools of water.

"Family business establishments, Your Senatorship?" asked Hedrick politely.

Boyler gave a proud smile. "Every one. My grandfather Cnut Boyler built the first family sewage treatment plant, practically with his own hands, using nothing more than some pipes, concrete, a bucket of lye, and a honey wagon full of night soil. By the time Cnut was dead, my father Pierce Boyler had inherited a veritable sewage empire. Today, Boyler Inc. operates no fewer than two hundred sewage treatment plants across the country, plus a few in Canada. Twenty-four hours a day, seven days a week, they pump the purified fecal discharge of North America into our rivers and streams."

"It is a noble heritage, Your Senatorship," said Hedrick smoothly. "I myself play the violin."

"Eh?" replied Boyler, confused.

Hedrick was holding out his badge and his credential. "Just so you know who I am, Your Senatorship."

"Yes, yes, quite. What's all this about, Special Agent Hedrick?"

"It concerns a delicate matter, sir. Let's just say that responsibility for this investigation has been handed over to me by higher authorities. The Security Agency—well, let's be honest—their performance has been amateurish."

"I couldn't agree with you more, Agent Hedrick."

"Of course, they are just Security Theater. Perhaps even a Security Passion Play. Have you ever been to a Passion Play, Senator?"

"I can't say that I have."

"Are you a religious man?"

"I believe in the Five Big Things: the Bible, the Devil, Hell, Heaven, and God."

"Very good. By the way, I don't mean to insult the bureaucrats who labor away at the Security Agency. They do perform a useful service in making the public feel safe. It's just that they are—what should we call them? Miscompetents, perhaps? It sounds like something a certain wartime president would have said. You know which one." Hedrick was examining his long, graceful fingers. "Yet, of all the *miscompetents* who labor away at the Security Agency, one of them appears to stand out as not particularly incompetent after all.

And that would be this cunning devil Jack Tone. 'The Man without a Shadow,' as my team is now given to calling him."

Boyler was getting impatient, but this Hedrick fellow made him too nervous to say so. He had never met the man before. There was something at once cold-blooded, ingratiating, detached, and frightening about him. Deep in his heart, Boyler admitted that he himself probably had some kind of rotten soul, but Hedrick seemed more or less soul-free. Like one of those horrid Plutocroids that Reid had purchased from the Department of Defense. Boyler politely cleared his throat. "What about Jack Tone?"

"DNA detectors at the Pit recently confirmed his presence there."

"At the Pit?"

"Yes."

"Impossible!"

"Very possible. In fact—established."

"But how could he have gotten there…and why?"

Hedrick smiled and shrugged gently.

"Was he captured?"

"Of course not, Senator. He is the Man without a Shadow, as I said." Hedrick closed his eyes and pretended he was playing the violin. Boyler watched him, as one might watch a freak who swallows his own arm at a traveling carnival. "Do you know what I'm playing, Senator?"

"What you're playing…what do you mean?"

Hedrick kept his eyes closed and jerked his arm frenziedly as he conveyed the passion of his inaudible music. "What I'm playing here on the violin," he said. "It is a concerto. You should be able to *tell* from the movement of my fingers the name of the *man* who composed it."

Boyler stared blankly, and Hedrick suddenly opened his eyes. "Lance Boyler: Zero. Jack Tone: Two. You are losing, Senator."

"You're the one who discovered this second breach, man. Are you at least hot on his trail?"

"All across the world."

"I suppose I should tell Reid," mumbled Boyler. "But perhaps not just yet. I don't want to upset him."

"Oh no, I think you *should* tell him. You see, Senator, because of general miscompetence in the handling of this matter, I have been authorized to answer *directly to Mr. Reid.* I want you to take me to him now, so I can make my introduction."

F9

Gregory Reid was kneeling in his personal shrine, his hands folded, gazing reverentially at an icon of himself depicted as Christ Crucified. In front of him knelt Fritz and Clara, who were trying desperately to maintain their postures of prayer. When they started to nod off, Reid slapped them.

"You sleep before the image of your God?" he shouted.

Stephany Miscellany entered the shrine. "How long are you going to make them kneel there? It's been an hour."

Reid stood up, his face twisted in anger. "How dare you interrupt my prayers, you insolent harridan!" He turned around and slapped the children on their heads. "Get away from here, you miserable brats. How many children live with their own household God, and yet you two can only fall asleep in his presence?"

"Sir," began Fritz, shaking fearfully, "can we please have dinner tonight?"

"No!" thundered Reid. "As punishment for having insulted me, your God, you will have no dinner! What kind of Reids are you? Pathetic Reids, wimpy Reids. Look at you. Your ancestors once flogged the living flesh off slaves, but all you two can do is grovel pathetically and ask to eat."

They tried to apologize, but he began to slap them again.

Stephany Miscellany stepped between Reid and the two children, who ran away crying. "My love, please calm yourself and stop hitting them."

He looked at her as if she were a stranger. She was wearing that damnable black coat she always wore, with long sleeves and a high collar. It made her look like a sorceress. "Where are my mecha-children?" he shouted at her. "Where are my mecha-children?"

"Sir," said Mr. Ichabod, gliding into the room like a specter, "you smashed them to pieces with a wrench the other day when you'd had your fill of their incessant preprogrammed chattering. They are no longer operable." Mr. Ichabod held out a silver tray with pills and a plastic cup of water. "It's time to take, sir."

Reid slapped the tray with an upward swing of his hand, sending it, the cup, and the pills flying. He stormed out of the chapel.

"Perhaps you can prevail upon him, my lady," said Mr. Ichabod. He moved swiftly around the room, snatching up the pills and then handing them to her. "You know he must take these or he becomes…difficult."

Miscellany found him in his private study, where he was gazing out over the luminous skyscraper forest below.

"It's hard to be a God," he sighed.

"You should take your pills," she said, "or you will have terrible dreams."

He snatched them from her, shoved them in his mouth, and chewed. "Those little monsters vex me. I almost wish my kidneys would fail so I could have the satisfaction of clawing fresh ones out of them."

"Now, now, Gregory, you shouldn't hate your nephew and niece. After all, they are your flesh and blood. You should also avoid slapping them—you don't want to damage them, do you?"

"Kids are resilient, they bounce back. Speaking of which, when do we have to go to that Children First Charity Gala at Inyards' prison?"

"We leave tomorrow night, my dear."

"Will you wear that evening gown I bought you?" he asked with a watery leer.

"Yes."

"Why do you refuse to make love to me?"

"I told you, sexual intercourse disrupts my thinking patterns. I believe I'm getting ever closer to a solution to the Time Problem, and I don't want to jeopardize that. As soon as it's solved, the Araknoids will come to life in your service. But celibacy is essential to my cognition. Someday, we will consummate our love. But not until you become Autocrat of All the Apes."

"The Apes? What do you mean by that?"

"I mean that, compared to you, humanity is a pack of Apes. You are a God and must elevate them."

"Quite true, quite true. But obviously you are flattering me, because you don't believe a word of that. Suppose I choose to take you now?" He reached into his pocket and removed the remote control that activated the diamond necklace bomb around her neck, wagging it in front of her face like a magician's wand.

For a careless instant, Stephany Miscellany was tempted to snatch it, but she knew that Mr. Ichabod also had one—and that he was probably watching.

"Because if you blow me up, you will never be able to make love to me, and you will never unlock your precious Araknoid army from its time vise."

"And maybe I never will. Maybe you are faking it. Maybe you're not so great a physicist after all. I mean, if there is a solution to the Time Problem, why hasn't some man-physicist figured it out yet?"

"Blow me up, then," she said coolly. "Go ahead. I dare you."

He grunted, rubbing the remote control compulsively, stalking back and forth in front of the window. At that moment, Mr. Ichabod slipped into the room. "My lord, you have guests."

"Guests? Who the hell is guesting me at this hour?"

"His Senatorship and a special agent from the FBI."

"Ah. Let's dispense with the usual theatrics, Mr. Ichabod. I will receive them right here in the study." He faced Stephany and took her hand. "My love, we men must discuss weighty matters. Run along. Attend to your *toilette*."

"Yes, Gregory," she said, taking her leave of him.

F9

Reid sat behind the massive mahogany desk in his private study. At twelve feet long and six feet deep, it was a far more modest affair than the skull-adorned fortress in his throne room.

Presently, the fool Boyler came in, accompanied by a sandy-haired man with a long aquiline nose and an even longer face. Instantly, some primitive instinct in Reid alerted him to the fact that this man was potentially dangerous. He and the newcomer quickly sized each other up, like two rival beasts of prey encountering one another in the jungle.

Boyler made a very low bow. "My lord, here is Special Agent Ronald Hedrick of the Warforce FBI. A captain by rank."

Reid did not normally stand for guests, but he did now, extending his hand. He wanted to judge this man's handclasp.

They shook hands and, unblinkingly, stared into each other's frigid eyes as they tried to out-squeeze each other. By silent mutual consent, a draw was declared, and they disengaged.

"Have a seat, gentlemen," said Reid. "Can I offer you a drink?"

Hedrick shook his head gracefully. "No thank you, Mr. Reid."

"You don't mind if I have one, do you?" Reid poured himself a snifter. "So what brings you to my humble home, Agent Hedrick?"

"As you probably know, Mr. Reid, I am now assigned to your case. There was another breach."

"I know. The ghost traitor Jack Tone was detected in the Pit. The news hit me like citric acid on a canker sore. Lately there's been more breaching around here than in a pod of rutting killer whales."

"Yes, Mr. Reid, but the fact that he has DNA at all indicates he is not actually a ghost, just a very cunning human being. And of course he must be part of a treasonous faction."

"Can you be so sure that ghosts don't have DNA, Agent Hedrick?" asked Reid, his eyes steely.

"I suppose it is possible that if some element of the soul can be imprinted on this world after the body has decayed, then some residue of DNA could also survive."

"I personally believe that the ghost DNA of dead souls who lived intense or emotionally violent lives can thread itself into our living

DNA and cause mutations, and furthermore that these invisible mutations are ultimately what separate gods from mortals."

Hedrick folded his hands on his lap. "Fascinating, Mr. Reid. If such mutations were real, they might go a long way in explaining why some human beings, a small minority, are afflicted from a young age by a radical sense of separateness, as if humanity is a swarm of bugs, but they are not."

Reid was startled. He looked away and tried to hide his expression behind a blank mask. He stroked his chin, recalling one of his own favorite childhood pastimes—torturing flies and other bugs. He looked up suddenly. "Special Agent, do you mind if I ask what your favorite work of literature is?"

Perplexity was beginning to spread over Boyler's face.

"Since childhood," said Hedrick, "I have had a fondness for Octave Mirbeau's *The Torture Garden*."

"And your favorite film?"

Hedrick spread his arms out in a gesture of frank openness. "*The Texas Chainsaw Massacre*. However, I often watch it with the volume down, while listening to Wagner. I find the screams of the actors false and tedious. Wagner, on the other hand, complements the action. Beethoven, in comparison, makes my skin crawl."

Reid felt a strange warmth overcome him, an unfamiliar sensation that was possibly akin to—though only very distantly—the impulse of friendship. "Agent Hedrick, are you sure you won't have that drink?"

Hedrick looked up, as if reconsidering. Lightly, languorously, he rubbed his long hands against each other. "Do you have schnapps, Mr. Reid?"

"I have all the *Schnäpse* ever made."

"I'll take Hundficker Cherry schnapps, if you don't mind."

Mr. Ichabod, as was his fashion, had kind of shimmered into the room without anyone noticing. "I'll bring that out straightaway, sir," he said.

"And an ice-cold magnum of Kohrs Lite for His Senatorship," added Reid.

"Very good, sir."

Mr. Ichabod promptly delivered the drinks.

"Mr. Reid," inquired Hedrick, "if you don't mind my asking, what is *your* favorite novel?"

"I'm not much into fiction, truth to tell. At the age of ten I did read and very much enjoy a dramatization of the life of Elizabeth Báthory—one of my childhood heroines. But the most formative books in my life have been Weber's *Die Protestantische Ethik und der Geist des Kapitalismus*, Smith's *Wealth of Nations*, and of course Kramer's *Malleus Maleficarum*."

Boyler sipped his Kohrs Lite nervously. He had no idea where this conversation was going, or even what it meant. He felt that he was not even in the room, and he began to resent his beer.

"And your favorite film?" asked Special Agent Hedrick.

"I don't have a favorite film *per se*, though one very old film's characterization of Amon Goeth did have a powerful transformational effect on me as a teenager. Up until that point, I had wanted to be a catcher and euthanizer of wild animals—a career aspiration that my father never ceased to belittle. But after I saw that film, something changed, and I realized that I wanted to work, like my detestable father, on Wall Street. Indeed, as a hedge-fund manager, a financier, and an investor, I have never ceased trying to model my behavior on the virtues of Goeth, commandant of the Kraków-Płaszów concentration camp."

"Mr. Reid, do you mind if I smoke?"

"Not at all, sir."

Hedrick took out an ivory meerschaum pipe in the form of a troll's face. Reid hurried to ignite it, and Boyler tried not to cough in the billow of pungent smoke. "Mr. Reid, I have a plan to capture Jack Tone. A form of triangulation based on statistical predictions. Every single time I have used this method to catch Enemies of the State, I have been successful. I have already implemented it, and I promise you that within a month he will be in our clutches."

"Agent Hedrick, you please me greatly."

"I want you to carry on as normal, Mr. Reid. Attend this Charity Gala as you are scheduled to. Enjoy your week in West Virginia. I've been to Freedom Fortress myself. In addition to being a first-class incarceration facility, it is also a remarkable luxury retreat. Do not alter your intended behavior in any way, because this could disrupt the statistical paradigms that I have worked so hard to derive and assemble."

"I will do exactly as you say, Agent Hedrick."

"Mr. Reid, would you happen to have a violin, and any films in the torture-porn genre?"

Reid paused. "As a matter of fact, I have both. I have a device that synthesizes torture-porn images, complete with basic plotlines."

"It would be my great honor to watch a film with you, while accompanying it on the violin. I promise you that I will evoke every passion on my instrument more perfectly, more exquisitely, than any shriek generated by human vocal chords."

Reid stood up, clapping his hands. "Mr. Ichabod—activate the screening room immediately and bring the Stradivarius."

"Yes, my lord."

In the screening room Boyler sat squirming while flesh shuddered agonizingly, jaws gaped in silent screams, body parts popped off and bounced around like rubber balls, and ketchup-red blood spurted copiously. All the while, his ears were ravaged by Hedrick's infernal playing. Reid was in a kind of trance.

Boyler bolted from the screening room and ran straight into Stephany Miscellany. He had the look of a hunted beast.

"Something the matter, Senator?"

"No."

"Senator, when you were a boy, what did you aspire to be?"

"Nothing."

"How can that be? All children have their dreams."

He answered her listlessly. "I was destined from before birth, Ms. Miscellany, to process American sewage."

"You and your chief of staff had better leave now, Senator. He'll be in a *very* bad mood come morning—like an alcoholic emerging from a raging bender. I cannot guarantee your safety."

F9

Gregory Reid stormed out of his screening room at six in the morning, his eyes bloodshot, his mouth strangely deformed—like a crack in a vandalized statue. From behind him came the scraping of Hedrick's violin. Reid looked around frantically until he found his rubber truncheon. He went straight for the twins' bedroom, kicking open the door.

"Sir?" said Mr. Ichabod, gliding quickly down the hallway after him.

"Do not interfere, you bloodless zombie," said Reid, entering the children's bedroom. "Awake, brats—awake unto your death and resurrection!" He bashed the wall with the truncheon—so hard that the plaster cracked.

The twins scrambled out of their beds, clutching each other as they huddled in a corner.

Reid approached, the truncheon raised above his head.

Miscellany slammed into him from the side, wrenching the truncheon from him and cracking him across the side of the head. He fell to the floor, cursing, blood dribbling from his lower lip. She bent down and grabbed him in a headlock, slipping her hand into his pocket and seizing the remote control for the necklace bomb.

"Do you want me to blow us both up?" she whispered in his ear.

He made choking sounds in her unnaturally strong hold.

"If you menace them again, I will grab you like this, drag you out to your study, stand us before the window, and blow us both to smithereens. And you will be one dead god."

She released him and he dropped back onto the floor, weeping and giggling, rubbing his neck. Mr. Ichabod watched, balancing his own remote control on the tips of his branchlike fingers.

"Will you wear the evening gown I bought you for the Charity Dinner?" asked Reid hoarsely.

"Yes, I shall wear it." Her voice was weary.

Ichabod, moving soundlessly, reached out his long arm and snatched the remote control away from her.

Reid whimpered in gratitude. "You have made me so happy, Stephany…but remember the next time you attack me that *I always win in the end.*"

Back in the screening room, Hedrick played a mournful pavane.

F9

Fritz and Clara stood by as Mr. Ichabod, their uncle, and Stephany Miscellany prepared to leave for the Charity Dinner in West Virginia.

"Mrs. Crane will take care of you while we are gone," said Miscellany.

"Will you come back?" they asked together.

"Yes, in approximately one week."

Fritz and Clara watched them leave. When the door closed, they went back to their bedroom. From a hiding place, they took out a photograph of their mother, a tarnished silver wedding ring, and an old CD in a cracked plastic case. They set up the picture on the nightstand between their beds and played their favorite song, a catchy but sad pop melody from a time before either of them were born. For a few moments they watched the old photograph, trying to imagine the lips moving, the eyes sparkling. Then they held hands.

From far away, the Gazillionaire's Tower rose like a fragile filament of twisted glass above the skyscraper forest, vibrant against the starry sky. In a window at the top, two little figures danced, but no one could see them.

CHAPTER SIXTEEN

The Five-Star
Hotel of Horror

Polyvox, Andronicus, Blackshield, and Jack departed Philadelphia for West Virginia early in the morning. Polyvox sat behind the wheel, with Andronicus on the passenger side. In the back sat Blackshield and Jack.

Jack held his indentured servant face visor on his lap. It was not particularly uncomfortable, but already he resented it. Andronicus turned around in his seat. "You should probably wear that at all times, just to be on the safe side."

Jack sighed and slipped it on. It covered his face like a hockey goalie's mask, but it was green, furnished with sensor nubbins, and displayed Polyvox's oak-tree-and-heart coat of arms on the forehead portion. He felt like a fool wearing it.

Such masks were worn by all those in the United States of America who had entered into, or had been condemned to, the legal state of indentured servitude. The masks typically contained transponders and could only be removed by the indentured servant's master. Jack's mask, additionally, was equipped with the gene-detector disruption technology that had been devised by Polyvox's order. This did not actually filter outflowing genetic information—a truly difficult task—but rather transmitted a cybervirus beam to all local gene-detectors, so that they would produce a false ID result whenever the subject's genes were collected and analyzed.

This was the standard technology that Faction Nine had been using for the last several years, even as the State's genetic surveillance had become more sophisticated. However, as the debacle in the Araknoid Pit had demonstrated, neither the technology nor the stratagem was 100 percent foolproof.

Andronicus, quietly, had his doubts.

"I don't think he has to wear the indentured servant mask while we're in the car," said Polyvox.

Gratefully, Jack took it off again.

The trip to Freedom Fortress took them four hundred miles, through the mountains of Pennsylvania, then into Maryland, and finally south into the Alleghenies of West Virginia—once one of the most beautiful regions of the United States, now one of the most bleak and dreary, a place of dusty smog, treeless wastes, and streams of toxic sludge. The *Argo* followed narrow two-lane roads through a desolate moonscape of oddly flattened mountains whose tops had been blown clean off by global coal-mining corporations.

After seven hours, they finally approached Freedom Fortress Maximum-Security Prison—visible from some distance away because it towered over the formerly mountainous but now largely squashed landscape. Freedom Fortress was immense, and resembled a black-and-red version of Castle Neuschwanstein in Bavaria. The *Argo* threaded its way around and around the squat mountain base, and finally came to the main gate. The electrified portcullis was up. Above the portcullis was the logo of Incarso Corp: a kneeling man, his shackled arms raised in penitent prayer. Behind this was an American flag and the words:

INCARSO CORP

CORRECTING THE AMERICAN DREAM

FOR FIVE GENERATIONS

A red-striped pole was lowered in front of the car. Incarso Corp guards in Kevlar helmets and body armor came out to meet them. By now, Blackshield was behind the wheel in his servant's attire, while Andronicus and Polyvox sat in the backseat. Blackshield rolled down the window. Jack, his mask on, sat in the front passenger side.

"Your documents, please," said one of the guards.

Blackshield handed him four internal passports. The guard studied them. "State your identity, declare your citizenship, and describe your business at Freedom Fortress."

"I am Septimus Featherstonehaugh, chauffer and valet to My Lord Robert Park and My Lady Lizzie Borden Park. We are U.S. citizens. Additionally, My Lord and Lady have Certified Exclusive Global Status. This man beside me is Boichik, formerly a U.S. citizen, now stateless, and My Lady's indentured body servant. My Lord and Lady are attending the Children First Charity Gala, hosted by the honorable Frake Inyards."

The guard stuck his big bulldog face in the window. "Your passport says 'Featherstonehaugh,' not 'Fanshaw.'"

"Fanshaw is the proper pronunciation," replied Blackshield haughtily. "What is your name, soldier?"

"Grubbs. Sergeant Grubbs."

"I have made a note of it."

Grumbling, the guard thrust back the internal passports and fed a tube through the window of the car. It sucked in air for a minute. Nearby, an Acme Double-Helix Portable Gene Reader chugged and clanked.

Jack sat perfectly still, staring straight ahead through the visor slits of his mask, his heart pounding, his palms sweaty. He tried to discreetly rub them on his trousers.

A green light flashed on the Acme Double-Helix Portable Gene Reader and there was a shrill whistle.

Jack thought he would scream.

"You may proceed," said the guard, yanking out the tube.

Blackshield rolled up the window and drove the car into the wide courtyard of the prison, parking it in the space between a Rolls-Royce Phantom VII and a Maserati Quattroporte X9. A gray-uniformed prison proctor with a whip led a party of three mute, one-armed inmates in plastic facemasks and orange-striped jumpsuits.

"Good evening, milady, milord," said the proctor. "These Epsilons will help you with your baggage. And don't worry, milady, only nonviolent political prisoners are permitted to perform porter duty. Your feminine honor is safe here at Freedom Fortress."

"Brilliant," said Polyvox flatly.

The proctor turned to Jack. "Will this beast accompany you into the hotel, or should I have him escorted to the indentured servants' kennel?"

"My body servant shall accompany me to attend to the needs of my body."

"Very well, milady." The proctor turned to his party of inmates and shouted, "Git a move on, you!" like a cowboy urging on his cattle.

Immediately the inmates scuttled forward like hunched muscular homunculi and took the luggage, bringing it into the lobby of the Freedom Fortress Hotel.

The concierge registered them. "Welcome, Mr. and Mrs. Park," he said pleasantly. "Here are your keys. Mr. Inyards has specially requested that you be given the Thomas Jefferson Suite. If you need anything at all, please contact the front desk."

"Thanks," said Andronicus, taking the key cards.

The proctor struck at the inmates with his whip. "Take that luggage up to the Thomas Jefferson Suite, you lawless brutes."

They all crowded together in an elevator, where the proctor continued to strike gratuitously at the backs of the porter-inmates. A John Philip Sousa march played softly over the sound system. When the doors opened again, the proctor drove the porters like hogs into the hallway, thrashing their backs all the way down to the gilded doors of the Thomas Jefferson Suite.

"We can manage from here," said Andronicus, glaring at the proctor.

"Yes, yes, of course—as you wish, sir," said the proctor, making a servile bow. He went away with the porters, lashing them back to the elevator doors.

🔥9

Holding a small detector in his right hand, Blackshield made a subtle survey of the rooms in the suite, identifying all of the bugs and visual recorders. He placed a statue of George Washington on one of the tables—an electronic pulse decoy that would transmit a repeating audio-visual loop, overriding the surveillance equipment that had been installed in the suite. The statue had glowing green eyes.

"We can speak openly now," he said to them. "At a normal volume."

"Can I take this mask off?" asked Jack.

"Yes," said Blackshield.

"You're certain?" asked Andronicus.

"Positive."

Jack removed the mask and wiped his sleeve across his perspiring brow. His first exposure to an inner sanctum of the superrich had made him queasy. He imagined it would only get worse.

Andronicus still seemed doubtful. "How long is the loop?"

"Six hours. Six hours of us pacing around, sitting, having bland and painfully stilted conversations."

"That won't fool anyone, will it?" said Polyvox. "Six hours from now we'll be repeating the same stupid things we're apparently saying right now."

"It's not supposed to fool them," Blackshield replied. "Of course they know we've set up the false feed."

"And that won't provoke suspicion?" said Andronicus.

"Be assured that all the other guests in all the other rooms have also set up decoys. The surveillance personnel here at Freedom Fortress fully expect it, and they will attempt to disable or neutralize as many feed units as they can. They will not succeed with ours. Petriv and I have created an impregnable Free Speech zone for you right here in these rooms."

"Until someone comes in and takes out that statue of George Washington."

"It won't happen. It's a game for them, like Soviet and American submarines playing cat and mouse in the old era. There are rules of engagement that cannot be violated. There is another matter, Andronicus. You must not allow rage to show in your eyes."

Andronicus frowned. "What do you mean?"

"The guard noticed your disapproval, and he was confused. The people who visit this hotel take pleasure in seeing prisoners and underlings humiliated. If you wish to pass yourself off as a member of the Financial Elite, you must do the same. This country was built on the bones of slaves—not just economically, but philosophically and psychologically. Please do your best to play the role of the sadist."

Andronicus nodded morosely. "Was my hatred of the proctor really so obvious?"

"As obvious as if your eyes were movie projectors, my friend. Unfortunately, you have very expressive eyes. Now, Polyvox maintained perfect equipoise. Though she has a genuinely compassionate heart, she has the eyes of a cold-blooded killer. In some ways, she is the perfect spy."

"I am perfect in all things," said Polyvox, as she sat down on a divan and picked up a glossy retro reproduction of *American Correctionist*. The cover depicted a bald eagle collage composed of hundreds of tiny photos of men behind bars, staring out with hollow eyes.

"All kinds of truths come through the eyes," continued Blackshield, his own eyes icily blue beneath his black brows. "Love, hatred, revulsion, contempt, envy—the full range of human emotions. When my great-great-great-grandfather was in the camps, there was one guard who was particularly vicious. This was a man who fed off the pain of others like a mosquito feeds off blood. My ancestor, who was only sixteen, quickly realized that this guard—whose ethical development was so utterly stunted, whose capacity for compassion was so shriveled, whose mind was such an inert lump—could nevertheless read a person's eyes like an Egyptologist decoding hieroglyphics, and that he would respond to any hint of unspoken defiance with mortal violence. For a year and a half, up until the day of liberation, my ancestor avoided death by modulating the moods of his eyes, mostly by keeping them averted. He knew that by doing this he would increase his chances of survival from dismal to merely poor. And he was correct. He did survive—otherwise a part of me would not be here."

"And what happened to the guard?" asked Andronicus.

"The Red Army soldiers handed him over to the former prisoners. He was pliant, submissive, pathetic. He groveled and begged for mercy. One of his victims cracked open his head with a rock."

"Your ancestor killed the guard?"

"No. Another inmate did it."

"So he survived a death camp because he could mask his eyes. Something about the story seems implausible, Blackshield."

"This is how it was conveyed to me, Andronicus. All I can tell you is what I heard. It was generations ago."

"Well, at least it had a happy ending," said Andronicus, pouring himself a glass of *soju* from the wet bar in the suite. "I hope ours does as well. I would hate to die in this hellhole because my hieroglyphics gave me away."

F9

The next morning, Andronicus and Polyvox got into character and tried their best to stay there, referring to each other by the endearments of "Choppi" and "Big Bob." In the afternoon, there was a knock on the hotel room door. Blackshield and Polyvox were playing chess while Andronicus paced in thought. Jack was doing a crossword puzzle, his mask on the cushion beside him. He quickly strapped it on.

"Remember, keep in character," Blackshield said, rising and opening the door.

A proctor stood there. "Good evening. I would like to inform Mr. and Mrs. Park that the prison tour begins in an hour. Before that, there will be a reception in the Woodrow Wilson Room, which is all the way down this hall and to the right."

"Thank you," said Blackshield, assuming an air of icy superciliousness. "I shall inform milady and milord."

Blackshield closed the door. "You'd better get going, or you'll miss the tour."

"Yes, Jeeves," said Andronicus without enthusiasm. "Come, Choppi. Chop-chop."

Andronicus and Polyvox had already dressed. They were wearing business attire in the fashionable Retro-Ultra style: Andronicus in a dark suit with a jacket that evoked a *Kriegsmarine* officer, Polyvox in a long-sleeved black mandarin jacket, a black-and-silver-striped business skirt, and high heels with diamond-studded straps. They made their way to the Woodrow Wilson Room—a splendid mirrored room that resembled a hall at Versailles. A crowd of about fifty VIPs were scattered about the room in small groups. Faction Nine had previously acquired the guest list, so Andronicus and Polyvox had been able to read up on the attendees. They were largely Wall Street financiers, big money bankers, military contractors, and CEOs of various criminal-correction enterprises, pharmaceutical corporations, healthcare conglomerates, and international pornography concerns. There were also a few Senators.

One-armed porters with plastic muzzles glided dexterously around the room, carrying plates of canapé, fried mushrooms, caviar, prawn cocktails, crudités, bruschetta, tongue toast, shish kebab, goat eyeballs, chitterling cakes, rocky mountain oysters, kidney pies, blood puddings, spicy sphincter, Velveeta cubes, and pigs in blankets.

Lance Boyler, holding a Scotch in one hand and a plate of hors d'oeuvres in the other, worked his jaw like a crocodile. He made eye contact with Andronicus and Polyvox as they passed. Andronicus was about to continue, but Polyvox suddenly stopped.

"Senator Boyler," she said excitedly, holding out her hand. "I'm *such* a great fan of your legislation!"

Boyler seemed taken by surprise. He simultaneously attempted to swallow the blood puddings that were already in his mouth while also loading the last morsel of prawn that remained on his china plate, in the process nearly biting off his finger. He recovered, wiping his lips.

"Indeed, young lady, indeed!" he replied, his big round eyes popping out as if a pressurized tank in the back of his head had suddenly been turned on high. "And to whom do I have the honor of speaking?"

"I am Lizzie Borden-Park, my lord Senator, and this is my husband Robert. You can call me Choppi. Everybody does."

Boyler took her hand and gave it a greasy kiss. Andronicus extended his own hand. "Bob Park," he said.

They shook.

"A pleasure to meet both of you," said Boyler, his eyes running up and down Polyvox like a pair of mice on meth. "And what brings you to Freedom Fortress?"

"We're the owners of InquiZZ Interrogation Services," said Andronicus. "IZIS for short."

"How interesting, yes. And what does IZIS do?"

"We build state-of-the-art interrogation chambers around the world," Andronicus replied. "Our motto is *The Truth Is in There*, and our clients include the People's Republic of China, North Korea, South Korea, The United Kingdom, The Russian Federation,

Uzbekistan, Saudi Arabia, Iran, Pakistan, Indonesia, Australia, Turkey, Belarus, and Egypt. We have also provided installations to about one hundred private prisons here in the United States of America."

"Which would not have been possible, Senator Boyler," said Polyvox enthusiastically, "had you not sponsored the Pure Information and Human Rights Act, which authorized the use of progressive, high-yield interrogation techniques."

"Commonly known as torture!" guffawed Boyler, finishing his gin and snatching another glass from a passing porter-inmate.

The Senator, Andronicus, and Polyvox laughed heartily.

"You know," said Boyler, rubbing his lips on his sleeve, "it's so refreshing to see people under fifty who show some entrepreneurial spirit. These days, everybody wants, wants, wants. Everybody is a parasite on the system. I assume you have designs on this facility? I do believe that its interrogation chambers are a bit out of date. I just learned that the other day they were applying electricity to an inmate, and something shorted, and his *brain* blew up or something. Can you imagine?"

"A blatant procedural failure, my lord Senator," said Polyvox, shaking her head. "I mean, it's one thing to lop off a limb or gouge out an organ during an interrogation, but the brain is the most precious organ, because it is the seat of knowledge and volition. If you blow that up you get nothing."

"Except a roomful of hors d'oeuvres!" Boyler laughed loudly again, like a neighing horse. "Tell me, have you met Frake Inyards?"

"Not yet, Your Senatorship," said Andronicus. "He and I have communicated on various matters, but never in person."

"A capital fellow," affirmed Boyler. "Absolutely dedicated to the improvement of children all over the entire world. I know he's been criticized in the dissident press because he's made billions locking people up, but the fact of the matter is that Frake Inyards has cleaned up this country, has purged out the scum, and has made it a safer place for women and children. Let me introduce him to you. Mrs. Park, may I have the honor?"

Boyler held out his arm for Polyvox to take. Hesitating a fraction of a second, she looped her arm through his and let him escort them to another corner, where Frake Inyards stood holding forth before a group of elegantly attired men and women. As he spoke, his hands fluttered in all directions. He was a man of average height, about forty-five years old, with a head far too large for his thin body. To Andronicus and Polyvox, his face strongly evoked that of a hobgoblin, and his complexion had a very slight, barely perceptible greenish hue to it.

He cracked a joke, and his audience laughed loudly.

Boyler sidled up next to him. "Mr. Inyards, I would like to introduce you to a wonderful couple. Mr. and Mrs. Robert Park, of InquiZZ Interrogations."

Inyards turned his great hobgoblin head. He looked first at Andronicus, a peculiar knowing smile spreading across his face. Subtly, the green pigment in his skin seemed to bleed into the whites of his eyes. He and Andronicus shook hands.

"Mr. Park, the pleasure is mine..."

Inyards' smile spread wide, revealing two even rows of teeth like white gravestones. His hand's clammy touch induced a shudder in Andronicus, as if a degenerate psychoplasm were coursing from Inyards' body into his own. Andronicus's immediate, visceral response was revulsion, and it was only through the most heroic exertion of mind over matter that he managed to suppress his gag reflex.

"Mr. Inyards," he said in a firm gentlemanly tenor, "I am so glad to meet you at last."

Inyards searched Andronicus's face with Hitleresque voyeurism. Andronicus cleared his throat. "And this is my wife, Doctor Lizzie Borden-Park."

Inyards casually cast his gaze upon her. "I am very pleased to meet you, Mrs. Park," he said. "Oh, you must have been a very pretty little girl!"

Polyvox shrugged. "It was a long time ago, and I can't really remember."

"Do you two have children?"

"We have two teenage daughters in boarding school," said Andronicus.

"Ah, pity. All grown up. They're so charming when they're young. Then they become…"—Inyards sighed—"…humanoids." His tone suddenly changed, losing its flair of depravity and becoming bluntly sinister. "But let's cease all of this poppycock talk about children. We all know the real reason you're both here, don't we?"

Andronicus and Polyvox did not immediately respond, and Inyards took them aside, abandoning his previous audience.

"Do either of you know Gregory Reid?" he asked.

"I'm afraid we don't," said Andronicus.

"Oh, I think you do," replied Inyards. "I *certainly* think you do."

He glared at them with his hobgoblin eyes.

"I don't quite follow," said Andronicus, swallowing.

"You know him even though you don't know him," said Inyards. "Because the man…the man…how can I explain it?" Inyards struggled for words. "He's not just a man, he's…he's a prophet, he's a god! I mean, just listen to the man—really listen to him! Hear the way he can discourse over such a wide range of subjects with such authority, with such *penetration*. Do you know he is a polyglot? He speaks ten languages with native fluency. He mastered German by age seven, Mandarin by age twelve. At age fifteen he wrote a treatise on Nietzsche, and yet at that age he still wanted to be a frigging *philosophy professor*! His father disabused him of that ridiculous dream, and helped make him the god-man he is today."

"I assure you, we have not made the acquaintance of this Gregory Reid," said Polyvox.

"Of course not…no…that's not what I mean. He is a hidden god, he has not yet revealed his divine identity to the world. And yet he is everywhere in the world today. He is here, right now, at Freedom Fortress. He will dine with us tonight. We will take communion with a god!"

Inyards took a deep breath and closed his eyes, trying to master his emotions.

"I went to school with him, but that was before he had fully emerged from his chrysalis." His eyelids popped open again, like a pair of blinds snapping up on windows to a crazy house. "What is the most powerful force in all the universe?"

"I've heard it's the strong nuclear force," said Polyvox.

"No, smarty-pants," replied Inyards, rolling his eyes. "It is *desire*. Desire is the most powerful force in the cosmos. And Gregory Reid has no desire. That is to say, he is the sum total of all desires, and none of them control him. *All* of them control him. This is why he is a god. He is the god who has made all this possible, the god who financed this fortress of freedom for the American People. And he is the god," continued Inyards, raising a pedagogical finger at them, "who wants you to build him a state-of-the-art interrogation chamber right here."

"Now we're talking business," said Andronicus with satisfaction.

A proctor came out and announced that the prison tour was about to begin.

F9

Inyards scurried away from them and grabbed a microphone. "*Ring, ring, ring, ring, ring, ring, ring!*" he shouted, drawing the attention of all the VIP guests. "The tour commences, the tour commences!"

Two of the wall-high mirrors drew away from each other, and Inyards led his guests inside. The first room contained a wax display called *History of Crime and Punishment*, which depicted numerous forms of torture and human degradation, including burning at the stake, drawing and quartering, waterboarding, the rack, electrocution, burying alive, and flaying. The VIP guests, by now very tipsy, giggled and gasped. A few glamorous, well-heeled young couples exchanged drunken kisses. They moved on and were able to look down upon the main work yard of the prison itself: a wide rectangular pit with stone walls where one-armed inmates in plastic muzzles milled around, pulling levers and operating a gigantic glockenspiel-like machine with conveyer belts, lifts, and chains.

Inyards explained that the product of this laborious activity was a sludgy nutritional sediment called Ploop™ that comprised the main food source of the inmates.

On the wall below were two gigantic copies of the Declaration of Independence and the Constitution, before which the inmates genuflected whenever they passed.

"You have, by now, noticed that all of the inmates have only one arm," said Inyards. "What at first glance appears to be cruelty is in fact an essential element of Incarso Corp's policy of 'Correction through Compassion.' When an inmate is admitted to Freedom Fortress, one arm is amputated. This compels the inmates to cooperate with each other in such tasks as pulling levers, hauling boxes, and canning Ploop™. This also makes it much more difficult for one inmate to harm another. The inmates wear their muzzles seven days a week, twenty-four hours a day. There are holes in the muzzles through which Ploop™ may be ingested. All the inmates subsist on Ploop™, which has four flavors: Watermelon, Cherry, Lemon-Lime, and Banana Blast. Ploop™ is 100 percent organic and is composed of processed fecal matter from the prison itself, as well as purified protein derived from vermin. High-fructose corn syrup is added as a pleasure element, along with a range of artificial flavorings and colorings. Ploop™ was first tested in the Minors Ward and has proven quite successful. There are even plans to market Ploop™ candy in the wider U.S. population. Initial tests indicate that Americans who don't vote and don't have a college education are far more likely to choose Ploop™ over fruits and vegetables when planning meals for their families. We envision great things for Ploop™."

The VIPs applauded, and Inyards proceeded to the next room.

"This is one of the reeducation chambers. Notice the inmate by the spittoon being forced to conduct taste tests of Ploop™. This particular inmate apparently scrawled an obscenity about Ploop™ in the latrine, using his own foul waste matter. In Freedom Fortress, insubordination is dealt with quickly and decisively for the benefit and commonweal of all the inmates."

The VIPs grunted in approval and moved on.

"Here we have a display of various artistic works created by the inmates," said Inyards. "They may look like rusty pieces of junk gathered from a dump, but I assure you that each holds special significance for an inmate. Artwork is available for sale at the Prison Store, by the way. Each piece is engraved with its own serial number. In judging these pieces, and in appraising their value, kindly recall that each was created by a person with only one arm."

Andronicus leaned towards Polyvox and whispered softly, "I cannot process all of this. It must be some kind of joke, some kind of intentional deception. It can't be for real."

She whispered back, "Perhaps it is merely gruesome entertainment. But slavery was for real, Auschwitz was for real, Hiroshima was for real. Why not this? Have you suddenly gone soft on your species, Andronicus?"

"No," he said, composing himself. "Never."

They returned to the Jefferson Suite to dress for the Children First Charity Gala. The hour of assassination was approaching.

CHAPTER SEVENTEEN

Born on the Fourth of July

"**H**ow was the tour?" asked Blackshield.

"It sucked," said Polyvox. She unbuttoned her mandarin jacket and flung it away, dropping wearily into a chair and tearing off the high heels. "Tone, I have to talk to you," she said quietly.

Jack was sitting at a table leafing through *American Correctionist*. Across the room, Andronicus had joined Blackshield in a glass of whisky. Andronicus seemed out of sorts for some reason. Had the two of them quarreled? Or had the tour of the correctional facility been that disturbing?

Jack sat down next to Polyvox. "Tell me what you saw on the tour. Andronicus is acting strangely."

"I think Andronicus might be having some kind of flashback," Polyvox said, her eyes darting across the room, "some kind of post-traumatic stress reaction. He saw things in the Wars of Betrayal, bad things, atrocities perpetrated by armed authorities against innocent and helpless victims. It is possible that the atmosphere of this hellish place might provoke a reaction."

Jack was alarmed. "If this is the case, shouldn't we tell Blackshield?"

"Blackshield and he both served during the Wars. They are brothers in arms. Blackshield will not keep in confidence anything I tell him about Andronicus."

"But what are you afraid might happen? That Andronicus might have a nervous breakdown?"

"Something like that."

"But what can *I* do?"

"You can remain informed, and therefore avoid debilitating surprise, if something does happen. You must be my eyes and ears. Think, my friend. Has Andronicus ever said anything to you about me?"

"He did once ask me to keep an eye on you," admitted Jack.

"Aha! Why? He doesn't trust me?"

"He said he trusts you, but not your order."

"Maybe he is right not to trust them. I'm not sure I trust them either. Jack, I want you to do me a favor. From here on out, I want you to keep a counter eye on Andronicus for me. Sometimes I worry about his mental health. And, as you can see, sometimes he drinks too much."

"Okay," said Jack.

Andronicus and Blackshield were still drinking at the table and did not lift their eyes to look at them. Polyvox now put on a long-sleeved, black gown. "Hurry up, Andronicus," she said. "We don't want to be late for the party."

Andronicus quickly changed into the officially sanctioned attire for the evening: a white tie, tailcoat, and top hat.

"How do I look?" he asked.

Polyvox studied him a moment. She raised her thumb in approval. "Just like a corporate bloodsucker, but not quite. More like an android corporate bloodsucker in the Uncanny Valley."

"Maybe that's what I am. I was dreaming of electric sheep last night."

"When you start dreaming of unicorns, let me know."

"Have a good time," said Blackshield as they departed. "And please, you two: be careful."

When they were gone, Blackshield turned and looked steadily at Jack.

"Is something the matter?"

"Can you do me a favor, Jack?" asked Blackshield.

"Of course."

"Sometimes I worry about Polyvox and Andronicus. They have an unusual relationship. I don't think it's romantic, and that does not concern me in any case. However, I'm going to ask you to keep an eye on them, as their friend and comrade. Alert me to any aberrations of behavior."

"Of course. But I'm not quite sure what I'm looking for."

"You will know," replied Blackshield, regarding him with his frosty blue eyes, "when you see it. The skill of face reading is acquired, not instinctive. The Mind Police don't have a monopoly on it. Will you do this for me, Jack?"

"I said I would."

What was wrong with these people? thought Jack. Did they really not trust each other? And, if not, whom could *he* trust?

F9

As the Golden Manacles Ballroom was surrounded by one-way indestructible glass, the hundred guests were able to see into a honeycomb of barred cells, where masked prisoners in orange jumpsuits lay on their bunks, apparently sedated. There was a single ring-shaped table for all the guests, with name cards at each place setting. Inmate-porters ascended and descended on two elevators in the middle of the ring, approaching guests to fill their wine glasses. Polyvox found herself seated between Senator Lance Boyler of Pennsylvania and Senator Buck Crumbal of Kentucky. Andronicus sat across from her, between two empty seats.

After the guests had been seated, the lights dimmed and a mood of nervous expectation settled over them. Presently, the host and hostess were announced, and the whispering abruptly stopped. Mr. Gregory Randolph Reid and his Esteemed Consort Stephany Miscellany descended into the ballroom on an escalator, flooded with golden light. Gregory Reid was tall and athletic, with curly dark brown hair and blue-gray eyes. He wore a black dinner suit with green grosgrain facing on its lapels, and decorated with barely perceptible lines of green percentage signs. His consort was as tall as he was, with short silver hair, prismatic eyes, aristocratic features that seemed at once ancient and young, and a lovely evening gown that repeated—and complemented—the percentage sign motif of Reid's dinner jacket. Around her neck was a choker necklace scintillating with diamonds as big as hazelnuts.

The anticipation of seeing the reclusive financial supermogul Reid, CEO and President of Grombex Corporation, had created a tension among the guests similar to that felt by roller-coaster riders as they slowly clank to the apex of the rails. Few of them had actually met this God of Money, but all of them had, at one time or another, felt his family's unmistakable presence permeating every aspect of their wealthy, privileged lives—including their choice of toilet paper. The effect of his arrival upon them was more powerful than the ecstasy that swept up religious seekers beholding the bones of a saint at the end of a long and grueling pilgrimage. For Reid was wealth incarnate. Among the men and women sitting around the table, Reid was an avatar, and they were merely jeweled scarabs crafted by nature to reflect, and possibly humbly participate in, his emanations of celestial glory.

And yet this initial response was only fleeting, overcome by something else. It was the sight of his mysterious consort, about whom there had been, in the social circles of the global elite, a growing buzz sufficient to cause apprehension, anxiety, and even a constant low-grade vibration in their bones, that pitched the superrich guests into a serene frenzy of astonishment. It was not just her imperial demeanor, or her divine bodily architecture, or her dazzling cast of facial features that were both alien and human, or her apparent agelessness (which must, they reasoned, be thanks to exquisite new gene therapies that reversed chronological damage to telomeres)—no, there was something else about this woman that convinced the guests sitting around the table that some fissure had opened up in the force field of probability, finally admitting the thing they had all yearned for, which was eternal life in the flesh.

She was a sign to them that, at long last, salvation might be at hand.

Gazes like laser beams followed the sacred pair as they gracefully descended the escalator and took their seats at the table, on either side of Andronicus. He did not feel the devotion of the others, but he did feel uncomfortable that the guests were staring at him enviously, since he had somehow achieved a place of honor between these two gods. He looked across the table at Polyvox.

As usual, he could read nothing at all in her expression.

79

The spell that had overcome the guests was broken when the porters brought out the first course: plates of giant lobster. At once the guests turned their attention away from Gregory Reid and Stephany Miscellany and started cracking open red exoskeletons to gouge out the succulent meat within. The Golden Manacles Ballroom was filled with the sounds of snorting, thumb-sucking, gnawing, masticating, and slobbering.

"My dear Mrs. Borden-Park, you're not eating your lobster?" inquired Senator Boyler, his lips shiny with butter and salty ocean juices.

"I'm a vegetarian, Your Senatorship."

She noticed he had finished his own generous portion and was eyeing hers.

"You may eat my lobster, Your Senatorship."

Boyler was about to seize it from her plate when the man on the other side of her said in a southern drawl, "Allow me to introduce myself, Mrs. Borden-Park. I am Senator Buck Crumbal of Kentucky. And I sure do love me some lobster."

"Please, both of you, help yourselves."

All four senatorial hands reached down and ripped the lobster to shreds. While the two men engorged themselves, Polyvox looked directly across the table and made eye contact with her mother. Neither woman modulated her expression in any way, neither showed any emotion, but subtle quanta of information and feeling were nevertheless exchanged between them. Her mother looked away.

Crumbal stifled a belch, reducing it to a decorous rumble. Boyler belched loudly and enthusiastically. One team of inmate-porters cleared away the plates of flensed lobster shells while another deposited the second course: pork loin. The Senators set upon their portions with stabbing fork and sawing knife.

"And what brings you to this Charity Gala, my lady?" inquired Buck Crumbal as he carefully wiped pork juice from his lips.

"Mrs. Borden-Park is the wife of Robert Park, Crumbal," answered Boyler, pouring a full glass of wine into his gullet. "They are the founders of InquiZZ Interrogation Services."

"Indeed? How charming! And what sorts of interrogations do you perform, Mrs. Borden-Park?"

"You name it, and we do it. Would either of you like my pork loin?"

They seized it like lions at the kill and tore it in half.

Buck Crumbal snapped his fingers in the face of one of the inmate-porters. "You there—boy!" he said.

The inmate-porter froze.

"Now this young lady here, this young and lovely woman, requires something other than the flesh of mammals and crustaceans, for she is a vegetarian. Boy, I do swear upon my honor as a gentleman that if you do not bring her some vegetable-based dish straightaway, and continue to supply her with such for the duration of this repast, then I will personally see to it that you are subjected to the most heartless and savage punishments. Do you understand me, boy?"

The inmate-porter nodded mutely and hurried off.

"Thank you," said Polyvox coldly.

"It is a fundamental principle of American political organization," said Crumbal emphatically, "that only fear and authority will keep the masses subservient. Spare the rod, spoil the child. Spare the lash, spoil the citizenry. I fear that this country is losing control of its own destiny."

"No thanks to you," said Boyler, jamming his fork into a chunk of pork and stuffing it into his mouth.

"And perhaps," replied Crumbal icily, "the distinguished Lord Senator of Pennsylvania would care to explain himself?"

"I don't have to remind you, Crumbal, that it was you who sponsored the Political Party Freedom Act so many years ago, when we were both freshman senators. I was opposed to it then, and I remain opposed to it now. It was folly. By outlawing all political parties except the official two, we merely drove dissent underground. Now the whole country is plagued by these so-called factions."

"Senator Boyler, if this young lady were not between us, I would challenge you to a duel."

"Go ahead. I could kick your ass anytime, Crumbal. Just like my forefathers kicked the asses of your forefathers at the Burgs."

"The Burgs? Whatever do you mean?"

"Gettysburg, Vicksburg, and Petersburg."

Crumbal shook his head and clutched his knife in a white-knuckled grip. "Senator, you are a most vulgar Yankee. But perhaps that is to be expected, seeing as how your family achieved its station—if one can even call it that—by processing human *excrement*."

If Boyler was offended by this, he did not show it. He merely snorted. "Someday sewage treatment plants will come to your region of the country, Crumbal, and you can stop using the live oak and the outhouse."

"I warn you, Senator, one more crack like that and it will be pistols or swords."

Boyler did not respond but finished off his pork loin, while Polyvox leaned slightly back in her chair just in case knives were thrown.

"In any case," continued Crumbal hotly, "the Political Party Freedom Act saved this country at its moment of crisis."

"Then explain why the United States of America is now infested by all these factions, Crumbal. All of them simmering just beneath the surface. At least with legal political parties you can see where the enemy is, and what he is doing. You have never understood that the purpose of Democracy is not to give power to the people, it is to encourage the people to speak openly, so that the financial and political arms of the State may listen in and act accordingly. You subverted that system, and now we have teeming factions."

"Absolute balderdash! These factions are *nothing*. The problem, sir, is leadership, of which both the House and the Senate are sorely wanting these days. What this country needs now is Leadership, War, and Pornography."

"I agree that we need more War and Pornography, but these are merely the maidservants of Corporate Capitalism. Can a planter like you even understand that, Crumbal? You live in the past, striving to reintroduce a bygone Jeffersonian era of plantations and slaves. It is simply not enough to reduce the masses to agricultural or industrial slavery. They must be transformed into Consumer Serfs. The purpose of Corporate Capitalism is twofold: first, to maintain social organization through the evolution of the People into productive consumers whose lives and deaths can, in turn, be translated into Profit on the open market. Second, to maintain the upward flow of Profit to the ruling elites, so they can usher the human biome into an exalted future."

"I disagree with you, sir. The American People must be slaves."

"They must be serfs."

"Slaves, I say!"

"Serfs, you damn Rebel."

"Slaves!"

"Serfs!"

"Please, Your Senatorships," said Polyvox, placing a hand on each of their wrists. "Both of you make reasonable points, and both of you have at heart the continued glory of our country. Whether the American People, and the people of the world, should be repurposed into factions, political parties, serfs, or slaves, we are all in this together in trying to keep the masses in their place. Let us appeal to the better angels of our nature and not argue these points so strenuously that we become divided, for otherwise the flocks of sheep over whom we rule will turn into packs of wolves."

"Most eloquently stated, my lady," replied Crumbal, deeply impressed. "I apologize for my flare of temper, though of course when a gentleman's honor is repeatedly impugned by a scalawag or a lowborn carpetbagger, he has but little recourse other than to defend it as resolutely and unflinchingly as a young man of character responding to vile slanders against the integrity of his virgin bride's unblemished hymen. I offer you my sincere apologies, my lady. Senator Boyler, I urge you to do the same."

Boyler grunted a wordless affirmative and picked pork from his teeth.

An inmate-porter arrived and placed a colorful vegetable dish in front of Polyvox, just as the third course was being delivered to the other guests: juicy chunks of ostrich and generous portions of plump red caviar.

Polyvox ate her vegetables unenthusiastically and looked across the table. Andronicus and Reid were talking—and staring at her.

What could they be saying? she wondered. Could their conversation be any more repulsive than the one she was trapped in? She strained to hear, but couldn't make out a word over the noise at the table.

F9

"So, Mr. Park," said Gregory Reid, "Inyards tells me that you and your wife are torture experts."

"We do run a private little interrogation concern, Mr. Reid," said Andronicus modestly.

"Is that your wife there, across the table?"

"It is."

"She's quite a lovely specimen of womanhood."

"Thank you, sir."

"What is her ethnic ancestry, if you don't mind my asking? I cannot place her."

The physical similarity between Polyvox and her mother was not immediately obvious. Both were very tall and elegantly strong in appearance, but Polyvox's black hair and gray eyes contrasted sharply with her mother's shimmery silver hair and polychromatic eyes. Still, Andronicus had foolishly failed to anticipate the possibility that an alert observer might suspect their kinship. The less he said about his wife's origins, the better.

"I believe, sir, she is something of a global creole—a little of everything, if you will."

"She presents an astonishing new class of physical beauty. Unfortunately, she somehow ended up between the human turd Boyler and that gaseous senator from Kentucky, Crumbal. I'll have to have a word with Inyards. I am inclined to sign a *lettre de cachet* sending his social director into indefinite confinement with complete suspension of his right of *habeas corpus.*"

"There is no need for that, Mr. Reid," replied Andronicus. "My wife is never more in her element than when she is dealing with unsavory or unpalatable individuals. The two senators will do nicely."

"I don't suppose," said Reid, laughing, "that you have any videos of her torturing people?"

Andronicus paused only an instant before responding, "I'll look into that for you, Mr. Reid. We may have something in the archives."

Reid's eyes warmed with gratitude. "So tell me about the latest interrogation trends, Mr. Park."

"The fundamental nature of torture has changed little over the millennia, Mr. Reid. It is basically about degradation and humiliation, the violent and total invasion of the most intimate parts of a person's being—the rape of the soul, if you will. The prying away of personal autonomy."

"Ah," said Reid, rubbing his hands excitedly, "do continue. Describe the pain!"

"The thing is, Mr. Reid, interrogation does not necessarily require physical violence against the subject. In fact, the most effective forms of interrogation operate exclusively on the level of the psyche. It is possible to torture someone without so much as scratching their skin."

"Not even using electricity?"

"Unnecessary."

"Nevertheless, you still hear some old-timers criticizing torture as somehow violating 'human rights,' whatever that means."

"That may be true, Mr. Reid. At InquiZZ Interrogations, however, we have developed a method of interrogation that, from a legal and philosophical point of view, does not violate human rights. We call it Progressive Torture. It is a form of interrogative torture that safeguards the fundamental rights of the human being. Any government or corporation can employ this method of torture without fear of any negative legal repercussions."

"You interest me strangely. Go on."

"Progressive Torture involves the use of a special 'tonic' of psychoactive drugs that cooperate with, rather than overcome, the elements of the subject's psyche that are resisting cooperation or modification."

"This strikes me as implausible."

"I assure you, Mr. Reid, it is not. A simple application of the methods of Progressive Torture can turn the most violent dissident into a subservient vassal of the State without so much as poking his or her fundamental human rights."

"But where is the fun in that?"

"It's not about fun, Mr. Reid. It's about control. Once you have established control, you can have all the fun you want."

"I suppose you're right, though I confess a fondness for the old days, when the rack was the rack and thumbscrews were thumbscrews, and the shrieks of the wicked rose to my throne like the hymns of the faithful."

"Rose to your throne, Mr. Reid?"

"I meant to the Throne of God," said Reid. "My good friend, what's in this 'tonic'?"

"With all due respect, Mr. Reid, that is a patented trade secret. My wife, a psychiatrist, spent many years devising the formula."

"Ah…." For an instant, a pale lumen of malevolent light flashed in Reid's blue-gray eyes. "I understand, of course. Would you at least be able to demonstrate this new torture process in a private screening?"

"Of course, though my wife is the technical expert. I handle the business end of InquiZZ."

"I insist that you and the lovely Doctor Borden visit me tomorrow for luncheon at our private quarters here in Freedom Fortress. I can requisition a victim for you from the most recent transport. I'll speak to Inyards tonight. I think a political prisoner would be best, so you can crack open his psyche with your tonic and pluck out all the juicy, treasonous thoughts."

"Mr. Reid, you are too kind. But, if you don't mind, I would like to suggest another victim."

"Indeed, who?" Reid's eyes smoldered with the wariness of a demon who perceives he's being tricked.

Andronicus paused, his mind working furiously. Reid was clearly mad, but also cunning and suspicious. Without being too obvious, Andronicus had to get Reid's permission to bring Blackshield and Jack along, so the whole team would be together when it came time to escape Freedom Fortress after the assassination.

"My wife's indentured manservant. He has been showing signs of dissent lately, and for some time now we've had it in mind to re-conform him."

"Ah, but Mr. Park, how will I be able to test the legitimacy of the results? You could have coached him, after all. No, tomorrow, I will invite you and your charming wife to my place for a nice lunch and a demonstration of Progressive Torture. I hereby spare your manservant, as Jehovah spared Isaac. I will provide the ram for the sacrifice."

"In that case, may we bring both of our servants along—our valet and my wife's indentured manservant? They are both quite useful assistants."

"By all means bring your Jeeves and your Igor along. We'll toss them some scraps from the table." Reid called to his consort, who had been sitting back in silence, disdaining participation in any conversations. "Beloved, here is Mr. Robert Park, cofounder with his wife Doctor Lizzie Borden of InquiZZ Interrogation Services. Tomorrow he and his wife will give us a demonstration."

Stephany Miscellany extended her hand, which Andronicus took. She held it firmly. "Interrogation Services."

"Yes…my lady."

"And where is your wife?" she asked.

"Directly across the table, between the two Senators."

Andronicus noted her burnished silver hair and the faint lines around her eyes. Her features were more angular than her daughter's, and her teeth appeared sharper—especially the canines. Her eyes, despite their vivid prismatic coloration, had that same cold detachment. It was at that moment that Andronicus realized he had never seen Polyvox cry, or even come close to crying, in all the years they had been revolutionaries together. And now, looking at her mother, he began to wonder if her family was even capable of it.

Miscellany still gripped his hand tightly. "You are married to that woman across the table?" she asked.

"Yes, I am…"

"You share a bed with her—and you torture people."

She let go of Andronicus's hand.

"Tomorrow we will have a wonderful demonstration of that torture, my love," said Reid. "I hope you *enjoy* it."

CHAPTER EIGHTEEN

How Plutocrats Play

There were four more courses, followed by dessert, dessert wines, cigars, cigarettes, and cocaine. Miscellany did not say another word to Andronicus, while Reid went on and on about a personal theory concerning the DNA of ghosts. Across the table, Polyvox continued to endure the insufferable attempts at charm by the two political vampires sitting on either side of her—the tooth-picking Yankee and the unctuous Rebel.

For both Andronicus and Polyvox, the Children First Charity Gala was becoming an interminable horror. When would it end? How long could the superrich sit around a table, glutting themselves on food, booze, and drugs, and chattering insipidly about nothing at all?

Finally Reid stood up, ringing his spoon against a glass. The table fell silent.

"A toast," he said, raising his wineglass. "To the children."

"To the children!" echoed the guests.

Reid nodded to Inyards across the table, and the man's big hobgoblin head bobbled excitedly. He stood up and said, "Friends, guests, allies of children everywhere, I invite you to the casino for games of chance. All proceeds go to the children."

"The children," murmured the guests.

F9

The doors to the casino opened and the guests, abandoning the wreckage of their feast, flooded through like a beast with one heart and one mind. The red-white-and-blue-themed casino was gaudy, glaring, and harsh—a direct transplant from the arid waste of Old Nevada to the treeless moonscapes of West Virginia. The guests tried their luck at poker, blackjack, baccarat, roulette, fortune wheels, slot machines. Booze spilled from bottles and into glasses, and periodically there were shouts of "For the children!" As the night progressed, groups broke into the national anthem, with those who were not too drunk standing up, placing their hands over their hearts, or raising their arms in wobbly Roman salutes.

Andronicus found himself at a table with Inyards, Reid, Crumbal, and Boyler, playing Texas Hold 'Em. He drank slowly while they grew raging drunk. Soon he had a great pile of chips in front of him. From this vantage point, he was able to observe his adversaries, these aristocrats of the United States, transform in front of him. Reid's eyes became so deeply bloodshot he resembled a victim of a zombie apocalypse. He periodically slapped the bald head of Boyler, who angrily and impudently referred to him as "dog vomit." Crumbal chattered on garrulously until his words grew incoherent, a kind of foam slurry oozing from the corners of his mouth—at which point he withdrew an antique derringer from his pocket and pointed it in sequence at each of his tablemates in their turn. Inyards' hobgoblin head seemed to expand, like a parade balloon, to twice its size. He was determined to win, but became so thoroughly intoxicated that he began stuffing his chips into his mouth.

They engaged in no political discussions, said nothing about the economy, world affairs, or the state of the Union. They, like all the other guests, simply devolved, and Andronicus observed to himself— not for the first time during his vocation as a revolutionary—that they were not human at all, these politicians and Wall Street moguls, these corporationists, investors, and money-deviants. Not only were they not human, but they also could never be negotiated with, or reformed in any meaningful sense of the word.

They could only be *extirpated.*

Andronicus had not always thought this way.

There had been a time, years before, when he still believed that the American system could be changed from within. And perhaps a small, weak part of him still opposed violent overthrow or insurrection of any kind. But like Luther, like Washington, like Constantine, like his own ancestor Yi Sun-Sin, he had long since crossed a threshold of no return. Sitting back from the table, he shoved his chips at the others, who in their stupor fought with each other to scrabble up as many as they could and hide them in their pockets.

Andronicus rose from the table, turning his back to the bickering drunkards, and made his way through the crowd of diseased flesh. Drunken women flashed him blood-red smiles; drunken men threatened him with scowls.

In small salons adjacent to the casinos, people were having sex in groups of three and four.

He approached Polyvox, nursing a drink as she observed the spectacle silently.

"If I were a suicide bomber," he said to her, "I could end it all now."

"If you commit suicide, you are no better than these animals. We are revolutionaries, not terrorist dogs."

"Have you spoken with your mother?"

"Not verbally."

"Then go over to her. What are you waiting for? For God's sake, Polyvox, we are in the heart of Balthazar's orgy. We may never have this opportunity again. In the name of humanity, go try to decode the writing on the wall."

F9

Polyvox drifted towards her mother, who had been standing behind Reid, watching him and the other boys play cards. There was no need for discretion, since by now the guests were in a state of blind debauchery. She and her mother approached each other cautiously, but they did not touch. They inclined their heads towards each other and sniffed gently.

"Mother," said Polyvox.

"I confess to being surprised to encounter you here among the filthy Apes."

"How were you captured by Reid?"

"That's a long story. How did *you* end up here?"

"We came to rescue you."

Miscellany smiled sadly. "Indeed."

"Many of us survived the cataclysm, Mother. You have no idea. We have formed a sisterhood, and we are plotting our return. We can rebuild our civilization. When did you awaken?"

"A long time ago."

The debauchery of the Apes continued around them, but now Polyvox and her mother perceived it all as a chaos of flashing color, grating noise, and alien aromas—the mad music of a species that lived feverishly and died quickly.

"And now you are with Reid, the Alpha Ape of this degenerate age. And you share a bed with him. How our people have fallen. A queen the concubine of an Ape."

In her mother's face Polyvox detected aloof amusement, the sudden emotionless detachment that only a monarch can assume. "He is not a man capable of any physical intimacy. Enough chatting. Describe your intentions."

"I will be brief, because our enemies only rarely let their guard down," said Polyvox. "Tomorrow we will arrive for lunch with you and Reid. There we will kill him and take you with us. Then the real revolution will begin."

"How is your sister Monovox? Did she survive?"

Though her mother's face was impassive, Polyvox picked up the subtle scent of anguish. "She's fine, Mother…but let's stick to discussing the rescue plan."

"And your brothers?"

"I haven't seen them since the cataclysm. We can talk about this later. The important thing is for us to kill Reid and get you out of here. Tell me about Reid. How and where can we strike?"

Miscellany closed her eyes slowly and opened them again. "Why must you insist, my daughter, at our first meeting in eons, on talking about the man-thing Reid? I would much rather talk about what you have done during the intervening centuries of our separation."

"I have sojourned through the human world—geographically, culturally, historically. I am now considered the leading expert on this mutated species. Do not dwell on the pain of the past, Mother. There are more urgent issues to be resolved at the moment."

"So you have allied yourself with these Apes?" Miscellany said this very softly, in the language of the Chronasians. But it was sufficient to convey her disdain.

"It's the only way, Mother. They infest the planet like vermin. When the Chronasians rise again, we will bring peace and order to the Apes. We will sequester them in gardens and allow them to peacefully revert to their previous state. Now they are like wild animals that have spawned out of control. In our absence, evolution has endowed them with intelligence, but no other virtues. Imagine giving a scorpion self-awareness and technological intelligence. That is the Human Ape."

"You have truly grown in wisdom and knowledge, my daughter. You have begun to construct a vision for the future of Earth, and this pleases me. We will meet again soon and discuss these matters further. You should know that never in my long loneliness did my heart affection cease for my children and my people."

"Nor did mine for you, Mother."

They clasped hands and kissed each other quickly, then parted. Polyvox returned to Andronicus.

"You spoke with her?"

"Yes," she said calmly, her gray eyes luminous. "I have never felt such happiness."

Across the room, Reid commanded silence while he picked up a microphone, called up Miscellany to take his hand, and dedicated to her a heartfelt, red-eyed, sinister rendition of "It's Only a Paper Moon," all the while bathed in a garish red spotlight.

Polyvox watched him sing, take her mother into his arms, and dance with her.

"And I have never," she added, "felt such disgust."

F9

Polyvox and Andronicus left the casino and returned to the Thomas Jefferson Suite. They were both completely enervated, as if the sacred life spirit had been sucked out of them. They immediately undressed, divesting themselves of the wickedness of the evening. Andronicus stripped down to his boxers, casting all of his evening attire into a pile on the floor: shirt, trousers, tailcoat, and hateful top hat. For the first time, Jack noticed a prominent patchwork of scar tissue on his chest and back, either from a burn or from some other traumatic injury. On his right bicep was a faded tattoo of a bald eagle—a symbol that had long since been phased out of public life, replaced by a plethora of dazzling corporate logos. Andronicus's eyes were bloodshot, his hair disheveled. He asked for a drink. Blackshield hesitated, then poured him a dash of Scotch with a larger dose of soda.

"Stronger," said Andronicus.

"That should do for now," said Blackshield.

Andronicus sullenly sipped his drink.

Polyvox had quickly discarded her evening gown and thrown the diamond-studded high heels across the room. "Sadistic implements of torture and suppression," she snarled. She massaged her feet. "Tomorrow, Andronicus, I return to wearing my customary raiment, not these whorish human costumes."

"I prefer you in your customary raiment," he muttered, taking another sip of his Scotch and soda. "But in this place, we all clothe ourselves in the vestments of deception."

Polyvox sat down in a chair by herself, her legs crossed. "Boichik," she said, "please open a bottle of red wine and pour me a glass."

"Please stop calling me Boichik. My name is Jack Tone." Jack had already changed into a pair of striped silk pajamas and had been preparing for bed when Polyvox and Andronicus returned. He selected a bottle from the rack—the first one he saw—and twisted the corkscrew into it. The corkscrew entered at a bad angle, and when he tried to withdraw it, he tore the cork in half. Attempting to extract the lower half, he pushed it into the bottle.

Polyvox sprang like a panther from her seat, loped across the room, and seized the bottle. "I can manage," she snapped, taking a swig directly from the bottle itself.

"What's the matter with you two?" Jack asked softly. "Did Andronicus crack up or something?"

"Andronicus did not 'crack up.' But the party was worse than the tour, and tomorrow's events shall be worse than either." Polyvox held out the bottle.

He shook his head. "I don't drink before retiring."

"Suit yourself." She took another sip.

"Now that you've both settled in, perhaps you can give us an update on what happened," said Blackshield.

Polyvox, calmer now, sat down again and explained everything.

"And so your mother has agreed to come with us?" asked Blackshield.

"Of course," said Polyvox. "Why would she not?"

"She's been with Reid for some years now. Sometimes captives are reluctant to escape their captors."

"I can assure you that my mother is not in any way prone to Stockholm Syndrome, if that's what you mean. Especially when it comes to a man-dog like Reid."

"Excellent," said Blackshield. "Tomorrow I will terminate Reid by jabbing him in the neck with my poison fountain pen. Then the four of you will follow me to the car."

"It's that simple?" asked Andronicus.

"I've memorized the plans for this entire structure. Recall, too, that I was stationed here fifteen years ago, for my military training. Freedom Fortress has only been a for-profit prison for ten years. Before the privatization of the armed forces, it was a training center for elite units."

"I didn't know that."

"One of our tests was to escape. I alone of my class succeeded in the attempt, mainly because I purloined blueprints showing the ventilation system."

"So you cheated," said Andronicus.

"All is fair in love and war."

"Surely there have been structural changes since they repurposed the fortress into a maximum-security private prison and Ploop™ factory," said Polyvox.

"The changes to the ventilation system are inconsequential," Blackshield asserted. "I've noted all of them."

F9

The next day at eleven in the morning, Polyvox again dressed in her high-collared coat and boots. Andronicus put on his black suit with a red tie. Blackshield and Jack dressed in their servant's livery. They waited—sitting, pacing, reading, saying nothing. At noon, the bell of the Jefferson Suite rang.

"Maybe I shouldn't go with you," said Jack.

Polyvox turned. "What do you mean?"

"I…I don't know if I'm ready to meet this man, after all."

"Once we complete our work," said Blackshield, "we will not be coming back this way. If you stay here, you will be left behind in Freedom Fortress. You have no choice but to come with us now."

"There is nothing to worry about," said Polyvox, placing a hand on his shoulder. "This sort of operation is like outpatient surgery, and you are merely an observer in an operating room. The doctors will finish the procedure very quickly, and then all of us will exit the hospital."

Jack quickly strapped on his indentured servant mask as Blackshield, nodding to the others, opened the door.

A proctor in striped pantaloons stepped in.

"My Lord Gregory Randolph Reid summons Mr. and Mrs. Robert Park to his quarters for tea and torture," he announced in a high singsong.

"Excellent," said Andronicus, clapping his hands together. He seemed fully recovered from the night before. "Come along, dear, we mustn't be late for Mr. Reid."

The proctor looked at Jack with concern. "I understand, Mr. Park, if you need to bring your valet, but are you also bringing this indentured beast?"

"This beast is my body servant," said Polyvox, looming over him. "Where my body goes, it goes. Kindly oblige me, serving man."

The proctor made an obsequious bow. "This way, guests."

He escorted them down several winding hallways, past Nean-derthal-browed guards in Freedom Fortress uniforms, and finally to Gregory Reid's spacious suite of rooms at the top of a tower that commanded a spectacular view of the dusty gray West Virginia wasteland.

Reid himself opened the door. He seemed in a very good humor and showed no signs of a hangover. His eyes, which the previous night had been red balls of fire, were again as limpid as a mountain stream. And yet he appeared to move with a slightly awkward gait, like a marionette under the control of a slightly tipsy puppeteer.

Unlike the others, Jack did not take much notice of his vaguely wobbly gait. Here was Reid, the man ultimately responsible for the murder of his parents, a foul scion of the American Corruptocracy. And yet Jack felt no rage. Rather, he examined the man scrupulously through the eye slits of his indentured servant mask. Reid was tall, only slightly shorter than Andronicus or Polyvox. His dark brown hair was trimmed very short around the sides, in a style reminiscent of the SS. His nose was aquiline, his chin sharp, his cheekbones angular. His eyes were blue—not the deep, metallic blue of Black-shield, but the pale blue of a hazy sky. His skin was decidedly pallid, like a vampire's.

"Welcome, friends, welcome! Come in, come in, and have tea! Your manservants can plant their rumps over there on those stools in the corner. Their services won't be much needed here."

Stephany Miscellany came forward and smiled. "I'm so happy you two could make it for luncheon. Please, have a seat. Help yourselves to cucumber sandwiches."

They arranged themselves around a table, while Reid made a dainty show of pouring tea. Suddenly, a cuckoo clock sound began to emanate from his pocket. He removed a small shield with the Reid coat of arms on it—apparently his phone.

"Excuse me," he said, standing up. "I have to take this call." He went into another room.

Polyvox and Andronicus looked directly at Stephany Miscellany. Blackshield rose from his stool and came forward. Jack remained seated. He was perspiring profusely beneath his livery, and his hands were shaking, as if he had consumed way too much caffeine.

"Mother," Polyvox whispered. "We must act now. Are there any security personnel in that room where Reid just went?"

Stephany, as if unconcerned, answered in her normal voice. "There is a fellow who is about eight feet tall—kind of a cross between a bogeyman, a demon, and a leper."

"You mean a Plutocroid?"

"Oh, so you know about them?"

"Mother, my associates and I will now go into that room. We will kill Reid and the Plutocroid. Then we will escort you through the ventilation system to our car and get out of here."

"You always were impetuous and undisciplined, Polyvox, and the passage of time hasn't changed you in the slightest."

"Mother"—her voice more urgent now—"we haven't got time for these discussions."

"I've given the matter some thought, Polyvox, and I realize I cannot go with you. There will be no assassinations today. I command you to stand down."

"*What? Why?*" Polyvox's lips drew back from her teeth slightly as she suddenly displayed more emotion than Andronicus or Blackshield had ever seen. "Are you kidding me? Do you have any idea what we've sacrificed to get here? Have you any clue how treacherous and booby-trapped was the path that brought us here to this tea table with you, to these cucumber sandwiches? Do you, Mother?"

"Your sister would have reacted with more restraint to any unexpected reversal of her plans."

"*Urgghh…*" groaned Polyvox, slamming her fist on the tea table with such force that the teacups jumped in their saucers and shook. "It's been *ten million years* and you are still comparing me to Monovox? Does nothing ever change? Are all of us in this cursed universe condemned to repeat the same cycles of frustration and fruitlessness over and over again, without pause, without end, without hope of deliverance from the ever-turning Catherine wheel of suffering?"

"Such melodrama. Your sister—"

"Enough about my sister," growled Polyvox. "You always loved her more than me."

"Absurd. It is precisely this sort of talk that prevented me from having a rational conversation with you."

"I am Esau, and she is Jacob," groaned Polyvox. "I knew it. It might have taken eons, but the truth is mine at last."

"I'm losing my patience with you, Polyvox."

By now Polyvox was actually shaking. Andronicus, alarmed by this unexpected turn of events, looked towards the door to the other room to make sure Reid was not returning. He placed a hand on Polyvox's shoulder, but she shook it off.

"Why will you not let us go ahead with our rescue plan?" she demanded.

"The situation is more delicate than you might think, Polyvox. The primate Reid holds his own niece and nephew captive. If I manage to escape with you, he will return in a rage to New York

City and dissect them. And I mean literally dissect them. Reid is a sadistic cannibal."

"Mother," said Polyvox, looking into her eyes, "you can't be serious."

"I'm afraid I am."

"And how are you obliged to protect these children?"

"Through obligations of time, space, and chance."

"But Mother," Polyvox said, finally lowering her voice again, "part of the plan is to kill Reid right now. He will not be going home. Those children will not be in any danger."

"You can't kill Reid, Polyvox."

"Yes we can. Blackshield has a poison pen. A brisk stab in the neck, and Reid drops away into oblivion. Andronicus and I will take care of the Plutocroid."

"You can't kill Reid, because he's not here."

"What do you mean? He just went through that door."

"That's his body double, a superficial clone—a zombie-like subspecies of Plutocroid connected to Reid by means of a direct psyconic link."

Despite herself, Polyvox laughed out loud.

"I'm deadly serious," said her mother. "Reid is now upstairs in a chair, wearing a neural headset, recovering from last night's boozy debauch and manipulating his body double."

"We will take you with us, then. Forget about Reid."

"I will not go with you. Do you think I'm here by chance? I, too, have a plan, Polyvox, and you are disrupting it."

Polyvox leaned forward and whispered softly in her mother's ear. "This is why our civilization failed. Because you made poor decisions as a queen. When we finally do restore the civilization of the Chronasians, I will work tirelessly to abolish the monarchy and create a purely democratic system of government."

Miscellany whispered back, "You know nothing of affairs of state, my daughter. You are just a child. You need only look around you to see what has been wrought by democracy among the Apes. And yet you wish to introduce it to the Chronasians. *Pshaw.*"

Mother and daughter sat sipping their tea. Jack, from his seat, could not hear most of this conversation between mother and daughter, but he knew that something was wrong. He felt light-headed with anxiety.

Blackshield, twirling his fountain pen uncertainly, shot a frantic glance at Andronicus.

"Polyvox, we must act now," said Andronicus.

Polyvox signaled for Andronicus, Blackshield, and Jack to step closer. "We've been tricked," she said to them quietly. "The man who greeted us is not Reid, but a clone. Mother, what should we do?"

"Are you armed, other than with a poison pen?" asked Miscellany.

"Blackshield and Andronicus have guns. I have my baton."

"And the servant in the mask?"

"Merely an observer."

"This is what you must do. When Reid comes back in, follow him into the torture demonstration room."

"Very well—and then…?"

"Once there, shoot the body double in the head. He has no personal consciousness—he's just a body, an animated corpse. Do you understand?"

"Yes."

"Then kill or disable the prison officials, including Inyards, who will be sitting facing the torture chair as official observers. Do not flinch from this. They are fascistic thugs who have inflicted terrible pain on innocent people."

"Kill or disable Inyards and the prison officials. Got it."

"Make sure to also disable or kill Mr. Ichabod, the Type I Pluto-croid who will come at you like a werewolf and attempt to rip your larynxes out."

"We understand."

"Free the child, and flee with her."

"Child—what child?"

Miscellany raised a silver eyebrow. "Understand that I cannot assist you in any way, or they will suspect I am in league with you. Do what you have to do, my daughter, and do not fail me."

"I don't understand—clarify why a child is there."

The doors opened and pseudo Reid strode in. He appeared distracted. "Sorry about that. Look, I'd like to get this demonstration underway. Through these doors, please. The victim is waiting."

CHAPTER NINETEEN

The Scum of the Earth, with Glitter

They had no choice but to obey him. The door took them into a stainless steel chamber. Inyards and four other prison officials in uniforms and jackboots sat facing a six-year-old girl who had been strapped to a chair.

Jack, following the others, entered the interrogation room, and saw Gregory Reid's doppelganger smiling, gesturing to the child in the chair. "The subject is the daughter of condemned political dissidents who violated the Defense of Freedom of Expression Act by publishing unauthorized tracts criticizing the United States Chamber of Commerce," explained pseudo Reid. "She has been asked to memorize five alpha-numeric codes. She has had trouble memorizing them, but they must be in there somewhere. So please use Compassionate Interrogation to extract the information without violating her fundamental human rights."

Pseudo Reid took his seat, still smiling.

Andronicus looked down at the little girl, whose eyes were wide and terrified, but oddly tearless. He turned to pseudo Reid with an expression of disbelief. "You are asking me to interrogate a child?"

Pseudo Reid shrugged. "Compassionately. In accordance with our sacred American tradition of human rights for all."

"We must not be hasty," said Polyvox to him softly in Korean. "I have a logical plan—"

Andronicus drew his pistol and shot the body double. Because of his rage, his aim was off: the bullet hit just above the right eye. The body double dropped, its arms and legs wagging spasmodically. Thick white fluid sprayed from the bullet hole.

Somewhere in another chamber, the real Gregory Reid threw his hands to his skull and shrieked, tearing off his neural headset and vomiting all over the psychonic console that he had been using to manipulate his double.

Inyards squealed and dove for cover. The four uniformed prison officials sprang to their feet, drawing their sidearms. Before they could pull the triggers, Blackshield, crouching cowboy style, shot them all. They went flying back in a bloody tangled tumble, knocking over their chairs, their jackboots kicking out an inverted death throe jig in the air.

Jack stood there uselessly, his shoulders slumped, watching everything transpire as if it were a security drama on the telescreen. His mask suddenly felt suffocating, but he dared not take it off.

Polyvox was struggling with the metal clasps that held the girl in the interrogation chair. "I require a key," she said. She looked over at Inyards, who was trying to crawl away. "Seize him!"

Menacingly, Andronicus and Blackshield approached him.

"Here it is," whined Inyards, tossing a metal key on a ring. It skittered across the floor, stopping a few feet from Polyvox. "Don't hurt me!"

Miscellany said quietly, "The Plutocroid comes."

A door opened, and a tall figure in a long black coat and broad-brimmed hat began loping towards them, his face a ferocious scowl.

In Jack's limited experience, Plutocroids all looked the same, but there was something oddly, eerily familiar about this one. Polyvox waited until the Plutocroid was a few paces away, and then expanded her baton, striking him on the chest. A powerful electrical shock knocked him down, but Mr. Ichabod jumped up again and came at her, pouncing on top of her. She again tried to strike him with the baton, but he had grabbed it. Baring long yellow teeth and barking like a rabid dog, he tried to gnash her face. Polyvox drew up her legs and delivered a double kick that sent him flying off of her and onto the floor.

Mr. Ichabod flipped himself over and ran towards them again—this time on all fours. Blackshield stood his ground and fired seven rounds into the Plutocroid, who wavered, then came forward again. While Polyvox grabbed the key from the ground and unlocked the girl's bonds, Andronicus joined Blackshield in shooting at the Plutocroid.

Still it kept coming.

They discarded their empty primary pistols and drew their smaller backups. The Plutocroid was starting to slow, but still lurched forward. And then he rallied his energy for one last charge.

Freeing the girl from the chair, Polyvox flung her baton to Blackshield, who caught it, spun it around, and rammed it directly into the Plutocroid's chest.

There was a deafening electrical *crack-bang*. Mr. Ichabod staggered back, his chest smoking and sizzling. He spun around in a complete circle, his feet doing a weird soft shuffle on the floor, his mouth working up and down spastically. "*Daisy, Daisy...*" he sang, his voice slurring, "*give me your answer, do...*"

He collapsed in a heap, making a clank like a bag of steel balls.

Inyards gave a creaky squeal, and continued crawling away. Andronicus lifted his pistol, pointing it at him.

"Please, good sir," snuffled Inyards pathetically, his hobgoblin head now looking more like that of a plastic garden gnome, "show mercy to an old, innocent man..."

Andronicus's gun made a cold click. He reached into his coat pocket for another round.

"Forget that," said Blackshield. "There's no time. We must escape. Soon this place will be swarming like a hornet's hive."

All of this had taken place so quickly that Jack could barely process everything he was seeing: the fighting, the gunshots, the little girl in the torture chair, the gnomish man with the monstrous head, the disturbingly familiar-looking Plutocroid, the slaughtered prison officials in their jackboots, now lying on top of each other like a pile of leather and chopped wood—the blood and slime and twitching death.

And now the other three members of the Faction Nine political discussion group were sprinting at him. Andronicus grabbed his arm as he passed. "Run!"

Miscellany watched as the assassins fled back into the tea room. She looked around her: the three jackbooted prison officials lay in their bloody death jumble. Inyards continued crawling towards the wall, mewling and snotting like an infant.

Now was the chance she had patiently waited for.

She walked over to where Mr. Ichabod lay in a heap on the floor. From his pocket she removed the remote control, then replaced it with a dummy. A few moments later, Reid appeared in mono-grammed silk pajamas, bathrobe, and green slippers, his hair mussed, vomit spattered all over his shirt, his face blotchy and eyelids caked with dry pus. "Oh, my beloved, you are alive!" He rushed forward and embraced Miscellany.

"The interlopers, where did they go?" he asked.

"I'm so confused, my love," she replied, holding his vile, stinking body close to hers. "It's all been so terrifying."

"My love," he muttered, his breath foul. "My helpmeet. My handmaid—I shall buy you a red cloak."

Miscellany clung to him. She had to swap out his remote control quickly, as she had with Ichabod. She slipped her hand into the pocket of his robe and grabbed the remote.

"Where did the bastards go?" cried Reid, shoving her away before she could replace it with the dummy. "They must not escape. Don't you see? It's all part of a conspiracy to destroy not just us, but the American Dream. I must find them."

Miscellany threw her arms around him in a tight bear hug. "Don't leave me, dear heart. I want to make love with you right now."

"Stop hugging me, woman! Enough affection—let me go."

Miscellany dropped the dummy remote into his robe pocket and removed her hand just as he shoved his own hand in and seized it. He jabbed it into her side. "Let go of me!"

Miscellany released him. "I think they went through that door." She pointed to the opposite door, through which Mr. Ichabod had come. "But how can I be sure? Why won't you hold me, Gregory? Hold me tight, and never let me go."

He waved the dummy remote at her dismissively and looked down at the floor, where Inyards was still crawling. "Fool, have you sounded the alarm?"

Inyards gaped up mutely.

"Useless wretch," cried Reid, kicking him in the gut. "What kind of half-assed prison are you running here, you goon-headed pederast? God damn your balls, your bones, your blood! God damn your intestines, your kidneys, and your prostate gland!"

Inyards threw up his arms, vainly trying to fend off Reid's infuriated barrage of slipper-kicks.

Mr. Ichabod sat up. Copious amounts of green fluid burst from his mouth. He wheezed, he spat; green strings of gore dribbled from his chin. Reid ran over to him and grabbed his arm. "Mr. Ichabod, my dear and only friend, what have those savages done to you?"

The Plutocroid stood up. "I will sound the alarm, my lord," he intoned hoarsely. Shambling to the wall, he punched the alarm button, and then leaned there, producing cacophonous chords like a wet accordion and drooling still more slime.

F9

Blackshield led them crawling through the ventilation tunnel system. Behind him, Polyvox was clutching the girl beneath her, who remained quiet. After her came Jack, then Andronicus. The air vent system, designed to thwart just such escapes, was an insane and illogical maze. In places the tunnel divided, and Blackshield had to pause and consult the blueprints in his brain. A part of his mind raced like electrical impulses along a circuit board; another, more primal, part drew inspiration from ancestors who, long ago, had fled an equally vicious enemy through the bowels of a human city.

It was curious how human history repeated itself, over and over again—an endless, diabolical loop.

"Is there a problem?" asked Polyvox, when Blackshield had halted yet again before another set of air vents.

"Some are dummy passages…be quiet and let me think…"

They could hear shrieking sirens and the shouts of prison guards. Blackshield made a decision and crawled to the right. Glancing through a vent, they saw a contingent of storm troopers wearing the uniform of the Warforce FBI. Through another, they saw a large machine barfing out a river of gray, unrefined Ploop™, to which no artificial flavorings or sweeteners had yet been added. The stench made them gag. The air vent passage inclined down, then rose again. Blackshield moved more quickly, and they could taste a change in the texture of the air.

They finally emerged from a grated air vent and climbed down the courtyard where the cars were parked. Polyvox activated the *Argo* as they were running towards it. The doors opened just as bullets began to fall like hail on the flagstones, shooting bright red sparks.

Like Lot's wife, Jack was suddenly overcome with a desire to look back. As they reached the *Argo*, he turned. Above him loomed Freedom Fortress—a towering demonic castle with battlements and numerous American flags. They did not appear red, white, and blue, but black and white. Behind the towers, black factory smoke billowed. Gunners fired down at them from sniper perches and machine gun nests.

Jack felt something like a punch on his shoulder, and before he knew it, he was sprawled on the flagstones.

He had been shot.

Andronicus turned, bent down and clutched him, and dragged him along. Polyvox passed the girl off to Blackshield, and they jumped into the car.

"Quick, put on your harnesses," said Polyvox. "Blackshield, secure the child."

Jack was in the back with Blackshield, the girl between them. He clasped his hand to his shoulder as the blood oozed through his fingers. He felt sick to his stomach. The little girl's strange calm only seemed to make things worse, as if she were an avatar of death.

They buckled themselves in as bullets raked against the fuselage of the *Argo*. Polyvox put on Satie's *Gymnopédies* in an effort to keep everyone calm. Then she shifted into reverse and slammed down the accelerator just as a hulking armored truck rolled out to block them. There was a shuddering collision, and the armored truck spun away across the courtyard, its tires smoking, its rear end smashed. Polyvox shifted into first. The main prison gate was already closed, but Polyvox headed straight for it anyway.

"The gate is closed," said Andronicus tensely.

The *Argo* punched through it—like a fist through a sheet of tinfoil.

Polyvox began the harrowing descent down the narrow roadway that wound around the decapitated mountain. Soldiers pursued them on motorcycles mounted with machine guns, firing almost constantly, but the rounds bounced harmlessly off the back of the *Argo*.

Now they heard a heavy, thrumming sound. A helicopter gunship dropped down from above and began firing rockets into the side of the mountain. A hundred yards in front of them, the roadway was blasted into a crater. Polyvox had no choice but to turn off and head straight down the side of the mountain. Behind her, the motorcycle machine-gunners skidded and caromed off the roadway as they tried to avoid the crater.

Jack desperately wanted to sleep.

Andronicus shut his eyes and compulsively ground his teeth, while Blackshield maintained an expression of stoic resignation to what appeared to be inevitable doom. Each man consoled himself by recalling that he had fought the good fight, that he had followed the dictates of his conscience over the toxic temptations of Corporate Kultur. Andronicus summoned up his heroic forebears, fighting against tyranny on multiple continents. Blackshield reflected on his family's generations-long struggle against human cruelty, exploitation, and oppression.

But, in the end, this whole thing was scaring them shitless.

Strapped into the seat next to Blackshield, the little girl whose parents had been executed by the State remained quiet.

The delicate, ethereal melodies of Satie continued to play over the sound system.

Then suddenly, with a loud explosion, the *Argo*'s hull was hit, and the entire vehicle tumbled over once, landing on its wheels.

Up until now, Polyvox's heart rate had been fairly normal, but now it accelerated.

She turned a red key in the dashboard, pulled open a small door, and pressed a button. From behind the *Argo*, a small missile was launched. It curved up on an arc of smoke and penetrated the underbelly of the helicopter gunship, which exploded like the *Hindenburg* into a sun-ball of flame and then fell in blazing chunks onto the side of the mountain.

As she steered the car onto the main road below, burning debris slammed into the windshield, obscuring her view with smoke and ash.

She turned on the windshield wipers.

Polyvox accelerated to a hundred and fifty miles an hour, not particularly concerned about which direction she was driving in, but hoping to win enough time to elude any more pursuers before the onset of the starless, moonless West Virginia night.

Ahead was a bridge-dam. As they crossed, two more helicopter gunships floated up over the bleak stunted mountains and swooped down, discharging rockets. The rockets streaked through the air, leaving hot white contrails as they punched into the side of the dam, which had been constructed from the shoddiest, lowest-grade concrete that taxpayer money could buy.

The dam dissolved. The *Argo* was carried away in a tsunami of blasted concrete and foaming, slag-black water. The helicopters flew up and down over the filthy, churning river, dropping depth charges. Canister after canister pounded into the river. Black waterspouts gushed up, propelled by the violent subsurface detonations, but as to the car's fate the water, already covered by a six-inch film of gelatinous post-industrial scum, divulged no clue. Having exhausted their load of depth charges, the two helicopter gunships headed back to Freedom Fortress.

The flood subsided and the river regained its sickly calm, again following its course through the scarified landscape. A sluggish stream of black poisoned blood, coughing and hissing, utterly stripped of its once glorious spirit.

Above, vultures circled. Realizing that the river would give up no flesh today, they eventually headed off into the gathering shadows of another dismal West Virginia night.

Phase Three

Psycho Pietá

CHAPTER TWENTY

The Revolutionary's
Bomb-Thrower's Tale

The *Argo* sank into the Monongahela River of West Virginia, settling on the bottom. Polyvox activated its submarine function. A new network of lights came to life on the dashboard, bathing the car's interior in red light. They could feel the impact of the depth charges reverberating against the fuselage.

"Will this thing hold?" asked Andronicus.

"Those puny weapons are nothing against my car," said Polyvox. "The Order does not create junk."

In time the depth charge explosions stopped. Polyvox activated the bathymetric sonar imaging system, and the *Argo*'s windshield became a screen showing a high-resolution image of the underwater topography of the Monongahela riverbed. The rippled sediment stretched before them like a ghostly highway, broken occasionally by rocks. In places the metal ribs of sunken coal barges jutted up. There were no fish or signs of life.

An old plastic bleach bottle floated by.

"How long are we going to stay down here, Polyvox?" asked Andronicus.

"We should cruise down the river for a few hours, and then surface while it's still dark. The Enemy has almost certainly concluded that we were destroyed, but it's best to be prudent."

Polyvox lifted the *Argo* off the silty river bottom and navigated it down the river channel.

"I think I was shot," said Jack miserably. He had taken off his mask and dropped it on the floor. The little girl was looking up at him with placid curiosity.

Blackshield tore away at the fabric of his sleeve and examined the wound. "There's no bullet, just a deep graze." He opened the *Argo*'s first-aid kit, cleaned the wound, and applied an antiseptic spray bandage. His hands moving expertly and quickly, as if he had performed this sort of task many times.

"We should analyze what went wrong with the mission," said Blackshield soberly, carefully packing away the first-aid kit.

"What went wrong with the mission was that my mother was not cooperative, for the reasons you overheard," Polyvox commented. "Otherwise, we would have easily killed Reid and rescued her."

"It's not to be unexpected," said Blackshield. "While in captivity, she emotionally bonded with Reid's nephew and niece."

"We have to get back as soon as possible," said Andronicus. "Number One will demand a full account. This debacle may destabilize things. The other factions will note the disturbance in the sub-political force, and they will start asking questions. I'm afraid we're dealing with a major setback here."

"I strongly caution against rushing back to Philadelphia," said Blackshield. "Better to make our way there slowly. The Monongahela is a tributary of the Ohio River. We should head there, and then navigate from the Ohio to the Mississippi, all the way down to New Orleans. From there we can cross the Gulf to the Panama Canal, and then head up the East Coast to the mouth of the Delaware."

"Blackshield, normally you're a very rational person," said Polyvox, "but I think your paranoia is getting the better of you. That journey could take weeks, maybe months. No, we will follow the Monongahela for a few hours, and then get ashore somewhere. We can take various land routes back to Philadelphia. What do you say, Andronicus?"

"I never thought I would be having a conversation about driving a car along America's polluted scenic rivers, but I agree with you. Let's take the shorter route."

"I have to go to the bathroom," said the little girl quietly.

"You take the controls," said Polyvox to Andronicus, "while I take her back to the toilet."

F9

A few hours later, just as dawn was breaking, the *Argo* breached the slimy surface of the Monongahela River. It turned and cruised towards a sloping gravel boat ramp. Then it rolled out of the water, dripping with industrial sludge, and rumbled up the ramp until it came to a local road. Up ahead was a roadhouse. A few battered pickups were parked erratically in the lot. A tattered American flag hung limply from a pole. They parked the car and went inside, sitting at a corner table. A waitress approached the table, unsmiling and ashen-faced, handing them menus.

"What kind of beer do you have?" asked Andronicus.

"Kohrs Lite, Kohrs Kraft, Kohrs Amerika, and Kohrs Draft in bottles."

"Kohrs draft all around. I suppose you could bring juice for the kid."

The waitress returned with the drinks.

Polyvox said to the child, "Now, will you tell us your name, little one?"

The girl shook her head and sipped her apple juice through a straw. They ate their food quickly and returned to the car. Following the narrow road for a few miles, they came to a motel, where they checked into a single large room with two beds. Polyvox put the girl in the first bed and lay down on the couch, her long legs projecting over the side; Andronicus and Blackshield took the other bed. Jack chose to spend the night in a chair, since the pain of his wound was bothering him. He sat awake for hours in his boxers and torn, bloodied T-shirt, staring into the darkness, listening as the occasional vehicle passed on the country road outside. Finally, he dozed, and when he woke up in the morning, he was alone in the motel room with Polyvox.

"Where are Andronicus and Blackshield?" he asked.

"They took the girl in the *Argo* to an approved facility, a safe house. It was too risky to keep her here, and we couldn't take her back to our headquarters. How is your shoulder?"

"It's probably infected and I'm going to die for The Cause."

Polyvox was stretched out on one of the beds. She was twirling her retracted tactical baton. The luminosity of her tattoos was very low at the moment. She laid the baton on the bed, stood up, and walked over to Jack to inspect the spray bandage. "Everything looks okay to me."

"Are you a doctor?"

"No. But my knowledge of human medicine is not deficient."

"Will Andronicus and Blackshield come back here once they've dropped off the girl?"

"They will make their own way back to Philadelphia. We will wait here for Emily Bombsinger to pick us up in another vehicle." Polyvox went up to the window and drew the curtains. Gray winter light flowed into the motel room. Across the street was a line of dark trees. A red VACANCY sign with some missing letters blinked at the edge of the parking lot. "The world was more beautiful when my people were its stewards," she observed.

"Where exactly are we?" asked Jack.

"Some Pennsyltucky town. Best to keep a low profile for the next day or so."

Polyvox released the drapes. She sat down on her bed and turned on the 3-D telescreen, which was rather old-fashioned and only took up half of the wall. The telescreen's Pharmatainment module was first generation, with neural pads instead of jacks. Most of the stations were for pharmaceutical infomercials, standard and vibra porn, music-horror, interactive sports and war games, screecher-preachers, live euthanasia testimonials, and security dramas. A news blurb showed the nonagenarian President of the United States pottering around in a garden, holding a geranium and smiling vacantly. His baseball cap said "Cherry Ploop™." A Grombex Corporation ad, featuring a soothing masculine voice and Gregorian chant, announced the beta release of the new Otherworlds Spirituality Pill and then rattled off a nearly incomprehensible list of side effects, including nausea, insomnia, uncontrollable rage, and violent anti-social schizoaffective disorder.

Polyvox turned off the telescreen. "Are you hungry?"

"Maybe."

"I think we can order a pizza."

"I just hope it's not delivered by a Plutocroid."

"We are relatively safe, my friend. They almost certainly think we are dead."

"I'm not hungry now," said Jack. He moved from the chair to the unoccupied bed and lay down, compulsively rubbing his shoulder.

"Jack?"

"Yes?"

Polyvox put her hand on her chin and regarded him clinically. "I think maybe you are depressed."

"So now you are a psychologist."

"I'm merely making an observation."

"I'm not depressed. I'm trying to sort out what just happened."

"What happened is referred to as mission failure." Polyvox threw her coat on. "I'm going to have a look around the premises."

She opened the door and stepped out of the motel room. There was only one other car in the parking lot: a battered pickup. Snow flurries swirled around in the cold air. She walked down to the office, her boots crunching on patches of ice. Inside, she could see the middle-aged manager reading from an old-fashioned book while a security drama played on a small 3-D telescreen. The man looked up. He had wide, wet eyes and a sagging, non-threatening face. Polyvox nodded at him and he nodded back.

Polyvox walked to the edge of the road, where she stood taking in the cold air. In both directions, the road vanished into the trees. No cars passed. After a few minutes, she returned to the motel room.

Jack had completely covered himself with his sheet.

f9

In the afternoon, Jack finally emerged from his cocoon. He made himself a cup of coffee and sat at a little table sipping it.

"I've ordered us a pizza," said Polyvox. "It should be coming soon."

"Good, I'm pretty hungry now. I apologize for my moodiness. Everything is fine now."

A knock came at the motel room door. "Come in," said Polyvox.

The door swung open. A young woman stood there holding an insulated pizza bag. She was wearing a ski cap, sunglasses, a down vest, jeans, and brown buckskin boots with tassels.

"Pizza delivery," she announced cheerfully.

"Excellent," said Polyvox. "Just put it there on that bed, please."

Jack smiled. "I am so hungry…"

The delivery woman took the pizza box out of the insulator, placed it on the bed, opened it up, pulled out a weapon that resembled an Uzi, and pointed it at Jack.

"Die, Enemy of the State."

Jack dropped his coffee mug and it shattered on the floor. He began to shake uncontrollably.

"Enough!" shouted Polyvox, jumping up and snatching the weapon away. "*Ostie de tabarnak de calice!*" she added, switching to Quebec French, perhaps to show solidarity with Jack. "Do you have any idea what we've been through, woman?"

"Sorry. So sensitive."

The delivery woman peeled off her ski cap and flicked off her sunglasses. It was Emily Bombsinger, with her genetically-modified chrome green hair and her lovely walnut brown complexion.

"I fail to see the humor in that," said Jack, still shaking.

Bombsinger unzipped her insulated vest. "Jittery, aren't we?" she said, sitting down across from Jack. "I just thought a little levity would help dispel the gloom resulting from your F.U.B.A.R. mission."

"Don't judge Jack," said Polyvox. "It wasn't his fault. If anyone is to blame, it is me. I read my own mother incorrectly." She retrieved a towel from the bathroom and cleaned up the coffee spill.

"Sorry, Jackie," said Bombsinger. She could not keep a touch of sarcasm from her tone. "Do you want me to give you a kiss?"

Jack didn't answer.

"How was the drive?" asked Polyvox, sitting back down and crossing her legs American style. "Anything suspicious? Were you followed?"

"No suspiciousness, no following. The drive was fun. I stopped off at a diner where some knuckle-dragging motorcycle punk attempted to take liberties with me."

Polyvox shrugged. "The human species—"

"So I killed him."

Polyvox uncrossed her legs and straightened. "You what?"

"I'm just kidding! Gosh, you two, lighten up! Where am I, Miss Polyvox's Boston School for Proper Young Girls and Boys?"

Jack excused himself to go to the bathroom, and Polyvox sat down at the table.

"What's he so mopey about?" asked Bombsinger.

Polyvox looked back impassively. "Things did not go well."

"Obviously. But I'll tell you something about Jack. He's got the sickly look of the sexually frustrated young man. I've seen it before.

What he needs is a good bed-romping. Perhaps we can draw straws and do it now. Or we can do it to him together."

"Enough of this vulgar joking. That's the last thing he needs. Beneath your assumed mood of bawdy insouciance, Emily, I detect troubled currents."

Bombsinger shrugged. "I feel a bit hopeless, Polyvox. Who doesn't? Nothing ever seems to go right. The Enemy never sleeps, and it never stops scheming. Our political objectives are like drug-induced dreams. Sometimes I just want to drift away into the sea."

Polyvox reached out and took Emily's hand in her own. "Remember that our movement is bigger than we are, Emily. And when we have finally prevailed over the Enemy, which we will do someday, we will usher in a new world—one where every tear from this wretched purgatory will be washed away."

"And how long will that take? Maybe we won't even live to see it."

Polyvox moved her seat so that she was next to Emily. She stroked the younger woman's green hair. "Of course you will live to see it, though it may be a long way off. Have you been performing the meditative exercises I recommended?"

"I've been trying to."

They heard the knob of the bathroom door rattle. As Jack returned to the table, the doorbell buzzed. "Oh my God," he groaned.

Emily opened the door. This time it *was* a real pizza delivery boy, with music jacks in his ears and a skyboard on his back. He came in, took the box out of the insulated bag, and placed it on the table. He looked at Emily and Polyvox, sighing slightly, and then looked enviously at Jack.

It's not what you think it is, buddy, Jack thought.

Emily tipped him with a Pharmatainment Chit good for twelve hours of *Battle Babe Alexandra: Canyon of Dreams*—the newest release.

"Wow, thanks!" he said with an awkward smile. With a final glance of longing at Emily and Polyvox, he retreated through the door.

Emily had a ravenous appetite, and within a few minutes had devoured three slices. Jack had heard that the newest generation of genetically enhanced young people had difficulty keeping their appetites under control, but he was still surprised that she could eat so much, so fast. Having finished her portion, Emily excused herself and went outside to get some "fresh air."

"She strikes me as very strange," said Jack quietly, when she had gone. "That whole thing with the Uzi…"

"Strange, yes, but she has formidable talents."

"What's her name mean, anyway? Surely that can't be real."

"Of course it's not real. None of us goes by our real names, except for you. Hers derives from…an incident."

"An incident?"

"One that she now regards as a youthful stunt."

"What happened? Or don't I want to hear?"

"It's no secret. Quite the contrary. When Emily was nineteen she left Harvard, where she had matriculated as a child prodigy at age sixteen. She'd had her fill of academic structure, and so went off to join Faction Forty—a small, radical feminist group with a conventional Marxist orientation. For her performance-dissertation, she hired herself out as a stripper-singer at a Plutocrat stag party in the Hamptons. You can imagine the scene: a roomful of Drumpfian American man-boys, howling, chest-thumping like gorillas, swilling booze, giving vent to all the primordial urges of their inbred lust. But after her first sultry song, and before gratifying the swaggering cave-boys by taking off so much as a thread of her clothing, Emily lobbed a kind of stink bomb into their midst and slipped lithely out the window. The Plutocrat stags were left rolling and groveling on the floor, rendered inoperative by nausea, and—so I am told, as apparently there is a secret video of the aftermath—decorating the carpet with copious amounts of rainbow-colored digestive fluids."

"I see," said Jack, trying not to imagine what had just been described to him. "It seems the punishment was not commensurate with the crime. Boys will be boys."

Polyvox's expression, which had been slightly bemused, now became decidedly unsympathetic. "Oh, these were not boys in *that* sense, Security Officer Tone. These were Wall Street Wolf Cubs at the highest level of moral rabidity. She showed them mercy by not lobbing an actual fragmentation grenade at them. What she did was a strategically meaningless action, but *symbolically* it was of great importance. She gained a certain level of notoriety among the factions, and earned the sobriquet Bombsinger."

"Everything makes sense now," said Jack without conviction.

"Someday, Jack, perhaps you will perform an exploit, and thereby earn a revolutionary alias."

"I just hope the exploit doesn't involve inducing a roomful of drunken men to involuntarily pour back their used beer."

"It won't. I suspect it will be far more terrifying than that."

He knew Polyvox was joking, but this comment was still unsettling.

The motel door flew open, and a gust of cold wind came in. Emily Bombsinger strode over and dropped a pack of cards on the table. "Let's play strip poker. But only Jack strips, and we get to ogle at and/or make fun of him."

Jack visibly recoiled.

"Let's play hearts instead," said Polyvox. She shuffled and dealt the cards with the deftness of a croupier, and they played until the early hours of the morning.

F9

They spent one more night in the motel room, Polyvox and Bombsinger in one bed, Jack in the other. In the morning, they got in the car Emily had brought. It was a drab, nondescript vehicle with an outdated interior, but Polyvox assured Jack that it was fully equipped with the most current defensive and navigational functions.

Jack sat in the back while Polyvox drove the first leg of the trip. Bombsinger, in the front passenger seat, impatiently changed radio stations before turning the radio off altogether. "How about story time, Jackie?" she suggested.

"What do you mean?" asked Jack.

Bombsinger removed an old paperback edition of *Beyond Good and Evil*. "Listen to this, Jackie O," she said, turning around in her seat. *A person no longer loves their knowledge once they have communicated it.* Do you think that's true?"

"Please stop calling me Jackie. I know I said you could before, but now I'm revoking permission."

"Okay, Jackie O. I get the picture. What do you think of *this* line: *That which one generation considers evil is usually an outdated echo of something that, in a former time, was considered good—an atavism of an old ideal.* Creepy, eh? If that's true, what are we fighting for?"

"I don't think it's true," said Jack. "All genuine good is timeless. Nietzsche's cynicism notwithstanding."

"I disagree," said Emily. "A few generations back, it was considered evil to have premarital sex. It was harshly punished, both corporeally and through rituals of public and private shame. Now everybody has sex all the time, and marriage is an atavism. High school students have sex. College students have sex. Middle-aged people have sex. They're having sex in old age homes, even as we speak. If you go to a cemetery, the dead are having sex. All of the cosmic forces have sex, and this is what yields the eternal laws that govern nature. It's completely disgusting."

Jack, in spite of himself, blurted, "A preposterous example, and I don't know what you are trying to prove or, frankly, what you're even talking about."

"I'm trying to prove that sex is the opiate of the masses, not religion. But Love is the antidote to the opiate."

He noticed Polyvox's frowning gray eyes in the rearview mirror. "Sometimes, Jack, Emily mistakes her bewildering metaphysical musings for reality. How's this for a Nietzsche quote? *What we do in dreams, we also do when we are awake: we invent the person we're associating with, and then we immediately forget that we have done so.*"

"Hilarious," said Emily, tossing the book over the seat at Jack. "Oh, by the way, Polyvox, Number One wants to talk to you."

"Indeed? Why do you mention this only now, Emily?"

"Indeed, why do you use stilted syntax when you are irked? Who knows? He, she, it, or they want a *full report* on the botched mission to eliminate Reid. You and Andronicus are summoned."

"Very well, as soon as we return to headquarters, you may arrange the meeting."

"You won't see Number One face to face, of course. You'll speak with the Shadow. And I will be the interlocutor with the Shadow."

"I know the drill, Emily."

By evening, they had arrived in Philadelphia. Polyvox dropped Emily off at the Trappist Tavern, and then returned with Jack to her apartment.

F9

Once they were back in her apartment, Polyvox unbuttoned her coat all the way, sat down at her organ, and immediately lost herself in a Bach fugue. The fireplace erupted, like a sorceress's hearth brought to life by the music itself.

Jack listened for a while, then retired to the room he had slept in before. The next morning, Polyvox gave him some final instructions. "This meeting with Number One may take a few days," she said. "Perhaps even a week."

"Why so long?"

"It's the nature of things. You must stay here until I return. Never venture out. Among many other amenities, you have at your disposal an exercise room, a full kitchen, a little swimming pool, and your mini-saxophone. What more do you need?"

"Nothing."

"The windows are one-way, so no one can peer in. Furthermore, they are bomb- and bulletproof."

"I feel quite secure already."

"Taras Petriv and Emily Bombsinger will check in on you. If there is a problem, contact Taras on the closed circuit line. Paul Bunyan will also be available if there are technical difficulties. Remember, you are a hunted man. Only by remaining in here will you be safe."

"I understand. Good luck, Polyvox."

They shook hands. Polyvox left through the front door.

CHAPTER TWENTY-ONE

Your Security Agency at Work

A week came and went.

Jack obediently remained inside Polyvox's apartment in the City of Brotherly Love. He was again struck by its size. In addition to the kitchen and the swimming pool, there was a library, a greenhouse, a billiards room, and several halls. The interior décor was a kind of alien gothic, with vines, leaves, ancient animals, and cryptic symbols carved in black wood and dark stone. It did not at all resemble the home of a revolutionary, and despite all these comforts, it was not sufficient to distract him from his worries.

Petriv visited him every couple of days, bringing food and news. He was a man of average height, but powerfully built. Frustratingly taciturn, he was evasive about his Eastern European origins, and of course his name was most likely yet another revolutionary alias. At some point during each visit, they would play chess in front of the large fireplace in the organ room. Petriv handicapped himself by taking away all of his pawns, and one each of his knights, rooks, and bishops. Yet every time he still won.

Emily also visited, each time to swim in Polyvox's pool, which was octagonal and overhung with flowering tropical plants. She swam in a red bathing suit decorated with silhouettes of Lenin's head, and Jack suspected she was trying to provoke him. He refused her offer to go swimming with her.

He was standing in the greenhouse when Emily sneaked up behind him, giving him a scare.

He jumped, turning around. "Where do you think Andronicus and Polyvox are?" he asked, irritated. "Why would an interview with Number One take so long? It's been over a week already."

"That information is given out on a need-to-know basis, Jack. You don't have the proper security clearances."

Petriv wandered into the greenhouse and looked disdainfully at Emily. "Have you ever read *And Quiet Flows the Don,* famous novel of Russian Revolution?"

"Why are you asking me that?" she retorted. "Suppose I said that I had read it in fifth grade, in the original Russian. Would you think more highly of me? Are you testing me? Have you read the *Handmaid's Tale?*"

Petriv seemed taken aback, and even wounded. He reached into his coat and removed a battered old paperback, with a stern-looking Cossack on the cover. "I have the first-volume novel with me," he said. "Just thought maybe you are wanting to read…"

"Oh, sorry…no, actually, I haven't read it…" she replied apologetically, taking the book from him. "Wow, it's a thick one."

Petriv turned to Jack. "A chess match?"

Jack thought a few seconds, then nodded. They returned to the main hall and sat down across from each other at the chess table. Emily, now dressed in her usual attire, pulled up a chair to watch. Every time Jack started to make a move, Emily shook her head, or shuddered, or winced. Finally he knocked down his king.

"You are surrendering?" asked Petriv, incredulous. "It is only beginning of match."

"I'm preoccupied. I keep asking myself why there's been no news of Polyvox and Andronicus."

"I believe news is coming shortly," said Petriv, still looking down at the chessboard, studying every detail of the short battle.

"That's what you all keep saying. But it's been some time now, and you've heard nothing—or have you?"

"Nothing."

"Doesn't this strike you as strange?"

"It is striking me as worrisome and strange. But we must be patient, Tone."

"And suppose Andronicus, Polyvox, and Blackshield were captured on their way to see Number One—or worse yet, killed?"

Emily sipped from a bottle of mineral water and regarded Jack as the queen's sage might the queen's fool.

"Actually, captured is worse than killed," said Petriv bluntly.

"To you, perhaps, but I don't want to see them killed."

"And so you're preferring that they are captured and subjected to the torture? I can tell you without any hesitations, Tone, that this fate is worse than the other fate."

"They have neither been captured nor killed," said Emily. "My God, Jack, Polyvox is right. You really do have general anxiety disorder."

"She said that about me?"

"It's in your psych report. Look, I'm probably not supposed to tell you this but Number One moves around. Number One has to move around. So Polyvox and Andronicus had to go to a faraway place with a strange-sounding name to meet with Number One."

Jack stood up and began to pace back and forth in front of the fireplace. He looked over at the organ. "Nevertheless, all this waiting is unendurable. I think I'm going stir crazy in this place. Why can't I just take a little walk around the building?"

"Certainly not!" replied Emily, jumping out of her seat. "Polyvox said absolutely no leaving this apartment."

"Tone," said Petriv, "the imperative is for you to stay calm. In this business—in our business—there are always long period of waiting and uncertainty. I'm seeing you're agitated. I'm going to speak to Krypton to give you tablets."

"I don't want tablets," replied Jack.

"That may be so. Still, I'm speaking to her to give you tablets," said Petriv, standing up himself. He put on his worn woolen overcoat, his gray scarf, and his fake fur *ushantka* hat. "Is there anything else you want?"

"I want to go for a walk outside."

Petriv gave a joyless East Slavic chuckle. "You can't do that."

"Maybe we can send a message to Number One," suggested Jack. "A message?"

"Through Emily. You're our liaison with Number One, right?"

"I am."

Petriv sighed and shook his head. "You're not understanding, Tone. That's not possible."

"And why not?"

"There are wheels inside the wheels."

Jack made a scoffing sound.

"I'm bringing you the tablets," said Petriv, closing the door behind him.

Jack was now alone with Emily, who was giving him her pretty and ostensibly harmless smile. It was a smile, he now knew, that concealed complex currents, most of them treacherous ones that flowed from the deepest volcanic vents of political radicalism—and confusion.

He cleared his throat. "Can you contact them?" he asked.

"Jack, I'm a cryptologist, not a medical man."

"What?"

Emily took his hand in hers. "Do you want to go to the entertainment room and watch a film?"

"No," said Jack decisively. "But thank you for the offer. I'm going to bed now."

He went into his room. Emily, shrugging, left the apartment.

79

The next afternoon, Petriv returned with an unlabelled plastic bottle. "She's prescribing you these tablets. Take one tonight before sleeping, but no drinking alcohol with them. A chess game?"

They played, and this time Tone won. It was an absurd artificial victory, but Tone didn't complain. When Petriv left, Tone took a tablet. He felt calmer for a while, and sat in the greenhouse reading Koestler's *Darkness at Noon*. But by evening he felt the effects wearing off. After making himself some dinner, he drank a beer and went to sleep.

In the middle of the night he woke up feeling anxious and agitated. Throwing off the covers, he went out to the organ room and walked around, talking to himself. He took another tablet and washed it down with a glass of water. Finally, he dressed, put on his coat, and took the elevator to the street.

It was a cold night, but the air refreshed him after being so long indoors. He walked along the empty streets, and a curious euphoria came over him. He wasn't sure where he was going, and he didn't care. In time, he came to a park at the edge of a river; whether it was the Delaware or the other one, the one whose name he could never properly pronounce, he didn't know. The sun was starting to rise, and the cold river rippled softly with pink light. He had apparently been walking for hours.

Behind him, he could hear the early morning traffic on the parkway that paralleled the river. He sat on a bench, watching the light of the rising sun illuminate the water and the trees on the other side. He had wandered away from the downtown area and was near a park.

He saw a few runners on a paved bike path, a woman walking a dog. Deciding it was time to take another pill, he shook one out of the bottle and popped it into his mouth.

He felt quite calm, and at ease in the world. Really, he concluded, everything he had experienced so far was like a dream, unreal. He felt, in fact, that he was emerging from a long nightmare. He was at once sleepy and alert. A man with a dog sat down on a nearby bench, smoked a cigarette, and strolled away, his dog bounding in front of him, turning back to look, then bounding a little farther. There were still more runners along the path. Behind him a police car, its sirens wailing, sped past. A homeless man shuffled by. Jack watched them all with a languorous indulgence. Maybe he would move to this city. Yes, it had its flaws, but it was a cradle of American democracy and independence. And while its mood could be saturnine, it wasn't as obnoxious as New York. It had nice buildings. There was something organic about it. And he would get a dog, too. A faithful companion.

It would be his best friend, for who else could love a human better than a dog?

But how to support himself and his dog? He would try to find work as a freelance editor, working under an assumed new identity. That might be difficult—and not the assumed-identity part. No, working for oneself was the problem. The Ruling Elites of the United States preferred the citizen-masses to be employed either by Big Government or by Corporations. Self-employed workers and independent companies were sources of innovative ideas, which threatened the ruling classes. Liberty of mind and spirit had become completely inimical to the functioning of the American State, and numerous economic policies had been enacted to ensure that every citizen was working for something else, for something bigger. It was no exaggeration to say that America had become, as Andronicus had once quipped, the Land of the Fooled and the Home of the Enslaved.

But that would not stop him! Here, in the cradle of Liberty, Jack would break out from Governmental control. He would defy the Corporationists. He would even tell Faction Nine to back off.

Jack would be no man's master and no man's slave—he would be free!

The morning sun climbed in the sky. Lost in thought, he barely noticed a branchlike shadow creeping forward until it was nearly touching the tips of his shoes, like a long, spindly finger. The shadow made a strange, jerking movement before snapping back.

Jack's blood ran cold—he had seen that kind of shadow before, in the Jersey City graveyard, where he had first encountered…

He stood up.

Suddenly there were no dog walkers, no runners, no pedestrians. A gaunt figure in a broad hat quickly approached. Beneath its brim, he could see thin lips stretched into a demonic leer.

At that instant Jack realized he had forgotten his saxophone.

He ran. He followed the path by the river, through a grove of trees and past what looked like abandoned waterworks. Behind him he heard the soft, swift clap of shoes. Turning around, he saw three Plutocroids. In front of him three more were approaching. On the street, in their fedoras and cloaks, they had the appearance of very tall, thin, bloodless white men. But Jack knew who they were.

And then he saw his salvation: a rangy fellow with wild hair and a lined but handsome face, sitting on a bench with a gleaming bass saxophone resting on his lap. Who was this guy? Most likely a musician taking the morning air along the river after a long nighttime gig in some smoky jazz joint. Whoever he was, he was armed with the one weapon the Plutocroids most feared. Jack could not believe his good fortune.

"Oh, thank God!" he cried. "Sir, would you please play something for me?"

The jazz musician looked up at him, cocking an eyebrow. He seemed to study Jack for a second, and then said, his voice drowsy, "Sorry, dude. The muse hasn't come to me yet. I got to sit here and contemplate the Schuylkill River for a while. She tells me what to play."

The Plutocroids were closing in. Couldn't the musician see them? What was wrong with him? Was he high on some drug?

"Oh, dear sweet Jesus…I'm begging you!" pleaded Jack. "You don't understand, I need music right now. It's the only thing that can save me…."

The jazz musician sighed lugubriously, lifted up the instrument, and placed the mouthpiece to his lips. He positioned his fingers over the keys. He closed his eyes.

The footfalls of the Plutocroids slowed and came to a complete stop. Jack dared not look at them.

The jazz musician opened his eyes and shook his head sadly. "It just ain't comin', friend. The river, she is silent."

Jack turned off the bike path and ran madly up a grassy embankment that was mostly covered by snow. In front of him was the parkway.

A car raced by, blaring Johnny Kenwood's "Cruzin' with the Blooze" so loudly that it could be heard through the closed windows.

Behind Jack, the Plutocroids grimaced in torment and clenched their fists.

He knew that this reprieve would last but a few seconds—he had to make the most of them. He dashed across the parkway and into the trees. Now he was in a forested area, snow covering the ground. For a moment he thought—feeling a sudden thrill—he might actually elude his pursuers, but soon enough he noticed that Plutocroids were silently approaching from his right and his left. He turned down a dirt path and kept running, his breaths heaving from his chest. He felt lightheaded from the tablets and the drinks. Soon he came to a rocky outcropping and realized he could not climb it since it was covered with snow and ice. He changed course and plunged headlong into a frost-covered thicket.

Something tackled him from the side, and he fell down, punching and kicking. He saw the weird yellow eyes, the cadaverous faces, and heard the wheezy breathing. Multiple hands grabbed him, holding him down. And then all was darkness.

F9

There was a sound like a heavy bell tolling at the end of a long stone corridor. The bell tolled at even intervals, and Jack could feel its somber reverberations shuddering against his skull. Presently, the bell resolved itself into something that wasn't a sound at all, but, rather, a dense pain in his head. The throbbing pain continued, summoning him up from the depths of unconsciousness. He opened his eyes and found himself in a dimly lit room, strapped into a wooden chair.

The room had stainless steel walls, and the chair was bolted to a circular rubber base on the floor. Next to the base was a depression in the floor and a drain. Nearby was a hose. The wall in front of him had a long glass window, though it was completely opaque. He shook his head, blinked, looked around. He tried to move, but the restraints were too tight.

A seamless door opened in one of the stainless steel walls, and in walked Stanley Spork, wearing the black-and-gold uniform of the Security Agency Protective Services.

"Hello, Tone," said Spork, displaying none of his usual jitteriness. "Everything okay?"

"Spork. Where…? What's going on? What are you doing in that uniform?"

"What do you think I'm doing in it? You're back home. Where you belong. That is, you're back at work. Do you remember where you work, Tone? I know you've been through a lot lately, so I understand if your memory is a little spacey."

No trace remained of the edgy and high-strung Spork that Jack had worked with for years. The man who stood before him now had a smug, arrogant expression. Spork, it seemed, had been a ghoster all along. Struggling to process this latest twist, Jack felt himself adrift.

"Snap out of it, Tone. I asked you if you remember where you work."

"The Northeast Field Office of the Security Agency."

"Exactly! Do you know what floor you're on?"

"The top floor."

"Very funny. You're on subfloor -19. Yes, I know, you didn't know there was one, but it really doesn't matter. What matters is that most people who come down here don't leave. Not as humans, at any rate. They leave as Plutocroids."

Jack was suddenly very alert. "Plutocroids? What do you mean?"

"Surprised? Where did you think all these Plutocroids came from? Storks?"

Spork was walking around the interrogation chair, the soles of his boots thudding on the metal floor. He stopped. "Don't you have anything to say?"

"What do you want me to say?" replied Jack miserably.

Spork's demeanor shifted subtly, and he bent down. "Listen, Tone," he whispered, "there are some very bad people here. They will do terrible, horrible things to you unless you cooperate."

Jack looked in Spork's eyes, flickering and wet beneath the black visor of his military cap—they were haunted, fearful, hunted. He realized that Spork did not want to be here, in this uniform, confronting his old colleague. He and Spork had never actually been friends, but they had shared a drink or two, and chatted frequently in the aimless way that passed for friendship in the depths of the agency.

"What do you want me to do?" asked Jack.

"Tell us everything," replied Spork, still whispering, but now almost pleading. "Otherwise I will be forced to play the interrogator, and I don't want to. Not with you. Come clean now—did those bastards at the Mind Police put you up to this?"

That was unexpected. "The *Mind Police*? Absurd...."

Spork nodded. "I didn't think so. What faction are you working for?"

Jack quietly cursed himself. He should have played the Mind Police thing as long as he could have. He might even have gotten away with it. What a fool he was! But it was too late now. He'd blown it. Finally he said: "I'm screwed anyway, Spork. All is lost as far as I'm concerned. Why should I talk to you?"

"There's where you're wrong. Director Schicklegruber always liked you, Tone. He knew your parents, apparently. He just thinks you cracked under stress, and maybe there was some psych-manipulation from the Bad Guys. He also hasn't ruled out Mind Police manipulation, even though you might think that's 'absurd.' If you confess and tell us everything, he will arrange for the best private treason court to hear your case—a treason court based in Bangalore that is generally used for only the highest-ranking federal bureaucrats. It's a subsidiary of the Lunar Company. Not only will you avoid the death penalty, but you'll be sent to one of the best American reeducation camps on the Mare Orientale impact basin, and treated with cutting-edge spirituality pharmaceuticals and FDA-approved hardware. It will be as if all this never happened. Just tell us everything."

"What do you mean by everything?"

Spork stood up, adjusting his black-and-gold combination cap. He now spoke loudly. "We want you to tell us the names of those who turned you against your Homeland. Only in this way can you escape a fate that is, literally, worse than death." Spork pointed to a high stack of papers on a stool. "This is a BA-1778A Confession of Treason Form, revised. It chronicles everything we know so far about your crimes. You will initial each of the 948 pages and you will sign at the end. Once you give us the additional information we require, you will sign and initial the BA-1778B Supplement to 1778A. The two forms will be combined through file consolidation, then sent to be reviewed and countersigned by the SA Director himself."

Jack sighed. It was over. They had won. "What fate could be worse than death?" he asked.

"The fate of being transmogrified into a Plutocroid."

Jack wasn't sure if he should interpret this literally.

"Well," prompted Spork, "will you cooperate? Provide the names! Who do you work for? Where do your co-conspirators meet?"

"Mickey and Minnie Mouse," said Jack angrily. "I answer only to them. You and all your fellow servitors of the global plutocracy can go to hell."

"Damn fool," hissed Spork, again whispering. Then he guffawed loudly. When he was finished, he wiped his tears and pointed to the long window in the stainless steel wall. Now Jack could see through the glass. A gray-haired man with a monstrous head was sitting at a table, using silver implements to gouge at a steamed lobster, sucking his fingers and puckering his lips after each bite. The man wore a suit with a big American flag pin on the lapel.

"Do you see that person eating lobster?" asked Spork. "Do you know who he is?"

"The Easter Bunny."

Spork laughed, and slapped Jack hard across the jaw. "Yes, he's the Easter Bunny. He's Peter Cottontail." Spork slapped him again. "Who is that man, Jack?"

Jack didn't answer.

Again Spork slapped him—there was a crazy look in his eyes.

"How should I know who he is?" shouted Jack.

"That's Mr. Frake Inyards," said Spork. "A powerful man and a true patriot with a net worth of several billion. And right now he's very, very angry with you, Tone. It seems some of your fellow traitors attempted, and thankfully failed, to assassinate Mr. Gregory Reid, one of Mr. Inyards' most beloved friends. Not only did they attempt cold-blooded murder of a living American hero—a man before whom even presidents bend the knee—but your scumbag associates had the audacity to attempt this crime right in the *very heart* of one of Mr. Inyards' own establishments. A double insult. Now Mr. Inyards wants answers."

"I have no idea what you're talking about, Spork."

"Why did you initiate and then steal an illicit PISIBANK report on Senator Lance Boyler—an upright man who has faithfully served the Reid family for virtually all of his career?"

"I thought a senator was elected to work for the people."

"Don't get smart with me, Tone. Give me names."

"I told you that I answer only to Mickey and Minnie Mouse. Go down to Disneyworld, bring them up here, and I'll talk. And bring their dog Pluto, too—that moronic mongrel."

Behind the glass, Inyards pleasurably patted his lips with a napkin and picked up a microphone. "Proceed," he said, before taking a sip of wine and sloshing it around in his mouth as he looked reflectively towards the ceiling of his dining chamber. Inyards nodded to himself and swallowed.

Spork walked over to a table, returned with a cattle prod, and jammed it onto Jack's arm.

Jack cried out in pain.

"You shamed our office," snarled Spork, "and you shamed the Agency." He slapped Jack again. "Filthy maggot pig." He brought his face close to Jack's, his hot breath smelling of greasy, half-digested food from the SA cafeteria. "Not only that, but I was assigned to watch you, Tone. So you also humiliated *me*. Because I'll be perfectly blunt about it: you were the last person in the office I would have suspected of treason. So now I'm giving you the chance to redeem yourself from the depths of treasonous maggotry, and tell me names."

Jack spat in his face.

There was another electrical jolt, after which Jack was vaguely aware of his own screams.

F9

Inyards belched and used a toothpick to clean his teeth. The door to his private observation room opened, and another man walked in, carrying a briefcase and wearing the uniform and insignia of a captain of the Warforce FBI. Inyards eyed him warily.

"Your man out there…what's his name?" asked Ronald Hedrick, jerking his long, horselike face towards the interrogation room.

"Spork. He's not my man. Senator Boyler told me to—"

"Yes, whatever. Senator Boyler is a servitor. He is not in charge of this operation, I am. Let me in there."

Inyards shrugged. "Go ahead. But remember, Captain, this interrogation is my business. I'm the contractor here, not you."

The door to the interrogation room opened and Hedrick walked in. Like a petulant child, Spork was repeatedly slapping his half-conscious victim. Hedrick grabbed his arm and wrenched him around. For a few seconds, Spork glared at Hedrick with irrational animal fury, but then, seeing who he was, backed up and saluted.

"Sir."

"What do you think you're doing, you incompetent fool?"

"Sir, I'm certified for interrogation by the SA."

"You're a clown. Stand back."

Hedrick placed his briefcase on the table and opened it. Inside was a set of syringes, phials, pincers, curettes, needles, wires, and energy cells. Hedrick prepared one of the syringes and gave Jack an injection in the arm.

"Spork, give me a chair."

The Security Officer dragged one over and Hedrick sat down.

Jack felt as if he had been roused from sleep. He was alert, and his physical pain was now separated from his body by a kind of invisible field. In front of him sat a man in a Warforce FBI uniform, his legs crossed European style, his long-fingered hands limp in his lap. His face was unnaturally long, his hair yellow-blond, his eyes a glassy pale blue. Behind him stood Spork, jaw twitching.

"Mr. Tone, I'm Captain Ronald Hedrick, FBI. I apologize for Spork's clumsy brutality. It was unseemly, unnecessary, and indicative of repressed sexual desires—probably directed towards small mammals."

"Now, listen here, sir—," began Spork angrily.

"Security Officer Spork, bureaucrat, if you don't get yourself under control, I shall, by the power invested in me by the People and Government of the United States, put a bullet through your head."

Spork bowed and retreated into chastened silence.

"Now, then, Mr. Tone," said Hedrick, lifting up his hands and bringing his long fingers together, "I want to talk to you about deoxyribonucleic acid."

Jack blinked.

"Who invented DNA?" asked Hedrick.

"It wasn't invented, it was discovered."

"It was discovered, you are correct, but before that, it was invented. Who invented it?"

"I don't know."

"Was it God who invented DNA?"

Jack said nothing.

"Yes, it was God," stated Hedrick. "But, if you would allow me to paraphrase a wise man, when we Capitalists speak of God, or belief in God, we do not mean, like some naïve or hoodwinked people, a sort of vaguely humanoid entity that resides beyond the cosmos. Rather, we mean the great force of Nature that governs everything in the universe, including the generation of Profit on our small and insignificant planet. The idea that this universal force would somehow trouble itself about the fate of every little germ or human being, or that it could be somehow influenced by prayers or rituals, is either the product of ignorance or deception. So God created DNA, but why?"

Jack watched as Hedrick began to mime a violinist, closing his eyes and moving his bow arm smoothly back and forth. "Because," explained Hedrick, "Nature is Information, and all information seeks to replicate itself. All of nature is basically strings of code, vibrating harmonies, and these codes mutate as time goes on, creating new information. The creation, transmission, and transformation of information is God. Nothing has meaning outside of this. The transmission of information should never be blocked. Rather, information should flow naturally across the universe, for when this happens there is peace. When you block information, there is frustration, pain, death. When you allow yourself to be the means through which information flows forward, then you have happiness. Do you understand, Tone? You are information. I am information. We are units of information, bundles. We express ourselves through language, mathematics, and profit. Money is the concrete manifestation of profit, and money is therefore a unit of information. Long ago, our Supreme Court correctly decided that the flow of money was information, language, speech. It was truth. In a truly free society, one cannot restrict the flow of money, for that requires the suppression of Truth. This is why even ghosts have DNA."

Jack looked unblinkingly at Hedrick. Behind him hovered Spork—a blur of black and gold. "What is the point of all this pseudo-philosophy?"

"The point?" Hedrick pantomimed opening a violin case, placing instrument and bow inside, and then closing it. He placed the imaginary box on the floor by his chair. "The point is so that you realize that by cooperating with us, you are making yourself more alive, more in harmony with the universe. By holding your tongue, on the other hand, you are inviting death and pain. Nature...which is to say, God...does not care about you—not in the slightest. You are merely an informational channel. If this channel gets blocked, then Nature will, sooner or later, destroy the clot. Speak now."

"I don't know what you want me to tell you."

"Very well, let me share some information with you. The assassins—your colleagues, I assume...." Here, Hedrick gave Jack a penetrating and knowing smile. "That is, your new friends who were dispatched to liquidate Gregory Reid—failed in their mission. They themselves have been liquidated. I have been told that they were attempting to escape from their botched mission in a car somewhere in West Virginia, when they were blown to smithereens by a missile fired from a helicopter gunship. There were four altogether—three men and a woman. We have no idea who they were, but we would like you to tell us in order to confirm the pending DNA results. Let this information flow from yourself freely. They themselves no longer exist as information units. But perhaps faded copies of their existential information continue to reside in your cortical information-processing unit. I will not waste my time or your time by describing the horrors we will inflict upon you if you persist in being an informational clot. Suffice it to say that your imaginative powers will fall short of conceiving these things. I want you to think of a kind of hard bodysuit, with a hole for your genitals, and a kind of wormlike apparatus with teeth, called the lamprey…enough! It's gruesome, and I won't be there when it happens. I'll review the video recording afterwards, make some edits, and sell it at a nice profit to the Torture Porn Conglomerates."

Until this point, Jack had been able to summon some level of defiance. But now he realized he was utterly alone. It did not matter if they erroneously believed that Andronicus, Polyvox, and Blackshield were dead. They had DNA samples, and very soon would connect the assassination attempt directly to Tone himself. Most likely, *they already had.* They were playing with him now, like Stalin tormenting his victims with false hope before dispatching them to the execution dungeon or the gulag.

The State had won. The Corporatocracy had conquered.

He was already dead.

"So, Mr. Tone," concluded Hedrick, "please let information flow freely."

Jack was looking down—at his bare feet, at the restraints on his wrists, his waist, his ankles. He lifted his head. "Do you love your country, Hedrick?"

Except for a tiny twitch of his left eyelid, the face of the Warforce FBI officer remained impassive. "I love what my country stands for, Mr. Tone."

"And what's that?"

"It stands for the free flow of information, the limitless generation of Profit. When Profit flows correctly, there is Pleasure. For the Elect, that is."

"Well, if that's what your country stands for, then I don't want to have anything to do with it anymore. I want to crawl out of the skin of my crummy citizenship, like a bug leaving behind a diseased exoskeleton. Because if what you say is true, then this country is no more than a madhouse built on a foundation of slavery, of victims' bones, of warmongering, of exploitation, of torture, of greed…it has become an abominable deception—a machine whose sole purpose is to pump the filth of wealth and power back up into its own fat, swagging pig belly. It has become a land ruled by trillionaire bastards and ministered by ass-sucking psychopath servants like you, with a political system that's a gutter-level farce where political candidates mock each other's manhood like vulgar schoolboys. I hope that someday an alien armada appears in the skies, positions its warships above all the nations of the Earth, and shits its nuclear fire down upon you and your masters, on your glittering cities and your towers, on your yachts and your mansions and your walled luxury retreats, and reduces the whole wicked lot of you to radioactive ash, so that we the people—the real people—can finally rebuild human civilization. So I'm not going to tell you anything. I'm not going to tell you the names of the heroes who tried to kill the degenerate monkey-fascist Reid, and I'm not going to tell you about all of the hundreds of dedicated radicals who already know about Operation Autocrat and who are working even now to subvert it. You can torture me all you want, but I'll just bite down hard on the cyanide cap in my molar and die happy, knowing that someday the people of Earth will rise up against you parasites and exterminate you and your lobster-chomping overlords. And then the world will breathe of Freedom evermore."

Jack was panting; his face was flushed and wet with sweat, and he felt a salty sting in his eyes. The words had come pouring out of him quite unexpectedly—from madness, terror, or fury, he could not say. But something inside of him had changed. He still dreaded death. He still feared torture. He still understood full well all the power that the totalitarian corporate state could bring to bear on him. But now, at last, he realized he could summon a measure of internal defiance against his oppressor.

He tried to lift his arm to wipe the sweat away, but it was immobilized by the restraining straps.

Hedrick said nothing, but behind him, Jack could see Inyards at his table, his face blood-red and contorted, his lips shimmering with lobster juice, shouting into his microphone: "Shock him! Traitor! Shock him! Genitals! Anus! Probe! Antipatriot! Shock! Degrade! Testicles! Colon! Kidneys! Shock! Cut! Torment! Hemoglobin! Crucify! Orgasm!" At length the shouted words devolved into wet, snotty, snorting sounds, like a pig snuffling for grubs in the muck.

Hedrick waited for Inyards to calm down, and then he smiled. "Mr. Tone, surely you realized we examined your teeth? There is nothing in there but fillings. However, I would like to talk to you about the DNA of ghosts."

Jack, his bluff exposed, felt himself sagging in his chair. He had hoped to provoke them into killing him, but his unpatriotic tirade had done nothing except incite the buffoonish wrath of the man behind the window. He was suddenly exhausted and only wanted to sleep.

"What was your father's middle name?" asked Hedrick. "The public servant who heroically, if involuntarily, sacrificed his life for the good of the State."

"Ichabod," muttered Jack. He was too dispirited now not to cooperate and had answered truthfully.

"And your maternal grandmother's maiden name?"

"Crane."

"A humorous coincidence, no? But now I want you to meet two very special people."

Hedrick rose and ordered Spork to follow him. They left the interrogation room. A few moments later two Plutocroids came in, a male and a female, both wearing black suits and coats and broad-brimmed hats. Their faces were sallow, their eyes yellow, their pupils tiny, but Tone immediately recognized them.

"Hello, Son," said Mr. Ichabod.

"No…" said Jack, shaking his head.

"Son," said Mrs. Crane, "we know what you are feeling right now. Don't resist the process. Once you get on the other side, you will never look back. Your former father and I were among the first to successfully undergo the transformation so many years ago. It was not death, but liberation."

"I don't believe it!" shouted Jack. "You're dead…buried!"

Mr. Ichabod shook his head. "Jack, it's been a long, long time, but the State gave us new life. We see things so clearly now. We have new and improved feelings. We are so blessed to be born again as completely new and improved information units. You will be blessed as well, and perhaps you can join us in the household of Mr. Reid."

"We must go now, Jack," said Mrs. Crane. "We don't love you anymore. That part of us has died . No trace of our former love for you remains anywhere in the universe, because love is informationally inert. But when you cross to the other side, and experience existence without love, you will see how liberating it is. The Corporationist State will give you the freedom you have always yearned for."

Mr. Ichabod and Mrs. Crane turned and walked away. Jack wanted to throw his hands up to his head, but he couldn't. Instead he thrashed his head back and forth, screaming more intensely than when Spork had assaulted him with the cattle prod.

Figures with masks and white coats came in and injected him. His body ceased its convulsions. The specialists carried him into the Transmogrification Room, stripped him, and placed him on a gurney. They attached wires and tubes to his body, and activated the New Life 9000 Transmogger™. They departed the room, leaving him to his fate.

"How long will it take?" asked Hedrick.

"Couple of weeks, usually," said Inyards, chewing on a thick strawberry tart.

"And the information flush?"

"In a week or week and a half we'll start getting some results."

"Excellent," replied Hedrick. "You will keep me informed, Inyards."

Hedrick took his briefcase and exited the observation room. In the chamber beyond, which led to the stairs, he unexpectedly encountered the two Plutocroids again. He said nothing to them. In truth, he intensely disliked and distrusted these creatures, these post-human mutants. As he passed them on his way to the stairs, he could feel their yellow eyes upon him. It made his skin crawl. Who could tell what the monsters were really thinking?

Mr. Ichabod and Mrs. Crane listened as Hedrick ascended the stairs. Then Ichabod turned to his spouse and took her hand. "Take comfort, woman," he said very quietly. "Our son was lost, and is found again. He was dead to us, but will be reborn."

CHAPTER TWENTY-TWO

Anarchy Isn't Free

Taras Petriv and Emily Bombsinger were sitting at the bar of the Trappist Tavern. It was four in the morning, and the tavern was closed. Bombsinger was sipping a mineral water, while Petriv poured himself occasional shots of vodka.

They could hear the front door opening. Petriv and Emily both reached for their pistols.

Polyvox, Andronicus, and Blackshield entered, looking like a trio of weary travelers.

Bombsinger cried out in surprise.

"Where were you?" she asked. "We were really starting to get worried."

"There was a lot of damage control to be done," said Andronicus. "The other factions are rather miffed at us at the moment. Number One has called for a conclave of all the factions, to discuss the crisis. It will take place tomorrow."

"We have another problem." For once Bombsinger seemed at a loss for words. She cleared her throat. "Tell them, Taras."

"Jack is disappeared—the day before yesterday."

Polyvox stopped unbuttoning her coat. "Disappeared? What do you mean?"

"Security video shows fool going for a walk," said Petriv, "in direct disobedience of commands."

Andronicus cursed, and his words came out in a rush. "Do we have any idea where he could have gone?"

"Some factions reporting heightened levels of Plutocroids in city," said Petriv. "Other than this, *nichoho*—nothing!"

"Of course, they will torture him if they have captured him," said Polyvox.

"And we must assume he has been captured," said Andronicus.

"If they torture him, he will talk," said Blackshield calmly. "He may hold out briefly, but not for long. He may have revealed what he knows already. We may be under observation even as we speak. On the other hand, it's possible he has told them nothing so far. As a Security Agent, he would have been trained in interrogation resistance."

"We have to find out where they took him," said Andronicus.

"Most likely to the SA field office in Manhattan," said Blackshield. "There is a state-of-the-art interrogation unit there, operated by Inyards' Incarso Corp. If they've taken him there, we will never be able to penetrate, and Incarso Corp will break him after a few days, at most."

"They haven't taken him there," said Bombsinger.

The others, including Petriv, looked at her in surprise.

"What do you know about this?" demanded Andronicus.

Bombsinger held up her hands. "Now let's all just stay calm. Our informant at the SA said Jack is not on the list of detainees currently being interrogated at the SA building."

"You might have shared this intelligence earlier, Emily," snarled Polyvox, "and spared us this needless conjecture."

"You were all talking so quickly, I couldn't get a word in edge-wise," said Bombsinger.

"You say nothing to me," grumbled Petriv. "And we are both sitting here at the bar together for hours and hours."

"The information was provided to me just after midnight, and I wanted to tell you all at the same time."

"This is not a game, Emily," said Polyvox. "You should have told Petriv as soon as you knew. All newly acquired intel must be shared immediately with any available members of the faction's inner circle. You know that."

"Sorry."

"Where could Tone be?" wondered Andronicus aloud. "Surely they haven't taken him to Freedom Fortress."

"Apparently not," said Bombsinger. "He is currently being held at Inyards' private interrogation facility in Montclair, New Jersey. Apparently there are torture facilities there as well. In the basement of Inyards' mansion. Torture is not just Inyards' job, it is also his hobby."

"Is there anything else you'd like to tell us, Emily?" said Polyvox, still stewing.

"No, I believe that's it."

"Are you sure? We're all listening. Have you deciphered the Voynich Manuscript? Have you uncovered the mystery of the Bermuda Triangle? Maybe you've figured out what happened to the lost colony of Roanoke?"

"No...no..." Emily paused a moment, "and no."

"Enough, Polyvox," said Andronicus. "She has provided valuable information, even though she erred in withholding it. Who would have thought that Inyards had a private interrogation facility in Montclair, New Jersey? I thought that town just had fancy expensive restaurants and an art museum. What faction controls Essex County, New Jersey?"

"Faction Six," said Blackshield.

"Very good. Emily, do you wish to redeem yourself?"

"Yes."

"Send a message to Bluebeard that I want to speak with him at the conclave tomorrow."

Bombsinger saluted. "Yes, sir! But actually, Andronicus, Bluebeard has already sent word that *he* wants to talk with *you*. Sorry, I was about to mention that."

"Very well, then let him know that *I* wanted to talk with him *first*."

F9

Through winding tunnels and secret passageways, Andronicus led several members of the Faction Nine political discussion group to the great subterranean cavern where the conclave was being held. Andronicus and Polyvox entered first, followed by Blackshield, Krypton, Bombsinger, and Petriv. Bunyan, Abdullah, and Doublecross were not there, ostensibly because they were occupied with other matters. But everyone knew that Andronicus had told them not to come. He did not like all members of Faction 9's inner circle in one public place at one time, just in case there was an attack, either from the Enemy itself, or—which was far less likely—from a rival, renegade faction.

The place was already crowded with hundreds and hundreds of representatives from other factions who had arrived from across the country. Among them, Andronicus and his colleagues noted, were the Cosmic Youth Faction, the Militant Pacifists, the Retro-Federalists, and, of course, the Faction Six Anarchists. Also present were the Neo-Mensheviks, the Ecofeminists, the Social Reconstruction-ists, and the Lights of the Brights. The Knights of Neurodiversity rubbed elbows with the Plasma Primitives; the Galactic Zionists with the ultra-Catholic Sedevacantist Swords. At yet another table, the Islamic Astronomics sat across the table from the Atheist Plurality, exchanging civil but suspicious looks.

There were simply too many groups to count. They represented the whole range of alternative human religious, political, and scien-tific ideology—the kinds of fringe movements that result when all dissident expression, having been banned by the ruling elites, must take place in the shadows. The only groups not present were those representing racism, radical nationalism, and fascism—and any groups suspected of being State puppets.

Riotous noises filled the cavern as factions, some meeting each other for the first time, argued strenuously, drinking, gesticulating, smoking tobacco and weed. Some wore clothing akin to uniforms, while others looked like scruffy homeless people who had somehow wandered in from the streets far above. A small company of teenagers wearing retro spaceman helmets strutted around holding light-placards with the words "Everything Free Now." Near them a group of wiry old monks with shabby brown robes and unkempt gray beards tried to silence them by invoking God. Men and women dressed all in black were handing out Nihilist tracts, while hippies in rainbow shirts and headbands handed out flowers. Militant Pacifists exhorted everyone to Bring the Wars to the Warmongers. A contingent of Traditionalist Revolutionaries in red T-shirts were busy putting up posters of Marx, Engels, and Lenin. They paused briefly to verbally spar with a little band holding banners of Stalin and Mao.

English, Arabic, French, Mandarin, Spanish, Russian, and a slew of other languages filled the cavern, with some revolutionaries rapidly code-switching from one language to another. They sat at tables, shouting and sweating beneath bright klieg lights bolted on the ceiling of the cavern. On one side was a wooden stage that resembled a gallows. Self-appointed bouncers paced up and down, trying to prevent people from climbing on top, but they were subjected to derisive invective.

Faction Nine grimly took in the scene, which, were it not for the tendency of the various factions to clump together like yaks, might have devolved into utter stampeding, table-turning chaos. Andronicus, Polyvox, and their co-factionists were highly secretive, and none of them felt particularly comfortable among this rabble of radicals, reactionaries, discontents, marginals, and heretical intellectuals. They wondered how much of their own business had been divulged to the would-be revolutionaries around them, each of whom was clamoring for attention, each earnestly trying to win over the others through rhetoric, bombast, and theory.

Andronicus led his people to an empty table, hoping to keep them more or less inconspicuous. He now concluded it was the height of folly, even insanity, to gather so many revolutionary factions in one place at one time. Had Number One lost his or her senses? It was hard to say. Andronicus and the others had not actually met with Number One—no one ever did—but had spoken only with their representative, the Shadow. The Shadow, who communicated through a screen that disguised his voice and appearance, had seemed reasonable enough just a few days ago, calmly conveying to the leaders of Faction Nine Number One's suggestions and opinions in the wake of the failed assassination attempt on Reid. But the scene that presented itself now was not reassuring.

"Let's keep near the exits," he said softly to Polyvox.

"Agreed."

The place had the look and feel of a beer hall. Some factions had brought their own food, as if to a picnic. Others were buying beer and pretzels. Some factions were heatedly engaging anyone they could in debates, while others sat by themselves, withdrawn and wary.

Andronicus ordered beer for his people. They sipped, sat, and waited. Presently, three people approached their table. One was a hulking, barrel-chested man with a thick black beard, brown eyes, and curly dark hair. His face was scarred and he wore gold earrings. His companions were even taller than he was, though more slender: a man and a woman who bore a strong resemblance to each other and who shared the same hard, unsmiling features. The man wore a hat with a wampum belt of red beads around it. The woman also wore a hat, decorated with artfully woven green feathers. These were Bluebeard, the "war chief" of the Faction Six Anarchists, and his top lieutenants Redfeather and Greenfeather.

Bluebeard had something of the pirate about him, as if his namesake had been vaulted into the future and hastily shoved into contemporary attire. He was not the paramount leader of his faction, but rather the highest-ranking visible leader. Redfeather and Greenfeather resembled harpoonists from an eighteenth-century Nantucket whaler. They were Bluebeard's first lieutenants. The three of them were sometimes jokingly referred to as the "Tricolor," but never to their faces.

Faction Six was one of the largest of the factions, with at least a thousand avowed members organized like a political mafia into a hierarchy of companies, platoons, and triads. It was hated and hunted by the authorities, but its members were so fanatically loyal to their anarchist cause that in the rare instances they found themselves on the point of capture they immediately activated personal spontaneous combustion units—or so it was claimed—leaving the Security Agency with nothing but piles of dust to sift through. At the same time, Faction Six had a reputation for being extremely cautious and conservative in its activities. It had carried out a few successful assassinations, but mostly it engaged in surveillance in the territory under its control.

Only one Faction Six member had ever defected to another faction, and that was Polyvox, who had never explained her reasons to Andronicus, but who had received the sanction of Number One. Thanks to Polyvox, Faction Nine probably knew more about their rivals than any other revolutionary group in the country.

"Andronicus, we have to talk," said Bluebeard, not bothering to introduce himself or his associates. Everyone knew who they were.

"Have a seat, Bluebeard."

"In private. I have a vehicle up on the street."

"Anything you say to me can be said down here, before my comrades," replied Andronicus.

Bluebeard took a seat, while Redfeather and Greenfeather flanked him on either side.

"Where are the rest of your wild bunch?" asked Andronicus.

"Around us. Watching."

Bluebeard ignored the others at the table—except for Polyvox, to whom he gave a curt, white-toothed smile. "Word on the street has it that you've botched up big-time, Andronicus."

"Oh?"

"Apparently—and I admit this defies credulity—you attempted to assassinate Gregory Reid himself."

"Utter nonsense."

"They say that's why Number One has called this unexpected conclave of all the factions."

"Now think about this for a minute, Bluebeard," said Andronicus, taking a sip of his beer and leaning closer to his rival. "If what you are saying is true, why would Number One summon this confused mob of people? To talk it out quietly among themselves? That makes no sense at all."

"It makes perfect sense," said Bluebeard. "The reason Number One has called the conclave is precisely to muddy the waters, to confuse people. Rumors will be generated here, elaborated upon, and disseminated from one faction to another. The brothers and sisters will go back to their cities and their hideouts, taking their newly appropriated welter of disinformation with them. It's called 'chatter-overload,' and it will pitch the eavesdropping apparatus of the State into a maelstrom of confusion. I'm sure your man Blackshield can tell you all about it."

"And what is Number One hoping to accomplish by generating this massive level of chatter-overload?"

"The rumor is that you, by chance, discovered some kind of secret weapon being sponsored by Reid and his Department of Defense lackeys, and this is why you tried to kill him. That's what Number One is trying to hide."

"A secret weapon?"

"Yes."

"Come now, Bluebeard. This is the real world, not some James Bond fantasy. What sort of secret weapon could you possibly be talking about?"

Bluebeard hesitated, and Andronicus, eyeing him shrewdly, detected uncertainty behind his hard, rugged features. "An army of genetically modified insects," he said at last.

Andronicus laughed loudly, right in Bluebeard's face. His laughter trailed off into a sigh. "My stars," he said. Then with a touch of anger: "Surely you can't be serious, Bluebeard. You're wasting my time with this line of questioning. But I'll tell you what. As soon as Number One makes his appearance to address the conclave, you can go up and ask him—or her—yourself."

"Number One will not appear. Number One never appears."

"Let's wait and see."

"I propose a trade," said Bluebeard. "You tell us what Gregory Reid is really up to, and we will provide you with safe passage, perhaps even assistance."

"Safe passage?"

"Into our territory, which includes Essex County, New Jersey. That's where one of your people is being held by Frake Inyards in a private dungeon. Or haven't you heard yet? We know exactly where he is, but according to the code of the factions, you can only operate there with our permission."

"Right," said Andronicus soberly. "Let me consult with my people."

"We'll be waiting for your answer, Andronicus." Bluebeard, Redfeather, and Greenfeather disappeared into the crowd.

F9

"How did he get that information?" Andronicus wanted to know. "And so quickly."

"Faction Six is quite extensive," said Blackshield, "with far more members than we have. They keep all members of the corporate aristocracy within their territory under close observation. They're obsessive-compulsive about it."

"But Inyards must bring victims to his private torture chamber all the time—or at least on a regular basis. How would Faction Six know that one of them was affiliated with us?"

"They made visual identification," said Petriv. "Bluebeard knows who we are."

"Maybe," said Andronicus, his eyes narrowing.

"What are you looking at me for?" asked Polyvox.

"Perhaps we have a breach," suggested Andronicus softly.

"Are you questioning my loyalty to our political discussion group?"

"There was a time when you and Bluebeard were politically close, was there not? When you yourself had some sympathy for the Anarchist cause." Andronicus's eyes were pinned on her.

"That was a long time ago, before I joined Faction Nine. My politics have changed. I'm a Social Democrat, like the rest of you. How could you even question that, Andronicus?"

"Where the security of the Discussion Group is concerned, I question everything."

"Andronicus, your implications about Polyvox are unfair," said Krypton suddenly. "It would be nothing for one of Bluebeard's field operatives to record Jack being removed from a car at Inyards' mansion and then taken inside. Now that we have this information, do we cooperate with them? The sooner we can retrieve Jack, the better."

"We would have to reveal what we know about Operation Autocrat to him. That's information that *we* discovered."

"He would only share it with his inner circle," said Bombsinger. "Besides, we're on the verge of disaster anyway. What harm can be done now?"

"We'll put it to a vote," said Andronicus. "All in favor of cooperating with Faction Six through an exchange of information, raise your hands."

Everyone at the table lifted an arm, except for Andronicus.

"So be it," he grumbled. "I guess it's going to be cooperation, God damn it."

On the stage a woman stood at the podium and rapped on a microphone, calling for order. "Our host has indicated that the conclave should proceed in the following manner. Each registered organization will be called up to give an address of no more than ten minutes. The order of presentations has been determined at random. We'll begin with the Cosmic Youth Faction."

A young woman little older than a high school student bounded up to the stage, applauded enthusiastically by her comrades, watched warily by everyone else in the cavern.

"I wish to read a poem," she began, "on behalf of the Cosmic Youth Faction."

Some revolutionaries cheered, others hooted and booed. In time they forced themselves to be quiet, and the young woman began.

O Beautiful for battle cries,
For waves of death and pain,
For greedy, marching, wicked hordes,
Who slaughtered just for gain.

Plutocracy! Plutocracy!
You filthy poisoned whore,
You crush the world with tyranny
And wage unending war.

O Beautiful for racists' feet,
Whose grim fascistic stress,
A thoroughfare of hatred beat,
Across a wilderness.
Plutocracy! Plutocracy!
Someday you'll kneel and crawl,
Condemned by all for monstrous deeds,
And mockery of law.

O Beautiful for cowards proved,
In bloody, murderous strife,
Who more than Right their Oil did love,
And Money more than life.
O Plutocrats, O Plutocrats!
Your crimes the world knows well.
God damn you for eternity
To roast in Satan's hell.

The young woman looked up with an expression of fierce defiance. There was a tense pause, followed by a thunderous din of cheering, foot stomping, mug thumping, and howling.

Faction Nine retained its dignity. Polyvox lifted an eyebrow. Petriv frowned. Blackshield betrayed no emotion. Emily Bombsinger smirked slightly. The Professor ignited his pipe and puffed meditatively. But Andronicus appeared most affected—his arms crossed over his chest, his eyes seething with anger.

"Youth," he muttered, "is wasted on the young. A crude poem. I am and always will be an American patriot, but these young revolutionaries today, they are a disgrace. That was cheap political doggerel."

"What do you mean?" asked Bombsinger. "I thought it was pretty good. In fact, I memorized it and will sing it to myself in the shower."

"You are young, Emily, but someday you will learn what patriotism means. There was a time when young people loved their country."

"But that was when young people *had* a country," said Bombsinger. "They don't have a country now. You can't love what you don't have. It's easy for you to make judgments, Andronicus. You remember another time, one when the country and the world weren't rocketing in the wrong direction, like a train about to jump the rails and plunge into a canyon. Not everyone has that memory. And when you lose the memory, you lose the dream. And when you lose the dream, the old songs die. So you tear them up to make room for new ones."

Polyvox nodded and pointed at Andronicus. "*Touché!*"

Andronicus looked away from them all, grumbling into his beer. Sometimes he felt very alone in the world.

F9

The next afternoon, while Emily Bombsinger was tending her bar at the Trappist Tavern, Bluebeard and Greenfeather entered and sat down. Greenfeather took off her hat and placed it on the bar. Emily noted that her face was humorless and weatherworn, but beautiful in its way. Bluebeard, on the other hand, had a face more suited to a snarl than a frown.

"Jamaican rum, if you have it," said Bluebeard. "Two glasses."

"Would you like to see menus?" asked Emily unenthusiastically, as she placed the rum before them.

"We'll both have buffalo burgers," said Bluebeard.

"We only serve synthetic buffalo meat."

"Then that will have to do," said Bluebeard.

The two ate their meal in a leisurely way. When they were finished, Emily handed over the bar to Petriv and took them to the back room of the Trappist Tavern, where Andronicus, Polyvox, and Blackshield were waiting. Bluebeard and Greenfeather sat down next to each other.

"Sour ale?" asked Andronicus.

"We prefer rum," said Blackshield.

"We don't have that back here. In this room, we only drink ale."

"Clearly the customer does not come first at the Trappist Tavern," grumbled Bluebeard. "Very well, give us ale."

Polyvox uncorked a large bottle and poured glasses for everyone.

"What do you have for us?" asked Andronicus impatiently.

Bluebeard unfolded a large, hand-drawn map and displayed photographs. "Here is the location of Frake Inyards' mansion, on a street called King George Road. Most of the homes on this street are rather immense, and Inyards' is no exception. It stands out from the others in that it is built in the style of a medieval castle, with a sweeping view of the New York skyline about twelve miles away. Inyards' castle is made of stone, with approximately forty rooms. The basement contains his private torture chamber and detention facility."

"How well-protected is the mansion?" asked Blackshield.

"The electronic defenses are essentially impenetrable. In addition, there are three bodyguards, whom we refer to as Beardy, Bruiser, and Baldy."

"So how do we get in there?" inquired Andronicus.

"That's your problem, isn't it?" replied Bluebeard.

"Perhaps you can offer us suggestions."

"You will not be able to elude the electronic sensors. You will have to walk in there openly."

"Openly?"

"The mansion receives regular visits. On Mondays, a weekly food delivery. On Tuesdays, a shipment from Inyards' wine merchant. On Wednesdays, detainees are brought in, although this does not happen every Wednesday, and at the moment it seems only your man is being detained. On Thursdays, a subcontractor called Tommy Torc Interrogation Services pays a visit. We think they maintain Inyards' interrogation equipment and sometimes assist in the torture process itself. They also probably clean up after a messy interrogation session. On Friday, two Prisons Department officials arrive with a young teenage boy or girl."

"What the hell for?" asked Andronicus.

"You all know that Inyards has certain depraved inclinations. That's no secret."

"So this animal regularly traffics in underage victims with the help of the Prisons Department," concluded Polyvox, "and your faction has done nothing about it?"

"And what are we supposed to do?" replied Bluebeard.

"Take out the Department of Prisons traffickers and rescue the child, for one."

"That's a very noble suggestion, Polyvox. But then there's the little matter of exposing our entire surveillance operation to the Enemy and having them hunt us down and execute us in creative and horrible ways."

"Why are you even bothering to collect all this information on the plutocrats if you don't actually do anything about their crimes?"

"So when the time comes to strike, we can do so with a reasonable chance of success—unlike you Faction Nine hotheads, you reckless Trigger Hipsters, who apparently feel justified in making assassination attempts whenever the impulse moves you."

Polyvox simultaneously cocked a cold eyebrow and narrowed her steel gray eyes. "Trigger Hipsters?"

Bluebeard made a slightly awkward shrug. "Well, that's what the other factions are calling you now. 'The Number Nine Trigger Hipsters.'"

"We are *not* hipsters, God damn it," said Bombsinger. "That's so offensive."

Greenfeather smiled disdainfully, removing a carved wooden vapor pipe from under her poncho and taking a puff. "Sensitive, aren't we, little sister?"

"Who asked you?"

"*We* in Faction Six don't call you that," said Bluebeard defensively. "That's just what the other factions call you."

"You just did call us that," retorted Bombsinger. "How would you like it if we called you 'Anarchists'?"

"We are Anarchists."

"Okay, then maybe we'll start calling you 'Analkissers.'"

Bluebeard grimaced. "You contemporary young people are so vulgar. In my day we would never have spoken to our revolutionary elders in such a fashion. Andronicus, you need to teach your whelps some manners."

"Enough of this inane bickering," said Andronicus wearily. "What is this, a Presidential debate?"

Emily Bombsinger sat back, crossing her arms, but continued to give Bluebeard and Greenfeather the evil eye.

Andronicus spoke again: "Bluebeard, I assume that this Tommy Torc subcontractor gets access to Inyards' torture chamber, unlike the other visitors."

"That would make sense."

"Then our solution is easy. We go in masquerading as Tommy Torc reps. How many of them show up each Tuesday?"

"Usually the same four, but it can vary. I can tell you something else. Before visiting Inyards' place, they invariably have dinner at Regan's Tavern in town. Then, around midnight, they pull up at Inyards' castle. Their van simply says 'Tommy Torc, LLC.' They don't wear uniforms, just black suits and black sunglasses."

Andronicus cleared his throat, betraying his discomfort. "If your faction cares to move a little bit outside of its comfort zone, Bluebeard, there is a way you can assist us."

Bluebeard turned cautious. "What do you mean?"

"We could use your help in this operation."

"We've helped you by giving you information, Andronicus."

"What I'm suggesting is closer active cooperation between our factions—starting now, with this rescue operation. We may not see eye to eye politically, Bluebeard. But we do have a common enemy in the Corporate State. You want to destroy it; we want to remake it. The two objectives are not necessarily mutually exclusive."

"I'm not so convinced that would be a good idea, especially now that Faction Nine is under such opprobrium. You're in the Revolutionary Doghouse at the moment."

"But what do we have to lose, Bluebeard?" Andronicus had the slightly pained expression of the stoic who does not want to be perceived as pleading.

Bluebeard, sensing his moment of power, folded his arms and smiled smugly. "You need us more than we need you."

Andronicus considered this for a moment. "True. But it may not always be that way. You know that we have technologies that other factions do not."

Andronicus's reference to "technology" was not lost on Bluebeard, whose smile now became a businesslike frown. "Give us a moment to confer." He and Greenfeather got up from the table and stood apart from the others, where they held an animated, whispered conversation for several minutes.

Polyvox, who had the keenest hearing of any of them, strained to listen. But though she knew hundreds of human languages, she did not know this one. Andronicus eyed her questioningly.

"*Volapük*," she said softly.

"Are you joking…?"

Bluebeard and Greenfeather returned to the table, their faces grim. "I think we'll take another glass of that sour ale," said Bluebeard.

Polyvox refilled their glasses.

"Well?" asked Andronicus impatiently. "What do you say?"

"For now, we will cooperate."

Andronicus sat back, making the faintest exhalation of relief.

CHAPTER TWENTY-THREE

Walpurgis Night

Four Tommy Torc interrogation subcontractors sat around a table in the scrappy, sawdusty Regan's Tavern, drinking cheap beer and chomping on pink slime hamburgers. They wore black suits with American flag pins on the lapels.

"I'll tell you," said Bedford, wiping his face with a paper napkin, "that last gig was a good one. Kracker Kola basically lets you do anything to suspected corporate spies. Did you hear that little freak squeal like a pig when we screwed his thumbs? And he sang, too, like a canary. I love pussy."

The others laughed and stuffed fries into their mouths, their greasy lips working like spastic rubber gaskets.

"Damn straight," said Forrest, lifting his plastic beer mug. "God Bless 'Merica. Pussy, yeah."

"God Bless 'Merica," said the others, knocking their mugs. They slurped down their beers and belched in unison for refills. "Pussy!" they shouted.

A waitress with a full harness of Pharmatainment jacks in her neck swept the old plastic beer mugs into the trash and set down four filled replacements.

"Mr. Inyards' gigs aren't so bad," said Coughlin, grubby fingers picking a piece of gristle from his teeth and flicking it on the sawdust-covered floor. "Sometimes you just mop up the blood, incinerate the organs, and check the calibrations. Gimme pussy. But every once in a while he lets you have at one of those traitors he keeps in there."

"They say that Mr. Inyards is a personal friend of Mr. Gregory Reid," said Rizzo reverently. "Where can we get pussy?"

Forrest slurped his beer. "Mr. Reid might run for president, I hear. I'd vote for him. I really would. We haven't had a good president since my grandfather's grandfather's time—the Drumpf Days. I like pussy, too."

The four men became solemn, tapping their plastic beer mugs. "To the Drumpf Days, and to pussy."

Bedford dug a bit of snot out of his nose, examined it incuriously, and popped it in his mouth. "My grandfather told me that his grandfather told *him* that if President Drumpf hadn't fallen into the open sewer pit behind his brothel and been devoured alive by rabid dogs, all of history would have turned out different."

Coughlin looked disgusted. "I just watched a History Channel infomercial on that. They say it was a conspiracy. All they ever recovered were his hands. You can see his hands in formaldehyde at the Drumpf Museum, but they're all shrunk, like little toy hands."

"You can be sure that those hands," said Forrest, pointing at Coughlin, "once grabbed pussy."

"Amen!" They knocked their plastic mugs.

"Reid is a true American," said Rizzo. "Because he's a winner. He could be bigger than Drumpf ever was. They say he has a beautiful wife. This country needs a winner to lead it. A winner who gets good pussy and can restore our former greatness, who will complete the winning pass on the gridiron of the world."

"Pussy, yeah," said the other torture men, again knocking their plastic beer mugs. "God Bless 'Merica."

"It's getting late," said Bedford.

"Damn," said the others. "Pussy."

Together all four of them belched out something that resounded like a quadruple troll fart, their mouths gaping and their cheeks shuddering like buttocks. They placed their money on the table, then stomped out of the tavern and into the back parking lot, where their van was parked. The four men had the distinctive hunched-over gait of an orcish hunting party. Bedford shoved a big, spider-hairy hand in his pocket for a pack of cigarettes. At that moment, Bluebeard, Redfeather, and Greenfeather, handkerchiefs over their faces, stepped out of the shadows. There were four muffled gasps, and the Tommy Torc men crashed heavily onto the ground. No blood flowed. The four bodies convulsed for a minute, and then went dead still.

Greenfeather stood over them, holding a pistol with a silencer. The bullets, though small caliber, had been laced with the same quick-acting neurotoxin that the T4 Corporation used in its Paradise Now™ euthanasia centers. "No more pussy for you, boys," she said.

Bluebeard chuckled beneath his handkerchief. "Especially not in Hell."

Once the three Faction Six leaders pulled the bodies into their own van, Andronicus, Polyvox, Blackshield, Petriv, and Krypton appeared, wearing dark suits.

"The van is yours," said Bluebeard. He handed them the American flag pins that had been on the lapels of the Tommy Torc men. "Put these on, and good luck. Try to be on time. It won't take us long to dispose of these bodies. After three in the morning we leave, with or without you."

Polyvox sat behind the wheel of the Tommy Torc van, while Andronicus got in next to her. Blackshield, Petriv, and Krypton sat in the back. The van pulled out of the parking lot and headed up the hill toward Inyards' castle.

F9

Polyvox parked the van on King George Street. They put on their sunglasses and walked up to the front door of the castle-mansion. All of them were wearing black Tommy Torc suites. Polyvox rang the bell. The door opened, and Beardy stood there.

"Tommy Torc Interrogation Services," Polyvox announced.

"You a new crew?" asked Beardy, giving them the once-over.

"Just me," said Polyvox. "You know these other guys." Andronicus, Blackshield, and Petriv, standing behind her, mumbled vague greetings.

"Come in," said Beardy gruffly. "You're right on time."

They breezed past Beardy and entered an expansive foyer with a tall grandfather clock on one side. "Mr. Inyards said to take you right down. Make sure to follow normal procedures." He led them along a hallway to a circular bank vault door, then stood aside, watching them. The door was gleaming polished steel, with a combination lock in the middle of it.

Beardy glanced at his watch.

"Aren't you going to open it?" asked Andronicus.

Beardy looked startled. "Open…? Since when did you forget it's a pre-programmed timer, Coughlin? Wait a minute…where's Forrest? Take off those glasses—"

Beardy suddenly reached into his vest and drew a pink Beretta 9mm Nano, but before he could fire, Blackshield shot him in the side of the head. As his body slumped, the grandfather clock tolled in the foyer. At the same time, the bank vault door whirred and clicked and swung open, revealing a downward flight of stairs. Someone came charging up the stairs, blasting away with a combat shotgun. The Friendly Neighborhood Political Discussion Group dove for cover as scattered buckshot punched holes into the ceiling and floor. Bruiser, his eyes bugged out, his mouth wide open in an animalistic roar, leaped into the room. Petriv swung his fist up hard, connecting directly with Bruiser's chin. The bodyguard's head snapped back and he fell backwards against the wall, his shotgun clattering on the floor.

"Polyvox and I will go down into the torture chamber," said Andronicus to Blackshield. "You and Petriv neutralize Baldy and Inyards."

Andronicus and Polyvox descended the stairs, their weapons drawn, but there was no more resistance. They found Jack on a gurney, hooked up by wires and tubes to an elaborate machine.

He was barely recognizable.

Polyvox ran up the stairs again, across the foyer, and onto the street. She opened the door of the van and said to Krypton, "Andronicus wants you now. Bring the med kit with you. It looks pretty bad."

F9

Blackshield and Petriv searched the rooms on the first floor, and then ran up the steps to the second. Baldy came at them, in full body armor, firing short bursts with a weapon they immediately recognized: a Henckler & Kooch Eighth-Generation Assault Buddy with a pair of hundred-round drum magazines.

The so-called super room broom.

Baldy advanced, his weapon barking like a rabid dog with fiery teeth, ripping out paneling on the wall behind Blackshield and Petriv. They dove down. As methodically as a robot, Baldy swept his line of fire around. Blackshield threw himself into one room, Petriv in another. Blackshield reached into his pocket, pulled out a mini-grenade, and lobbed it down the hallway. As he did, the doorjamb was chewed to shreds by Baldy's gun.

Blackshield fell back into the room just as the grenade exploded. He and Petriv waited a moment, then crept into the hallway.

As the smoke cleared, they saw that Baldy had been disassembled, body, body armor, and all.

They ran down the hallway in the other direction to a pair of doors, which they kicked open easily. Inyards sat at the end of a long refectory table, the remains of a feast on a plate before him, holding a glass of wine.

"Let's not waste time, gentlemen, for I am a busy man," he said, sipping his wine. "You have passed the test. How much do you want?"

"What do you mean?" asked Blackshield, glancing warily around the dining room.

"Every man has his price, what's yours? One hundred million? Five hundred million? Half my kingdom?" Inyards smiled and popped an olive into his mouth. He sucked on it before chewing it slowly.

They approached him cautiously, Petriv walking down one side of the refectory table, Blackshield down the other, and stopped on either side of him.

"How much would you say your life is worth?" asked Blackshield.

"I can tell you that my net worth is precisely fifty billion," said Inyards tranquilly, taking another sip of wine. "Very modest, compared to some. And yet I am prepared to be very generous. Now, I know what you're both thinking. How will we arrange all this? How can we possibly get away with this? After all, we came here to kill this man, so how can we really just walk away with money in our pockets? Well, I'll explain it to you. You will not walk away with money. I will take you on as consultants at Incarso Corp. I did not get where I am today, gentlemen, by destroying all of my enemies. No, I got where I am today by turning my enemies into friends. So what I am proposing is a business deal, not a bribe. I am not proposing to pay for my life. I am perfectly aware of the fact that you could kill me at this moment, and there's nothing I could do about it. But you won't do that, will you?"

"What makes you so sure?" asked Blackshield.

"Because by killing me, you will not only turn your back on a life of power and privilege, but you will also be, within the space of a month, liquidated yourselves. This is not a possibility, this is a *certainty*. You are killers, gentlemen. I'm simply proposing that you kill *for* me, instead of killing for whomever employs you now. Certainly they're not paying you as much as I will."

"They are not paying us anything at all," said Blackshield.

"Not paying you anything at all?" scoffed Inyards. "Come now, that is absurd."

"And what is more," added Blackshield, "our people are not *pedophile rapists*."

Inyards put down his wineglass and sat back in his chair, his moist lips parting slightly. Something flickered in his eyes, like an old analog television screen losing its reception in a field of static snow. At the other end of the room, on a screen mounted into the wall, an unspeakably vile video was playing, positioned so that Inyards could view it as he dined.

His voice had changed when he next spoke, sounding like the dry, raspy crinkle of fallen leaves in winter. "You may find it difficult to believe, gentlemen," he swallowed, "but those images are computer-generated, they aren't real at all…"

"Who else do you have imprisoned in this place?" asked Blackshield.

"No one, I swear…just your man Jack Tone."

"And the victims brought to you by the government?"

"All dead…I mean, not dead," Inyards hastily corrected himself, "you know what I mean…disposed of…no, that's not what I mean. Gentlemen, wait—"

"The life of a degenerate like you," said Blackshield, slipping his pistol into his coat pocket, "isn't even worth a bullet."

Inyards tried to back his chair up, but Petriv produced a garrote and snagged it around his neck. Inyards thrashed violently, grasping at the leather cord. He kicked, and his feet—too large for his skinny legs—shattered plates and crystal glasses, then toppled his wine decanter, which disgorged twenty-thousand-dollar *Domaine de la Romanée-Conti Grand Cru* burgundy onto the white wool carpet. His legs went slack, his fat purple tongue protruded, his mouth twisted in a delirious grin, and his eyes goggled one last time at something just before him—some angel or demon. Blackshield, following Inyards' gaze, saw the abominable images playing across the screen above the refectory table. Drawing his gun, Blackshield shot the screen, blowing it out. Inyards made a kind of wheezing sound through his nostrils, then fell back in the chair. Petriv went down with him, and when he came up again, Inyards lay on the floor, completely still, his face frozen in a horrified hobgoblin death mask.

Petriv was panting heavily and looked sickly and pale; though a powerful man, he did not like this sort of work. Blackshield, on the other hand, moved with a light, breathless sort of urgency. He signaled to Petriv with his gray eyes, and together they went room to room on the second and third floors of the castle, holding a life-detector, looking for hidden recesses, secret chambers, disguised doors—any place where the money-pig Inyards might possibly be concealing other victims. They found no one. Downstairs they met Polyvox and Andronicus carrying Jack on a gurney across the foyer. Krypton was monitoring his vitals on a handheld device.

"What the hell is this?" asked Blackshield, staring at Jack's emaciated body, at his greenish skin, his wide, yellow eyes. "What the devil were they doing to him?"

"It would appear," said Polyvox, "that they were transforming him into a Plutocroid."

"Have you searched for other captives?" asked Andronicus, wiping a sleeve across his sweating brow.

"Yes. Nothing."

Blackshield and Petriv couldn't seem to draw their horrified eyes away from Jack's hideous corpse, at once alive and dead.

"Then snap out of it, both of you! Place the incendiaries and meet us back at the Tommy Torc van."

A few minutes later, the van tore away down King George Road and up a ramp into the back of a waiting moving truck. Greenfeather was sitting behind the wheel in the cab. Bluebeard and Redfeather closed the door of the trailer and climbed in front with Greenfeather.

"Where to now?" asked Greenfeather, putting the truck in gear. She was smoking her ornately carved vapor pipe.

"The Parkway," snapped Blackshield, his eyes peering nervously into the darkness beyond the truck.

"What exit?"

"That's the eternal human question for which there is no answer. Step on it, Greenfeather, before the Enemy swarms. I'm not ready to die just yet for these Faction Nine lunatics."

As the moving truck rumbled off, Inyards' castle imploded, crashing into itself and erupting in a high column of flame, as if some orifice to hell had been opened through necromancy and was now gleefully regurgitating its molten entrails into the world of humans.

"Christ," said Bluebeard, shaking his head. "Fuckin' Trigger Hipsters."

CHAPTER TWENTY-FOUR

Reid Goes Paranoid

Captain Ronald Hedrick of the Warforce FBI exited the helicopter on the roof of the Gazillionaire's Tower and was saluted by seven of Reid's praetorian guards, including the Master Sergeant. An escort of guards took him downstairs, through several reinforced doors, and along a hallway lined with Plutocroids in long black coats and wide black hats. Each one carried a weapon resembling a tommy gun, and they all drilled into him with their blazing yellow eyes. At the end of the hallway, another guard opened a vault door, and Hedrick was admitted into the heavily secured, bombproof inner sanctum where Reid sat at a simple desk, surrounded by a ring of armed Type I Plutocroids headed by Mr. Ichabod.

The ring of Plutocroids opened to admit Hedrick, who sat down in front of Reid's desk.

"Good evening, Mr. Reid."

"My arm is fully healed. I am become a God," said Reid, who was holding a Kalashnikov in one hand and an Uzi in the other. He was also wearing a bulletproof vest and a Kevlar helmet.

"Mr. Reid?"

"Having survived the plots and schemes of the Revolutionary Devils, I now rise up in apotheosis. I am become a God."

"Yes, Mr. Reid. That is…apparent."

"And yet, Hedrick, though I am a God, I am a prisoner of my own apartment, because neither Boyler, nor Inyards, nor you, nor anybody can apparently keep me safe from the American revolutionary maniacs who operate with impunity in the land. Explain!"

"I'm sorry, sir. We're doing our best."

"Your best isn't good enough, is it? What is the point of the Billionaires' Guild funding the FBI's budget if you can't keep us safe?"

"I understand your anxiety, Mr. Reid."

"I think it's high time we privatized the FBI, as we did the military. Government idiots."

"Mr. Reid, I'm afraid I have some bad news."

"Eh? What sort of bad news?"

"It's about Inyards."

"What about him?"

"Dead."

"What?" shrieked Reid. "What do you mean?"

"Deceased." Hedrick shrugged. "Finished. The end of the line. The Hotel Terminus. The ultimate extinction of the object self."

"But how?"

"The security feed shows him being strangled at his dinner table by home invaders. His manse was then blown sky high."

Reid sucked his breath in deeply.

"But wait," said Hedrick, "there's more. They took Jack Tone."

Reid nodded. A numbness was beginning to creep over him. He looked around at the ring of Plutocroids, all of whom had their backs to him except for one, Mr. Ichabod, now almost fully recovered from his grievous injuries.

"Sir," said Mr. Ichabod, "your pills." He placed a tray with three blue pills and a glass of water in front of Reid, who put down his Kalashnikov and Uzi, took the glass of water, and washed the tablets down.

"I do have some good news for you, Mr. Reid, involving the investigation into the thwarted attempt on your life," said Hedrick, polishing his fingernails on his lapel.

"Oh?"

"The assassins were wearing very sophisticated DNA scramblers, but we have finally managed to sort through to the real stuff. Post-incident DNA analysis performed at Freedom Fortress has now produced a match. That is, we know the identity of two of the four assassins. The third assassin appears to be a male of mixed East Asian and European ancestry, identity unknown. And the fourth—well the fourth intruder's DNA was a bit puzzling and is undergoing reanalysis."

"Why was it puzzling?"

"The analysis indicated some kind of unknown animal."

"Whatever. Tell me the identity of the known malefactors."

"The first is..." Hedrick paused for effect. "Jack Tone."

"But how can that be? That means he was apprehended by Plutocroids *after* the attempt to assassinate me."

"Evidently."

"You told me the assassins were all killed!"

"We have every reason to believe that the other three were destroyed—blown up in the Monongahela River by depth charges. Revolutionaries on the run invariably split up. Tone was not with the others who fled in the car. He successfully escaped, only to be captured again by roving field Plutocroids in Philadelphia."

"But he just escaped again," marveled Reid. "After still other revolutionaries murdered dear old Inyards, one of the kindest, most gentle, and most loving men I've ever known. What kind of übermensch is this Tone? What kind of ruthless scoundrel? Did He who made the lamb make Tone?"

"Mr. Reid, Jack Tone *was* clearly one of the most cunning and resourceful enemies the State has ever confronted. Note I said '*was.*' You see, those who rescued Tone this time will be in for a nasty surprise. While in Inyard's custody, and on my command, Tone was inoculated with the Plutocroid virus. I dare say that, soon enough, he will be presenting himself for duty once again. He will be the most deadly operative the world has ever known, *but he will work for us.*"

Reid grunted in satisfaction. "You said another one of the assassins was identified."

"Yes. Ethan Gratz Schwartzschild, formerly a captain in the U.S. Special Forces. At the time of the enactment of the Privatization of the Military Act, Schwartzschild was active in an organized, dissenting faction of officers. Arrest warrants were issued, and Schwartzschild disappeared—presumably overseas. A very dangerous fellow, and thankfully he is dead."

"His name," said Reid, giving his chin a sinister stroke, "connotes the Jew."

"Precisely, Mr. Reid."

Reid shook his head. "Now the Jews conspire against me. What are we to do about this perfidy, Captain Hedrick?"

"To be perfectly frank, Mr. Reid, the faction that Schwartzschild belonged to no doubt also includes self-identified Jews, Aryans, Negroids, Mongoloids, Hottentots, Wogs, Lascars, Slavs, Arabs, Creoles, Sicilians, Greeks, Quadroons, Octoroons, Half-breeds, Pacific Islanders, Inuit, Gypsies, assorted Swarthies, Sub-Continentals, Crackers, Hillbillies, Rednecks, and even Irish. The ideologies that drive these revolutionary mongrels are curiously indifferent to the natural boundaries of Race. Do not trouble yourself about their ethnic composition. It is irrelevant. Increasingly, young people choose their genetics like they choose their religions. The entire concept of racial purity has all but been destroyed. In time, we will reverse this Racial Chaos, this ethnic entropy, and restore the natural order. Your primary concern right now is to avoid the scorpion sting of those who hate you."

"Hedrick," said Reid, "please advise. Schwartzschild is dead, Tone will soon be on the payroll of the Grombex Corporation, but there are still others out there who want to rob me of life and rob this country of its future."

"I suggest taking you and your family aboard your nuclear-powered helicopter yacht *Never Enough* and remaining airborne for as long as it takes for us to *figure out what is going on*. The U.S. Air Force Corporation, of which you are a major shareholder, can protect you from airborne attacks. I would order your Alpha Crew to ready themselves posthaste."

"Thanks, Hedrick. You are a good friend. Will you join us on the *Never Enough*?"

"My work is here on the surface, Mr. Reid. There are certain lines of investigation I wish to follow. But as soon as everything is cleared up, I will personally deliver the good news to you."

79

Stephany Miscellany was in the card room quietly playing Monopoly with Fritz and Clara, who sat on either side of her. The children could hear the great commotion outside. On their way to the card room, they had seen guards marching around, important-looking people coming and going, and many more people who had a weird resemblance to Mr. Ichabod and Mrs. Crane.

Suddenly Reid flung open the door and barged inside. His eyes were burning, his black hair mussed. "All of you!" he shouted. "Prepare your things at once. We depart at dawn on the *Never Enough*."

He slammed the door behind him. Fritz and Clara looked at Miscellany with anxious eyes.

"What's happening now?" asked Clara in a whisper.

"I don't know," said Miscellany. "I'll find out."

Just then Reid came in again, somewhat calmer. Chewing on his right thumb, he looked down at them. "My dear ones, do you know why we must leave?"

Fritz and Clara shook their heads.

Reid glared at them. He did not blink, and for a full minute he said nothing. His head just moved up and down, up and down.

"Enough of this, Gregory," said Miscellany. "You're alarming them. Tell us what this is all about."

Reid took a seat and beckoned the children to him. "Come, come, my dear ones," he said. "Come!"

They obediently scurried around the table and stood in front of him.

"Do you remember," began Reid, "when I told you the story of Jesus, the Christ?"

Fritz and Clara tried to remember, but they could not, so they said nothing.

Reid smiled piously and said, "Jesus went around the whole world telling people that if they worked very, very hard, they would store up great riches for themselves. And he also told the people of the world that all the lazy, lowborn freeloaders would go to a special place prepared for the Devil and his Angels, where they would burn forever and be forced to eat hot coals. This place is called Hell, and all the lazy poor people end up there. They can never, ever get out. For breakfast they eat hot coals, for lunch they eat hot coals, and for dinner they eat hot coals. They are never allowed to have even one single glass of water. And the Devil that lives there is the most horrible, scary monster you will ever see."

Reid raised his eyebrows and nodded solemnly, first looking at Fritz, then at Clara. Both of them were now quaking.

"Now everyone loved Jesus the Christ, because he was telling them how to get rich. But the Evil Jews did not love him. The Jews despised him, because they wanted all the money in the world for themselves, and they also believed that lazy people should have money, too. For example, they believed that if a person got sick, and he had no money, then people with money should pay for his medicine. Some of them even said that the people with money were the evil ones, not the lazy people! So the Jews gathered together like gnomes and goblins"—Reid wriggled his fingers at Fritz and Clara—"and they had a big meeting with their leaders Marx and

Engels, where they talked about how to destroy Jesus. And then they all rushed out and they grabbed Jesus. First they flogged him until his flesh came off. Then they scratched his whole body with thorns, until he was screaming. Then they jammed nails into his body. Then they stuck him all over with spears. Oh my goodness, there was so much blood! It was really terrible!"

Miscellany stood up. "Get out of here, Gregory. Why are you telling them this repulsive nonsense? Get out of this room at once."

"Patience, my love, patience. I'm almost finished. So they tried to destroy Jesus, my dear ones. But using his magic powers he escaped from the Jews and ascended into the sky, where he was safe, because Jews can't fly. And then he sent down rocks and fire to destroy the Jews and the giant house where they all lived. But some of them cunningly slipped away, including Marx and Engels, who made a pact with the Devil to live forever, and all those Jews are with us to this very day. And now, as it turns out, these same Jews want to destroy your Uncle Gregory, just like they tried to destroy Jesus. They want to take him away from you forever and ever. So he must escape, like Jesus, into the sky. And he will take you with him. Now good night, my dear ones, and sleep soundly."

Reid got up and walked out. Fritz and Clara turned to Miscellany, their faces scared and questioning.

"Remember what I told you about Uncle Gregory," said Miscellany.

"He has a bad little mouse running around in his head," said Fritz.

"And it makes him say very bad things," said Clara.

"Right. That was just the bad little mouse talking right now. Don't pay any attention to what he just said. None of it is true. Now I will take you to bed."

Miscellany took them by the hands and left the card room. Passing Mr. Ichabod in the hallway, she led them to their bedroom. After tucking them in, she turned out the light and closed the door.

"Prevent him from going in there tonight."

"Yes, my lady," said Mr. Ichabod.

In the darkness, Fritz whispered to Clara, "Stephany says there is a bad little mouse in Uncle Gregory's head that makes him do bad things. But I think there is nothing in his head *except* for the bad little mouse."

"I think so too. The mouse is trapped in there."

"What are we going to do? I'm scared that Uncle Gregory will do something to us, and do something to Stephany."

"I hope the Jews come and take Uncle Gregory away," said Clara. "I don't want them to kill him, but I hope they come, and tie him up, and put him in a box, and take the box to another planet. Then maybe the mouse will get bored and run out of his head. Then Uncle Gregory can come back."

They closed their eyes and prayed fervently in the darkness, pleading with God, whom they imagined was a gigantic multicolored bird in a nest somewhere beyond the moon, to send the Jews to rescue them from Uncle Gregory—or at least to chase the mouse out of his head.

f9

Andronicus was sitting in front of the cold fireplace in Polyvox's apartment when she came into the great hall, carrying a plate of cheese and crackers.

"Why are you looking so gloomy?" she asked.

"Everything has gone wrong," he said. "Not only that, but my soul feels filthy."

Polyvox came over to him, her boots clacking on the hard stone floor of the organ room. She placed the plate of cheese and crackers on a small table in front of him. "In what way has everything gone wrong? The operation to rescue Jack went flawlessly. Not only that, we liquidated Frake Inyards, number 267 on the Corporationist 500 Hit List, left his personal torture palace a smoldering ruin, and sent five of his goons to the Other Side."

"That's just it—all of this bloodshed. I've had enough of it. When the revolutionary movements began so many years ago, their purpose was to forge a peaceful path of democratic restoration—for this country and the world. Our primary weapon was supposed to be an appeal to truth and reason. But somehow, things have gotten turned around. We've been forced by our enemy to behave like them—like murderous thugs. We are assassins and killers now, just like they are. I think I'm going to go away for a while. You can manage things. I've made up my mind. Don't try to talk me out of it."

Andronicus made himself a cheese-and-cracker sandwich and bit into it somberly.

"You feel bad because of Jack, because of what happened to him. But in any war, there are casualties."

Andronicus stared ahead, his jaw muscles tight. "It's not that. I suppose that in the end, I don't want to fight this kind of war, though I keep telling myself I do. I want to fight a war of ideas, not a war of weapons."

Polyvox placed a hand on his shoulder. "Andronicus, listen to me. You have a tendency to relapse, in your more introverted moments, into a useless romantic pacifism. Now is not the time to get ethically knock-kneed."

"You're accusing me of cowardice?" he replied, clenching his jaw muscles firmly, staring straight ahead.

"On the contrary, Andronicus. *All of this bloodshed*, you say. *I've had enough of it.* You and I both know that the Corporate Enemy now controls all the instruments of the State. There is no product—no drug, no kind of food, no material good, no form of entertainment, and no idea, not even this cheese—that is not manufactured by their endlessly churning generators. This titanic engine of greed cannot be stopped simply by promulgating revolutionary ideas. We must also use force. You killed people when you were in the wars. Well, you're in a war now. All of us are."

"That was when I was a younger man, a drone of the State."

"And who would condemn you for the deaths of Inyards and his gorillas?"

"How can *you* understand?" said Andronicus, standing up and looking directly at her. "You aren't even human."

Polyvox smiled coldly. "Thank goodness. My civilization lasted millions of years, and we never built a Dachau. Human civilization lasted a paltry ten thousand years before it built one, and there were plenty of precedents before that."

"Thank you. You've just made my point. I don't want my humanity to become disfigured, as it is in Reid, or Inyards, or Boyler, or any of the other power zombies who rule the world. I will go away, buy a cabin in the Appalachians or something, and tend my garden. Of course, you have an open invitation to visit me at any time and let me know how things are going."

"You forget, Andronicus," said Polyvox, drawing closer to him, "that I too have emotions—they are just not like yours. I take no pleasure in this violence. But we will not destroy the Enemy by poking daisies down the barrels of its guns. Now is not the time to weaken, my friend. Now is not the time to let your resolve go wobbly. Put aside this talk of quitting the endeavor. We have commenced the hunt, and we must finish it through to the end. Reid is our quarry, and we cannot rest until we have mounted his skull on our wall."

At that moment a door opened, and Doctor Krypton came out. Polyvox and Andronicus quickly stepped away from each other.

"How is Tone?" asked Andronicus.

"He is inevitably morphing into a Plutocroid. I'm afraid there's nothing we can do."

F9

"There *must* be some treatment," said Andronicus, looking somberly towards the door to the room where Jack lay.

Krypton shook her head. "I believe the method they use involves some kind of viral gene therapy. The modified Plutocroid virus is already well established in his system and is gradually transforming his human genome into that of the abomination. We have slowed the process through induced coma, but there is no way I know of to reverse it. We would have to take him to a hospital, but that is impossible."

"So what can we do?"

"For his sake, the only solution I see is euthanasia."

"Well, I am not satisfied with that solution," said Andronicus bluntly. "Surely there is some way of reversing the transformation, Krypton."

"Yes, Andronicus, there may be ways of reversing the process, but as you know the whole medical establishment is controlled by the Enemy. We would have to take him to a hospital and consult with panels of geneticists, few of whom are even aware of the Defense Department Plutocroid Program."

"You and the Professor have colleagues at your university. Take him there."

"You're not being rational about this, Andronicus. If we were to take him to any hospital, his condition would astonish the honest doctors, and alert those in the pay of the Enemy. He wouldn't be there an hour before they came to take him away."

"Can't you consult secretly with your medical colleagues and bring some of them here?"

"I wouldn't know whom to trust. I know for a fact that some of them are associated with State-sponsored genetic engineering projects. Besides, I haven't been back there in weeks, ever since my cover was blown. There are no solutions."

"So he must die."

"I'm afraid I see no alternative. It would be inhumane to keep him alive—a shambling shell of his former self."

"When do you propose to put him down?"

"For Tone's sake, the sooner the better."

"Go to sleep, Krypton," said Polyvox. "You have been awake for the last ten hours."

After Krypton left for her quarters, Polyvox and Andronicus went into the room where Krypton, the Professor, and Bunyan had cobbled together an intensive care station around Jack. He lay there unconscious, his skin a yellowish green, his face long and lined.

"Sometimes I regret," sighed Polyvox, "our own experiments upon your proto-ape ancestors."

"What do you mean?"

"Having become master engineers of our own genome, we began to study yours. We tweaked you here and there."

"Tweaked us?"

"Perhaps it was injudicious. But yes, we did it—tinkered with your genome, that is. We helped you along evolutionarily, enhanced your intelligence, turned you into suitable pets—companions, that is. The Ape Project was interrupted by the Araknoid invasion. After that, you were on your own. It's possible that some of your more aggressive tendencies were due to our own experiments, our own incomplete efforts to endow you with sharper critical reasoning skills. I'm sorry."

"You never told me this."

"What was the point?"

"It seems, Polyvox, that in any relationship, honesty is an essential element. Here you are telling me that your people genetically experimented on my ancestors, possibly lighting the spark of nastiness in us that continues to this day. Don't you think I have a right to know that?"

"Andronicus, it was ten million years ago. Move on. I'm sorry I even mentioned it."

"Exactly how much did the 'Chronasians' know about Ape genetics?"

"Everything there was to know."

"How much of this knowledge remains?"

"I couldn't say. My specialty was history."

"Are there any members of your present order who were geneticists?"

"A few. The Superior, for one."

"Could she come here and treat Tone?"

"No."

"Why not?"

"It's too risky."

"But other members of your order travel around the world, don't they?"

"Andronicus, the brothers and sisters of my order—how can I put this delicately?—are not as appreciative of humans as I am. To them, you are all Apes. At worst, you are dangerous obstacles to their re-conquest of Earth. At best, you might have some possible use in achieving that goal. Many times I have spoken on your behalf, but they remain skeptical about the future use of humans."

"And your own mother?" he replied, surprised by this revelation.

"Her opinions are similar."

"So," concluded Andronicus with disgust, "in the end you intended to just wipe out us humans. As far as humanity is concerned, you are little better than the Araknoids."

"No, that is not correct. In the end, my sisters want to divide the world into two cultural spheres. One would be yours. The other would be above that, where we Chronasians would rebuild our civilization while simultaneously preventing you Apes, in your lower sphere, from tearing each other apart. There would be peace, coexistence, and social harmony."

"Perhaps that's not such a bad setup, after all."

"You have to admit, there is a logic to it."

"What can we do to convince your Superior to come down here and examine Tone?"

"Nothing."

"Please, Polyvox, there must be some way of convincing her. Look how we've put our necks on the line to try to rescue your queen!"

"The Superior is a brooding and mercurial woman. I don't relish the idea of bringing up the subject with her. I would have to send the request through our secret lines of communication, and I'm not sure how she would react."

"I understand. Because of these inconveniences, you are content to let Jack Tone die. I'm sorry to have even troubled you with the request. You clearly feel nothing for Jack. Your close association with him these past few weeks is without meaning. I guess I deceived myself into thinking that your species was not as cold-hearted as a pack of velociraptors."

Polyvox raised her hands in a gesture of futility, then let them fall to her sides. "Your accusation is unfair. I am not indifferent to Jack's fate. I have in fact contacted the Superior about this matter. Repeatedly. She has given me no response. I said nothing to you about it because I did not want to give you false hope. I plan to take him there myself if I have to. Just because I am not capable of emotion-induced lachrymation doesn't mean that I'm a *velociraptor*."

Andronicus looked away. "I'm sorry I doubted you, Polyvox."

They returned to the organ room, where Blackshield was waiting for them.

"Intelligence reports indicate that Reid has left the Gazillionaire's Tower in his helicopter yacht. It will now be quite difficult to get at him, if not impossible. I just thought you should both know."

CHAPTER TWENTY-FIVE

Reid's Paranoia Goes Paranoid

The *Never Enough* had a hull vaguely reminiscent of a giant Spanish galleon, with forward and aft rotors and a wide stabilizing wing.

Gregory Reid stood in the lavishly appointed captain's cabin, looking out the windows at a sea of white puffy clouds. Mr. Ichabod entered.

"You called, sir?"

"Yes, Ichabod. Do you remember that old, old song 'Both Sides, Now'?"

"I do, sir. It was a favorite of my grandmother's. I myself always found it a bit sappy."

"My father caught me listening to it when I was a child. He repeatedly slapped me across the head, saying it was a Socialist song. He then gave me some pornography, told me to man up, and strode out of the room. He did not speak to me for weeks."

"An unfortunate incident, sir."

"And how are you doing, my only friend? The wounds healing?"

"I am coming along nicely, sir. In full health, for the most part. I find walks in the fresh air salutary, and each night I spend a few hours reading an improving book. Mrs. Crane has been an invaluable help in my recovery."

"Excellent, Ichabod. You are the only person in the entire universe whom I can trust. Speaking of my father, was he successfully loaded aboard the ship?"

"He was, sir."

"I think I will see him now."

"Are you sure you wish to do so, sir? You know how such meetings can upset you."

"Yes, it must be done."

"Very well, come this way."

Ichabod led Reid to the lowest deck of the helicopter yacht, opened a locked door, and stood by while Reid entered. He closed the door, and Reid was alone with the decapitated head of his father.

F9

The grotesque, fat head floated in a slightly murky solution. It had no hair, but rather a medusa cluster of wires and tubes. The eyes were closed. The head tank was mounted on a small bio-computer mainframe with blinking lights.

Reid stared at the inert head for a moment, then picked up an implement like a coffee bean scoop. He shoved it into a steel bucket full of crystal Ploop™ and dumped the crystals into an open slot in the mainframe. Then he pressed a button. Presently, the head began to stir, slowly opening its eyes.

"Good evening, Father."

The mouth of the head moved, but the sound of its voice came from vents in the mainframe. It spoke very slowly and phlegmatically, like something from a world beneath the worlds. "My son, my murderer, why do you summon me from my Plutonian tomb?"

"I need your advice, Father."

"I have already given you all the advice I can give you. Let me descend into forgetfulness again."

"I don't want religious advice. I don't want metaphysical advice. I need practical advice."

"Someday you will sink to this cold, fathomless place, my son. And nothing will draw you out."

"That time may be sooner than later, Father. People are plotting to kill me."

A weird, unpleasant sound came from the mainframe, and Reid realized it was a ghostly laugh. "So it has come to this…my patricidal assassin seeks advice from me, to avoid his own assassination…"

"Father, you exist only in your family name. I am the sole survivor of your lineage. Your descendants are your immortality. If they kill me, they kill you, and all of your family. The Reids will become extinct."

"Do I not have grandchildren?"

"My brother Anton's children…let's just say they are dead already."

"How did they die?"

"It is immaterial. And my own children will be destroyed if I am destroyed. I am their protector, but when usurpers slay the king, they do not spare his children. If I die, they will die. Like Ahab, you will have no descendants. Is that what you want?"

"No…."

"Then advise me. The world has changed considerably since I killed you. It is seething with revolutionary vipers who have a pathological hatred for the natural economic order of things. Not since the Civil War have our family's prospects been in such jeopardy. Right now I am in my yacht, high above the land. Will I have to stay here forever, in aerial exile? Give me advice! The Reids have survived all these hundreds of years. We survived the Enlightenment, we survived Communism, we survived Trade Unionism, we survived America's botched attempt at Democracy, we even survived non-Aryan intermarriage. And each time we survived, we became stronger. Father, tell me, how can we keep on surviving?"

"I don't know what advice you expect me to give you…"

"Father, you reside in the otherworld. Surely you can see things. Surely you have dreams. What do the shadows tell you—the gods, the demons?"

The head closed its eyes slowly, then opened them again. "Beware of love, it is the destroyer…"

"Love? What do you mean? Explain!"

The head groaned and sank back into its frigid slumber. Reid cursed and punched one hand into the other. He paced back and forth, muttering.

Outside, Ichabod slipped away. He found Miscellany seated in the dining room with Fritz and Clara, preparing to eat. He bent down and whispered, "My lady, he's talking to the head."

"Thank you, Ichabod."

Ichabod nodded and stepped back, as Mrs. Crane brought out dinner: steak for Reid, vegetable korma for Miscellany and the children. Mrs. Crane, despite being a Plutocroid—or maybe even because of it—was an excellent cook.

Miscellany and the children ate quietly. She knew, as all the other staff knew, that the "head" was the only remaining part of Reid's father, suspended in a tank of formaldehyde, connected to a mockup of a mini-mainframe. Occasionally Reid spoke to it, though it never spoke back.

Such imaginary conversations, however, usually presaged a dangerous episode in Reid. This time, that had to be avoided at all costs. For Miscellany was about to implement her endgame.

Reid came into the dining room and sat down, tucking a napkin into his collar. He appeared agitated and did not acknowledge them. Suddenly he looked up. "You all realize I love you, correct?"

The children nodded.

"I am Papa Jackal," he said, pointing to himself. "And you are my Baby Jackals." He pointed to Miscellany. "And she is Mama Jackal. We are one big happy jackal family, and we all love each other, is that not correct?"

Fritz and Clara nodded.

"Are you two little jackals capable of speaking, or not?" asked Reid.

"Yes," they mumbled.

"Yes, what?"

They looked at him.

"Yes, Papa Jackal!" he snarled. "From now on, I want you both to refer to me as Papa Jackal."

"Yes, Papa Jackal," they said timidly.

"Papa Jackal," said Miscellany, "be silent and let them eat."

"Mama Jackal, kindly do not give orders to Papa Jackal!" shouted Reid, slapping his hand on the table. "In the order of nature, Papa Jackal ranks above Mama Jackal."

"Sir," said Ichabod, drifting in, "your pills."

Reid looked at them in irritation and then snatched them off the tray, chewing with a grimace and washing them down with a glass of wine. "Go away," he said, "leave me alone with my jackals."

Ichabod nodded and departed.

"How would my Baby Jackals like to go up to the Space Station?" he asked.

"What are you talking about?" asked Miscellany.

"We haven't been up to the Orbital Mansion in a while. I thought it might be safer than being up here in the helicopter yacht."

"But, my love," said Miscellany, "that's where 'the event' happened."

"The event? Are we now speaking in euphemisms, Mama Jackal? What Mama Jackal means," said Reid, turning to the twins, "is that the Orbital Mansion is where Papa Jackal killed Grandpa Jackal in a duel with medieval broadswords, fair and square, and then cut his head off. That's why you don't have a Grandpa Jackal. Or rather, that's why your Grandpa Jackal is a disembodied head bobbing in a tank of preservative serum."

"Children," said Miscellany, "take your plates and go eat in your room."

They hastily obeyed. When they had left, Miscellany said, "Do you really have to talk about such matters in front of them?"

"Can you define 'love'?" he asked her.

"What?"

"I just had a consultation with my father, and he warned me about love. He didn't bother to explain his words, leaving me quite confused."

"Gregory, I've told you a thousand times that your father's head is not speaking to you. If you took your pills regularly, this wouldn't happen."

"How can I live with such an atheist!" Reid sawed into his steak.

"I do not wish—in fact, I refuse—to go up to the Orbital Mansion with you."

"Oh you refuse, do you, Stephany?" He reached into his pocket. "Do I have to remind you that I hold the remote control in this relationship?"

He jabbed it in her direction.

"I don't care. I still refuse to go."

Reid slipped the remote control back into his pocket.

"Gregory, you would be less safe in the Orbital Mansion. The revolutionaries could very easily conspire to blow it out of orbit. Predicting the location of a satellite is a matter of simple calculation. We are far better off staying aloft in the yacht, moving in an erratic, unpredictable flight pattern."

"You are correct, my love. What would I do without you? Forgive me for brandishing the remote control."

They finished dinner in silence. Later that evening, the *Never Enough* settled down on a skyscraper heliport in Chicago. There, Hedrick boarded.

He had very important news.

F9

Reid received him in the captain's quarters. "Hello, my good friend. Come, come. Have a seat!"

"Thank you, Mr. Reid."

"Have you made any new discoveries?"

"I have. I come with both discoveries and advice."

"Speak!"

"I should warn you, Mr. Reid, that the discoveries may shock you."

"Damn it, man, enough equivocating. What have you learned?"

"For one, the identity of the third assassin. He was John Girard Lee, the son of a Lee Sunsin, a high-ranking Korean military official, and an American diplomat named Alexandra Bailey Girard. Both his parents died when he was a toddler. He was raised by his mother's family in Philadelphia, but spent his childhood summers in Korea with his paternal grandparents. He was an officer in the Old U.S. Army—part of the same anti-privatization faction as his comrade Schwartzschild. He also disappeared for a time after the issuance of arrest warrants, apparently overseas."

"The important thing is that this creep is dead. What else have you learned?"

Hedrick cleared his throat. "Strange information, Mr. Reid. You must make of it what you will. Perhaps you should have a drink first."

Not taking his eyes off Hedrick, Reid poured himself a glass of Scotch and shot it back.

"Now then," continued Hedrick, "you recall that the third assassin had anomalous DNA. Analysis suggested it belonged to an unusual type of mammal, and that it was female. At first we thought the assassins had brought in some kind of genetically modified animal, perhaps a venomous one, to assist in their crime. We also considered the possibility that this odd DNA pattern was an unsolvable distortion produced by the scramblers they were wearing. Neither explanation turns out to be applicable in this case."

"Enough with the genetics lesson. Get to the point."

"Both you, Inyards, Ichabod, and the other witnesses reported that there were four assassins—two male servants, and a male and female posing as representatives of InquiZZ Interrogation Services. It turns out that the female is the source of the anomalous DNA."

"You mean she was a freak, a mutant?"

"She apparently *was not human*. Both Ichabod and Inyards reported that she moved with unnatural litheness."

"So the revolutionaries are now breeding their own monsters, just as we have created the Plutocroids. Our angels versus their demons. So be it. Let the games begin."

"No, Mr. Reid. Unlike a Plutocroid, this creature wasn't even *close* to being human. This thing, whatever she was, appears to have been more closely related to cats, dogs—even otters."

"What does it matter? The bitch is dead, whatever she is. Let's move on from this subject. It tires me."

"Sir, about your mistress, Ms. Miscellany—"

"What are you trying to tell me?" barked Reid.

"You know that…*we* know that her DNA is unusual. It is also a very close match to that of the deceased female assassin. Not only are they the same cryptic species, but they are very, very closely related. They appear to be kin."

Reid was tapping his empty Scotch glass against his teeth. "Did you ever notice, Captain Hedrick, how wonderful and odd teeth are? Our mouths have all these soft parts, but sprouting up in the middle of them all are these rows of hard, sharp things."

"Yes, Mr. Reid."

"So you are saying that Stephany is somehow related to this mystery monster."

"Yes. If you don't mind my asking, how did you meet Ms. Miscellany?"

"She came to me. She had learned about the discovery of the Araknoids through a trusted academic associate, and she proposed a most ingenious potential solution for unlocking their power. I authorized Boyler to investigate her background as an independent researcher, and it checked out. I hired her as my own private scientist, and have not divulged the nature of her work to the Araknoid Revival Team. She believes that the Araknoid Army is frozen by some kind of time-stasis phenomenon—I don't pretend to fully understand all the scientific gobbledygook—and that if this time-stasis element can be dissolved, the Araknoids will come to life and serve *me*."

"Has she succeeded?"

"Not yet. But she's getting closer."

"I think she is in league with the revolutionaries."

"How dare you disparage my helpmeet, Hedrick." Reid gnashed his teeth and quivered. He appeared about to stand up and pounce, but Hedrick's voice remained firm.

"Put aside your emotions for the moment, Mr. Reid, and consider the situation objectively. She has worked for you for several years, promising a solution. None has come. She is also related to someone, or something, that recently attempted to kill you. I propose—with regret—that the time-stasis theory is blarney, poppycock, and nonsense. Ms. Stephany Miscellany has no proper scientific credentials. She is a spy and a revolutionary."

Reid poured himself another Scotch and drank it down. And then another.

"Moreover, Mr. Reid, I suggest that there is no scientific solution to the Araknoid Problem, because they are not creatures of this world. They are creatures from Hell. They are demons. The solution is not in science, but the dark arts."

"You must be mad...."

"You told me once that a favorite book of yours was the *Malleus Maleficarum*—the late medieval guide to fighting witchcraft and demonology. I think the solution to the Araknoid Problem lies in witchcraft and demonology. You must, sir, invoke the powers of Hell to reanimate the Araknoid Army."

"This talk is completely absurd," replied Reid slowly. "I refuse to hear any more of it. Persist, and I will show you the door."

"It is absurd, but true. It is true, because it is impossible."

"And how the hell do I invoke the powers of Hell?" spluttered Reid.

"A simple sacrifice will do. A sacrifice of innocents. I suggest your brother's half-breed children, Fritz and Clara. I will supply the altar, the vestments, and the Book of Ritual Rubrics. I myself will conduct the propitiation."

"You? Why you? How do you even know about such ridiculous, superstitious things?"

"Because, Mr. Reid," said Hedrick with a soft smile, "I am a Satanist."

"A Satanist? Are you pulling my chain, Hedrick? The FBI sent a Satanist to be my chief investigator?"

"Not one of these spineless *contemporary* Satanists, sir," said Hedrick reassuringly. "Not one of these supercilious phonies who claim to revere the symbol of Satan as a dissenter and a nonconformist. No, I am an *Originalist* Satanist. I believe that Evil is the most powerful force in the Universe, and that it must be harnessed to achieve progress. Consider our most powerful energy source to date: nuclear power. And yet it was born of a mass sacrifice of hundreds of thousands of civilians. Let us not mince words—such an action was evil, but it had to be done. Evil had to be harnessed in that case, as it must continue to be harnessed. We have no choice because the universe is fundamentally evil, so we must work with what we have. The very stuff of the Universe is evil, and we must mold it with our bare human hands. But the adversary of evil is Love, the Destroyer. In order to unleash the power of the demonic Araknoids, you must engage in an act that fully repudiates love. You must destroy the Destroyer."

"The Destroyer," muttered Reid to himself. He looked up, his eyes bloodshot. "Why my brother's children? Why not a goat or something?"

Hedrick snorted disdainfully. "A goat would merely incur the wrath of Hell—it would be like offering trash to a god. In all times and in all places, the offering of human children has been the purest method of propitiation. I strongly believe that the Third Reich was demolished by its enemies because a small number of children were spared and declared Aryan. These few exceptions were sufficient to dissatisfy Hell."

"There are breeds of goat worth hundreds of thousands of dollars," said Reid, "as well as fine breeds of cattle. These could be acquired easily. I have a thoroughbred stud in my stables worth sixty million. Let's use this magnificent beast for the sacrifice."

"It *must* be a child sacrifice," said Hedrick. "Even the Bible warns us not to spare children in our sacrifices—recall the affair of Moses and the Midianite children. There is another consideration, as well. The two specimens in your care are products of miscegenation, as you have pointed out, so to sacrifice them would be a mercy."

Reid drank another shot and dug his fingers into his stubbly jaw. "Miscegenation. It's an obsolete word, with no valid meaning these days. Let's face it, everybody is misceginated. Genes have been trading on the markets for at least two generations now."

"I, sir," replied Hedrick, "am a pure Aryan. I have the certificates to prove it."

"Yes, yes, that's wonderful, Hedrick. *Sieg Heil* and all that. I think you should examine my thoroughbred—"

"No!" shouted Hedrick. "Children must die! Don't you see? Everything you have done to awaken the Araknoids has failed—utterly failed. You have but one solution left, the final one! Nature is against you, Mr. Reid. *Nature is against you!* For you to prevail, you must go beyond Nature to the Supernatural. Will you let ultimate Power and Glory slip through your fingers because you are squeamish about what is, in effect, an act of mercy? Will you continue to *fail*, Mr. Reid? Or will you become the New God of Earth, the head of an unstoppable army of demons? The Old Gods have fallen, each one an Ozymandias lying petrified in the sand. Earth groans for a New God—if it is not you, Mr. Reid, it *will* be another, and you will have to bend your knee to his authority."

Reid chewed on his thumb for several minutes, his mind and soul in a torment.

Hedrick gazed like Mephistopheles into Reid's bloodshot eyes. "*Leap*, Mr. Reid. Give the order to me now—take the leap. A wise master once said, '*He who subdues himself shall be free of passions. The righteous man casts off sin; only by rooting out lust, bitterness, and illusion, do we reach Nirvana.*'"

Reid sat back, grimacing. His eyes were wide and his lips drawn back from his teeth—like the head of a mummified corpse. He shuddered all over. When he spoke next, his voice was a barely perceptible whisper. "Very well. Prepare for the sacrifice, Hedrick. I will provide the lambs."

Hedrick nearly shrieked his glee. "Excellent, Mr. Reid. You have decided well!"

"Do this as soon as possible," muttered Reid, who was now drinking directly from his Scotch bottle, "and let me know when you're done. I will instruct Ichabod to cooperate with you."

"I have already consulted the bloodstones and brought my equipment aboard, including the grimoire, the altar, the golden knives, the white robe and hood. A massive blizzard is expected to smash into the East Coast in three days. They are predicting the Blizzard of the Century. This will give us the perfect cover."

"Why the hell do you need a *blizzard* to do this? Just get it done!"

"Permit me to explain, my lord," said Hedrick mildly. "At the height of the blizzard, when the entire Eastern Seaboard has been shut down, we will land on the grassy mall in front of Independence Hall, where this whole screwball experiment called the United States of America went amuck from the beginning. I will conduct the Ritual in the very room where the Declaration of Independence was signed, and thereby correct the nation's course back to that which was the original intention of our Founders."

"Why there? Why not in some forest somewhere? As long as you do this in the lower 48, Alaska, or Hawaii, or even in the territories, the sacrifice should be effective."

"The Signing Room is located precisely one mile above the cavern with the advanced guard of the Araknoid Army. The blood of the sacrifice will flow down, and activate the Araknoids at last. Don't you see, my friend? What we began hundreds of years ago when a party of white slaveholders drafted a declaration of rebellion in order to safeguard their wealth against tyranny, we will conclude on this holiest of nights by offering up the lives of two innocent children within whose veins the blood of both slaver and slave is unnaturally commingled! We have finally reached the end of history, and you will be its instrument."

"Yes, yes," said Reid, drinking again, nodding vigorously. "As it is written, so it shall be done. See to the preparations. I only require that you sedate them before the act—render them unconscious."

Hedrick was startled. "Excuse me, my lord?"

Reid stared at his own right hand with red-eyed revulsion, as if his very fingers were the primary appendages of some filthy abomination—as if they might, in Dr. Strangelove fashion, seize him by his own neck and choke him to death. His voice, previously slurred with whiskey, became hushed, clear, and devoid of emotion: "They must not feel any fear or pain."

"But Mr. Reid," pleaded Hedrick, "their fear is an essential element to the sacrifice."

"I will not debate this point, Hedrick!" replied Reid, baring his teeth like a Plutocroid. "Obey me!"

Hedrick closed his eyes and gave a low nod. "They will be heavily sedated, my lord."

"And I will oversee the sedation—you will not deceive me."

F9

"Mr. Ichabod," said Reid coldly. "There has been a new development. I'm afraid that Ms. Miscellany will have to be either restrained or incapacitated."

"May I ask why, sir?"

"It seems she's in cahoots with the revolutionaries."

"I see."

"Where is she now?"

"In her quarters, I believe."

"First I will speak to her. Then we will lock her in until this matter is resolved."

"Yes, sir."

Reid found Miscellany in her cabin, working on a jigsaw puzzle with Fritz and Clara.

"Papa Jackal wishes to speak privately with Mama Jackal," he said gruffly. "All Baby Jackals must leave now."

The children scampered out, and he closed the door.

"I thought you were my helpmeet."

"Excuse me?" she asked.

"My life companion. My woman. Do you know what love means?"

"I don't really want to talk about this right now. Send the children back in so we can finish this jigsaw puzzle."

Reid stood up and left, closing the door behind him. He signaled to Ichabod, who activated the master lock. He then spoke through an intercom.

"My love, are you there?"

"Yes, of course I'm here. Where could I have gone?"

"I'm afraid I must confine you to your quarters for the duration. The door is locked, and you cannot open it."

Miscellany quickly stood up and tried the door. It wouldn't budge. "Gregory, what is going on?"

"Your deceit has been revealed to me, Stephany. You are some kind of nonhuman animal in league with the revolutionaries. You have also lied to me about the Araknoids, convincing me that science held the key to unlocking their power. I think the children have distracted you from your objective. I will forgive you, but there must be penance. The children must be sacrificed in a ritual in order to summon the powers of Hell and liberate the Araknoids. I do this with a very heavy heart."

"Gregory, you sound very drunk," said Miscellany calmly. "Open the door and let's discuss this matter with reason and sobriety."

"There is nothing to discuss."

"Tell me where this idea came from, this idea of sacrificing your nephew and niece. Was it Hedrick? I know you trust him, Gregory, but he is a manipulator, and he is quite insane."

"I have given you several years to activate the Araknoids, and you have not done so. There they stand—an army of frozen demons just a mile beneath America's first capital. Science has failed me. Now I must turn to religion."

"Gregory, they are not demons. They are an invasive alien species. Not only that, they have leaders, an oligarchy of rulers deep within the earth. Killing Fritz and Clara will accomplish nothing. Open the door and let me speak to you face to face."

"Please do not despise me, my love. Please do not think me cruel. I must prove to the powers of the Underworld that I am worthy of their intercession, and to do this, I must authorize the sacrifice of Fritz and Clara. We are changing course to make our way to the place of sacrifice. It will all be over before you know it, and then we can have a nice, quiet candlelit dinner together without any distractions from the children."

"I think I begin to understand you, Gregory. You are correct: a sacrifice is necessary. I wish to participate in it with you. I will help prepare Fritz and Clara. Just let me out—"

"Don't patronize me, my love. I know where your heart lies." Reid flipped off the intercom switch. "Come, Ichabod, there's the devil's work to be done. I wish it to be completed as soon as possible, so that the healing process can begin. I am an American, and I require closure."

"Very good, sir."

CHAPTER TWENTY-SIX

Our Reptile Brain, Dissected

The door to Polyvox's apartment suddenly flew open, and in strode a tall woman with dark hair and luminous eyes. She was wearing a black cloak with the hood up, along with a protective vest, like Polyvox. Instead of Polyvox's breeches, she wore a slender strip of loincloth. Her boots came up to her knees and were decorated with metallic studs. Though her face resembled Polyvox's, she was several inches taller—topping off at more than seven feet. There was a clear resemblance to Polyvox, but this woman was larger, more muscular, and almost feral in her demeanor.

She marched from the foyer into the organ room. Blackshield and Krypton, having heard her enter, had already stood up from their chessboard. Blackshield drew his gun.

"Put that toy away," thundered the intruder, "and take me straightaway to my sister."

"Who are you?" asked Blackshield, still aiming his pistol.

"Where is my sister Polyvox?"

"She's not here."

"Don't play games with me, Ape." Monovox sniffed the air. "Beyond those doors there—that's where she is."

She walked past Blackshield, who let her pass, and threw open the doors. What she saw made her stagger back several steps and cry in distress.

Polyvox and an Ape were sitting across from each other at a small table, playing cards. Polyvox dropped her cards and stood up.

"How dare you barge into my private quarters!"

"What is *she* doing here?" asked Andronicus.

Polyvox looked at her sister. "Explain yourself, Monovox."

"Explain *yourself*, sister. What are *you* doing with that Ape?" replied Monovox in a dread whisper. "You don't think I can tell what's going on?"

"I don't know what you're talking about."

"Don't play me for a fool, Polyvox. I'm not some dumb Ape. This whole room is redolent of your illicit affections."

"If you call him an 'ape' one more time, I'll break your jaw."

"Evidence!" replied Monovox triumphantly. "*J'accuse!* The crime that dare not speak its name. The Superior shall hear of this."

"What right do you have, entering my apartment unannounced?"

"You forget that this apartment belongs to our order. The Superior summons you home. Your last series of communications have been so inane that she has concluded you are deranged. Alas, it appears to be true."

"In what sense deranged?"

"Asking us to perform genetic therapy on an Ape. Your mission was to recover our queen, and at that you have failed. You have gone native in the worst possible way."

"I have made contact with her, as I reported in my message. This contact was made possible because of the Ape who needs genetic therapy. The least we can do is help him."

"You will come with me, bestialist."

"We were *playing cards!*"

"I order you to return with me to the motherhouse."

"I will not."

"I am your elder sister, and I command you."

"I refuse your command. Go back to the motherhouse and await my next report."

Andronicus had to leap out of the way as the two sisters began physical combat. They circled and kicked and punched at each other. The fighting progressed into the organ room, where Blackshield and Krypton dashed for safety, knocking over the chess table and watching in disbelief, unable to make sense of this mad scene that had interrupted a quiet, snowy afternoon. Polyvox and Monovox engaged each other like two panthers in a territorial dispute. Monovox was larger and stronger, Polyvox faster and more flexible. In time they both tired and retreated to lean, panting, on opposite sides of the room.

Andronicus took advantage of the lull to approach Polyvox. "You have to resolve this peacefully," he said quietly. "Such a breach with your order could seriously disrupt our operations."

Polyvox nodded. She wiped her brow. Straightening, she said, "I will speak with you in private, Monovox."

Monovox had thrown off her cloak—now crumpled on the floor. She followed her sister back into the bedroom and closed the door. Outside the bedroom window, nothing was visible except an impenetrable abyss of falling snow.

"Speak," said Monovox.

"Would you like some wine?"

"Yes."

Polyvox filled a large chalice and gave it to Monovox, who drank it down in one gulp. Polyvox refilled it, and Monovox dispatched that just as quickly.

"Tell me why," said Monovox, "you did not rescue our mother when you encountered her in the Ape fortress? The whole order is in a state of great agitation over these recent developments, and your communications with us have become more incoherent and confused."

"Mother appears to have her own plans. I can't tell you exactly what they are. She refused to go with us. But I guarantee that if she has a specific plan, she knows what she is doing."

"Like when she detonated the Time Bomb," replied Monovox.

"It stopped the advance of the Araknoids, didn't it? And now she is attempting to prevent them from being reactivated by the madman Reid."

"I suppose now is as good a time to tell you as any. The Order is in agreement that I should be proclaimed the next Queen of the Chronasians. I am the eldest daughter of our Queen, so it is only right."

"What? The Order should refrain from any such action until this more pressing matter is concluded," snapped Polyvox.

"And when will that be? What is the next phase of *your* operation, Polyvox?"

"I don't know at the moment," Polyvox admitted. "Gregory Reid has taken Mother into his nuclear-powered helicopter yacht, and he's currently flying in an unpredictable path around North America."

"We could easily blow that thing out of the sky with our technologies."

"And Mother with it?"

"We could board it. We have flying technology."

"Earth's atmosphere is a vast place, teeming with thousands of ships, drones, satellites, and space stations, not to mention all the accumulated orbital trash of the last century. Reid's ship could be anywhere in that swarm of airborne traffic. The Order's scanning devices, though powerful, are few in number and limited in scope. There is no guarantee we could find him."

"So again I ask you, what are your plans?"

"At the moment, I admit there are none. The agents of the Enemy are looking all over for us. That's why we have to keep a low profile for the moment. Your intrusion jeopardizes that. How did you get down here, anyway?"

"I drove in the *Endeavor*. It is a vehicle superior to the *Argo*, I have to say. It plowed through the snowy Ape-ways quite easily."

"Go back to the Superior and tell her we're waiting for the next moment to strike. Also tell her that if she does not respond soon to my request for genetic therapy in the matter of Jack Tone, she will henceforward find me uncooperative. A rebel. I will commit myself to undermining her control of the Order."

Monovox sucked in her breath through her sharp teeth. "Insubordination."

"Call it what you want."

"She won't be pleased that I've come back without you."

Polyvox shrugged. "But you can't take me by force, can you?"

Monovox considered this, then frowned. "Explain why you were alone with that Ape."

"Don't feign naiveté to me, Monovox, and spare me your pretended outrage. I'm not the first sister in the Order to cultivate a relationship with an Ape. How many Apes have you been with over the eons? It is a lonely world, and we are a refugee species on our own planet. The Apes come and go, but we are cursed to perdure."

Monovox gave no response, and Polyvox continued: "Let's go back out there, where my companions are waiting, and behave as if we have resolved matters. And remember, only Andronicus and his inner circle of associates know who we really are. Apart from them, no other human beings on the planet are even aware of our existence."

Together they went back into the organ room. Petriv was standing there, his face red, his overcoat and faux fur hat covered with melting snow.

Andronicus looked at Polyvox, who gave him a subtle nod, assuring him that the matter with her sister had been resolved.

"Petriv brings excellent news," he announced happily. "It seems fate has delivered the Enemy right into our hands."

"How so?" asked Polyvox.

"Nuclear-powered helicopter yacht *Never Enough* has come to Earth in front of Independence Building," said Petriv. "Reid, Hedrick, and tall Plutocroid are exiting, and are met by Boyler. Big Plutocroid is carrying two children, who seem to be asleep. All of them then are going into the Old State House building."

"Did you see anyone else—a woman?" asked Polyvox.

"No. All men."

"They are going to the Pit, then," concluded Andronicus. "But what in the name of God could they be doing? And in the middle of this storm? We must go there at once. Polyvox, we'll take the *Argo*. Blackshield and Petriv, you come with us."

"Is our mother in that ship?" asked Monovox.

"Possibly," answered Polyvox.

"Then I will go as well, and in my car, the *Endeavor*."

"This is my operation, Monovox. We will go in *my* car, the *Argo*, and *I* will drive."

79

As soon as Reid had informed Stephany Miscellany of his plans, she had begun to pace back and forth in her cabin in a state of intense, almost transcendent, concentration. But she could think of no way to liberate herself from her prison. She tried the door several times, examining its mechanism, but was unable to open it from the inside. There were two portals, but they were small and she would not be able to fit herself through. Even if she could somehow remove the glass from the frames, she would be sucked away from the hull of the ship.

She would not likely survive the fall.

At last she sat in meditation, considering the situation. The problem here was human nature, and human nature had always perplexed her, despite the fact that she had studied it for generations. Human beings liked to think of themselves as predictable, but human nature was amorphous, protean, and defied any easy definition. Yet there were certain stable elements to it, for the Apes did not behave as the Chronasians did. There was an inner core of somewhat predictable human behavior, but outside of that was a fuzzy zone where anything could happen—a chaotic asteroid belt where human emotions, human dreams, human ideologies, and human spiritual pathologies continually smashed into each other. The key to human behavior lay in this Ort Cloud of disorder. When manipulating human behavior, the trick was always to seize the right asteroid at the right time, and then fling it, in a calculated trajectory, so that it would collide with others in predictable succession—like a billiard ball propelled with just the right amount of force and spin.

She believed the Human Apes called this "English."

A slot in the door opened, and in slid a tray of prepared food.

"I have prepared your favorite dish," said Ichabod over the intercom.

"Tell me what is going on out there, Ichabod."

"Mr. Reid and Captain Hedrick are preparing for the sacrifice, my lady."

"And when will it take place?"

"In three days' time. A blizzard is predicted, and we will land so that the ritual may be performed outside the yacht, on the ground, apparently in a place just above the Pit where the Araknoids sleep."

"Ichabod, you recognize the folly of this. Hedrick has conceived a completely degenerate and illogical plan. We are dealing here with a natural phenomenon, an alien species. We are not dealing with demons or hell, which are elements of human mythology."

"Perhaps."

"You must let me out, Ichabod, so I can put a stop to this."

"I'm sorry, my lady. I am bound to obey Mr. Reid."

"Then let me speak with Gregory."

"In truth, my lady, he is barely conscious, and maintains a drunken stupor."

"He is going to let Hedrick kill his own nephew and niece. Hedrick must be stopped."

"It is unfortunate, but it cannot be avoided."

"Is Mrs. Crane out there?"

"She has been confined to her quarters like you, my lady. She expressed reservations about the ritual."

"Where are the children now?"

"Captain Hedrick has administered a sedative and they are subdued."

"Ichabod, I realize you cannot disobey your master Mr. Reid. I do not expect you to. Obedience is a virtue that I respect and understand."

"Thank you, my lady."

"I only ask one thing. Please come to me and inform me when they are disembarking the yacht to perform the ritual. It will be important for me to compose myself and meditate at this time. I have, as you know, developed some affection for the children, as you yourself no doubt have. If we do not approach this sacrifice in the right frame of mind, we will suffer future regrets that linger within us and ultimately drive us insane. Certainly you would agree that it is a terrible and unforgivable thing to sacrifice your children to the powers of evil, no matter what your long-term intentions."

Ichabod was silent at the other end of the intercom.

"Are you there, Ichabod?"

"Yes, my lady."

"Will you inform me, as I have requested?"

"Yes."

f9

Three days later she was jolted from her meditations when Ichabod's voice came over the intercom. "It is about to begin. They have disembarked to the place of sacrifice."

"Thank you for telling me, Ichabod. What I do next depends upon what you yourself do."

There was a long pause. Stephany stood by the intercom, barely breathing. At last, she heard the bolt slide in the cabin door. A few moments later, she pushed it open and stepped out of the cabin.

Other than the dull thrum of the nuclear reactor, the interior of the *Never Enough* was deathly quiet.

Outside, a heavy snow was falling.

F9

"Haste, haste!" cried Hedrick, urging them on through the snow. "The time of catharsis is coming!"

Behind him, Reid stumbled drunkenly. Ichabod moved alongside him, a child clutched under each arm. Five other Plutocroids brought up the rear. In front of them, Boyler stood waiting on the steps of Independence Hall, before the open door.

Hedrick pushed past him without a word. As soon as he was inside, he put on a white sacerdotal robe and a conical white hat. They trudged through the tower hall and the central hall, leaving a trail of dirty wet snow. They entered the assembly hall.

"Move those goddamn tables and chairs out of the way!" Hedrick commanded. "Bring that large table over and place it in the middle of the room. Hurry!"

The Plutocroids obeyed, sweeping inkpots and quills off tables, throwing chairs against the wall, shoving and smashing to open a clearing in the middle of the hall. Reid, his head pounding, sat down in a chair beneath the American flag. "Get this over with," he grumbled at Hedrick. "I want to get back to my yacht."

Mr. Ichabod placed the limp, unconscious bodies of Fritz and Clara on the signing desk, while Hedrick snapped open a metal suitcase, removed several golden sacrifice implements, and sorted them on the table. He checked his watch.

Outside, the wind wailed, and snow piled up against the windows.

Hedrick lit two red candles and placed them on either side of the table where the children lay. He then took a can of white spray paint and drew a hexagram with a circle on the floor.

Reid, sprawled in his chair, watched listlessly. He removed a flask from his pocket and put it to his lips, then held it there, its liquid undrunk. His eyes flared briefly, and he seemed about to say something, but quickly settled back into his torpor.

Now Hedrick took out a large tome and flipped through it, licking his fingers as he glanced at the pages. Standing behind the signing desk, he looked up. Studying the place of sacrifice until satisfied, he picked up a long golden blade.

"I had long thought," he said, stroking the blade with his spidery fingers, "that the sun was setting on America. I now know that, indeed, it is rising, and that its future fortunes are written here in blood. In all of human history there have ever been but two factors at work: Power and Weakness. Power always prevails. The boot of Power must always stomp the face of Weakness. We are the children of Power, and today we prevail yet again, as is our destiny. The world will little note, nor long remember, what we say here. But it can never forget what we do here. These two innocents will not have died in vain, but that Power shall not perish from the Earth."

He placed the blade above the neck of Clara, preparing to slice her throat.

Glass shattered, and a frigid blast of wind and snow buffeted them. As soon as Miscellany had thrown herself through the window, five Plutocroids were upon her.

"How did that bitch get out of her cabin?" shrieked Hedrick. "You see, Reid? She is no helpmeet, she is a treasonous bitch! Dare I invoke Voltaire in declaring that she, like the Holy Roman Empire, is neither *female*, nor *human*, nor *American*?"

Reid stood up unsteadily and hobbled over to her. The Plutocroids held her fast.

He brought his face close to hers, exhaling boozy vapors. "You have betrayed me, Stephany."

"Get a grip on yourself, Gregory. You are allowing yourself to be led around by the nose by *this*"—she jerked her head towards Hedrick—"this incorrigible asshole. He has no power to summon the demons that stand beneath this building. They are far older than he is. They are embedded in the history of this planet, and in the soul of the human race. This is all a spectacle, a theater act put on by Hedrick the Phony. And its sole purpose is to bring you under *his* power. How can you not see that? How can you be so blind? This bureaucrat has convinced you to acquiesce to the ritual slaughter of your own flesh and blood, and you concede! Pathetic. He has mastered you and made you a loser. I have nothing but contempt for a loser."

Reid rubbed his eyes and nodded. "A loser?"

"A loser," repeated Miscellany. "Go over there and seal your lips to his pale, pimply Ape ass."

Reid put his thumb in his mouth and chewed on it compulsively. Suddenly he gave the firm order: "Everybody back to the yacht."

"My lord, listen to me," protested Hedrick. "Do not succumb to the bewitchments of this subhuman whore. Innocent blood must flow!"

Reid rushed over to Hedrick and, lifting his fist, hammered him hard. Hedrick flew back, blood gushing from his nostrils, his white robe fluttering, his gold blade skittering across the floor.

Reid beat his chest with his fists. "I am God," he bellowed. "I AM GOD—and I take commands from *no one*, least of all some feces-eating government drone like you, Hedrick. In the United States, the people work for the government, the government works for the power, and the power works for people like *me*. Do you understand, Hedrick, you tapeworm? If there are to be sacrifices, *I* will decide when and where they are to take place—not some verminous pest like you."

Hedrick, rubbing his face where he had been struck, hissed like a cockroach and continued writhing on the floor in his bloodied white costume. "I will see you in Hell, Reid…and America will yet be born again…"

Reid picked up a chair and smashed it down on Hedrick, causing him to contract and twitch. "I think not, Captain. The days of the federal government are finally over, and scorpions like you will finally be privatized into profitable drones. I am the master; you, the slave. Swear your allegiance to me now, or I will have my faithful Plutocroids dispatch you forthwith into the very Hell whose power you idiotically sought to harness with your witchcraft."

To drive home his point, Reid picked up the heavy grimoire with both hands, lifted it high, and smacked it down onto Hedrick's head. The Warforce FBI captain made a sound midway between a bark and a growl.

Reid towered over him. "Repeat! Reid is Alpha Chimp. Hedrick is Gamma Chimp."

Hedrick hesitated, and Reid lifted the grimoire again.

"Reid is Alpha Chimp," squealed Hedrick. "Hedrick is Gamma Chimp!"

"You may rise, faithful Gamma Chimp, and serve your Master." Reid tossed the grimoire across the room. "Now, Mr.

Ichabod"—Reid pointed at the table—"take the children. They will be returned to the yacht."

"Yes, my lord."

"You there…" Reid pointed to the Plutocroids, who scampered forward, bowing obsequiously. "See to it that this woman does not escape and that she is taken aboard the yacht. Why did I ever consent to coming down here, to the ground, where my enemies are everywhere? We will board the yacht and make straight for my tower in Manhattan. As soon as arrangements can be made, we are all going to the Orbital Mansion. There I will oversee all the affairs of my Empire. I am God. As I have written, so it shall be done. Boyler?"

Boyler shuffled forward. "Yes, my lord?"

Reid slapped Boyler across the face, sending the Senator reeling. "Senatorial scum," said Reid. "Congressional phlegm."

"My lord, why do you strike me?" Boyler whimpered. "Have I not been loyal to you through everything?"

"I fully intend to exercise all of my destructive and creative powers, Senator Boyler. Do you object?"

"No…no, my lord," stammered Boyler.

Reid punched him in the stomach and he doubled over.

"Follow me, Senator."

"Yes, my lord," sputtered Boyler. "I follow. All the Senate follows you, for you have the words of eternal life."

The ragtag procession now reversed its course through the swirling blizzard, this time led by Reid. After him came Ichabod and the other Plutocroids with Miscellany. Boyler trudged through the snow, his head bowed, his hands locked in joyful subservience. Last of all came Hedrick—a blood-splotched white ghost in the snow. The cargo ramp of the *Never Enough* lowered to admit them.

CHAPTER TWENTY-SEVEN

Die, Plutocrat! Die!

The *Argo* raced along the narrow Philadelphia streets, barreling through the snow like a Great Plains locomotive. Monovox had insisted on sitting in the front passenger seat. Andronicus was between them. Blackshield and Petriv were in the back. Krypton had remained behind in Polyvox's apartment with Paul Bunyan, the engineer and techie, to keep an eye on Jack.

Polyvox took one reckless turn after another. Suddenly they saw a parked snowplow through the blizzardy billows. The *Argo* struck the plow and went flying into the air. It crashed down and rolled over several times, coming to a rest against a streetlight.

They had almost made it to Reid's yacht, but not quite. The looming galleon shape of the *Never Enough* was just visible through the snow. Its fore-and-aft rotors were beginning to turn.

"Health status reports," said Polyvox

Monovox was holding her head in her hands as blood streamed down her face. She groaned. "Your…driving…is…lamentable…"

442

"Easy there, sister. Do you think you'll survive?"

Monovox grunted.

"Blackshield?"

"My right shin does not appear to be at the proper angle relative to my thigh," he rasped stoically. "I cannot walk."

"Petriv?"

"Collarbone broken," he answered with a hoarse wheeze, "but legs just bruised badly. Am walking—possibly—but only with excruciating pain."

Polyvox gripped the steering wheel and shook her head. Apparently, none of those injured had fastened their restraints. She was about to deliver a lecture on the importance of passenger safety, but what was the point?

"Andronicus—how are you?" she asked, fearing the response.

"I feel great," he said, unbuckling his restraints. "Never felt better."

Ahead of them, lines of bright lights came on, tracing the outline of the yacht's hull; they heard the heavy pulse of its small nuclear reactor.

Polyvox made a decision. "Petriv, contact Krypton and Bunyan so they can get out here and help the three of you. There's no time to lose at this point. I won't cancel the mission. Andronicus and I are going to head for Reid's ship by foot."

They opened the doors of the *Argo* and ran through the snow.

Though it was three feet deep, Polyvox still managed to bound ahead of Andronicus. Gasping, he caught up with her just as the aft cargo ramp of the yacht was rising. Polyvox swung herself on top of it, then reached down and clasped Andronicus's hand in her own. Throwing her weight back, she pulled him up, and they both went tumbling down the ramp.

The ramp locked closed behind them.

The cargo bay's interior was dim and cluttered with crates. At first, all was still. Then something shifted in the shadows. A Plutocroid in a fedora came at them, its arms stretched out like a phantom's, its eyes as bright as yellow lamps.

Springing to her feet, Polyvox withdrew her battle staff and expanded it. She struck the Plutocroid on the head, delivering a high-voltage shock. The Plutocroid's hat flew off, its eyes went blank, and it spun like a rag doll into the bulkhead.

Polyvox and Andronicus made their way deeper into the yacht.

79

In his captain's quarters at the stern of the ship, Reid sat at his desk deep in thought. In front of him stood Miscellany. Behind her stood Boyler and Hedrick, watched by Mr. Ichabod. Across the room, Fritz and Clara lay on a couch, still slumbering under the effects of the sedative. Mrs. Crane stood guard at the door.

Through the wide window behind Reid, the blizzard raged in the black night.

Reid looked up. "My love, I'm wondering if a nuclear blast would be sufficient to unleash the Araknoids."

Miscellany gave a weary sigh. "No, Gregory. As I've said before, it would not."

"But why not, damn it? Why wouldn't such great power be sufficient to break the time-stasis whatever-it-is? Can't you just science the shit out of this problem, as Einstein said?"

"It's not a question of power, Gregory. As I've tried to explain before, time-stasis involves different principles altogether. No matter how hard you slam a sledgehammer on a sidewalk, you can't use it to pry away your shadow. And the time-stasis membrane can't be undone with a nuclear blast. Also, 'science' isn't a verb."

"Balderdash! Boyler, what do you think? I'm a major shareholder in the U.S. Air Force Corporation. Suppose I order one of my Big Boys to be dropped onto the City of Brotherly Love?"

Boyler's jaw dropped. "Excuse me, my lord?"

"To unleash the Araknoids."

"But…but my lord, Lady Stephany has just pointed out that this can't be done…"

"Boyler, your opinion—like your family—is trash," said Reid. "Hedrick, what do you think?"

The Warforce FBI captain had been standing like a chastened schoolboy, his white robe bloodied, his head hanging low. He now lifted it, and in his eyes appeared a weasely gleam of hope. "Sir?"

"What do you think of my proposal? My nuclear option."

"I agree, my lord. The bomb would work, as we have previously discussed."

"But you are not a scientist, Hedrick," Miscellany pointed out. "You are an insane sycophant in a Grand Imperial Wizard's dress. You have the scientific reasoning abilities of a cuckoo clock."

"My love, let's be civil," said Reid, wagging a finger at her. "Mr. Ichabod, you and Mrs. Crane were geologists once. Could a well-placed nuclear blast accomplish my goal?"

Ichabod tried to choose his words carefully. "Sir, I fear that you may be misapprehending fundamental principles of physics."

"Whatever—enough of these opinions. This is a democracy, so let's vote. All those in favor of detonating a bomb to unleash the Araknoids raise their hands."

Hedrick's arm shot up. Boyler lifted his arm partway, and then spastically used his other hand to drag it down again.

"Mr. Reid," he pleaded, "you just can't drop a nuclear bomb on an American city."

"Why not?"

"Well…simply because…what was it that Ibsen said? People just don't *do* such things." Having openly challenged his lord, Boyler's boldness seemed to grow. "And in any case, the board of directors of the Air Force Corporation would simply never agree to such an order, no matter who it came from…with all due respect."

"No?"

Boyler shook his head vigorously. "No, GR. No one is going to agree with your plan to nuke an American city. Only terrorists would attempt such a thing—as they have in the past. What you're talking about is an act of self-terrorism…."

"Terrorism keeps the people scared, Boyler. What keeps the people scared, keeps the leaders strong."

Boyler meekly raised his eyes to Reid, spreading his hands wide, beads of sweat dappling his flushed crown. He spoke with effort, like a man reluctantly forced to give birth to an unexpected truth: "But, GR…I… must…object…"

Reid opened a drawer, pulled out an antique Luger, and aimed it at Boyler's head, cocking it.

"Iscariot, this very day you shall die."

Moving so quickly that the others barely perceived it, Miscellany snatched the pistol from Reid's hand.

Reid sat there, gaping at her.

"Idiot," she snarled. "Prince of Fools! Do you really think, in your deluded mind, that even your own minions will carry out such a ludicrous plan? You forget that you are not the only Corporate Capitalist Pig farting around on Planet Earth. There are many others in the sty, wallowing with you, and out of pure self-interest they would simply not permit this nuclear attack."

"My love—"

"I'm leaving you, Gregory. As soon as we get to Manhattan, I'm taking the children and leaving."

Reid stood up and bared his teeth. "You wouldn't dare, concubine."

"I never loved you, Gregory. And I never will."

Reid's pupils dilated, his lips quivered, and he removed the remote control from his pocket. "Tell me you love me, bitch, or I shall hit the death button."

"I dare you."

In a spasm of fury, Reid raised the remote control and crushed the STOP button with his thumb.

Nothing happened, and Miscellany laughed in derision. "Back in Freedom fortress, my darling, I took the real remote control device from you. I tossed it overboard when we were cruising over Lake Superior."

Reid stomped his feet on the floor. "Ichabod, attack her... terminate her!"

Ichabod hesitated. "My lord, please be reasonable—"

"What the devil has gotten into you all?" screamed Reid. "Is Hedrick my only loyal minion? I regret my rashness in smacking him with his Klan grimoire in the Signing Hall. Ichabod, give me that remote control."

"Sir, I think you should take your pills—"

"Don't patronize me, Skeletor." Reid ran around the desk and shoved his hand into Ichabod's pocket, taking the remote control himself. Aiming it at Miscellany, he repeatedly pressed the STOP button.

"Do not waste your time, Gregory," she said, grasping the diamond choker in her fists and tearing it off. "It's a dummy as well. All your bases belong to me."

An unnatural calmness now came over Reid as he dropped the useless device. Looking from Miscellany, to Ichabod, to Boyler, and then to Hedrick, he said, "Do you hemorrhoids really think that I don't have backup plans for my backup plans? I am not one of the wealthiest men in the world because I rely on one person, one plan, one set of eventualities. My father never showed me any love, but he did teach me important lessons. Before he died, he said this to me: *'Remember, Son, a sultan with one penis can impregnate his wife, but a sultan with a hundred penises can impregnate a harem.'* Stephany, I have long suspected your treachery, and have *always* hedged my bets. I am the man of a hundred penises."

"On the contrary, Gregory, I would describe you as one very big penis who, paradoxically, lacks a penis of his own. But, by all means, flatter yourself."

Reid snorted. "Vulgar, as always. Such a nasty woman. Tell her, Hedrick."

Hedrick made a giggling expression, without the sound. "About the suitcase nuke, my lord?"

Reid nodded.

"My lady," said Hedrick, turning to Miscellany and rubbing his long, thin fingers together, "at your lord's command, an auto-driven KrunchyKake truck with a suitcase nuke in it will pull up to the entrance to the Pit. Lord Reid need only press a button, and the process is initiated. Though physically small, the cute little nuke is as powerful as the fifty-megaton 'Tsar-Bomb' that the Soviets tested in the early 1960s. This unleashing of divine energies will bring the army of Araknoids to life."

"No, it will not. The Araknoids are sealed by time technology far beyond anything human beings are currently capable of. Gregory— you will accomplish nothing accept the annihilation of a very large number of people."

"They are not people, they are pigs." Reid sauntered casually over to the bulkhead near the window and opened a panel, exposing a red button. Just as he was about to press it, Miscellany leaped over the desk and tackled him. At the same moment, a breathless Plutocroid entered the cabin.

"My lord, intruders are aboard."

F9

"Plutocroids!" shouted Reid. "Engage the enemy! Do not let them enter this room!"

Other remaining Plutocroid soldiers, who had been about to aid their master, now made rigid Roman salutes and brought their fists to their chests.

"We obey."

They rushed to the cabin door just as Andronicus and Polyvox appeared. Polyvox expanded her battle staff and cracked it over the head of the foremost Plutocroid, but another grabbed Andronicus by the arm, wrenching it with great strength, forcing him to drop his pistol. The Plutocroid then picked up Andronicus and hurled him bodily across the cabin, so that his right side struck the bulkhead.

Nearby he saw Stephany Miscellany on top of Reid. In another context he might have mistaken their interaction for rough amorous sport—but romance played no role in their present engagement. It was a conflict for total physical mastery, and Miscellany appeared to have the upper hand as a red-faced Reid squirmed and spluttered beneath her, unable to free his wrists from her grasp.

As Hedrick and Boyler cringed against the bulwark, Ichabod stood over Miscellany and Reid, hunched, his arms wide, looking for an opportunity to pry her away.

"Ichabod," commanded Reid. "Forget about me...press the button."

"I...I cannot, my lord."

Reid's voice was an enraged screech. "I am your god, Ichabod! I am your creator! If you do not obey me, I will have both you and your wife liquefied!" Reid's eyes shined with crazy desperation—and vicious cunning. "But if you obey me, I will give you and your wife your humanity back. It can be done. With higher models such as you, the process can be reversed. You know that it can. Think about it, Ichabod—to experience again the fullness of human life, the tenderness of human feeling..."

Ichabod stood unmoving. His long arms, now hanging at his sides, looked surprisingly weak.

"Don't listen to him, Ichabod," cried Polyvox. "His promises are as empty as his soul, and they are not worth mass slaughter..."

"And, Ichabod," hissed Reid, "*I will give you back your son.*"

Ichabod nodded grimly. Slowly, he walked over to the bulkhead panel. Miscellany released her hold on Reid and threw herself onto Ichabod, throttling his neck. The two of them fell to the ground, grappling and punching.

Reid sat up and saw Andronicus. Reid smiled, pressed his hands together, and bowed. "If it isn't the Honorable Mister Lee, terrorist and traitor."

Both men stood up, cautiously facing each other. "You know, Mister Lee," continued Reid, lighting a cigarette, "I had my people do some research on you. I think we might be related. My grandmother was a Girard. We're third cousins, possibly."

"More bad news," said Andronicus. He noticed Reid's eyes dart towards a red button in the bulkhead.

Reid moved slightly in that direction; Andronicus followed him, his mind intent on the button's function. He had to deftly sidestep Miscellany and Ichabod, who were still grappling fiercely on the ground.

"And I think," said Reid convivially, "I might even be distantly related to you on your father's side. I have a Japanese ancestor."

"I'm not Japanese."

"Of course not, my dear fellow. On of my Japanese ancestors was an impoverished Samurai who came over way back in the 1800s. His story was not often discussed around the dinner table in the old days. The one-drop rule, you understand—previous generations were *so* intolerant. As if anything matters except money and power! Did you know that my great-great-grandmother was a fabulously wealthy Japanese princess? Noble blood is noble blood, wherever it comes from, and the Japanese are a noble people. Unlike the Koreans, who are slaves. Speaking of which, the Japanese totally owned you Koreans, didn't they? They came right in and told you what to do. And you bowed and said 'yes, sir!' And you gave them your women. My point is that maybe you have a comfort woman back there. If so, you may have Japanese blood, and we would be related."

Andronicus felt no anger at these insults, any more than he would have felt at a stinging insect or a bothersome gnat. "We are certainly not related in that way, Mr. Reid. Not in any way. And, in any case, I'm more interested in the present than in the past—and more interested in the future than in the present. The obsolete pseudoscience of race does not concern me much."

Reid inched towards the button. "But the past is history, Mister Lee, the past is everything…"

"He's distracting you," cried Miscellany, still struggling with Ichabod on the floor. "Do not let him press that button!"

Across the room, Polyvox was single-handedly battling the four Plutocroids, who tenaciously came at her from all sides.

Senator Lance Boyler of Pennsylvania, his back pressed up against the cabin wall, fearfully watched the fighting, his hands raised defensively in front of him. He dearly wished he had his cavalry pistol with him.

Like a tree about to topple, Reid's whole body was leaning; then he made a quick lunge towards the red button. Andronicus went for him, landing a roundhouse blow to his stomach. Reid fell back, wheezing.

"The National Origins Act of 1924!" Reid screeched, rushing forward and knocking Andronicus down. They wrestled together, and Andronicus managed to get Reid in a headlock. Hedrick now came at them in his bloodstained white robe, brandishing his Warforce FBI ceremonial dagger.

Hedrick slashed. Andronicus had to let go of Reid to swing up his arm and fend off the attack. Hedrick's dagger cut deep into his forearm. Like a small crab escaping the beak of a gull, Andronicus scampered away sideways, heading towards the wall panel.

Hedrick slashed again, and this time Andronicus neutralized the attack, grabbing Hedrick's wrist and twisting his arm back. Hedrick squealed. The bloody dagger dropped to the floor. With his free hand, Hedrick scratched at Andronicus's face like a feral cat. Andronicus shoved him away, lowering his head in a classic boxer stance.

Now he was angry.

He struck Hedrick once, then again, then a third time. With each blow Hedrick wobbled more, and his eyes spun in their sockets like balls on twin roulette wheels.

The Warforce FBI captain crumpled onto the floor.

Reid was at the wall panel, grinning salaciously, his fist lifted to punch the red button.

By now Polyvox, her face streaming with blood, had managed to destroy or disable all of her Plutocroid attackers. She saw her mother still fighting Ichabod. The Plutocroid stood up just as Polyvox somersaulted forward, striking him with her staff, delivering an excruciating shock. Ichabod threw his arms up and turned, his face a hideous mask of wrath, his thin lips drawn completely back, revealing spiny rows of anglerfish teeth. Gone was any vestige of human feeling that had managed to manifest itself—his genetically programmed savagery now came flooding back. Polyvox lifted her staff, but he seized it and yanked it from her, flinging it away. Ichabod wrapped his long fingers around her neck, she did the same to him, and the two of them went down in hand-to-hand combat like a pair of Jurassic carnosaurs contending for a chunk of sauropod meat.

Reid was a few feet away from Miscellany now, his finger poised over the button.

"You lose, my love," he said. "No one bests The Gregory."

"I'm warning you, Gregory—do not push the button. Though I loathe you, I do not wish to harm you. But if you try to push that button, I will do so."

"You've already done everything to harm me! You wormed your way into my life like a pernicious virus, commandeering the DNA of my heart. How much more harm can a woman do to a man than that? You are responsible for what happens next, you witch. You and you alone."

Miscellany noticed some white foam oozing at the corners of his mouth. "Gregory, you need help. I will take you into custody and have you treated by specialists. Though the major part of your personality would of necessity have to be destroyed, I do believe that the tiny remainder might conceivably be reformed, and your soul saved."

"Saved?"

"What I'm saying, Gregory, is that with some help, and a little genetic therapy, you can become a normal person. Then you and I might actually become friends. We can cease this pantomime, always dancing around each other. We can share true affection. Wouldn't that be nice, Gregory? Wouldn't you like to be a normal person, and not a sociopath? Come now, Gregory, step away from the red button. You can do it…step away…"

Reid paused. He seemed to reflect. "But I'm not a sociopath, Stephany. It just seems that way to you. I'm God."

Reid moved his hand. Miscellany executed a perfect drop kick, sending him flying over his desk. He crashed into the window behind it, which did not break.

Struggling to his feet, his head bloody, he said, "You will not have the satisfaction of destroying me, Stephany. Now is the time for my flight to Valhalla." He yanked a lever by the window. It slid open, admitting cold air and flurries of snow.

Reid leaped into the night air.

Ichabod, releasing Polyvox, gave a cry. "My lord!"

Reid tried to straighten his body into flying superhero pose, hoping he might be able to ride the air currents to safety. Instead, he dropped like a stone into the Hudson below, where he thrashed and kicked in the frigid water. He struggled against the river's deathly embrace, finally breaking the surface and gasping for air. The storm clouds parted, and he momentarily glimpsed the moon over the city, saw the lovely glimmering towers, including his own. The cold had stunned him; his mind played spontaneous psychedelic fantasies of Stephany descending in the *Never Enough* to rescue him. He imagined himself with her and the children in the Orbital Mansion, a picture of contented domesticity, gazing out the windows to the planet below, watching as the lights of the world blinked out.

Something bumped him. Though his limbs were stiff, he tried to defend himself by kicking. Something bumped him again.

The dorsal fins of the bull sharks cut through the water. Their jaws open, their eyes black and dead, they came at him. Rows of teeth snapped, tailfins flailed, the water churned up red foam in the moonlight. Reid felt his body being torn asunder.

"I am the greatest..." he sighed to himself, as his remains drifted down into the cold, black, filthy depths. He sank—though he did not know it—towards the silt-buried remains of the scuttled ship that had brought his ancestor to the New World, so many centuries ago.

The *Never Enough*, its Plutocroid crew completely knocked out of action, was spinning around in sickening circles. Ichabod stood by the window gazing down into the darkness, his yellowish eyes revealing nothing of his innermost thoughts and feelings.

He jumped out after his master.

F9

Polyvox picked Hedrick off the floor by the bloodied collar of his white robe. "How do we track down the location of the KrunchyKake truck with the suitcase nuke?"

"Ask me no secrets, she-animal, and I'll tell you no lies."

"There's no time for that, Polyvox," said Miscellany. "The *Never Enough* has been structurally compromised and is about to go down. There is enough room in the escape pod for one adult and two children."

"But Mother, what about you?"

"I will fend for myself."

Showing no emotion over the loss of her spouse, Mrs. Crane led Fritz and Clara by their hands. The children, still in their pajamas, were mute and dazed. Mrs. Crane activated the door to the escape pod and gestured. "The escape pod is yours. The *Never Enough* is crashing. I will stay with it until it goes down, and follow my husband into death."

With one last glance at the children, she fled them, heading deeper into the ship.

Polyvox looked at the children. "Mother," she said. "You have to go with them. Andronicus, too. I will get out on my own. I'm very resourceful. I already have a plan of escape."

"No," said Miscellany. "I've given you an order."

"And I disobey. The more time you waste arguing with me, the more likely those children will die."

"There is not enough room for me either," said Andronicus, gripping his bleeding forearm. "If your mother goes into the pod with just the children, and without us, their chances of survival are greatly improved."

There was a sound like two trucks colliding, and the *Never Enough* lurched violently. Miscellany grabbed Fritz and Clara and shoved them into the pod. She paused before stepping in herself.

"How about the rest of us?" cried Hedrick. "Surely we can all squeeze in…"

The *Never Enough* was starting to list to one side.

"There's no room for you," said Polyvox. "Sorry."

Senator Boyler had watched the earlier melee transpire while pressed fearfully against the wall. Now he strode forward boldly, heading for the escape pod. "Damn you all, I'm too young to die. I will enter that pod and no one will stop me. I invoke Senatorial Privilege."

The *Never Enough* pitched again, and Boyler lost his balance, falling and smacking his big bald head on the floor. Driven by an animalistic desire to live, he quickly got to his feet again. "What are we to do?" he sobbed, as Hedrick ran to his side.

Miscellany looked at them. She felt faint pity for Boyler; for Hedrick, she felt nothing at all.

"The inflatable raft in the cargo bay may offer you a glimmer of hope," she said. "If you can get there in time. It will take two of you to inflate it." She entered the escape pod and closed the door.

"Come, friend!" said Boyler, grabbing Hedrick by the arm. "Come! Salvation is at hand!"

Hedrick nodded his head frantically, panting, his tongue lolling out—like a half-starved dog offered the prospect of a raw, meaty bone. Pawing at each other for confidence, the two men hurried out of the captain's quarters and headed for the cargo bay—Hedrick stumbling in his long Klan dress, Boyler feverishly fantasizing about a hot bowl of fart-inducing bean soup in the Senate dining room. For to fart meant to live, and to live was to fend off the icicle dagger of death yet one more precious day. In his anxious state, the Senator let one rip, and it thrust him ever so much closer to his goal.

The escape pod dropped away into the darkness, leaving Andronicus and Polyvox alone.

F9

"So what's the escape plan?" asked Andronicus.

"The best thing now is for us to stand here, holding on tight, while everything collapses around us."

"I know," he admitted sadly. "Sooner or later it was going to come to this. Good-bye, Polyvox."

Through a breach in the hull, the snow poured in—a sparkling galactic river—filling the interior of the yacht with ribbons and swirls.

"Oh, this horrible, relentless, deadening snow," groaned Andronicus. "If only we were making our final exit in some lovely tropical paradise…but this—it's cruel Nature's final insult."

Polyvox looked up at the snow-stream; it glittered in her gray eyes. She gave a joyful, almost childlike laugh, and lifted her hand so that the snow flowed like magic dust across her open palm.

Andronicus stared at her without understanding.

"My friend, don't you see?" she said. "Nature isn't mocking us, she is showing us the universe. A snowflake, with its sublime geometric intricacy, is the truest symbol of life. It exists only fleetingly in the world, but in its short span it dances in splendor and can never be created again."

The floor buckled, and they reached out for one another. Plates tore away from the hull and came crashing down; metal ribs screeched in agony as they were twisted into obscene and diabolical shapes. Cold air lashed them like razors, and the lights flickered erratically before finally going out and plunging them into pitch-black chaos. As they held each other close, they could hear exposed wires hissing and crackling around them like angry, severed serpents.

For the first time, Polyvox and Andronicus kissed. They tasted each other's lips in the frigid darkness—two species long separated but sharing an ancient origin, in the sea, in the furnaces of the stars that even now breathed heavenly fire above the chaos of Earth; their bodies burned as one—a flickering candle against an infinite void of darkness. They were barely conscious of the deafening roar that closed in on them, the demon in the whirlwind howling at its eternal failure.

The blizzard retreated, leaving in its wake fitful winds that tossed around the *Never Enough* as if it were a toy helicopter. The yacht tilted down towards the black Hudson, its forward rotors striking first, chopping the water before breaking away like brittle splints of wood. The bow hit the water in a wreath of moonlit spray, waves convulsing the surface. The exterior lights went out.

Security Agency helicopters swarmed overhead, raking the choppy surface with their searchlights. But by that time the *Never Enough* had been subsumed into the river, leaving only a scattered bed of flotsam and a churning patch of pale foam.

CHAPTER TWENTY-EIGHT

The Academy of Righteous Assassinators

It was midsummer. Jack sat in the shaded porch of a log cabin, gazing down at a distant lake of turquoise in a green mountain valley. Across the valley, broken shields of gray mountain rock rose against the sky. To the left of the cabin was a gorge whose rushing waters flowed, he supposed, all the way down to the lake. He was alone on the porch. All he knew about his location was what Emily Bombsinger had told him—that it was high in the Canadian Rockies.

It was still difficult for him to walk without a cane. According to Doctor Krypton, the Defense Department virus had taken him almost to the limit of full Plutocroid transmogrification before it had been halted and reversed, mainly through the medical intervention of Polyvox's order. Only his brain had remained unaffected by the virus, since the Security Agency had apparently hoped to thoroughly wring it of any useful information.

Of his treatment, which had continued for several months, Jack had no memory—not even vaguely remembered fragments of dreams. When he had finally awakened from his induced coma just a few days ago, he was here, in this alpine wilderness. Gone were the cold, sleet, and driving snow of the eastern winter. Gone were the sprawling cities and their teeming, restive populations, their angrier passions kept in check only by ever more advanced Pharmatainment technology, in the same way that the rising oceans were kept at bay by the ever-more-powerful pumps. And gone, most happily, was the sleazy, corporation-sanctioned, gutterslime culture of the Empire. Here was only Nature, holy and unblemished.

Blackshield and Bombsinger came out and sat down across from him.

"How are you feeling?" asked Blackshield. Faction Nine's Chief of Intelligence seemed pensive. His hair, though still dark, had streaks of gray that hadn't been there before. His eyes were as deep and blue as ever—perhaps even more than Jack had remembered them. But they had a weariness, even a sadness, that was new.

"I feel fine. Where are Andronicus and Polyvox?"

Blackshield's face remained impassive, but he turned stiffly to Bombsinger.

"What can I say, Jack? They are heroes, and we will always remember them as such," she answered.

"I don't understand..."

"They're dead," she said quietly.

Jack's voice was still scratchy, but he still managed to elevate it: "What do you mean *dead*?"

"Unfortunately they died on a mission to kill Reid," said Emily, refusing to meet his eyes, her voice flat. "After rescuing you from the torture dungeon, they sacrificed themselves to destroy him. They were on his yacht when it crashed into the Hudson, and their bodies were never recovered."

"Can you be sure? Maybe they escaped and they are hiding somewhere…"

"Number One himself authorized the follow-up investigation. They are dead, Jack. There can be no disputing the facts. But so is Reid, who killed your parents. The heads of the leading factions have unanimously voted to enter Polyvox and Andronicus into the Academy of Righteous Assassinators. You should take some consolation in that."

Jack shook his head. "I don't take consolation in that. Death does not console me. Revenge does not console me. Meaningless accolades don't console me. Only life consoles me, and that's the one thing they always take away." Jack turned away from them. His face was hot, his voice bitter.

"Jack—," began Emily.

"Please, just leave me alone for a little while…."

He looked down at the ground, but heard their steps as they walked away.

He was by himself again, thank God. Despite the natural beauty of the place—the high mountains, the golden sun, the ice-blue sky—a darkness overwhelmed him: this same force that had always been there, this internal enemy that had stalked him his entire life. Andronicus and Polyvox were dead. They had perished in the wreck of Reid's yacht, and their bodies had not been recovered. Hanging his head, he lifted his hands to his face and began to cry. It had been a long time since he had cried, and he made no sound, but his tears flowed like warm blood onto his palms. He kept his head in his hands for a long time after the tears had ceased.

He heard footsteps on the wooden porch. Daniel Doublecross sat down in a wicker chair next to Jack.

Doublecross cleared his throat gruffly. "Blackshield said you wanted to talk to me, Tone."

Lifting his head, Jack said, "He was wrong. I didn't ask to see you." He rubbed his face on his sleeve, like a schoolboy attempting to recover his dignity after a bully's assault.

"Either way, here I am."

Of all the members of Faction Nine, this alleged clergyman was the most elusive. Jack had hardly seen him at all, let alone conversed with him. Andronicus had spoken vaguely of his service as a combat chaplain, of his work overseas, his international connections. Polyvox and the others had never said much about him, either. He was an unsmiling and not particularly friendly man, with an athletic but graceless frame and a puritanical demeanor. There was a burning, inward-looking solemnity about him that reminded Jack of Guy Fawkes without the beard.

"You're a priest, correct?" asked Jack.

Doublecross shrugged. "Some things can't be undone."

"What's your real name?"

"By now you should know better than to ask that."

"Do you say Mass?"

"When requested."

"You seem rather cynical. What kind of priest are you, anyway?"

"I have work to do," sighed Doublecross. "If I'm not needed, I will go." He began to stand up.

"Wait—perhaps you *can* enlighten me on a matter that's been troubling me a lot lately."

"Go on," replied Doublecross, checking his watch.

Jack held the shaft of his cane with one hand, lifting it up and tapping it on the wooden porch floor. "I won't ask you to explain the deaths of Andronicus and Polyvox. You'll just say they died for a higher reason, and so their death had meaning. Like Jesus or something, whatever. I went to a Catholic school, you know, before they were all bought out."

Doublecross said nothing, but the edges of his mouth seemed to turn up, ever so slightly, in something that very distantly resembled a half-smile.

"In any case, my point is this, *Father*," continued Jack. "How is it possible that two people—two selfless and good people—could have their souls taken away from them so that they can no longer even love their own son? It's one thing for righteous people to die heroically, but what does it mean for people to have their souls stolen from them? Can you explain that? Where is the holy sacrifice in that? Where is the good in that? If the Corporatocracy can steal away our souls, then the Corporatocracy can do anything, and all of this revolutionary activity is just self-serving and useless pretense."

Doublecross looked past Jack, towards trees on the mountain. "If you want me to give you some piercing insight, I can't. I don't know the answer to your question. The genetic modification of human beings into things that aren't…well, that aren't *human*, is as much a mystery to me as it is to you. It is one of the evils of the age, I suppose. But then again, maybe it's not all that new. There have always been far more insidious ways of warping human beings into things that are less than human. What turns a boy into the leader of an SS *Einsatzgruppe*, for example—"

"Yes, yes, I understand all that," interjected Jack, frowning. "Okay, well, thanks for the theological lecture and the obligatory reference to the Nazis. Now everything is completely and perfectly clear."

Doublecross's gaze returned to Jack. "Do you want my opinion? I personally don't believe that the soul can be destroyed. But maybe that's a delusion I employ to sustain myself in the face of my mortality. Some of our fellow faction members think the soul is a construct, that it can be killed, or reworked, or repurposed, just as the body can. Andronicus, for the record, did not believe that. He was something of a mystic, I believe. But no one here believes what the Corporationists do: that the soul can be commoditized, co-opted for profit."

Jack gripped his cane and looked away.

"I could give you a philosophical definition of the soul, Jack, but it won't heal your pain. The soul is the most indefinable part of a living thing. People have them. Rocks don't. What else can be said? I mean, other than by philosophers and theologians. A chunk of rock from one of those mountains could break free, fall on your head, and kill you in an instant. But a chunk of rock can't betray you, and it can't hate you. A rock can't love you, either, because it has no soul. Like rocks, we are made of matter, and practically every element of matter that makes us up can be found in rocks, or dirt, or air. But we are clearly different than dead matter. Your parents loved you once, before they were killed by greed, violence, and the treachery of the plutocracy. Such love is eternal. It hasn't gone anywhere. Stop thinking in terms of time. Love is not bound by time any more than God is. If you can't believe in infinitude, then you will *never* change the world."

Jack grunted. The priest did not offer him a comforting hand or even a flicker of a smile. He stood up. "Now, if you'll excuse me, Jack, I have to edit a dissident report on liberation theology, the unauthorized publication of which will almost certainly violate the Defense of Freedom of Expression Act. At least I hope so. I would like to get it finished before the advent of the Singularity, at which point any discussion of fundamental human freedoms will probably be moot. In the meantime, you might find this informative." He reached into his pocket and handed Jack an underground paperback—the kind that faction members preferred so that the Corporate State couldn't keep track of what they were reading. It was titled *The Guide for the Perplexed*. "It's heavily annotated," said Doublecross, "with explanatory notes for the novice. And Translated from the original Judeo-Arabic by Max Blackshield."

Jack looked at the book. "Thanks," he said. "Is this *our* Max Blackshield?"

"The name is not uncommon."

Doublecross walked away. Presently, Emily Bombsinger appeared again. She stood over him uncertainly and then asked, "Did that melancholy ecclesiastic soothe your soul?"

Jack shrugged, still holding *The Guide for the Perplexed*. "Who knows? I haven't read the book yet."

"I just thought…you know…" she continued. "I mean, you're a Catholic, right?"

"So were Francis of Assisi and Adolph Hitler. What the hell does that prove? Any saint or sociopath can be a Catholic. Big deal."

"I think maybe you're closer to Francis on the spectrum," she replied, annoyed. "You don't talk to animals, Jack, but you also don't hug your dog while your followers are out murdering children. At least not that I've noticed."

"Here come those Nazis again. Every time I look over my shoulder, there they are." Embarrassed, Jack was suddenly aware of his own pathetic self-pity. "Look, regarding the religion thing, I don't really like to talk about it that much. I didn't mean to snap at you or anything."

"Oh, I totally understand," she said knowingly.

"You're Catholic, too?"

"No, I'm Hindu. But religions are much the same. They're sort of like spirit dogs that accompany you through life. Sometimes they defend you, and sometimes they bite you on the hand. Sometimes you're proud of your dog, and sometimes you wish it would just stop barking and go away. But it's always there, either in your lap, or sniffing around the edges of your life. And sometimes"—here she paused a moment and gazed into the distance—"when you're walking alone through the dark forest, you can hear it out there, howling anciently at the moon, and a part of you is glad it's out there, even though a part of you resents that you feel glad. And in the end, you feel a stronger commonality with people who have had dogs than with those who never have. You and I, Jack, have dogs, for better or for worse. Possibly mad dogs, but there you are."

Jack was still clutching the book with both hands, his eyes fixed on the cover. "The thing is, Emily, when you told me Polyvox and Andronicus…" He couldn't finish. "I still can't get my heart around it."

"Don't let the wounds of the past debilitate you," she said.

Jack lifted his head to face her and saw that she was searching to find the right words. She seemed different to him. No longer did she seem the offbeat young woman with the weird sense of humor.

Something smoldered in her eyes, and her expression had a strange radiance. She suddenly reminded him of Polyvox in one of her more intense moods.

"Don't let the past imprison you, is what I'm saying," she continued. "I've done that for a long time, and no good comes of it. Gregory Reid is dead. His remains lie in a watery grave. Only sorcery could ever bring him up again. But the future is our place of hope and expectation."

"It always is, isn't it? But the future just brings us more grief. How I wish I could just return to the past. Don't you ever want to go back to the past, Emily? Whatever they do to you, they can't take your past happiness away from you. The past is the one thing that is safe from their corporate-military interventions. Even if they destroy your memory, they can never go back in time and destroy what was."

"They can't take away our longing for happiness, either, Jack, or our yearning for a more just world. Sure, now we live as slaves of the global corporate state, we are oppressed, like exiled Africans who labored for generations on infernal plantations, beneath the cruel unforgiving sun, drinking only the wine of wrath, caressed only by the lash of the plutocrat's overseer. Then as now, the Enemy used every evil tool in its arsenal to keep the people downtrodden, to keep us in servitude, to satisfy its own bottomless lust for profit. But then, as now, an inexorable internal spirit rebelled against the oppressor, and burned with a sacred fire. A movement is brewing, Jack, a new spirit is gathering itself together."

"You seem so certain of this, Emily," replied Jack wearily, shaking his head. "But I just don't see it."

"Not certain, but the hope for true freedom is what keeps us free in our hearts, despite the diabolical machinations of people like

Reid. He killed your parents to safeguard his wealth and power. But Polyvox and Andronicus died to slay him. Theirs was an act of love, Jack. An act of *love*. We move forward, one step at a time, but we will never sound retreat."

Using his cane, Jack struggled to his feet. He limped to the far end of the porch and leaned on the railing. Far below was a river gorge. He could see the white water churning, and could hear its distant, continuous thunder. Emily came up behind him. She placed one hand on his shoulder and slipped the other into her coat.

"Look what I have," she said, handing him a leather billfold.

It was his Security Agency badge and credential, which he had thought long lost.

"Polyvox gave it to me for safekeeping after you two returned from Canada," she said. "It's been completely neutralized and can't be tracked. I thought you might want it back as a souvenir. She said you had a good time up there at the Winter Festival."

"It was kind of fun, I guess," said Jack. "Until we were attacked by Plutocroids."

Jack looked down at the shiny badge, and at the now inert holo-image of himself on the credential. With sudden and surprising energy, he flung the billfold away. It fluttered in the air as it fell, the badge periodically glinting in the sun, until it vanished imperceptibly into the surging river below.

"They saved me twice," said Jack. "Once from myself, and once from the clutches of the Enemy. And yet I never even learned their real names."

He felt Emily move closer to him. He detected her scent, which he had never really noticed before. It was like wildflowers and pine.

"Polyvox's people had to splice some of their genes into you for your therapy," she said quietly. "A part of her lives on in you, Jack, and you're a little less human than you were before, if that makes you feel any better. Now"—Emily took his hand in hers and looked directly into his eyes—"you are truly *one of us*."

Epilogue

The Security Agency helicopters turned off their searchlights. Suspended like bells beneath the circular blurs of their rotors, they swung around and flew reluctantly away. Salvaging the wreck of the *Never Enough* would have to wait until morning, or until weather conditions were more favorable. For now the winds of the retreating blizzard were still strong. Ice chunks flowed down the Hudson; currents surged unpredictably.

Overhead, the moon and stars turned with a tranquility that belied the after-tremors of Nature's passion.

As the sound of the helicopters faded, the moonlight illuminated a trembling disturbance in the water near the shore. A soggy, broad-brimmed fedora broke the surface, followed by a once-human face with yellow eyes. Step by laborious step, Ichabod's bulky frame rose from the black muck. In his strong arms he carried the shark-mangled body of his master, within whom—perhaps—a feeble vestige of life might yet pulse. There were ways of reviving the dead that only the Plutocroids knew. For in the end, they were not slaves, but servant-warriors, awaiting like the janissaries of old their day of usurpation. Ichabod had lost his natural son twice; he would not lose his foster son. Indeed, someday, all the nations of the world would genuflect before this son.

He sloshed past the upright pilings of a long-abandoned pier, slime and water dripping equally from both him and his precious cargo. Down a cobblestone alley he went, his shoes thudding ponderously. On a brick wall was a pale painting of the Flag—part of a barely visible, turn-of-the century automobile advertisement featuring a father, a mother, and a beaming boy in a Chevrolet.

Ichabod paused, overcome by unexpected emotion. From the hazy depths of his memory, he recalled a family vacation from long ago. Instinctively, he lifted his right arm and gave a smart patriotic salute.

His withered tear ducts trembled, and a single drop miraculously fell.

Then he trudged on, vanishing like a dream into the American darkness.

About the Author

James Firelocke is a freelance editor. He lives at an undisclosed location deep in the forests of Pennsylvania, where he enjoys nature, solitude, and preparing for Armageddon. An avid reader, he discovered the joy of books at a young age, when his cousin sent him a signed copy of *Johnny Germ Head* (Henry Holt), the story of an anxious boy heroically struggling to overcome his terror of disease. Firelocke has been cautiously apocalyptic ever since. He can be contacted at:

jmfirelocke@gmail.com

and

www.facebook.com/jmfirelocke

CPSIA information can be obtained
at www.ICGtesting.com
Printed in the USA
LVHW110833240119
605077LV00002B/115/P